LOVE'S CAPTIVE

All too late, Clay realized his mistake. Reina slammed against him, her slender curves pressed intimately close to his body. He could feel every inch of her as he held her pinioned and he froze, suddenly, achingly aware of her as a woman.

"Let me go!" Reina seemed to sense a sudden change in him. She gasped at the intensity she saw in his gaze. "Let me go, Clay."

"I can't," he groaned. "Not now. Not when I've finally found you . . ."

"No, Clay . . ." She began to protest, but she had no time to say more as Clay's mouth descended to hers, claiming her lips in a demanding kiss. This was no longer Clay, her captor, but Clay, the man. "Don't . . ." she whispered in hoarse protest as his mouth left hers; but he ignored her.

When he bent to seek the sweetness of her throat, a small whimper escaped her. She shivered at the ecstasy of his touch. Long-denied passion exploded within her. With a groan of surrender, she ceased her struggle and melted willingly against the hard wall of his chest.

Caught up in a ~~whirlwind of need, they~~ drank of each other, tasting ~~the sweetness. In a~~ full, flaming kiss, Rei ~~na felt she would die in a~~lmost exquisite agony.

"Clay . . ."

"Ah, Reina," ca~~me his whispered reply. It~~ was a moan of pure pleasure. "I want you mo~~re than I've~~ ever wanted any woman."

"I want you, too," she whispered, drawing him back for another kiss. She didn't want to talk. She only wanted Clay, and the joy that would come from knowing him fully.

THE BEST IN HISTORICAL ROMANCES

SWEET SILKEN BONDAGE

BOBBI SMITH

ZEBRA BOOKS
KENSINGTON PUBLISHING CORP.

ZEBRA BOOKS

are published by

Kensington Publishing Corp.
475 Park Avenue South
New York, NY 10016

First printing: May, 1990

Printed in the United States of America

This book is dedicated to four very special ladies I love and admire . . . Judy Courtois, Evelyn Gee, Audrey Hercules and Jody Lennaman.

A special note of thanks to Aunt Ree and her cohorts for all their help and loving guidance in assisting me with Reina's big adventure.

A note of appreciation, too, to Mr. Kevin Feeney of the San Fernando Mission Archives for his help with research, and to Mrs. Elaine Donaldson of San Antonio for her assistance.

Prologue

Louisiana, 1842

The lean, dark-haired youth and his thoroughbred
black stallion moved as one around the corral near the
stables of the Windown plantation while a grizzled,
seasoned stablehand looked on approvingly. At thirteen
and only a few inches over five feet tall, Clay Cordell
was not yet full-grown, but he handled the horse with
the ease of a master, guiding him through his paces
with a light touch. When Clay had taken the mount
through all of his exercises, he reined him in to a slow
walk to cool him, all the while stroking the intelligent
beast's sleek neck and praising him for his grace and
ability.

"Good boy, Raven," Clay told him, his wide, gray
eyes dancing with excitement. He had trained the two-
year old stallion himself and was more than pleased
with Raven's progress. "What do you think, Ab? Will I
make a racehorse out of him yet?"

The old black man grinned at him as he answered, "I
think so, Master Clay. Ol' Raven's comin' right along.
Yes, sir, he sure is." He was proud of the boy and the
job he was doing with the horse.

"Thanks." Clay beamed under Ab's much-sought-
after-little-given praise. He respected Ab's opinion
more than any other man's, except his father's.

7

"You just keep doin' what you're doin', and Raven'll be ready for the track real soon."

"Honest?" he asked, with youthful exuberance.

Ab nodded, his expression growing more serious. "But just because Raven'll be ready, don't mean you will be. The racetrack ain't no place for a boy, Clay."

Clay immediately sobered. "I know."

"Good, you remember that," Ab remarked as he swung the gate open to let him out. "Now, take him on in and rub him down."

Clay did as he was told, seeing to Raven's comfort before even giving a thought to his own. As he methodically rubbed the stallion down, he let his thoughts wander. Ever since he could remember, there was nothing he wanted to do more than race horses. His father had known that, and though there had never been a lot of money available, he'd managed to get enough together to buy Raven for him. At the time, his mother had protested the extravagance, but his father had overruled her, to Clay's great relief.

Clay fully intended to prove to both of them that the money hadn't been wasted. The purses at the tracks were large, so if he could just start racing Raven and win . . . Then, when Raven's racing days were over, they could put him out to stud and build up their stocklines. Clay had the future all plotted out in his mind. Cordell horses would be the talk of Louisiana, and he would be rich beyond his wildest dreams.

Clay had just finished caring for Raven and was starting from the stable when he caught sight of his mother's carriage coming up the front drive. He was delighted that she was back from her three-day shopping trip to New Orleans and he could hardly wait to see her again. The maturity he had displayed while dealing with the horse disappeared as he raced eagerly for the main house.

Clay idolized his mother, the gorgeous Evaline Cordell. He thought her the most gentle, loving, beautiful woman in the world, and while most of society was in accord with his assessment of her beauty, the other qualities he endowed her with were not as quickly agreed upon. Dutiful, adoring son that he was, Clay was too young to realize that there could be another side to her — another woman behind the motherly façade she presented him. He knew only that he loved her with all his heart and that he was anxious to see her again after being apart.

Evaline Cordell, an ebony-haired beauty of porcelain complexion, entrancing gray eyes and statuesque figure, stared out the window of the carriage at the main house as the vehicle made its way up the drive. Her expression was filled with loathing and disgust as she studied the structure. *Plantation home indeed!* she thought nastily. True, it was a sprawling, two-story frame home with verandas front and back, but size was the only thing it had in common with the other, finer plantation houses in the area. It boasted none of the finer amenities her neighbors had, and the faded and peeling paint gave silent testimony to its owners' desperate lack of funds.

Evaline knew it was a tribute to her pride and strength of character that she'd managed to last this long, living in what she considered to be such squalor, but no more! She'd had enough! Her little "shopping" excursion into New Orleans had proven that. She was done with this unending life of poverty, and more importantly, she was done with her husband, Philip. She'd wasted too much of her life already listening to his empty promises.

Ever since she'd left New Orleans and her secret lover, Evaline had been preparing herself for her upcoming confrontation with Philip. Their marriage was over now, and he was going to have to accept it. She was leaving him, and she was never coming back. As the carriage pulled to a stop in front of the house, she smiled cunningly to herself. Soon this farce of a life she'd been living would be finished, and she would finally have everything she'd always wanted . . . always deserved. Once she left Philip, she would never have to do without again. From this moment on, her life was going to be perfect. With confidence, Evaline descended the conveyance and started up the front steps.

Philip Cordell was deeply involved in trying to figure out how to keep the plantation running and still meet his bills when the study door opened. He didn't appreciate the interruption, and, scowling, he looked up in annoyance. His frown of irritation faded immediately, though, as Evaline swept into the room. All thoughts of his financial woes vanished before the glory of her loveliness.

"Evaline, darling, you're back." Philip came to his feet to greet her, his brown-eyed gaze darkening in appreciation. He still loved his wife with the same passionate devotion he'd had for her on their wedding day, and he had missed her desperately during her time away.

"Philip," Evaline said coolly, not responding to the warmth in her husband's tone.

Struck by the iciness with which she'd spoken his name, Philip stopped in midstride. "Is something wrong?"

"We must talk," she answered quickly, wanting only to get the interview over with. She had things to do . . . places to go . . . people waiting for her . . .

"Of course, but first let me welcome you home properly," Philip said softly as he reached for her. All he could only think of was the excitement of holding her again, of tasting of her wine-sweet kisses and making her his once more.

Evaline was well aware of the effect her striking good

10

looks had on Philip. He had often told her that her mouth with its full lower lip just begged to be kissed, and she could tell by his avid approach that he was intent on doing just that right now. She, however, was in no mood to suffer his pawings. When Philip tried to take her in his arms, she shifted away.

"No, Philip," she dictated sternly.

"Evaline? What is it?" Philip asked.

Evaline knew she had to get this over with as quickly as possible, and she turned on him, her manner haughty, her expression icy. "I'm leaving you, Philip." Her words were dripping with contempt.

By the time Clay reached the steps to the wide front porch, his mother had already disappeared inside. Knowing what a stickler she was about proper appearances, he paused just long enough to catch his breath, straighten his clothing and run a taming hand through the thickness of his windblown hair. Hoping that he looked presentable, Clay hurried indoors only to discover that she had already gone into the study where he knew his father was hard at work.

Clay was tempted to barge right in after her for the door was standing partially open, but caution held him in restraint. Earlier that morning, his father had commanded him not to interrupt him for he had some important paperwork to do. Remembering the admonition, Clay waited impatiently behind the door just out of sight, trying to listen to their conversation so he could know when it was safe to go on in and welcome his mother home.

"I'm leaving you, Philip."

His mother's declaration washed over him, draining all the color from his face as his stomach sank in a sudden, lurching motion. *She was leaving?* She'd just gotten home. Why would she be leaving again? He frowned, trying to understand what was going on.

11

Within the room neither Philip nor Evaline was aware of their son's presence.

Philip was staring at his wife, dumbfounded. "You're leaving?"

"Yes, Philip, I've only returned to pack my things."

"But I don't understand . . ." he said slowly, in total confusion.

"Of course you don't," she told him scathingly. "You've never understood me, and you never will!"

Philip reeled from her cruel verbal blows. His whole life was centered on his wife. She was his world. "Evaline, tell me what's wrong . . . I'll do whatever I can . . ."

"It's too late for that, Philip."

"Too late? What are you saying?"

"I've met another man . . ."

"Who, Evaline? I swear I'll kill the bastard!"

"He's someone who'll take care of me, Philip. Someone who will give me all the things you promised you'd give me when we married!" She threw the words at him accusingly.

Philip stared at his wife in disbelief and growing fury. *She'd been with another man?* When she faced him fearlessly without showing any shame, his anger exploded. He grabbed her by the upper arm and jerked her to him. "Who's dared to steal you from me?"

"I never belonged to you, so I can't be stolen," Evaline snarled. She was enjoying putting him through this torment, for she believed it little enough pay-back for the humiliation she'd suffered through the years. She'd been raised in a wealthy home, and Philip had vowed that he would provide the same for her. He'd lied.

"Evaline, I won't let him take you from me . . ."

"The idea to leave you was mine, Philip. *Mine!* I want to leave you!" Evaline smiled at him, coldly, viciously.

"I'll kill any man who touches you!"

12

"Don't bother, Philip," she sneered, twisting free of his bruising hold. "It won't change how I feel about you or how I feel about living here at Windown."

Philip had always placed his wife on a pedestal. He'd adored her unquestioningly, thinking her the most perfect woman in the world, but his blind love for her shattered in that instant. For the first time, he saw her for what she really was—a self-centered, spoiled woman who cared for no one but herself. It wounded Philip to think he could have been so wrong for so long, and the realization stunned him. "Why you little . . ."

"Spare me your condemnation, Philip," she dismissed his rage with an unconcerned wave of her delicate, perfectly manicured hand as she glanced back at him. "I don't care what you think of me. I'm sick of you and of this hovel you call a plantation!" Evaline's face was a mask of disgust as she stared about the room, noting the threadbare drapes, the worn carpet and the old furniture. "We've been married for fourteen years, and all I've got to show for it is this!"

"Don't do this, Evaline. Give me more time! I know I can make Windown a showplace! Just give me a few more years!"

"A few more years?" she scoffed. "You're a fool, Philip. This broken-down farm is never going to pay off!"

"No, I've got plans." He wanted to tell her of his plans to make Windown into the best horsebreeding plantation in the state, but she wouldn't listen.

"I want to live, Philip," she said. "I want to enjoy life, not grow old before my time! I've found someone who'll keep me the way I want and deserve to be kept, and I'm going to him."

"What about our vows? You know I love you!" His voice was strangled as he spoke. He was a proud man who'd never begged for a thing in his life.

Evaline gave him a pained look. "I don't love you, Philip," she declared. "Sometimes, I honestly think I

13

never did."

At her words, Philip blanched and his heart turned to stone in his chest.

"As soon as I pack my things, I'll be leaving," Evaline said.

"What about Clay?" Philip almost whispered this last plea.

"What about him?" She shrugged indifferently. There was no room in her heart for more than her own indulgent self-love. She considered her son more of an annoyance than a godsend. True, he was a handsome boy, but what would she do with a child? "He'll be fine here with you," she dismissed.

"For God's sake, Evaline, think about what you're doing!"

"I have thought about it, Philip! I've thought of nothing else for months now! I can't stand being poor any longer!"

"I won't let you go!"

"You really have nothing to say about it." Her eyes narrowed dangerously, their gray depths shining almost silver as she thought he might try to stop her. "Don't try to prevent me from going or bother coming after me. It won't do you any good! I've made up my mind."

With that, Evaline turned her back on her husband and her past life and left the room, closing the door behind her. Outside, to her surprise, she came face to face with Clay.

"You heard?" She'd hoped to leave without seeing Clay, but realized now that there was no way she was going to be able to avoid talking to him.

"Yes," Clay stammered in bewilderment.

"Good," Evaline said coolly. She was glad he'd been listening; now she wouldn't have to go through it again.

"Can I go with you?" he asked, his voice filled with hope. Though he loved the plantation and his horse, at that moment he loved her more.

14

"No," she snapped without even considering his request. The last thing she wanted or needed was a child clinging to her.

Her reply was so abrupt and so cold that wild emotions jolted through Clay. His hands tightened into fists at his sides as he fought to control them.

"But why not? I'll be good, Mother, I promise . . ." he pleaded with heartfelt emotion. He didn't want to be separated from her. He wanted to stay with her. He couldn't understand why she didn't want him.

"I said no, Clay, and that's final. You stay here with your father." She started to walk away from him, effectively dismissing him from her life, but he clutched at her arm, not wanting to let her go.

"Did I do something to make you mad? If I did, I'm sorry, Mother."

Evaline cringed at his clinging and shook him off. "For God's sake, act like a man!" she scolded him cruelly. "You'll be fine here with your father."

"But I want you to be here, too," Clay insisted with childish determination.

"Sometimes, Clay," his mother replied with cold precision, "we don't always get what we want in life."

"But Mother . . ." he started to say more, but stopped as he saw the icy indifference in her expression.

"Your father will take care of you," Evaline told him. Then without another word or gesture, she headed up the staircase, leaving her young son standing there alone. She did not bother to look back. The life she'd suffered through here at Windown was behind her now. All she cared about was her future, and it promised to be a happy one.

Pale and shaken, Philip stood rigidly in the middle of the study, trying to deal with the shock of what had just transpired. In the course of a few minutes, his entire

15

world had been destroyed. Evaline had always been his sole reason for living and now . . .

Needing something to strengthen him, he strode to the liquor cabinet in the corner of the study and grabbed up the bourbon. Not bothering with a glass, he drank straight from the bottle. As the fiery liquor burned down his throat, Philip wondered desperately how he was going to go on. Life had no meaning any more. There was no reason to go on without Evaline. He was so lost in thought that he didn't hear the door open or Clay enter the room.

"Papa?"

Clay . . . The sound of his son's voice so close behind him shook Philip to the core, and he desperately tried to get a grip on himself. How on God's earth was he going to tell Clay what had happened? Setting the bottle aside, he paused to draw a deep steadying breath and then finally turned around to confront his son.

Clay was standing just inside the door, his expression questioning and fearful.

"You heard?" he asked.

"Yes." Clay nodded.

"I'm sorry, son." It hurt him even more to know that Evaline had caused this sorrow in his son.

"But I don't understand."

"Neither do I," he replied uneasily. "I guess your mother needs some time away from us."

"She's going to come back, isn't she?"

The hope in Clay's voice caused Philip to agonize. He knew his son was desperate for some reassurance that everything would be all right, and he wasn't sure how to answer. He was torn between love and hate for Evaline, between wanting her desperately and hating the very thought of her. Her brutally vicious words and actions stabbed at the love he had for her over and over again, and as that tender emotion died, his hate and rage overwhelmed him.

Still, Philip knew he couldn't hurt his son that way.

He couldn't tell Clay that his mother was an amoral slut, who loved no one but herself and cared only for her own pleasures. Motivated by a fatherly desire to protect what was left of his innocence, Philip put a reassuring arm around Clay's shoulders.

"We'll just have to wait and see, son."

It was later that afternoon when Clay stood unnoticed in the shadows of the porch. He watched in silence as his mother climbed into the carriage and pulled the door shut behind her. He wanted to run to the carriage and cry out to her not to go. He wanted to convince her to stay with them, but he knew it would do no good. She was leaving. As the conveyance moved off down the long, front drive, effectively taking her out of his life, his eyes burned with unshed tears, and a knot formed in his throat. He swallowed against the strangling sensation.

Clay's thoughts were in turmoil as he searched desperately for a way to make things right again. Again and again, he reviewed the conversation he'd overheard between his parents, hoping to find some clue there to help change things. His expression grew grave, and his gray eyes turned dark and stormy as he remembered her words. She'd claimed that Windown was a hovel. She'd told his father that she wanted to be wealthy, and it dawned on Clay, then, that money had to be the key. Money! With a child's logic, he reasoned that if his mother had gone away because they weren't rich, all he had to do was to make a lot of money and she would come back.

A surge of fierce pride and determination filled him, and he turned away from the sight of the departing carriage. In an unconsciously adult gesture, Clay squared his shoulders as if preparing for battle. Somehow, some way, he was going to make enough money so his mother would come home. He didn't care what it took, he just knew that he was going to do it. Once he and his father had made Windown into the best plantation on the river, his mother would come back. It was that simple. Yet, as Clay walked slowly toward the stable to see Raven, he couldn't help but wonder why he felt so empty and so very much alone.

Chapter One

New Orleans, 1848

Clay looped his horse's reins through the hitching post and hesitated a moment to stare up at the spacious, three-story house with its wrought-iron balconies and wide, airy windows. It was a dwelling that spoke of elegance and style, of gracious living and easy money. It was his mother's home.

Several years ago when Clay had first seen the mansion, he'd been intimidated, but today he was not. Today, he knew he could face his mother proudly, as an equal. Today, he had come to tell her that the Cordell fortunes had been reversed, that they were now one of the richest families on the river and, most importantly, that she could come home.

Clay was proud of the fact that he'd reached the goal he had set for himself so long ago. He had worked tirelessly with his father to make their stables into the finest racing stable around, and it had paid off. To his way of thinking, his mother would no longer have a reason to stay away. She had wanted wealth, and now they had it.

Clay had tried to convince his father to accompany him for he was expecting the moment to be a celebration of sorts, but Philip had been adamant in his refusal. Still, he had not tried to prevent him from coming, though, and so Clay honestly believed that if his mother agreed to return to Windown, he would be happy about it. He had often seen his father staring at her picture, and Clay felt certain that he was still in love with her. It seemed to Clay that everything was about to work out just the way he'd wanted it to.

Clay's mood was alternating between eagerness and nervousness as he climbed the stairs to the porch. Though he had seen his mother only a few times since their separation, his opinion of her had not changed. He still thought her the most beautiful, most wonderful woman alive, and he was firmly convinced that she would be pleased with Windown's success. After all, they could now give her exactly what she wanted.

As Clay paused before the front door, he took a deep breath and fought to keep his youthful excitement under tight control. He considered himself a man now, and he knew from his father's example that men did not give their emotions away. He knocked, ready for the joyous moment he'd been waiting for for years.

Evaline had been just on her way upstairs to bathe and get ready for her dinner engagement with her current gentleman friend, when the knock sounded at the door. She was in a hurry to begin her toilette, but since there was no servant around, she decided to answer the door herself. She didn't know who she expected to find on her doorstep, but it certainly wasn't her son.

"Clay? What are you doing here?" Evaline blurted out, her tone reflecting her surprise. She had only seen Clay a few times since she'd left Philip and that had been fine with her. Her life was a wonderful round of parties and high-living now, and she wanted to keep it that way. She wanted to put the past behind her once and for all.

Clay had thought he had his emotions under control, but her hostile reception left him stammering and unsure. "Mother . . ." he began awkwardly, "I, uh . . .

was wondering if I might speak with you for a few minutes?"

"I suppose, as long as it doesn't take too long." Evaline was dismayed by his request and let it show in her voice and mannerisms as she stepped back to gesture him inside.

"No it won't. I just have something important to tell you," he assured her, moving into the hall.

Neither of them said any more as she closed the door behind him and led him into the sumptuously appointed sitting room. Clay's gaze clung to his mother, and he relished just being near her again. In his eyes she was as beautiful as always. He didn't notice that she was no longer as freshly pretty as she had been before. He wasn't aware that her once smooth skin was now aging, and her once magnificent figure was now less than firm. Instead, he was caught up in the remembrance of the elusive scent that was especially hers.

A thrill of anticipation coursed through Clay. Soon everything was going to be fine. He just knew it. He found himself almost smiling at the thought of what he was about to tell her, but he controlled the impulse. He was a man, not a young boy eager for praise, and after her less-than-excited welcome, he was a little cautious about how to begin.

Evaline seated herself on a single wingchair and waved Clay into the chair opposite hers with a careless flick of her wrist. She observed him from beneath lowered lashes as he took his seat. Clay's presence was as unwanted as it was unexpected, but a part of Evaline couldn't help but admire what a handsome young man he'd become. At over six feet tall, his broad-shouldered, slim-hipped form and dark good looks made him an improved, refined version of his father, and Evaline understood with sudden, insightful clarity just what it had been about Philip that had encouraged her to leave her wealthy family. Physical attraction. It was a powerful force, but, as she knew now, by itself it would

21

only wither and die with the passing of time.

"Well? What is it you want?" she asked sharply, forcing her thoughts away from Philip. She wanted to be done with this interview so she could get on with her own plans.

"I have something important to tell you," he offered eagerly.

"Yes, what?"

"Everything's changed at home," he declared in triumph. He was ready to tell her how hard they'd worked to make Windown a success. He wanted her to be proud of the fact that the Cordells had finally come into their own. They were rich now, and money would never be a problem for them again.

"Oh?" Evaline returned with less than enthusiastic interest. She didn't want to encourage him in this conversation. She just wanted to get it over with so he would leave. Her lover, Boyd Charleton, would be coming to pick her up in a little over an hour, and she liked to be ready when he arrived.

Her indifferent tone left Clay apprehensive, but he went on undeterred. He'd waited too long for this moment to let anything stop him. Clay was certain she would be delighted with the news. It never in his wildest dreams occurred to him that she would be less than thrilled. "Yes. We've done it. Father and I have made Windown into a paying proposition."

A sudden, uneasy feeling washed over Evaline. "How nice for you."

"For all of us," Clay finished. "There's no reason for you to stay away any longer, Mother. There's enough money now. You can have anything you want. You can come home."

Evaline blinked, regarding Clay in complete astonishment. *Home? Had he said she could come home?* "Why would I want to do that?"

"Why?" Clay repeated, frowning.

"Yes, why?" Evaline rose from her seat and crossed

the room, distancing herself from him.

"Well, I thought . . ." His veneer of maturity began to crack, fractured by her surprising reaction to his good news.

"You thought, what?" She turned to look at him, her expression mocking.

"I thought that you loved us and . . ."

He didn't get to finish as she erupted into derisive laughter. "You thought that I still loved your father and you?"

The sarcasm in her laughter crushed Clay's very soul. He sat there without speaking or moving as she spewed forth the venom of truth about her feelings. The venom that Philip had known all these years, but hadn't had the heart to tell his young, idealistic son.

"My dear boy, when did I ever give you the impression that I wanted to come back to you?" she asked in disbelief. "Did you really think I would run back to Windown after all this time just because you made a little money?"

Clay's jaw tensed at her jibe.

"I can see that that's exactly what you expected, but I'm afraid that's not what's going to happen. Did your father put you up to this?"

"No!" Clay blurted out.

"So this was all your idea?"

"Yes," he answered tightly, tension gripping him as he regarded her across the room. He had waited a long time for this moment. He had often imagined how this conversation would take place. How he would offer her untold riches and how she would take him in her arms, tell him that she loved him, and return to Windown with him where they would all live happily together as a family. Now that it was actually taking place, however, it was nothing like what he'd imagined. *She* was nothing like he imagined. As he stared at her, he wondered when it was that her beauty had started to fade and when her eyes had turned so cold?

23

Evaline gave a cynical chuckle as she came to stand before him. She lifted one lily-white hand to pat his cheek indulgently. "Darling, no matter how rich you and your father become, I will not return. I'm happy. Why in the world would I want to go back to living in that hellhole?"

Clay bristled as he came to his feet. "Windown is no hellhole!"

"It's all a matter of opinion." Evaline shrugged. "I hated living on that stupid farm. I hated it from the first moment I saw it, and I hated your father for taking me there. I have everything I've ever wanted now, Clay. I'm happy with my life just the way it is. I have no desire to change it. You can keep your money. I have no need for it."

Clay stood, his entire body rigid. "But I've worked for years so I could give you what you wanted . . ."

"Clay, the only thing I wanted from you was my freedom, and I've had that since the day I left," she said it with pointblank cruelty, bored with the conversation. "You are my son, but I suppose I'm the type of woman who should never have had children, let alone a husband."

He cringed inwardly at her words. "But you and father never divorced . . ."

"A mere technicality, Clay. I fully expected him to divorce me for desertion, but when he never took legal action . . ." She lifted her shoulders in an elegant gesture of nonchalance. "I never really worried about it. I vowed to myself long ago that I would never be trapped into marriage again, so it really didn't matter."

"I see," he managed through clenched teeth. An icy, helpless rage was slowly overwhelming Clay as he came to understand the truth. She didn't love him or his father. She didn't want to come back, now or ever, and she probably never had. All the years he'd devoted to winning her back had been for nothing. His dream of their being a family again was just that — a dream, and a childish one at that.

An understanding of his father's attitude dawned on Clay then, and he realized what a wise man his father really was. His father had known all along how his mother felt, but had refused to shatter his son's innocent illusions or poison his mind against her. He had let Clay find out the truth for himself, and that painful lesson, so vividly taught, impressed him more now than all the lectures he might have given.

"I hope you do," Evaline continued, moving toward the hall. She paused in the archway of the open parlor door in an obvious effort to get him to leave. "I have my own life now and have no wish to change anything."

Clay stared at her for a moment as pain coursed through him. He realized what a fool he'd been, and he swore to himself right then and there never to allow another woman to ever become so important to him. Clay's gray-eyed regard turned glacial as he committed to memory the sight of her standing there and with such utter disdain as she ushered him out of her life once and for all. It was a bitter mental portrait he would carry with him the rest of his life.

Drawing on every ounce of willpower he had, Clay allowed his eyes to meet hers. In the silver depths so like his own, he saw no reflection of any warmth or hidden affection. He gave a slight incline of his head as he started for the front door. "As you wish." When he passed her, he almost called her mother, but choked on the word. Instead, he bid her a curt, "Madam."

"Good-bye, Clay," was all Evaline said, and she shut the door behind him without a second thought.

Clay kept himself under control as he descended the steps and untied his horse. He had expected to be leaving here and returning home right away, triumphant, but now, all thoughts of returning home were banished. The pain of his heartbreak and humiliation was too great. He needed time away . . . time to think.

Swinging up into the saddle, Clay turned his mount

and headed for the riverfront and its section of wild, rowdy saloons. It was not the usual area of town he frequented for entertainment when he was in New Orleans, and he was glad. He didn't want to risk running into anyone he knew right now. All he wanted to do was to find forgetfulness in the numbing solace of cheap liquor.

Clay managed to open his eyes to a squint and was immediately blinded by the harsh noonday sun that was blazing through the dirt-streaked window. Pain throbbed sharply through his head at the unexpected, searing invasion of his senses, and he groaned out loud as he threw a protective, shielding forearm over his eyes.

"*Mon cher?*" a slurred, thickly French, female voice sounded from very close beside him.

Clay started in surprise to discover he was not alone. The nauseating scent of heavy perfume and stale liquor assailed him, and his stomach gave a churning lurch. In a tangle of semi-drunken, semi-hungover confusion, Clay wondered distractedly just where he was. The agony that was pounding in his head screamed to be eased, and the distant memory of a half-empty bottle of whiskey called out to him with sickening seductivity.

"Gimme the whiskey . . ." Clay growled. He needed something to clear not only his head, but his mouth as well. It tasted terrible, like the bottom of a backwater bayou.

"Here," came the voice again as the bottle was pressed into his hand. "Shall I help you sit up?"

Clay looked around for the first time, and his eyes fell upon the woman stretched wantonly out on the mattress beside him. She was a pretty girl with long, dark hair and a lushly curved figure, but for the life of him could not remember how he came to be here naked in her bed. With a groan, he tilted the bottle to

26

his lips and took a deep drink.

"Let me help you . . ." she offered again, her tone husky with implied meaning. Though she was only nineteen, Monique LaPointe had known many men, yet in all her experience not one of them had excited her the way this one did. This Clay, as he had called himself, was one handsome, virile young man, and she silently mourned the fact that, had things been different in her life, she might have had the chance to marry a man like this. He was a man who could be kind and gentle, a man who cared that she shared his pleasure. She'd enjoyed every minute they'd had together since he'd come to her room two nights ago, and she hated to see him leave.

"No," Clay refused her offer, pushing himself up into a sitting position as he glanced around the room. Still not sure where he was, he lifted the bottle to his lips for another quick dose of artificial strength.

"That isn't what you said last night," Monique said a bit playfully, hoping to arouse his considerable ardor one more time. He'd been an insatiable lover, and she'd taken great delight in pleasing him. She reached out to caress the leanness of his ribs, but he snared her hand before she could make contact.

"No more," Clay said flatly, knowing that he had to get out of there. "What time is it?"

"You're worried about the time? Shouldn't you be asking me what day it is?" she asked archly.

"Day? What are you talking about?" Clay frowned.

"You've been here with me for two days."

"Two days?" The shocking news had a very sobering effect on him. How had he lost two whole days of his life? His movements were jerky as he set the bottle on the floor and got up. He wondered what had happened during that time, and he was embarrassed as he grabbed his clothes and began to dress. "I have to go."

"Pity," she cooed, watching in disappointment as he pulled on his pants and buckled his belt. "It's still so early . . . we could . . ."

"Here." Clay dug a hand into his pants' pocket and pulled out his remaining cash. He quickly tossed a goodly amount on the bed next to her, and he watched as her eyes widened in appreciation.

"Ooh, thanks. But for this much are you sure you wouldn't like to. . . ?"

"Forget it." The only thing Clay wanted to do was to get out of there. "Where's my horse?"

"He's in the stable out back."

"Thanks." Clay gave a nod as he finished buttoning his shirt and then picked up his hat. He was opening the door when she spoke again.

"Will you be back?"

There was a wistfulness to her tone that made Clay pause as he started from the room. He glanced back at her and saw the flicker of hope in her eyes.

"No," he said solemnly, "I won't be back."

Somehow Monique had known his answer before he'd said it. She realized all along that he didn't belong there with her, even though she longed to keep him with her if she could. He was from another world. A world she dreamed of, but knew she never would belong to. Tears burned in her eyes as she watched him expectantly, waiting for him to leave. But when he turned from the door and came back to the bedside, she held her breath. With a gentle touch, Clay reached down and drew her to her knees before him on the bed. In a sweet, tender gesture, he kissed her cheek. He left her then without saying a word.

There was a touch of sadness in her voice when she called after him, "You take care of yourself . . ." But he had already gone, shutting the door behind him.

It was long hours in the saddle later when Clay turned his mount down Windown's main drive. Since leaving the city, he'd been sorting out his thoughts, and it had been painful for him. No longer was he the young innocent who'd left the plantation several days before. He'd faced the ugly truth of his life now, and as his beloved home came into distant view at the end of the winding road, he knew what he had to do.

Clay reined his horse in beneath one of the spreading oak trees bordering the drive just to enjoy the view of the house for one last time. Six years ago, the house had been a modest, but decaying, wooden, two-story structure with little magnificence or character. Today, the pillared, glistening, whitewashed brick, three-story mansion was the crowning glory of all his father's, and his own, hard work. They had both struggled and fought to make Windown into the success that it was, but, Clay realized with a sickened heart, all his work had been for nothing. His mother would not be returning . . . not now . . . not ever.

A great weariness of soul claimed Clay, and he closed his eyes against the memories that threatened to overwhelm him. He didn't want to think about how, up until just a few days ago, he'd held onto the dream of hearing the sound of his mother's footsteps in the hall once again or catching the scent of her sweet, light perfume as she swept through the rooms. That was over. Finished. Part of the past.

Still, Clay knew that if he returned to Windown, those memories would haunt him forever. The dream of his mother coming home had been his driving force all this time. Everything he'd accomplished had been done with that goal in his mind, and now he realized that goal was unattainable.

His dream shattered, Clay knew that he had to get away. The woman he'd cherished and strove to please all these years had never really existed. The mother he'd loved had been purely a figment of his naive, wishful imagination. *Well,* Clay told himself firmly, *he was naive and wishful no longer.* He would leave Windown and the pain of its memory-shadowed glory. Clay

29

mounted up again and rode on toward the house, ready to face his father with the news.

Philip did not try to disguise the tears that clouded his vision as he watched Clay pack his saddlebags the following day. He had argued with his son long into the night, trying to convince him not to leave, but his efforts had been futile. Clay had become as stubborn a man as he himself was. Once he was determined to do something, he would not be deterred.

"I'm going to miss you, son," he told Clay, his voice choked with emotion.

"I'm going to miss you, too," Clay replied, looking up from his task to find his father's sorrow-filled eyes upon him.

"Are you sure you're doing the right thing?"

"I'm doing the only thing," he reaffirmed his conviction to go. He knew that his father didn't want him to leave, but this was something he had to do. "Who knows what I'll find out west? I may end up in California and try my luck at the gold fields. I might even strike it rich . . ." Clay let the thought drop without further comment. Wealth was the last thing he was concerned about right now. He had learned for a fact that riches didn't bring happiness. All he wanted was inner peace.

"You'll come back?" Philip desperately needed to know that Clay would one day return; without that hope to cling to, his life stretched before him in one endless sea of pointlessness.

"I'll be back," Clay promised.

"Windown is your home. No matter where you are or what you're doing, remember that."

"I will."

The moment was a poignant one as their gazes locked. Philip knew his son was a man now, but he couldn't stop himself from throwing his arms around him and hugging him. Clay returned the embrace without reserve, feeling all the love and affection his father held for him in that one heartfelt moment. When they moved apart, there was no embarrassment, only a true depth of caring.

Clay picked up his things then, and they started from the room. They made their way to the front of the house without saying anything more.

"You be careful and take care of yourself," Philip urged as they stepped out onto the wide front porch.

"You, too," Clay replied. They clasped hands one last time. After a final glance at the house, Clay descended the stairs to mount the waiting Raven. Putting his knees to Raven's sides, he headed off down the drive, a solitary man.

Philip watched his son ride away, his heart filling with an acrid bitterness for the woman who was responsible for all their misery.

"*Evaline* . . ." he spat. Her name was a curse on his lips as he silently reviled her. He'd despised her ever since that fateful day six years before. Evaline — so selfish, so vicious, so destructive. The pitiful part of it was, Philip knew she had no idea of the heartbreak she'd caused her son. The woman was completely without conscience.

During the last six years, Philip had been tempted to tell Clay the truth about his mother, but had refrained. Clay had loved her deeply with a child's devotion, and he had not wanted to take that last vestige of innocence from him. As he watched him disappear from sight, Philip wondered if he'd been wrong in trying to protect him. Guilt assailed him for keeping his silence, but he dismissed it. Clay had been bound to find out about her for himself, and now that he knew the truth too, neither one of them would ever be hurt by her again.

Righteous anger blossomed in his bitterness, and as Philip turned back into the house, he knew it was time to take action. There was no longer any reason to allow

31

Evaline to continue to sully the Cordell name. He would send word to his attorney in New Orleans and have him start divorce proceedings immediately. Since Clay knew the truth, it didn't matter any more. He didn't have to continue to pretend that there was hope. He wanted that remaining tie between Evaline and himself cut as quickly as possible. As Philip sat down at his desk and began to write the missive to his lawyer, he felt a lightness of spirit that he hadn't experienced for years, and he knew instinctively that he was doing the right thing.

Chapter Two

Monterey, California, 1858

With shaking hands, Reina Isabel Alvarez adjusted the skirts of the long-sleeved, high-necked white dress she'd just changed into.

"Here, now put this on," her friend, Maria, a petite, pretty, dark-haired girl, instructed solemnly as she held out a floor-length garment that was to be worn bib-like, front and back over the loose-fitting dress.

Reina did as she was told, slipping the unusual piece of clothing over her head and feeling as if she'd been enveloped by a tent when it was in place.

"Here, Reina. This is most important . . ."

Reina reached for the stiffly starched, waist-length, black veil that Maria offered. She was about to don the headpiece when her gaze fell upon the pile of her own hastily discarded clothing on the small bed nearby, and she hesitated. Staring at the fashionable emerald-green riding habit and fancy petticoats, Reina's expression was tinged with regret. She loved beautiful clothes, and it pained her to think that she had to give them up. The memory of her purpose reasserted itself, though, and her dark eyes hardened with their intent. With a strength of will inherited from her father, she put on the veil, tucking her long, raven tresses beneath it. That done, she turned to face her friend, who'd been watching the final transformation in silence from across the room.

"Well, Maria, what do you think?" Reina asked nervously, taking care to keep her voice soft and low. Only Maria knew she was there in the convent, and it was important that she not be discovered.

Maria, Reina's friend since childhood stared at her in awe-struck wonder. "Take a look for yourself," she urged in a whisper, pointing to the small mirror over the washstand in the corner of her tiny, spartanly-furnished bedroom.

Reina swallowed tightly as she turned to the mirror. *This had to work! It just had to!* She lifted her gaze to look at her reflection and was startled by the vision of the woman who gazed back at her. It was she, and yet, it wasn't!

Reina studied her mirror image in disbelief. The eyes were her eyes, wide, dark brown and expressive as they reflected the uncertainty she was now feeling. The mouth was her mouth, full and mobile, given to quick pouts and even quicker smiles when she was given her way. The chin was her chin with its determined tilt that revealed so much of her fiery, stubborn personality. Yet, despite recognizing all these individual features, with her hair hidden beneath the concealing veil, she looked entirely different. She looked like a nun.

"I don't believe it . . ." Reina breathed, staring at herself.

"Believe it. You look as if you were born to a vocation," Maria said in a low voice, wondering how the haughty, flamboyant Reina Alvarez, only daughter of the richest ranchero in the valley, could change her image so completely just by donning a nun's habit. Reina looked positively devout, and if there was one thing Reina wasn't, it was devout. Not that she was a bad person. It was just that for as long as Maria had known her, Reina had been too full of herself, too much in love with the joys of living her life to the fullest to give much thought to anything besides her own pleasures.

"Perhaps I should consider joining you here?" She glanced back over her shoulder at her friend.

"Don't jest about something so sacred," Maria reprimanded her firmly. She knew full well what Reina's thoughts were about the religious life, for she had tried to talk her out of joining the order several times. Maria had not listened to her, though, and had just been professed after completing her required year as a novice.

"Who's jesting?" Reina returned petulantly. "Even a life here would be far preferable to being forced to marry that disgusting American!" She practically spat the word "American," so deep was her dislike for the man her father had so unexpectedly chosen to be her betrothed.

A shiver skittered down Reina's spine as she remembered how only three nights ago her father had announced his plan that she would marry the American, Nathan Marlow, in just six short months. If that hadn't been shocking enough, he'd refused to listen to her objections, and his uncharacteristic, callous disregard for her feelings had hurt her. Still, at the time, Reina had felt certain that she would eventually be able to convince him to change his mind, for, after all, he had never denied her anything before. But when her father had gone ahead and made the surprise announcement that very night at the party they were giving at Rancho Alvarez, she'd been trapped.

Furious over what Reina considered to be her father's betrayal, she'd been forced to act out a charade of happiness for their guests with the smiling, gloating Nathan at her side. When the crowd of well-wishers who'd gathered around the happy couple had dispersed, she'd been helpless to object as the blond-haired American businessman had maneuvered her out onto the patio for a few minutes alone. Reina had

35

tried to maintain her calm, but when Nathan had boldly kissed her and then attempted to caress her, she had fought him tooth and nail. Reina had had her fair share of kisses from her many suitors, but there had been something about Nathan's touch that had repulsed her, and she wasn't quite sure why.

Reina grimaced inwardly now, as the memory of his derisive laugh and taunting words *"Don't worry, Reina, I can wait for our wedding night. You'll be mine soon enough!"* echoed threateningly through her. Again, Reina shivered, and, realizing that Maria was talking to her, she dragged her thoughts away from the misery of that night.

"I don't understand how you can say Nathan Marlow is disgusting," Maria was saying. "I've seen him, and he's not an ugly man."

"If you think he's so handsome, you marry him!" Reina told her heatedly, knowing she would never be able to stand having him touch her again.

"Reina! You know I'll never marry! I was just saying that Nathan's not unattractive. He's rich, too, isn't he?"

"I don't need money, and I certainly don't need a husband!" Reina faced her friend, her eyes flashing with indignation. "I just don't know how my father could have done this to me! How could he have pledged me in marriage without first considering my feelings?"

"It's true, this doesn't sound like your father," Maria agreed, puzzled. "Did you try to talk to him about it?"

"I tried, but he wouldn't listen!"

"What reason did he give you for his sudden decision that you should marry?"

"That's what's so strange. He wouldn't give me a reason. He just said that it was time I got married and that Nathan was perfect for me. I'm only nineteen, Maria, hardly a spinster!" Reina agonized. "I've always dreamed of marrying for love, but now . . ."

"Is there some other way you can make your point with him?" Maria suggested hopefully, trying to discourage her from this wild scheme she'd concocted. Yet, even as she tried to dissuade Reina, she knew her obstinate friend was not about to be deterred.

"No, I've tried everything already. When Father locked me in my room and—"

"I don't believe it! He locked you in your room?" Maria was shocked. She had known Luis Alvarez all her life, and it was not like him to be so harsh with his daughter.

"Yes, and he threatened to keep me there until I agreed to do as he ordered." Reina felt suddenly tired, and she sat down on the small bed. "I stayed there for one whole day, but it didn't sway him at all. When I tried to talk with him again, he still refused to listen to reason. That's when I knew I had to do something drastic just to let him know how serious I was."

"So you came here . . ."

"It took me almost a full day of traveling by horseback, but it was worth it. Father will never look for me here, and, with this disguise, I should be able to make it safely to New Orleans. I have friends there who'll help me."

"You're planning on traveling to New Orleans alone?"

"I am." She bristled at her friend's unspoken criticism. Nothing was going to stop her from escaping the fate her father had planned for her, nothing!

"But you can't!" Maria insisted, coming to sit beside her. "It isn't safe for you to travel unescorted."

"God will be my escort," she replied with flourish. "I'm a nun now, remember? No one's going to bother me."

"I wish I could be as sure as you are."

"You can be sure, Maria. Nothing's going to happen to me." A rueful smile curved Reina's lips as she stared down at the relatively shapeless garment she wore. She had always prided herself on her extensive wardrobe, making it a point to be perfectly gowned for every occasion. *Certainly*, Reina decided, *this was the perfect gown for this occasion*. Since the habit reflected an image of purity, chastity and godliness, Reina was sure that no man would even look at her, let alone give her a second thought. It was the total opposite of her usual way of thinking, and yet, she was immensely pleased by the idea. To make her getaway, she had to travel unnoticed.

"I hope not!"

"Everything's going to be fine once my father realizes that I'm not about to marry Nathan," she declared, believing in her heart that her father would come around to her way of thinking.

There was a sound in the hall outside Maria's closed door, and the young nun's eyes widened in sudden panic as she realized the precariousness of their situation. She had smuggled Reina into the convent when she'd come to her for help, and she could not afford to have anyone discover she was there, especially not wearing one of the other sister's borrowed habits.

"Shhh . . ." She clutched Reina's hand as she glanced nervously toward the door. "If we get caught now . . ." Her stomach knotted at the thought. Her Mother Superior wouldn't look kindly on her activities with Reina.

Maria's warning reminded Reina that her victory over her father's unbending domination was not yet insured, and she went a little pale.

"We'll have to be extra careful," Maria warned.

"How soon can I leave without anyone seeing me?"

"Maybe another hour . . . everybody's usually in bed by midnight. We can sneak you out then."

"Good, then all I have to do is make it onto the stagecoach without being caught. After that, it'll be easy."

"I hope you're right, Reina."

"Of course, I'm right. By the time father discovers where I've gone, he'll have realized what a foolish

38

mistake it was to try to force me into marriage. He'll be so happy to have me back that he'll agree to anything," Reina explained simplistically. Yet, even as she tried to convince herself that it would happen as she hoped, she couldn't help but wonder about the unusual way her father had acted in regard to the betrothal. It was totally out of character for him to coerce her into doing anything; yet, in the face of her adamant refusal, he had not backed down. Instead, he had become even more insistent and had even punished her! She prayed that her plan would work for if it didn't—

It occurred to Reina that things might never be the same, and the prospect deeply frightened her. Stiffening her resolve, she banished all thoughts of failure. Her father was going to come around. He had to!

"What about money? Have you got enough?" Maria asked.

"Yes, I've got plenty. In fact, here . . ." Reina searched through the small reticule she'd brought with her and then handed Maria a substantial amount.

"What's this for? You're going to need all the money you've got."

"That's for the two habits," she told her, smiling a bit guiltily. "I don't want to go through life with the sin of stealing from a nun on my soul. Leave it where Sister will find it."

Maria grinned back at her. "I will."

"Is there anything else I need to know?" Reina had made it a point never to pay too much attention to religious matters. It troubled her now that she knew so little about being a nun.

"Do you think you can keep from flirting?" she asked in good humor, knowing how much her friend enjoyed the attentions of all the handsome young men who were always vying for her favors.

"You needn't worry about that. Right now, men are the last thing on my mind," she answered seriously. "All I want to do is to get to New Orleans."

"Then you'll be fine. Just don't forget who you're supposed to be while you're traveling. You're no longer Reina Alvarez. You're Sister Mary Regina now. Remember that."

"I will."

"Here." Maria moved to her small chest of drawers to get the final accessory she would need to make the habit complete, a fifteen decade rosary. "Attach this rosary to the belt at your side."

Reina stood up and did as she was told with great care, then cast one last glance in the mirror. The transformation was complete. The real Reina Alvarez had all but disappeared, and in her place stood Sister Mary Regina, a woman of patience and love, a woman of kindness and humility, a woman who was devoting her life to service for others.

"Now, you're perfect," Maria encouraged.

"Maria, thank you. You don't know how much your help has meant to me," she told her with heartfelt emotion.

"You're my friend, Reina. I just hope everything turns out the way you want it to."

"It will," she answered and then added under her breath, "it has to."

A short time later, Maria watched from the window of her room until Reina had disappeared from sight on her way into town. She said a quick prayer, asking God to help Reina and to protect her on her trip back East.

"We've found no trace of your daughter, Señor Alvarez," Juan Sanchez admitted cautiously as he stood, sombrero in hand, before his fearsome boss. He knew of Luis Alvarez's volatile temper, and he had been dreading informing him of their lack of progress.

A tall, distinguished-looking man of some fifty years, Luis stood rigidly behind his desk as he faced his hired man. His accusing, black-eyed gaze was fixed unwaveringly upon Sanchez as he repeated in a slightly threatening tone, "Nothing?"

"Nothing, Señor Alvarez. We have looked everywhere that you told us to and have found no trace of her."

A violent rage threatened to consume him, but Luis fought to control it. Fury vibrated through his whipcord-lean body as he bit out savagely, "That's not good enough, Sanchez! Go back and check again! Reina couldn't have just disappeared off the face of the earth!"

"Yes, sir," Juan replied quickly, fearful of his boss's angry mood. "We'll head out again right away." He backed from the room, anxious to escape his displeasure.

"Sanchez!" Luis called out sharply just as the other man was about to flee from the study.

"Yes, Señor Alvarez?"

Luis's tone was only slightly less vicious as he commanded, "Make sure that you remain discreet in your inquiries. I want her found, but I do not want it to be commonly known that she is gone."

"Yes, Señor," he answered respectfully. He hurried from the room, feeling sorry for the girl who would, no doubt, face the full force of her father's considerable wrath when they finally did bring her back.

As soon as Sanchez had closed the door behind him, Luis slammed his fist down on his desktop and muttered a vile curse. Reina's defiance had taken him by surprise. Love her though he did, and he did adore her, he could not allow her to get away with this unscathed. She had left him looking weak and spineless. What man couldn't control his own daughter? He was a proud man and not used to being made the fool.

Besides that very personal humiliation, Luis also had to worry about Nathan Marlow. He had not told the rich Yankee of Reina's disappearance, and he had no intention of doing so. Too much depended on the marriage taking place as had been announced. He couldn't risk angering Marlow and having him back out on the deal they had made—the deal that would save his deed to Rancho Alvarez from being contested in the American courts and possibly, ultimately, stripped from his ownership. He had seen it happen to several of his friends, and he would not let that happen to him. He loved his daughter, but the rancho was his whole life.

Nervously, Luis stalked to his liquor cabinet and splashed a healthy dose of whiskey in a tumbler. He took a deep drink as he began to pace the room. He was not used to being out of control, but until Reina was found and brought back, that's exactly what he was.

At the thought of his offspring's defiance, he swore out loud again. How dare she defy him over the one thing he'd ever demanded she do? Hadn't he given her everything she'd ever wanted? Hadn't he always tried to please her in every way? Luis realized now that he'd made a big mistake in spoiling her so, but it was a mistake that he would take great pains to rectify once she returned. He was going to teach her that no one defied him and got away with it. No one!

Draining the last dregs of whiskey from his glass, Luis strode from the room intending to go to work on the ranch. He hoped that the distraction of a hard day's labor would keep his thoughts from straying to Reina and his desperate fear that Marlow would find out about her disappearance before he had time to find her and bring her back.

A wide, satisfied smile curved the hard line of Nathan Marlow's thin lips, and his cold blue eyes flashed with triumph as he saluted his companion with a glass of champagne. "Everything is going exactly according to plan. In just six short months the Rancho Alvarez will be as good as mine." He made the announcement with supreme, almost arrogant, confidence.

Lilly Bascomb, a tall, voluptuous redhead, was sitting on the loveseat in the parlor of her splendid home on the outskirts of Monterey listening avidly to his every word. She gave a throaty chuckle as she returned his salute with her own glass. "You're a genius, Nathan. Although, I have to admit that I did have my doubts in the beginning," she continued. "Luis Alvarez has always been rather hostile to Americans, and I feared you might not be able to convince him to change his way of thinking. But, as usual, you've succeeded brilliantly. How do you do it, darling?"

"It's a simple matter, really," he said expansively. "You just find out what a man values most and threaten to take it away from him. Negotiations begin from there." Nathan's expression turned cunning and his smile, sharkish.

"Ah," Lilly murmured in understanding, "that just shows you how differently men and women think."

"Oh?" he asked, intrigued, as he took a drink of the fine bubbling wine.

"Yes, darling. When I make plans such as yours, I find out what the man wanted above all else, and I give it to him," she explained in a husky tone.

"Is that how you caught me in your web?" Nathan asked, his gaze darkening with the heat of remembered passion.

A small, self-satisfied smile curved Lilly's perfect lips as she stated coolly, "I have no web, Nathan. You know you're free to come or go whenever you choose." She was well aware that Nathan was the type of man who wanted no ties upon him, so she made no demands of their relationship. She enjoyed what they shared with no thought to the future. Rich widow that she was, she had no desire or need for another husband.

"So well I know," Nathan answered, moving to take her glass from her and set it aside with his own. "I intend to become the richest man in California, Lilly, and I want you by my side all the way. Obtaining Rancho Alvarez is just another step on my ladder to the top."

"And the Alvarez girl . . . your soon-to-be-bride?" His plot to marry the Alvarez girl amused Lilly, and she wondered how the proud, young woman was going to react when she found out that her husband had a mistress.

"She's merely an inconvenience in my overall scheme of things, Lilly." Even as he spoke the words, Nathan knew that he was lying. Reina had stirred his passion by refusing his affections the night of the party. He was not used to being denied, and her indifference to him had whetted his appetite for more. He enjoyed a challenge, and he would take great pleasure in showing his wife the power he had over her, body and soul. Theirs would definitely not be a marriage in name only, but Lilly didn't need to know that. They were both beautiful, desirable women, and he was sure he could keep them both completely satisfied. "You know how good we are together. Reina's not going to affect what we share in any way. Surely you're not jealous?"

"Hardly," she scoffed, "you know how I abhor the thought of marriage. The few years I spent tied to Bascomb were torment enough." She stood up and linked her arms around his neck. "Pretty though she is, it would take more than that little chit to worry me, Nathan. She's too young and innocent to know how to please a man like you. What we have is quite special."

"Indeed," Nathan agreed as he bent to kiss her pouting lips.

As his mouth moved hungrily over hers, a wild animal passion exploded within Lilly. They had been apart for several days while he'd been out at the Alvarez ranch, and she'd missed him tremendously. She was a very sensual woman, and she always eagerly anticipated the time they had together. Nathan was, without a doubt, the most ardent lover she'd ever taken

44

to her bed, and she could hardly wait to be with him again. Moving sinuously, erotically against him, Lilly enticed him to forget everything but the lusty pleasure she could give him. When Nathan groaned at her brazenness, she drew away.

"I've had enough talking for the night . . ." she told him in a sultry voice, leading the way to the privacy of her bedroom.

"So have I," he agreed, following Lilly from the room. Having never been a man to stay with one woman for long, he supposed the reason he'd never tired of her during their year together was because they were so much alike. She was a woman who knew what she wanted in life and took it. Her boldness pleased him and he wanted her, yet as he closed the bedroom door behind them, he could not put thoughts of Reina from his mind.

Chapter Three

Rafael Casita's expression was shocked when Luis finished explaining his situation. "I don't believe it! Reina has run away rather than marry the American?"

"Yes, but once I find her and bring her back, she'll change her mind. Reina will marry Marlow, mark my words," Luis snarled in angry frustration as he faced Rafael across the desk in his law office. The silver-haired, heavy-set attorney had been his friend for many years, and it was to him that Luis now turned for counsel.

Rafael gave a slow, disbelieving shake of his head as he studied his old friend. New, deep lines of worry were etched into his dark, handsome face, and there was exhaustion and a touch of fear haunting his eyes. "This doesn't sound like Reina at all."

"I know," Luis said bitterly. "She has never defied me in her life. Why should she choose to do so now, when what I've asked of her is so vitally important?"

"You say your men have searched everywhere?" he digressed.

"Everywhere," Luis confirmed. "That's why I'm here. I came to double check myself. But they were right. There's no trace of Reina to be found."

"What are you going to do next?"

"I don't know," he responded tightly. "You know my problem. I must make this alliance with Marlow if I am to have any hope of keeping the rancho intact."

"We could always fight the challenge to your owner-ship of Rancho Alvarez in court," Rafael suggested, hating to see his friend backed into a corner this way.

"There's no point to it," Luis despaired. "I've seen my friends mortgage everything they own to prove the validity of their land grants and deeds in the American courts, only to lose anyway and end up in poverty."

"I see your point." The attorney agreed reluctantly. He knew well the unfair workings of the new American judicial system. The general feeling among the gringos ever since they had started trying to take over the state was that it was unfair for so much land to be owned by only a few dirty Mexicans. The newcomers had begun challenging the ownership of many of the various ranches, forcing the Californios to prove their claims, even though the land may have been in their families for many generations. Very few had been able to win their cases. Many had lost just about everything.

"There's no use in beggaring myself to fight a losing battle. That's why I've worked out this arrangement with Marlow. With a rich, powerful Yankee for a son-in-law, my holdings will be safe." Luis's expression grew thunderous as he turned his thoughts once again to his daughter. "If I can just find Reina, everything will be all right."

They were both lost in thought for a moment, Luis imagining himself locating Reina and dragging her home and Rafael wondering how he could help him in his search. Silence stretched heavily between them until the lawyer remembered the man he'd encountered at the jail earlier that afternoon.

"I have an idea . . ." Rafael offered tentatively, not sure how his friend would react to what he was about to suggest.

"What?"

"I'm not sure you'll like it . . ."

"Rafael, I'm desperate. I'll listen to anything that

47

might help."

"Clay Cordell's in town. I saw him at the jail today while I was there meeting with the sheriff."

"Clay Cordell? Who is he? I've never heard of him."

"He's one of the best bounty hunters in the state. He and his partner, a big Irishman named O'Keefe, brought in Ace Denton today," Rafael supplied.

"Ace Denton, the gunfighter?"

"Yes. They tracked him down and brought him back alive to stand trial."

"You think I should hire this bounty hunter to find Reina?" Luis was doubtful. He knew what kind of men bounty hunters were.

"You need help, Luis. Reina's very clever, but Cordell could find her. I'm familiar with his reputation. He's good at what he does."

"But I must keep this quiet!"

"The man makes his living tracking people down. I'm sure for a price you could hire him to find Reina *and* keep his mouth shut while he's doing it." When Luis still looked unconvinced, he went on. "What have you got to lose? You won't be able to keep her disappearance a secret forever. What will happen if Marlow finds out that she's gone?"

"I know, I know," he agonized. "All right. I'll do it. Where can I find this gringo?"

"He and O'Keefe are probably in one of the saloons celebrating their good fortune. Cordell's a tall man with dark brown hair and a beard. He was wearing all black when I saw him earlier. O'Keefe's almost as tall as Cordell, but he's brawnier. He's clean-shaven and black-haired."

Luis got slowly to his feet, his reluctance obvious. He knew he had to do it, for Reina had left him no other choice. If hiring this stranger to find her was the only way he could get her back in time to avoid a scandal, he would do it.

"I'll be waiting to hear from you," Rafael said as he

walked him to the door.

"I'll come back after I speak with him."

"Good, by the way . . ." He put a hand on his arm to stop him from leaving. "I almost forgot to tell you. While I was speaking with the sheriff, someone came in with the news that Pedro Santana is dead."

"Pedro?" Luis was startled by the news. Santana had not been a close friend, but they were acquaintances.

Rafael nodded. "He was found out at his ranch north of town. He'd been shot in the back."

"Pedro was a good man, well liked and respected in the community," Luis mourned. "Why would anyone want to kill him?"

"Robbery, I guess. No one knows for sure. No witnesses have come forward yet. I'll let you know if anything develops."

"Please do. I liked Santana, and I want to see his murderer brought to justice."

With that, the two men said good-bye, and Luis headed off to find the man he hoped would be able to track down his wayward daughter.

"You boys ready for anything else?" Josie, the blonde, buxom saloon girl, asked as she sidled up to the table where the two strangers sat in the crowded, noisy bar. Though both men were covered with trail dust, they were the handsomest things to grace the Perdition Saloon in a long time. She knew from experience that men who'd been on the trail as long as they obviously had were ready for a little feminine company, and she was more than ready to supply what they needed.

"What have you got to offer, sweetheart?" Devlin O'Keefe asked in his deep, booming voice, his blue-eyed gaze hot upon the lowcut bodice of her scarlet silk and black lace dress.

"What d'ya want?" she returned archly, leaning toward him a bit to give him a better view of her barely

49

restrained breasts. "More whiskey?" She had served them a full bottle a short time before, and it was already better than half-empty.

"The whiskey will do for starters, then come back and join us, and bring a friend," Devlin instructed expansively, glancing back to the bar where another girl stood.

Josie's eyes lit up at the prospect. "I'll be right back." She sashayed back to the bar to place her order and to speak to Frenchie, the other barmaid.

"What do you think, Clay?" Devlin teased. "Are you in the mood for a blonde or a brunette?"

Clay shrugged. "One woman's the same as any other, Devlin. Seems the blonde's caught your eye, so I'll settle for the brunette."

Devlin grinned wickedly at his friend as he finished off his glass of whiskey and poured another. "Your generosity knows no bounds."

Clay returned his smile as he, too, refilled his glass. "Anything for a friend."

The girls approached the table then, carrying another bottle and the extra glasses, and Clay reached out to snare the dark-haired saloon girl around the waist. She gave a squeal of delight as he hauled her down onto his lap, then quickly threw her arms around him and planted a hot, wet kiss on his mouth. She'd been watching this one since he'd come in a short time before and definitely thought him the handsomest of the two, with his broad-shouldered, narrow-hipped physique. She even found his beard intriguing, although she imagined he'd look even better without it.

"What's your name, handsome?" she cooed when she came up for air.

"Clay, what's yours?"

"Frenchie," the brunette told him with a wide, inviting smile.

"Well, Frenchie, let's have a drink and see what kind of excitement the rest of the night might bring."

Frenchie giggled loudly as she wriggled her hips suggestively in his lap. "I can hardly wait to see what comes up . . ."

Josie did not wait for Devlin to grab her but went willingly into his arms. She kissed him excitingly as she lay half-prone across his lap. Without preamble, she took his hand and pressed it to her ample bosom, not caring that most everyone in the saloon was watching.

"We're going to have a good time tonight," Josie promised him in a husky voice, unaware that an elderly, distinguished-looking Californio had approached their table and was watching them with something akin to distaste.

"Excuse me."

The stern precision of the intruder's tone stopped both Clay and Devlin in their playful pursuits. Both men glanced up in annoyance at the stranger who'd dared to interrupt them. The last, long weeks they'd spent tracking down Denton had taken their toll on them. They were here to relax for a while, to live it up and enjoy life, which they were obviously trying to do.

"What can we do for you?" Devlin asked, eyeing the dignified, Hispanic man and wondering what he wanted.

"I'm looking for a gentleman by the name of Cordell—Clay Cordell, to be exact." It irked Luis to think that this dirty looking, bearded man might be Cordell, but he certainly matched Rafael's description.

"Who wants to know?" Devlin demanded.

"My name is Luis Alvarez, and I have a business proposition to discuss with Mr. Cordell. If one of you gentlemen is he." Luis tensed, annoyed that this lowlife, who was so boldly and openly fondling the whore sprawled across his lap, would dare to question him.

Clay maintained an aura of coolness as he studied this Alvarez. He kept one arm nonchalantly around Frenchie's waist, yet his gun hand was resting on the handle of his revolver, just in case this man's business

51

proposition wasn't friendly.

"I'm Cordell," he answered curtly, his gaze never wavering from the man's face.

"I must speak with you, Mr. Cordell," Luis announced in his usual imperious tone. "Alone."

Clay, however, took orders from no man, and this man's attitude put him off. "I don't think so, Mr. . . . What did you say your name was again?"

"Alvarez, Luis Alvarez," he snapped, unused to such treatment.

"Well, Mr. Alvarez, I'm a little busy right now, as you can see. Why don't you look me up tomorrow? Maybe we can talk then." Clay dismissed him.

"I have a very profitable business offer to make to you, Mr. Cordell. It can't wait until tomorrow," Luis insisted, though it infuriated him to have to plead his case to a man such as this.

Frenchie's eyes had widened as she'd recognized the name. She leaned closer to Clay to whisper. "This is *the* Luis Alvarez!"

"So?" Clay responded indifferently as he took another drink of his whiskey.

"He's a very rich, very powerful man in these parts. He's not one you'd want to anger, and it might be worth your while to listen to what he has to say," she encouraged.

Clay leaned back with seeming negligence in his chair, giving Luis a cursory look. "I'm a reasonable man, Mr. Alvarez, and since you seem to think that this can't wait, what exactly is it you want?"

Luis stiffened visibly. He did not want to discuss his personal affairs in the middle of a crowded saloon. "I must speak with you privately."

"What's wrong with right here?"

"I prefer to keep it just between us," he replied with what dignity he could muster. He would not beg for anything.

"You can use my room," Frenchie offered.

"All right," Clay agreed.

The saloon girl stood up and, taking Clay's hand, pulled him up from the chair and started across the room to where the steps led upstairs.

"Wait a minute." Clay resisted her lead long enough to grab the new bottle of whiskey off the table. He flashed Devlin an easy grin when his friend would have protested. "It might be a long meeting, you never know."

"I suppose if Josie, here, keeps me busy, I won't even miss you," he returned, pulling the more than willing saloon girl up for a kiss.

"Let's go," Clay urged Frenchie and Luis, and they disappeared upstairs.

"This is it," she told them, opening the door to a small room that contained only a single bed and small wash-stand. She drew Clay inside, but Luis hesitated in the hall.

"I need to speak with you *alone*, Mr. Cordell," he insisted again, looking pointedly at Frenchie.

"Get lost, Frenchie. I'll call you when we're through talking," Clay told her.

"I'll be waiting downstairs." She ignored Luis's icy regard and kissed Clay one more time before strutting from the room.

Luis watched her move off down the hall, waiting to make sure that she went back down to the saloon, then entered the bedroom and closed and locked the door behind him.

There was something about Alvarez that Clay didn't like or trust, and always being one to rely on his instincts, he monitored the man's every move—just in case. Though Clay appeared relaxed and at ease, in truth he was tense and on edge. Bottle in hand, he stretched out comfortably on the bed, bracing himself against the headboard, and took a deep drink.

"What can I do for you, Mr. Alvarez?" Clay's eyes narrowed as they watched the old Californio come to stand at the foot of the bed.

"I understand that you make your living 'locating' people, Mr. Cordell."

Clay gave a short laugh. "I guess you could describe it that way."

"In that case, I want to hire you." Luis's pride was taking a battering, having to deal with a man like Cordell, but he knew there was no other way out.

"You want to hire me?" Clay repeated. "I don't usually hire myself out."

"I'll make it worth your while, sir. Name your price."

Clay couldn't believe what he was hearing. *Name his price?* Only a fool or a very desperate man would give a man the power to name his own pay. He was intrigued, but he was also growing more and more uneasy. He was not a hired gun, although he didn't hesitate to use force if it was necessary. "Just what is it you want me to do?"

Luis looked uncomfortable, but he answered honestly. "I want you to find my daughter."

"You what?" Clay's expression reflected his surprise at the request. He'd been anticipating any number of possibilities, but this had not been one of them.

"I want you to find my daughter. She's run away, and I want her brought back home."

"I see." Clay paused to take another drink, musing on the strangeness of his request. It almost struck him as absurd. "And just what is it your daughter is running away from?"

"That doesn't concern you, Cordell."

"You're expecting me to risk my life for you and not know the reason? Sorry, Alvarez, no deal."

"This wouldn't be a dangerous job, Mr. Cordell," Luis said haughtily. "I merely want you to locate her and bring her back to me. It should be quite simple, actually."

"If it's so damned simple, why don't you do it yourself?" Clay countered, knowing there was something the man wasn't telling him.

"I have already searched the immediate area, and she

54

is not here. It's important that no one knows she's gone."
He hesitated, not wanting to reveal too much.

"Suppose you tell me why? Then maybe I'll consider it. Otherwise . . ."

Luis saw the steely glint in the bounty hunter's eyes and knew he had to explain further. "My wife died when Reina was just a baby, and I've raised her by myself, Mr. Cordell. She's a very beautiful young woman, and, as I am a man of considerable means, it has always been my pleasure to cater to her whims. I spared no expense through the years, yet it sorrows me to say that my daughter has grown into a very self-centered, very spoiled young woman. I realize now what a terrible mistake it was for me to grant her every wish, but I love her . . ."

As he spoke, Clay felt sickened. His daughter was a beautiful, spoiled little rich girl . . . *just like his mother. This Reina didn't like her life so she ran away, and she didn't care who she hurt in the process.* Clay knew already that he wanted no part of the old man's scheme.

"She is betrothed and the wedding date is set for less than six months away. For some reason, she's decided she doesn't want to marry her fiancé, and so she ran away. I want you to bring her back."

As he finished relating his story, Clay became even more firmly convinced that he wanted no part of Alvarez's offer at any price. There was no amount of money that could convince him to go after the girl. He'd dealt with a woman like that once, and once had been enough.

"Sorry, Alvarez," Clay said flatly. "I feel real sorry for you and for this fiancé of hers, but it's not my problem. I'm not interested."

Luis couldn't believe that Cordell was actually refusing him. "But there's no danger involved, and I said you could name your own fee! All you have to do is find Reina, bring her back and keep quiet about it while you do it."

"Like I said, I'm not interested."

"Money is no object."

"You're right," Clay agreed, taking a drink of whiskey to try to wash away the nasty taste in his mouth. "Money doesn't even enter into it. Your daughter's your problem, Alvarez, not mine. Find yourself another errand boy."

Luis grew livid at his refusal. "Two thousand dollars!"

"Sorry."

"Three!"

"Do you understand the meaning of 'no,' Alvarez?" Clay was annoyed by his persistence. "I'm turning you down. My partner and I've got better things to do than chase all over the countryside after your daughter!" He took another deep swallow of the powerful liquor.

"Like drink yourselves into oblivion, Mr. Cordell?"

"You're damned right, Alvarez! Now get outta here and send Frenchie back up on your way out. She's the only kind of woman who interests me. She's warm and willing and undoubtedly a real good lay. Probably everything your daughter isn't!"

Luis sputtered with fury as Clay went on.

"Think about this, Alvarez. Maybe her fiancé is the lucky one. Maybe her taking off is the best thing that could ever have happened to the man. She'd probably have brought him nothing but misery anyway."

At Clay's bluntness, Luis stiffened, feeling almost as if he'd been struck in the face. He blanched first and then his face flushed with color as rage consumed him. He was Luis Alvarez! How dare this American talk to him so and say such things about his precious Reina!

Luis's black eyes narrowed dangerously as he stood at the foot of the bed, staring at the lazy, drunken gringo sprawled there. The fool! He obviously didn't know who he was dealing with. *Well,* Luis decided with cold, determination, *he would just have to show him.* Since Rafael had told him Cordell was the best, he would have Cordell. It just remained to be seen how he would

56

manage it.

"I wouldn't refuse so completely, Mr. Cordell. Take some time to think about my offer, and I'll be back in touch with you later." Luis turned and walked to the door.

"Don't waste your time or mine, Alvarez," Clay responded. "I'm not interested."

"We shall see, Mr. Cordell. We shall see," Luis said under his breath as he let himself out of the room.

Chapter Four

The door to the room Devlin had taken for the night upstairs at the Perdition Saloon opened silently, and the large, shadowed form of a man crept inside. The soft, diffused light from the hallway silhouetted the intruder as he hesitated just inside the doorway, listening, waiting, fearful of being caught. When the low, steady sound of Devlin's drunken snoring came to him, proving to him that it was safe to go on in, the invader closed the door behind him. With soundless tread, he crossed the room to the bounty hunter's discarded clothing. After a minute of searching, the infiltrator found what he was looking for and, silently and meticulously, did as he'd been instructed. That task completed, he moved to Devlin's other belongings. Without making a sound, he took the small package he'd been given from his own pocket and planted it deep in the bottom of the other man's saddlebags. One last look around assured him that he was finished, and he backed from the room, pleased that everything had gone so smoothly.

It was late the next night when a sudden, near violent pounding on the door woke Devlin from a sound, sex-sated, liquor-induced sleep. Beside him

Josie, too, stirred and came awake.

"O'Keefe! We need to talk with you!" a deep, commanding voice called out.

"Who is it, Dev?" Josie whispered fearfully, wondering who would come looking for him at this ungodly hour of the night.

"Damned if I know . . ." he grumbled. It took him a minute to get his bearings as he groped in the darkness for his gun. The drunken haze that enveloped him was slowing his reaction time, and he gave himself a hard mental shake, trying to clear his mind. Once he had the familiar weapon in his grasp, he finally shouted back, "Yeah . . . who is it?"

"It's Sheriff Macauley, O'Keefe, and it's important that I talk to you now!"

"Hell . . ." Devlin muttered, agitated. He slammed the gun back into the holster and pushed himself wearily from the bed. He threw the sheet more completely over Josie's lush curves, and then grabbed his pants and tugged them on. "Cover yourself up. God only knows what he wants. Maybe Denton escaped." Dev stumbled across the dark room and unlocked the door, throwing it wide. "What's so damned important that you've gotta come—"

He never got to finish his sentence, though, as Macauley burst into the room, gun drawn, with two armed and ready deputies following him.

"What the—!" Devlin exclaimed, taking a jittery step back from the unexpected force of their entry.

"Stay right where you are, O'Keefe!" the sheriff ordered. "Carter, light that lamp so we can see something! Will, take a look around!"

"Sheriff!" Devlin protested in complete confusion. "What's going on? What the hell do you want?"

"As if you don't know," Macauley sneered, keeping his gun trained on the man he believed to be a cold-blooded murderer.

"I *don't* know, Macauley!" he argued. "What are you

looking for?"

"I got it, Sheriff! It's just like you said!" One of the deputies held up Dev's silver-tooled belt.

"Let me see that!" Macauley snatched the belt from him to study it closely. When he looked up, his expression was filled with loathing. "You're under arrest, O'Keefe!"

"Under arrest?" Devlin repeated stupidly. "For what? Drinking too much?"

The sheriff's look turned scathing. "For murder. Carter, get his gun and rifle. Will, bring the rest of his things."

"Yes, sir."

"Murder?" Devlin continued to argue. "Whose murder? I haven't killed anybody! What the hell are you talking about?"

"Shut up and finish getting dressed. You can ask all the questions later from your jail cell!" the sheriff snarled, clutching the silver belt in his hand. "Gather up the rest of his things, boys. We'll go through them back at the office."

Moments later as they practically dragged him from the room, Dev called out to Josie who was watching the whole scene in astonishment from the bed, "Josie! Go get Clay! Tell him what happened!"

Clutching the sheet around her, Josie rushed from the bed to close the door, then hurried to begin dressing. She had to let Dev's friend know what happened right away. When she'd finally managed to throw on her clothes, she ran from the room and down the hall to Frenchie's.

"Frenchie!" she cried out as she banged on the locked portal with all her force.

"What is it?" came the other woman's sleepy response.

"Frenchie, open up! Something terrible's happened!"

The panic in her friend's voice sent Frenchie rushing to the door clad only in a silken wrapper, and she opened it quickly to let her in. "What's wrong? What happened?" she asked worriedly as she drew Josie inside.

Josie glanced over to where Clay lay, awake and alert, in her bed. "They took Dev, Clay! You've got to hurry! You've got to get over there!"

"Somebody took Dev?" Clay frowned in confusion as he quickly sat up. "Who? Where?"

"It was the sheriff! He came barging in my room just a minute ago and arrested him."

"Arrested him?"

Josie nodded nervously. "He said it was for murder . . ."

With that, Clay nearly vaulted from the bed and began to dress. "Tell me exactly what he said, Josie," he pressed urgently. He knew Dev and he knew how he would react to being locked up.

Dev had been just a boy of ten when his parents had fled Ireland. Neither of his parents had survived the rough ocean-crossing to America, though, and he'd arrived in New York with very little money and only an uncle to rely on for help. The uncle had taken him in, all right, but he had spent all his money and had nearly worked him to death. When Dev had dared to complain, his uncle had beaten him and then locked him in a closet until he was ready to go back to work. As soon as he was big enough and strong enough to take care of himself, Dev had left the East Coast and headed west to the gold fields. Still, to this day though, Clay knew his friend couldn't stand being cooped up in a small area. That's why he had to get him out of that jail cell right away.

"I don't know; it all happened so fast," Josie was saying. "I mean, he woke us up from a sound sleep."

"Just tell me what you can remember," he urged, stuffing the bottom of his shirt into the waistband of his pants.

"It had to do with his silver belt."

"The belt?" Clay gave her an incredulous look as he finished dressing.

"Yes. After they found it, Macauley arrested him for murder! He even brought two deputies along with him. I guess he thought Dev might be dangerous."

"I don't believe any of this!" Clay was still stunned as he strapped on his gunbelt.

"Believe it!" she insisted. "He told me to tell you right away."

"Thanks, Josie," he said as he picked up his hat and started from the room.

"Clay . . ." Frenchie's call reminded him of her presence.

"I don't know when I'll be back," he said, and then he was gone.

Clay reached the sheriff's office to find that his friend had indeed been arrested and was locked up in one of the cells in the back of the jail. "Macauley, I want to know what's going on."

Sheriff Macauley had been expecting Clay, and he greeted the other man coolly. "You mean, you don't know?"

"All I know is what the girl at the Perdition told me—that you'd arrested Dev for murder."

"You got your facts right, Cordell."

"What murder?"

"It's amazin' how much you two sound alike, Cordell. Maybe I should look around some more. Maybe you were in on this, too!"

"In on what?"

"A real nice man named Pedro Santana was murdered a couple of days ago out at his place. He was shot in the back."

"So what's that got to do with Dev?"

"I was out there investigating early this morning, and I found these." Macauley tossed the two small silver medallions on the top of his desk for Clay to see.

"I remembered that your friend was wearin' a real fancy silver belt the day you brought in Denton, so I thought I'd check it out. Seems I was right."

Clay immediately recognized them as having come from Dev's hand-tooled, leather and silver belt. It was a one-of-a-kind keepsake that he'd had made for himself while they were down Los Angeles way several years before. "There's got to be some mistake." Clay looked up at the sheriff, puzzled.

"I found those at the scene of the crime, and . . ."

"Sheriff!" Carter's excited call interrupted them. He had been going through Dev's things while they'd been talking. "Sheriff, look at this . . ." He pulled a thick wad of money from the bottom of the saddlebag.

"Well, well, well." Macauley fixed an accusing glare on Clay. "Maybe you can explain to me what your partner's doing with over four hundred dollars cash on him, when you haven't collected your reward for Denton yet? Where were you two or three days ago?"

"We were . . ." Clay fell silent for a moment as he remembered the day they'd trapped Denton out in the wilderness. He and Dev had been separated for about eight hours as they'd circled around the cunning, elusive outlaw before finally managing to trap him. "We were south of town, rounding up Denton. Look, Sheriff, you've got the wrong man. There's no way Dev could have done this!"

"Then how do you explain the fact that I found these in the very place where the bushwhacker must have been standing? Were you and O'Keefe together the whole time that day?"

"No . . . we were apart for a while when we were closing in on Denton," Clay admitted slowly, hating to think what his testimony was going to do to Dev's chances of getting out of jail. He knew Dev as well as he knew himself, and he was positive that his friend would never kill anyone in cold blood, never.

"Then how do you know what your partner did or

didn't do?"

"Because I know Dev!" he argued vehemently. "He's not a killer!"

"Well, we'll just have to see what a jury has to say about that, won't we, Cordell? I'll tell you one thing, with the evidence we've got, it doesn't look good for him."

"I want to see Dev now," Clay demanded.

"You can have five minutes. That's it. Leave your gun here," Macauley instructed and then waved Clay on to the back of the building where Dev was imprisoned.

It was a shock to see his friend locked up next to the deadly murderer they'd brought to justice themselves just a few days before. Denton was watching the goings on and found Dev's situation highly amusing.

"What's the matter, O'Keefe? You gotta have your friend Cordell come and rescue you?" the killer taunted with obvious glee.

"Shut up, Denton, or I'll save the sheriff the trouble of hiring a hangman," Devlin threatened angrily. He'd been listening to the killer's abuse ever since they'd thrown him into the cell a short time before and he'd about had all he could take. Dev looked up then and was greatly relieved when he saw Clay coming. "Clay! What the hell's going on? Get me out of here!"

Clay quickly explained what the sheriff had just told him about the silver medallions from the belt, and Dev looked deeply frightened.

"I don't understand it," he said worriedly. "I didn't even know the medallions were missing, let alone how they got out to this Santana's place. Hell, I wasn't anywhere near there!"

"I believe you, damnit!" Clay swore. "But I've got to prove it to the sheriff. The way things look right now, it isn't going to be easy. Just sit tight. I'll do what I can."

Dev knew he could count on Clay. He felt a little

better, but he was still scared. "Clay," he begged in a low, desperate voice, "I didn't do it! You gotta get me out of here!"

"I know," Clay sympathized. "Just tell me where all the money came from."

"Money? What money?"

"They just found about four hundred dollars in your saddlebags, and it seems that money was missing from this Santana's ranch, too."

"I didn't have any extra money in my saddlebags—" Dev was completely dumbstruck by this revelation.

"You didn't?"

"No! Where would I get that kind of cash?" He could see the concern clouding Clay's gaze, and he asked, earnestly, "You believe me, don't you?"

"Of course I do. I've just got to figure out what's going on around here . . ."

"Time's up, Cordell," the sheriff called, forcing him to end their conversation.

"Right," he responded. "Look, Dev, try to get some rest for now. Let me see what I can find out. There's got to be some explanation."

"All right," Dev said slowly, already feeling caged and restless. He watched Clay leave the jail and then sank slowly down on the small, lumpy cot to wait.

It was dawn as Clay made his way back upstairs to his room at the Perdition. He'd spent the last hour going over everything that had happened to them over the last few days, but he could find no answer to Dev's dilemma. It seemed too pat, too simple, but oh, so damning. The whole scenario upset Clay, for he found himself doubting Dev for the first time in all the years he'd known him. *There was no way Dev could or would have done it. He'd had the time and the opportunity while they'd been apart that day, but he wasn't the kind of person to do a thing like that.* Clay allowed himself to follow that train of thought for only a few minutes before summarily dismissing it. He trusted Dev completely. There was no way the Devlin O'Keefe he knew could cold-bloodedly murder a man. No way.

Clay thought back to the first time he'd met Dev. It had been nearly eight years before when he'd been trying his own hand at prospecting. He'd had a little success, but nothing spectacular. Then one day on his way into town to see the assayer about a new vein he'd uncovered, he'd been wounded in an ambush. Clay knew he would have been killed that day had Dev not come along and interrupted the would-be robbers in the act. Not only had Dev saved his life, he doctored him up and helped him go after the two men responsible.

It had taken them several weeks to track the outlaws down, but they finally had done it and brought both men to justice. When they'd returned from chasing down the outlaws, Clay had discovered that his promising vein was so poor it wasn't worth the money and effort it would take to dig it out. So he'd sold his claim to another miner, and they'd left the gold fields behind. He and Dev had decided then to take up their present vocation, and they'd been working together ever since. They were as close as two men could be. Clay knew he owed Dev his life.

Troubled, Clay returned to his room. It was still too early in the day to do much in the way of investigating the charges against Dev, so he was hoping to get a few hours of much needed rest before checking further into the allegations. Clay did not expect to find anyone in his room, especially not Luis Alvarez, and he stopped just inside the doorway, tensing visibly at the sight of him.

"Alvarez . . ." Clay growled his name in surprise, glaring at the man who stood so casually across the room from him with a look of supreme confidence on his dark, Hispanic features. "What the hell are you doing here?"

"Mr. Cordell," Luis responded with a cool smile. "I'm glad to see you finally made it back. I've been waiting for some time to speak with you, and I was beginning to wonder if you were going to return."

"Oh, really?" he drawled sarcastically, not believing the gall of the man.

"Yes, I understand you and your partner ran into a little trouble with the law last night."

"What do you know about it?"

"Why, nothing, nothing at all. Frenchie, I believe her name was, told me what had happened, that's all."

"Look, Alvarez, why are you here?" Clay demanded, resenting his intrusion and wanting to get rid of him. "What do you want?"

"I'm here because I wanted to repeat my offer to you, Mr. Cordell. I want to hire you to find my daughter."

"And I told you before that I'm still not interested in your deal. Now, go on and get out of here." Clay's concern for Dev was foremost in his mind, and he wondered in annoyance if this man would ever give up. He had refused his business proposition point blank. He'd told him that he didn't want anything to do with chasing down his errant daughter, and yet here he was, back again.

Luis smiled even wider. "Ah, but Mr. Cordell, I've raised my offer again."

"I said I wasn't interested—not at any price!" Clay just wished the man would leave and let him get on with what he had to do. He had to concentrate on getting Dev out of that jail cell.

"Not even to save the life of your friend?"

Clay went completely still at the question, and he slowly raised his gaze to meet the Californio's. "What are you talking about?"

"I'm talking about Mr. O'Keefe. I understand he's been arrested for murder."

"Yes, so?"

"So, perhaps there's something I can do to help you. I am not without influence here in Monterey, you know."

"Sorry, Alvarez. I'm not interested in bribing anyone. Dev is innocent, and all I have to do is prove it."

"Ah, but Mr. Cordell, Pedro Santana had a lot of friends here in town, and vigilantes have been known to storm jails and wreak their own type of justice. Who knows if your friend O'Keefe will stay alive long enough for you to prove that innocence?"

"Why you . . ." The implication of his words infuriated Clay, and he took a menacing step toward Luis.

Luis held up one well-manicured hand to stop him as he dictated with a steely calm, "I wouldn't if I were you, Cordell." He waited to continue until he was certain the bounty hunter had his fierce temper under control. When he spoke again, it was in a conversational tone, "I think it's a more than fair exchange, don't you? My daughter returned for the life of your friend."

"You set this up, you no-good, son-of-a—"

"As it is now," Luis interrupted his tirade, "all the evidence against O'Keefe is circumstantial. As long as it stays that way, I'm sure he'll be safe enough in jail. Of course, should you refuse to take my job offer, there's no telling what other evidence might unexpectedly turn up against him."

Clay was holding himself under rigid control as he ground out the words, "I want Dev out of that cell today!"

The Califórnio's smile turned cruel. "Sorry, Cordell. No deal. He stays put until you get back with my daughter. Once Reina's home with me, I'll see that your friend is cleared of all charges and released. Until then, he stays right where he is. He's my insurance, you see." He watched the growing anger and frustration mirrored in Clay's eyes and was pleased. "Of

course, if you're not interested in taking on the job —"
Luis enjoyed power-plays, and after the way this gringo had talked to him previously, he was taking great pleasure in making him crawl a bit. He started to leave the room.

Clay was trapped, and he knew it. It enraged him that he was helpless to do anything more to free Dev, but Alvarez seemed to be holding all the aces. In temporary defeat, he demanded, "What do you want me to do?"

Luis's thin lips curved triumphantly. "I have here a small portrait of my Reina . . ."

Chapter Five

Four days . . . We've only been on the road four days and already it seems an eternity. Reina's thoughts were grim and miserable as the poorly-sprung stagecoach continued to rumble and jounce along on the last leg of its southward journey to Los Angeles. Scrunched in between a small, fair-haired, eight-year-old girl named Melissa and the hard, unyielding wall of the coach, Reina struggled miserably to keep her seat and maintain her dignity at the same time. This was not an easy thing to do considering that her habit, once so pristinely clean and white, was now dusty and wrinkled, and the veil that had once been so perfectly starched, was now wilting pitifully in the growing heat.

"Kinda a rough ride, eh, Sister?" the grizzled, skinny, good-natured, old cowboy named Poke who was sitting across from her in the coach asked.

"Yes, Mr. Poke, it is a very rough ride," she agreed, fighting to keep up her pleasant demeanor. When the stage unexpectedly hit another big bump and slammed her against the wall, Reina almost lost her temper with the obviously ham-handed driver. Couldn't the idiot see where he was going? Didn't he know how to drive? If he kept this up there wouldn't be an inch of her body that wasn't bruised and battered. She was about to shout at him and tell him what she thought about his ability to handle his horses, when Maria's words of caution about presenting the proper image at all times echoed through her mind. Annoyed, Reina squashed the urge to put the driver in his place. She was Sister Mary Regina now, not Reina Isabella Alvarez.

"I done told ya, Sister, ya don't hafta call me 'Mister' anything. I'm just plain Poke." He grinned at her, showing uneven, tobacco-stained teeth.

"All right, Poke." Reina finally gave in. She'd wanted to keep an aura of aloofness about her to dissuade any attempts at familiarity by the other passengers, but ever since they'd pulled out of Monterey this cowboy had been persistent in his efforts to draw her into conversation. There was nothing threatening about the old man, it was just that she didn't want to be bothered, not by him or anyone else. Even so, she realized now in agitation that nothing short of a withering look and a cold, cutting dismissal would discourage him, and Sister Mary Regina couldn't do that.

The cowboy smiled widely as if some great event had occurred. "How far ya going, Sister?"

Reina was annoyed, but drew on some deep inner resource to manage to give Poke her most serene smile. "I'm traveling to Fort Smith." It occurred to Reina that she had never had to smile so much in her whole life, as she had since she'd donned this habit. She almost felt as if her face was going to crack into a thousand pieces from the falseness of the effort. No matter how beatific she appeared, there was nothing rapturously happy about her. Still, it amazed Reina how others responded so openly to her display of seemingly tranquil spirit. It was almost as if they were drawn to her.

"Fort Smith?" Poke gave her a look of even greater respect. "Oooh-wee, Sister, that is one hell of a . . . er, uh, excuse me, ma'am, uh . . . ladies." He looked a bit shamefaced as he realized what he'd said in front of the women, and he hurried to apologize to Reina, to the young Melissa and to her matronly mother, Ruth Hawks, who was sitting on the other side of her.

"That's all right, Poke," Reina said graciously, and it amazed her to see him almost beam at her forgiveness. His reaction gave her cause to think. All her life she had demanded imperiously that her wishes be met, and they had been. Now, seeing how this cowboy responded to her sweetness, she realized she might have accomplished the same thing at home without all the tirades.

"As I was sayin', Sister," he went on after clearing his throat, "that is one heckuva long trip for a lady like yourself to be makin'."

"Yes, I know," she agreed, fighting to keep from sounding too disgusted over the thought of at least another ten days of travel in this miserable vehicle. "But, one must do what one is called to do." She thought smugly that her response sounded suitably reverent.

"What are ya gonna be doing back there?" Poke refused to let the conversation die.

"God's work, of course," Reina responded, pleased with her inspired answer, yet wondering just how much longer she could keep deflecting his queries without seeming rude. Knowing how much men liked to talk about themselves and sensing that Poke had no intention of shutting up any time soon, she turned the questioning to him. "How far will you be traveling?"

"Me?" He seemed surprised that she even cared to ask. "Oh, I'm only goin' as far as Fort Yuma."

At this news, the precocious little Melissa spoke up with childish enthusiasm. "My Mama and I are going there, too! My father's there, and we're going to meet him."

"I'll bet you're excited aren't you, little one?" Reina asked knowing that Sister Mary Regina would show interest.

"Oh, yes! Papa said in his letter that I can even have my very own horse once I get there! Right, Mama?"

"Right, Melissa," her mother answered, giving her an adoring look.

"That's wonderful," Reina responded and then found

herself adding almost wistfully, "When I was at home, I had my own mare. She was a beauty, too."

"I bet you miss her, don't you?" Melissa sympathized.

"Yes, you know I do. But it seems so long ago now since I left home . . ." Reina gave herself a mental shake. It had only been four days since she'd run away, and yet it felt like an eternity.

"Couldn't you have taken her with you?"

"No, I'm afraid not," she answered honestly. Dorado, her beautiful palomino, was so distinctive that she would have been easily recognized had she tried to bring her along.

"Then why did you leave her?" Melissa asked, expecting a simple answer in her childish perception.

"Sometimes, other things become more important in life." Reina clasped her hands tightly in her lap as the terrible memories of her last encounter with her father rifled through her. She had managed not to think about it for some time now, but the remembrance renewed the pain of her parting. She loved Rancho Alvarez. She'd never wanted to leave, but her father had left her no choice.

Melissa saw Reina's expression turn melancholy, and she quickly apologized, "I'm sorry, I didn't mean to make you sad."

"I'm not sad," she told her, managing a weak smile. "I'm just a little homesick, I guess."

"I can see by your habit that you've already professed your final vows," Ruth said gently and with the utmost respect. "But you look so young, Sister, have you been with your order a long time?"

"Long enough," Reina returned all too honestly, wishing with all her heart that none of this had ever happened. "I suppose I should be used to being away from home by now, but I'm not."

"I understand, but I'm sure you keep busy."

Reina thought of her mad dash to the convent and then her hectic, secretive trip into town to catch the stage. "That's true. It seems there's never a dull moment anymore."

"What do you do?" Melissa wondered with open curiosity.

"Oh, I pray a lot," Reina replied vaguely with a smile meant to disarm the little girl's interest. She really didn't want to talk about life in the convent for fear that they might ask too detailed a question. Maria had counseled her extensively before she'd fled into the night to make good her great escape, but Reina was well aware that there was a lot she still didn't know about being a sister. "In the convent we have morning prayers followed by mass, then vespers in the evening and meditation . . ."

"That's all you do? Pray?" the youngster repeated in disappointment, thinking a life of such holy devotion sounded terrible. "Why would you want to do that when you could be home riding your horse?"

"Melissa!" her mother scolded. "You mustn't talk to Sister Mary Regina that way."

"Yes, Mama," she responded contritely and then apologized. "I'm sorry, Sister."

"Don't worry, Melissa. I remember I felt the same way at one time," Reina told her. *Had she ever! When had it been? Twenty minutes ago?*

"What happened to change your mind?" the inquisitive child wanted to know.

"It occurred to me almost overnight that this was the only path to my salvation," she answered calmly, knowing that what she was telling her was the complete truth.

"Oh." Melissa frowned, trying to understand, but meeting with little success. "Still, it must be kind of awful wearing all those clothes all the time. Don't you get hot?"

"Melissa!" Again Ruth was shocked by her question. "Sister, I'm sorry. Melissa's never had the opportunity to talk with a nun before. She doesn't realize . . ."

"Believe me, Mrs. Hawks, I understand," Reina

soothed the embarrassed mother, then looked to the young girl. "Yes, Melissa, it does get very hot." Reina tried not to think about the sweat that was beading her brow and trickling miserably down her back. "But it's well worth it. The rewards for tolerating such a little inconvenience and discomfort will be tremendous," she assured the child, dwelling not on the terrible heat and resulting misery, but on the glory of reaching New Orleans, safe and undetected.

"Betcha you're gonna get even hotter before we get to Fort Yuma," Melissa declared knowingly. "Papa always writes and tells us that it gets real hot down there."

"I'm sure he's right," Reina replied. The thought of the long miles across the territorial badlands after leaving Yuma had her more concerned than the trip to Yuma. This habit she'd borrowed was downright stifling, if the truth be told, and she wondered how she was going to survive the desert climate dressed like this since it certainly wouldn't do for her, Sister Mary Regina, to start stripping off layers of clothes just for the sake of coolness.

Reina thought of the comfortable, loose-fitting skirts and blouses she'd left at home then, and the many hours she'd spent relaxing in shaded coolness of the patio of Rancho Alvarez with its splashing, gurgling fountain, and another wave of homesickness threatened. With an effort, she put it from her. She had made her choice, and she would see it through. No matter what, she would not go back unless she was assured that she wouldn't have to marry Nathan.

Reina was dwelling on that thought, when suddenly and unexpectedly, the sound of rapidly fired gunshots ruptured the quiet of the afternoon. Taken by surprise, the driver reacted instinctively, lashing furiously at his team. Spooked by the gunfire and stung by the whip, the horses responded, whinnying in terror as they took off at a dead run. Within the coach, Reina and the others were thrown from their seats as the stagecoach gave a maddening lurch and then took off.

Poke recovered first and quickly drew his revolver as he tried to get a look out the window. Seeing the bandits galloping at top speed in pursuit of the stage, he ordered tersely, "All of you stay the hell down! Sorry, Sister!" He began shooting out the window in an attempt to drive them off, but the jouncing of the stage made his shots far less than accurate.

The robbers saw that someone was shooting at them from inside the coach, and they shot back. Bullets exploded into the wood around the window where Poke crouched, and he ducked down by the women, taking a minute to reload.

"Sister, you'd better start prayin', 'cause these look like some real mean bastards!" he said seriously, meeting her dark-eyed gaze full on.

Reina saw the seriousness in his regard, and a shiver of apprehension frissoned down her spine in spite of the heat. "I'll pray for you, Poke."

"You damn well better pray for all of us," he growled as he finished shoving the bullets into his gun's chamber and then maneuvered himself back up to the window.

Clay slowed his horse to a walk as he neared the small pond. Except for a couple of hours sleep the night before, he'd been riding almost non-stop since leaving Monterey a little over a day ago. He was agitated and angry, but knew it did little good to cater to those emotions. He had to concentrate on the job at hand. He had to find Reina Alvarez, and he had to find her fast. It was the only way he could save Dev from being caged like an animal in the jail cell.

As he drew to a stop at the water's edge, Clay dismounted and allowed his horse to drink its fill. His thoughts were determined as he surveyed the surrounding area, trying to calculate how far he'd come and just how much farther he had to go. He'd been cutting

76

across country, making every effort to catch up to the stagecoach that had departed Monterey for Los Angeles two days before him.

It wasn't sheer speculation that had convinced Clay to track down this coach, but a good deal of checking and double-checking with Alvarez and his men before he'd left. Their thorough, but fruitless search had led him to believe that the girl had fled the area. When he'd informed his employer of his opinion, Alvarez had immediately suggested that Reina might be on her way to New Orleans where she had close friends. Inquiries at the stage depot had turned up the fact that there were four passengers on the stage that had pulled out two days earlier — two women, both of them relatively young, an old man and a child. Clay had felt almost certain that one of the women had to be Reina, and he'd decided to act on that hunch. So here he was, out in the middle of nowhere, trying to catch up with the stage he suspected Reina Alvarez had taken.

Leaving his mount to finish drinking, Clay moved off to sit down in the shade of a nearby tree and try to relax for a minute. Try as he might, though, thoughts of Dev's perilous situation haunted him, and not for the first time since he'd been trapped into taking this job, Clay silently cursed the woman who was the cause of it all.

In anger and annoyance, Clay pulled the small oil portrait of Reina Alvarez her father had given him from his pocket. He stared down at the picture of the beautiful woman, studying her every feature, committing this vision of her to his memory. Though the old man had cautioned him that the portrait was two years old, Clay doubted he would have any trouble recognizing her. In the tiny painting, she was wearing a fashionably low-cut, emerald green ballgown, and the expression the artist had rendered on her lovely features was quite regal. Her ebony hair was drawn up and away from her face, and then left to fall, unbound in a black, silken cascade about her slender shoulders. Her eyes, Clay realized, were her most attractive feature. Wide, dark and fathomless, they were the kind of eyes a man could lose himself in. Her complexion was flawless, her nose perfect, her mouth definitely kissable, and he wondered . . .

Clay suddenly realized the direction his thoughts were taking, and he grew even more irritated. Gorgeous though she might be, he wanted nothing to do with her. Forcefully, he reminded himself just what kind of a woman she was. She was a greedy, selfish witch, exactly like his mother, and he would not allow himself to forget that ever again. He would find her, and he would take her home to her father and loving fiancé, and that was all he wanted to do with her.

Agitated and knowing he shouldn't be resting and taking it easy while Dev was stuck behind bars, Clay got to his feet and strode purposefully to his horse. He paused there only long enough to stuff the picture of the Alvarez girl in his saddlebag, then gathered up the reins and vaulted easily into the saddle. He had just put his heels to his mount's sides when he heard shots being fired in the distance. He didn't know what was going on, but it sounded like trouble. Urging the horse to a full gallop, he raced off in the direction of the gunplay to see what was happening.

The outlaws had gained ground on the stage, and when Poke appeared at the window, one of the villains fired with deadly accuracy. Poke cried out in agony as the bullet hit him in the shoulder. Driven backward by the force of the shot, he sprawled half across the seat, half on top of the women.

Ruth and Melissa screamed in terror. Only Reina had the sense to act. She pushed herself free of his weight and maneuvered to see if she could help him. Reina helped him shift more completely back on the seat and then looked to his wound.

"Poke . . ." she murmured in concern and horror as she saw the blood staining his shirt. She ripped the garment away from the wound and seeing how serious it was, immediately tore a strip of cloth from her petticoat. Wadding up the material, unmindful of the gore that would get all over her white habit, she pressed it firmly to the injury, applying the necessary pressure to staunch the flow of blood.

"Damn . . ." Poke gasped, half out of his mind in his agony. "Sorry, Sister . . ."

"Hush, Poke!" Reina scolded, wondering how he could be in such obvious pain and still worry about the language he used around her. "Just hang on, I'll take care of you." She had no more time to speak as the stage suddenly began to slow down.

"Oh, my God! The driver's going to stop!" Ruth shrieked.

"Mama!" Melissa cried, and her mother gathered her close to her bosom to try to shield her from the terror she knew was to come.

As the stage ground to a halt, Poke made a superhuman effort and grabbed up his gun from where it had fallen to the stage floor beside him. He thrust it into Reina's hand. "Here . . ." he choked. "Don't let them varmints near you . . ."

Reina stared down at the weapon in surprised wonder. She knew how to shoot a sidearm. Her father had taught her well, but could she actually use it to shoot someone? Poke saw her confusion and misread her thoughts.

"It ain't no sin to save yourself," he argued weakly. "Use it if you have to, Sister . . ."

Poke passed out just as the stage door was thrown violently open. It banged loudly against the side of the coach as the hulking figure of a man loomed menacingly in the doorway. Big and ugly, the lower half of his face hidden behind a bandana, he leaned into the coach to get a better look. His pale, blue eyes glittered triumphantly as he saw the nun hovering over the cowboy.

"Heh, heh, heh . . ." The evil sound of his laugh echoed through the stage sending shivers of fright through Reina and the others. "Get out of the way," he snarled, giving Reina a hard shove to push her away from Poke.

Reina's wide, fearful gaze was fixed on the villainous-looking robber as she scrambled to sit on the opposite seat. Despite her terror, she had presence of mind enough to keep the gun hidden in the folds of her voluminous skirts.

"Good shot, Duke! You got him good!"

"Is he dead?" Came the gloating answer from outside.

"Not yet, but he will be soon," the vicious Vic declared with something akin to glee. "These others ain't, though."

"Others? You mean we got more passengers?"

"Yep, and they're all women, too." Vic backed away from the stage, but kept his gun trained on the door. "Get on out of there!" he ordered coldly.

"Sister . . . ?" Ruth turned desperate eyes to Reina, hoping for guidance.

Reina remembered Poke's warning that she should pray for them all, and she wondered what good a prayer was against men like these.

"We'd better do as he says," she urged. "Let me go first . . ."

Terrified, Ruth nodded as she momentarily closed her eyes and buried her face against her daughter's hair. Mustering a semblance of outward calm, Reina descended to face their attackers.

Though Reina had never before known true fear, she knew it then. Her father had often spoken of the vicious, lawless men who were ravaging the countryside attacking unwary travelers, and standing here now, looking at these two ruthless desperadoes, she realized exactly what he'd been talking about. While Vic remained nearby, the one named Duke still sat his horse a short distance away, his rifle aimed point blank at the chest of the fear-frozen, unmoving stage driver. He was a mean-looking man, and his obsidian eyes were devoid of emotion as he regarded her. The disguising mask he wore covering his mouth and chin only served to give him an even more dangerous look. Reina knew instinctively that these men were men without morals who would kill indiscriminately without thought or care. The chilling realization made her brush her hand against the reassuring hardness of her hidden revolver.

"Well, what ya got there, Vic?" Duke called out as he stared at her in amazement.

"We got us a nun," he responded.

"What d'ya think, Sister? Think your God's gonna help ya now?" Duke guffawed at his own humor as he dismounted, still keeping his rifle trained on the driver.

Though her basic, fiery instincts urged Reina to go for her gun and start shooting, she knew it would be useless. Even with the element of surprise on her side, she was outnumbered two to one. Forcing herself to continue her role, she fixed a cool, steady gaze upon him and refused to respond visibly to his taunt. When Ruth and Melissa joined her outside, huddling near her, she put a protective arm around them both.

"We're no threat to you," Reina told the outlaws. "Take what you want and go."

"You're right about one thing, lady, you ain't no threat to us. But maybe you got somethin' even more excitin' than money, eh, Vic?" The lecherous Duke eyed Reina hungrily. He'd always wondered about these religious women who always looked and acted so pious. He wondered if she was as cool as she looked. He took a menacing step toward her, his barbarous mind filled with thoughts of sating his perverted lust on her.

Chapter Six

Fred, the stagedriver, was fearful of what the outlaw intended to do, and he spoke up quickly, hoping to deter him. "Take the strongbox and get out of here!" He threw the heavy box to the ground.

"If you want to live to see sundown, you'll shut your mouth!" Duke commanded, and he gave a victorious, derisive laugh as the driver immediately fell silent. His interest in Reina secondary to his interest in money, he waved his companion toward the box. "See what we got, Vic . . ."

Vic hurried to do as he was told and quickly shot the heavy padlock off the box. He threw the lid open, and his eyes widened greedily. "Look here, Duke! We done hit the jackpot!"

"Hot damn!" Duke saw the bags of gold coins and promptly forgot everything else. Rushing to grab his saddlebags, he hurried to his comrade's side. Together, they began stuffing the bags full of loot.

Fred was warily eyeing his own rifle where it lay just out of reach. Since the two bandits were obviously distracted, he wondered desperately if he could reach it and shoot them before they could get him. He was about to go for the gun, when Vic finished packing away the last of the money and looked up.

"I wouldn't do it if I were you," Vic sneered, accurately reading the desperation in the driver's expression. "Just throw that rifle on down here real easy-like."

Scared and knowing that he didn't stand a chance, Fred did as he was told.

"That's the way to stay alive," Duke chided sarcastically, getting to his feet and walking slowly toward where the two women and the child stood. The heavyset woman and her little girl held no interest for him, only the pretty nun intrigued him. "Now, I think I want to have me a little fun . . ."

Ruth and Melissa cowered in horror, while Reina alone faced him without flinching.

"Leave us alone," Reina commanded using her usual arrogant tone. "You've got what you came after."

"I just decided there's another prize here I want besides the money . . ." Duke remarked, his gaze hot upon her. "You're awful young . . ." he said, leering at Reina. "Let's see if the rest of ya is as pretty as your face. Let's see what ya got hidden beneath all those ugly robes . . . what d'ya say?" He reached out to her.

"Don't touch me!" Reina ordered imperiously, ducking away from his hand.

"Oh, I'm going to do more than touch you . . ." he told her lasciviously. "You ever been with a man?"

"No," she answered, trying to keep her voice steady. "I am a bride of Christ."

Her words had no effect on the amoral, decadent bandit. He was too eager to see what kind of woman she really was.

"Good. That'll make you even sweeter . . ." Grabbing Reina by the arms, he tore her away from Ruth's and Melissa's clinging embraces.

"No! Don't!" Ruth cried out.

Duke ignored her and hauled Reina to him, pinning her against his chest. With one hand, he pushed his bandana down off his face and then bent to kiss her. His mouth ground down over hers in a punishing exchange.

Reina struggled violently to break free of his awful, degrading hold. She had no intention of allowing this

83

filth to touch her. She fought madly, trying to get her right hand free so she could grab her gun, but to no avail. The sound of Vic hooting and howling in obscene pleasure as he watched them, infuriated her. When Duke tried to deepen the vile kiss, she bit down on his lip as hard as she could.

When he suddenly broke off the kiss, Reina cried, "Get your hands off of me!" She tried to kick out at him, but the heavy skirts impeded her success.

Duke was not fazed in the least by the pain of her bite, and her continued struggles only seemed to amuse him. He controlled her easily and laughed as he glanced over at Vic. "Look at her fight! Ain't she a feisty little piece? You want some of this when I'm done?"

"Leave the Sister alone! You got your money!" Fred yelled in frustrated fury. He didn't know how anyone could even think of harming a religious woman.

"Shut up!" Duke snarled, dragging Reina back into his arms despite her efforts to the contrary.

Frustration filled the driver, but he knew there was nothing he could do.

Duke started to kiss Reina again, and Vic gave an excited hoot in anticipation of having his own turn at the young woman. It was then that something unexpected happened. A shot rang out of nowhere, and Vic's hollers of excitement turned to screams of agony as a deep, burning pain seared through his chest. He stood motionlessly for an instant, then his gun and the saddlebags dropped from his suddenly numb hands. Vic pitched face forward into the dirt, dead.

"What the hell. . . ?" Duke kept his hold on Reina as he spun around to see his friend drop to the ground, a bullet hole in his back. "Vic!" he bellowed in disbelief.

Suddenly more bullets were blazing around him. In a panic of self-survival, Duke shoved Reina to the ground and dove for cover himself behind some rocks. He caught sight of his assailant on a ridge overlooking the trail, and, drawing his gun, he began to shoot back at the intruder.

Reina was stunned by the sudden turn of events, and she lay on the ground, shaken. Ruth and Melissa ran to hide behind some nearby boulders as Fred jumped down from his perch to hide behind the stagecoach.

"Sister, you've got to take cover!" Fred shouted to her over the din of the gunshots. He wished that he had a gun to help out, but unarmed as he was, there was nothing more he could do.

His warning shook Reina from her dazed state of mind, and she quickly scrambled to safety with Ruth and Melissa behind the rocks half-way between the stage and the place where Duke had hidden. Fighting for breath, she stayed down low.

"Are you all right?" Ruth asked worriedly.

"I think so," she gasped.

"Who's up there?"

"I don't know," Reina responded breathlessly, "but whoever it is, he must be a godsend!"

The gunfire had stopped as Clay had raced across the countryside, and he hadn't even been sure he was heading in the right direction until he'd crested the ridge. He'd reined in abruptly at the sight of the robbery being acted out on the road below. Clay hadn't been able to tell if Reina Alvarez was among the passengers, but that hadn't mattered, for the shocking sight of the villain assaulting the helpless nun had enraged him. Filled with righteous fury, he'd swung down off his horse's back and taken his rifle from its case.

Clay had sought his most advantageous position behind one of the big boulders. The passengers had been clustered so close together that he was fearful of hitting one of them, so he took extra care to make certain his aim was true as he'd squeezed off his shot. Clay had watched in satisfaction as the outlaw who'd been standing slightly away from the others was felled by his marksmanship. When the other bandit quickly released the nun and made for cover, Clay kept up a barrage of bullets to give the women and the driver time to seek refuge. When he was certain they were momentarily safe from the outlaw, Clay dropped down behind the rock to reload. That done, he shifted his position to get a better view of the scene below.

More frightened than she'd ever been in her life, Reina's hands were shaking as she pulled Poke's gun from her pocket.

"Poke's gun . . . I'd forgotten!" Ruth's terrified gaze met Reina's. "Do you know how to use it?"

"My father taught me when I was young," she answered.

"Have you ever shot anyone before?" Melissa asked, her eyes wide with a mixture of respect and horror at the thought.

"Well, no . . ." Reina hesitated, knowing there was a big difference between shooting at a target and shooting down a man. She wondered if she could really do it. "But I have no intention of letting that man anywhere near us again."

"You're right," Ruth agreed, fearing for their very lives.

Reina peeked over the top of the rocks, hoping to get a clear shot at Duke. The outlaw had chosen his hiding place well, though, and she found it was impossible to even come close. Knowing she had only a few bullets left, Reina dropped back down beside Ruth and Melissa.

"No chance?"

Reina shook her head. "He's too well hidden. Maybe if he moves, I can, but right now, there's no way."

Clutching Poke's gun tightly in both hands, she leaned back against the sharp edges of the rocks and waited. She thought of the old cowboy then and of his advice that it wouldn't be a sin to defend herself, and she smiled slightly. He had been wounded defending them of his own free will. No one had hired him to do the job. No one had commanded that he risk his life for them, and yet he had. Then, despite his own severe injury, his thoughts had still been about their safety. He was truly a gentle, generous man, and she hoped, if they managed to get out of this, that he would be all right.

The protection Duke had sought behind the rocks was so good that Clay couldn't get a direct shot at him. Clay knew he had little hope of flushing the bandit out from his current position, so he decided to move to a better vantage point. To cover himself, he fired a salvo in the desperado's general direction as he made a run for a small grove of trees about thirty feet away across a small clearing.

When it came to saving his own hide, Duke could be a very patient, very vigilant man. He wasn't concerned in the least about the women or the driver for to his way of thinking they were unarmed. Instead, he was watching and waiting for the intruder to make a mistake. Whenever he did, Duke was going to be ready.

The extended silence troubled Reina, and once more, she tried to see what was going on. In the distance, she caught sight of their unknown protector trying to make a run across a small open area on the ridge, and she cried out in horror as gunfire erupted from where Duke was hiding. To her terror, the man was struck by one of the outlaw's shots and fell. Reina couldn't tell if he was still alive or not, and her grip tightened on Poke's gun—their last line of defense against the bloodthirsty Duke.

"What happened?" Ruth asked.

"Duke shot him." Reina admitted as she sat back down beside her.

"No!"

The two women exchanged knowing looks, and Reina felt ice encase her very soul. It would all be up to her now . . .

"Well, it looks like things have worked out jes' fine, don't they?" Duke called out confidently. He believed they were all unarmed, and he was sure the intruder was dead. Duke was a little troubled by the fact that his friend, Vic, had been killed, but the prospect of keeping all that gold for himself eased whatever grief he was feeling.

Duke was gloating over his triumph as he stood up, but he knew he had to change his plans a bit since he was now working alone. He figured he'd still take the nun with him, but first he'd have to tie up the others, release the horses from the coach and get the loot. Then, when he was sure he'd be making a clean getaway, he would get the hell out of there.

At his taunting words, Reina grew even more frightened. She knew her own shooting ability was their only hope, but serious doubts ran through her mind. *Could she do it? Could she really shoot a man, even if it was in self-defense?*

"C'mon, ladies, I know where you're hidin'," Duke chided Reina and Ruth a little angrily. "Get out here where I can see you. You, too, driver! Step out from behind the stage so I know just where you are!" When none of them responded immediately, he became incensed. "I said get the hell out here! Now!"

"Damn!" Clay swore softly through gritted teeth as he clutched his upper arm. Sweat beaded his brow, and he closed his eyes for a moment as he fought for control over the pain.

Clay had somehow managed to keep a tight grip on his gun, and he was glad for at least that much. Despite the agony that throbbed through him, he knew the wound wasn't life-threatening. Even so, it was bleeding heavily and that in itself was a danger. Grabbing his bandana from his back pocket with his good hand, he tied it tightly around the wound to help stop the blood flow. There was no telling what the outlaw might do next, and he had to be ready.

Clay had stayed down since being shot, but the sound of Duke calling out to the women jarred him to action. He put his own pain from him and levered himself up on his good arm. Fighting for control, Clay brought his gun to bear. He would have a good shot at him as soon as he took a step clear of his hiding place. Clay only prayed that he would be accurate enough to take advantage of it.

"C'mon!" Duke snarled viciously again, waiting for Reina and the others to show themselves. He was almost ready to drag the women out, but he didn't trust the driver with the rifle and Vic's gun lying there so close by the stagecoach.

Reina could tell by the outlaw's tone of voice that the time had come. She could delay no longer. She had to make her move, and she had to do it now.

"All right . . ." she called out, standing up slowly and keeping the gun hidden in the fold of her skirts. A hurried glance around told Reina that she still didn't have a decent shot at Duke and that worried her. She knew she could hit a target, but she didn't trust her marksmanship enough to try to hit the bandit where he was standing. She had to draw him out into the open.

Reina walked slowly away from the protection of her hiding place, and relief flooded through her when Duke did the same. As he stepped clear of the rocky barrier that had protected him, Reina knew she had to act. Desperate to catch the overconfident desperado off-guard, she moved quickly, raising the gun and firing without hesitation. To her heart-stopping horror, the shot went wide, missing Duke completely. He stood, unscathed, staring at her in shocked rage.

"What the hell?" Duke roared at the discovery that

the nun was armed with a gun and more than willing to use it. "You got a gun?"

"Sister!" Ruth and Fred cried out, miserable in their frustration at being unable to help her. They felt sure that the end was near for all of them now.

Reina saw the cold-blooded, murderous glint appear in Duke's eyes as he glared at her, and when he raised his gun and took another step toward her, she knew she had to shoot at him again or die. Once more, her finger tightened on the trigger and the explosion of gunfire deafened her.

As Duke had taken that fateful stride toward Reina, he'd moved into Clay's range, and Clay fired. He watched in satisfaction as the outlaw was dropped in his tracks.

Ignoring the throbbing pain in his upper arm, Clay got to his feet and ran back to his horse to mount up. He knew he had to get down there and make sure that the desperado was dead and that the women were all right. Putting his heels to his steed's sides, he raced down the incline to the stage.

Reina had squeezed off her shot at exactly the same time Clay had fired, and she'd watched in horror as Duke collapsed and lay unmoving in the dirt. When she realized that he wasn't getting up again, all the tension that had been sustaining her drained away. Her hands dropped weakly to her sides, and the gun, suddenly too heavy to hold, slipped from her trembling fingers.

Both Ruth and Melissa had shrieked as the sounds of the gunplay erupted around them, but when they saw that Reina was unhurt, they cried out in tearful joy.

"Sister! Thank God you're all right!" They ran to embrace her in thankful excitement.

"But I . . . I didn't . . ." Reina stared at the dead outlaw in disbelief, watching the growing stain of blood that was spreading across the back of his shirt. She realized in some confusion that she was not the one who'd shot Duke at all. He had been shot from somewhere else . . . somewhere behind him. "I couldn't have . . . I mustn't have . . ."

Fred hurried out to join them, dropping to his knees beside Vic to make sure he was dead.

"Look!" Melissa's urgent cry drew their attention to the rider coming down the hillside, heading in their direction.

Fearing more trouble, Fred quickly snatched up his earlier discarded rifle as he turned to face the unknown man. Reina and Ruth, still standing close together, turned to watch his approach, too.

Their savior was a big man, and Reina felt a shiver run down her spine as she studied him from afar. He was dressed all in black, from the shirt that stretched tautly across the powerful width of his broad chest and shoulders to the tight-fitting pants that clung to his lean, muscular thighs. He wore his black Stetson pulled down low over his forehead so that it shadowed his eyes, effectively shielding them from her probing gaze, and the rest of his features were equally hidden beneath a slightly overgrown beard that was the same color as his dark brown hair. He sat his horse easily, almost as if he'd been born to the saddle, and he still held his gun at readiness as he rode toward them. Reina thought the man looked savagely dangerous; yet at the same time, she realized that he had to be a good man or he wouldn't have bothered to help them.

"He dead?" Clay called out brusquely to Fred, gesturing at Vic as he rode in. He did not look at the women yet, but kept his gaze riveted on the outlaws. He knew better than to trust the likes of Duke and Vic, and he would not relax his guard until he was sure they were no longer among the living.

"This one is," Fred answered.

"Good," his response was curt as he reined in close beside Duke's inert form. His movements were slow and deliberate as he dismounted and then knelt down beside the outlaw and to check and see if he was still breathing.

"Is he. . . ?" Reina finally managed to ask in a voice that was tight with strangled emotions.

Clay heard the upset in the nun's voice, and he hastened to reassure her as he turned the dead man over for a better look at him. "Yes, Sister, he's good and dead. But you don't have to worry. It wasn't your shot that hit him. It was mine."

"Thank heaven . . ." she breathed.

"I'll go check on the other passenger," Fred said.

"There was another passenger?" Clay asked sharply, glancing up at the driver as he started off.

"Yes, and he was wounded trying to fight these murdering thieves off!" Ruth told him.

At the sound of "he," Clay knew the other passenger wasn't Reina Alvarez and disappointment washed through him.

"Sister," Ruth was saying, "I'll help Fred with Poke. You rest for a few minutes. You look terribly pale."

"Thanks, Ruth . . ."

"Sir, thank you for your help," Ruth told Clay. "Without your intervention, they might have killed all of us."

"You're welcome, ma'am."

Ruth gave him a warm smile and then hurried away with Melissa to aid Fred. When she'd moved off, Clay glanced up at the nun for the first time just to see how bad she really looked. Across the little distance that separated them, Clay's gunmetal gray eyes met Reina's dark, velvety brown ones, and he felt a shock wave reverberate through him clear to the depths of his soul. *This was no old woman!* he realized with great amazement. *Why, this nun was young and very beautiful!* The discovery left him momentarily speechless. *How could he ever have thought she was old?* Clay got slowly to his feet to face her.

Reina, too, was jolted by the unexpected charge of electrifying sensual recognition that exploded between them as their gazes met and held. Her breath caught in her throat, and time suddenly seemed suspended as she was nearly overwhelmed by the sheer animal force of this man's magnetism. The sensation enthralled her even as it left her puzzled and very discomfited.

Reina was not completely inexperienced where the opposite sex was concerned. She was a born coquette who loved to flirt. Yet, despite all the parties and balls she'd attended and all the suitors who'd courted her, not one of them had ever affected her the way this man had with just a single look.

Reina wondered what it was about this stranger that could disturb her so. Certainly, it wasn't just because he was particularly good-looking. Lord knows, she'd had dozens of handsomer, and definitely cleaner, men vying for her affections. This man was no more than a saddle tramp, a drifter of no obvious means, and yet his very nearness set her senses to spinning. She was pondering this perplexing thought as her dark eyes remained locked with his, and it was only Ruth's vaguely heeded call that restored her to sanity.

"Sister Mary Regina! Poke's still alive!"

Chapter Seven

Reality returned with jarring distress, and Reina found herself blushing a bit as she realized that she'd been very close to gawking at this man. As she tore her gaze away from his, she gave herself a fierce mental shake. *She was Sister Mary Regina now,* she scolded herself angrily. *Surely, no self-respecting nun ever oogled a man!* Trying to regain her composure, she glanced back toward the stagecoach.

"Poke's alive?" she repeated.

"Yes," Fred called out in answer. "He's not conscious, but his pulse is steady. As soon as we get him bandaged up here, we'll head for the nearest waystation."

"Thank goodness," Reina said with heartfelt emotion, surprising herself to find that she really cared what happened to the old man.

Clay had been totally captivated as he stood there gazing at Reina. Though he could only see her face, there was no doubt in his mind that she was absolutely gorgeous. Her complexion was perfect, her mouth soft and inviting, her eyes wide and dark and so intriguing that he was sorry when the other woman had called out to them, interrupting the moment and causing her to look away from him.

It was only then, when Clay saw Reina blush, that he realized he'd embarrassed her by staring so boldly. A wave of guilt washed over him. *She's a nun, for God's sake!*

he berated himself, trying to distract himself from his thoughts of her beauty. Yet, even as he fought to dismiss the attraction he felt for her, he couldn't understand why a woman of such obvious loveliness would want to join a convent. Surely men must have pursued her before she'd taken her vows. He wondered why she had chosen to lock herself away from the real world. Puzzled, he moved to holster his gun, and it was only then, when the pain stabbed at him, that he remembered his wound.

His painstaking action drew Reina's attention, and for the first time she noticed the makeshift tourniquet on his arm and the blood on his shirt. "You've been hurt!"

"It's only a scratch." Clay tried to discourage her concern, but Reina knew simple scratches didn't bleed that heavily.

"You must let me bandage it for you," she offered quickly.

"No, there's no need."

"There's every need, Mr. . . . ?"

"Cordell, Clay Cordell," he answered.

"You risked your life for us, Mr. Cordell. The least I can do is tend to your wound. Come over here," she insisted, reaching out to his good arm in an effort to urge him toward the stagecoach. The feel of his strongly muscled arm beneath her hand sent a tingle of awareness through her. The sensation was so strong that she almost let go as if burned by the contact, but she knew she couldn't do that without creating a scene. "Why don't you sit down here in the shade, while I get a canteen and see if there's anything we can use for bandages," she directed.

"Fine," Clay agreed. He sat down and leaned back against the wheel of the stage, closing his eyes for a minute as he fought for control. The gentle touch of the nun's hand on his arm had wreaked havoc on him, and he was glad she was leaving him alone for a minute. She was too pretty, and there was something about her that stirred feelings within him he didn't want to deal with.

"Ruth, Mr. Cordell has been wounded, too. Is there anything I can use to wrap his arm?" Reina asked as she hurried to the door of the stage.

"Yes, Sister," the other woman answered from where she and Fred were busily tending to Poke. "Here . . ." She held out some strips of cloth she'd torn from a petticoat Melissa had retrieved from their suitcase.

"Thanks." She took them, got a canteen of water and started back to Clay.

"Do you need any help?" Ruth asked, since they had done just about all they could for Poke under the circumstances.

"No, I'll be fine," Reina was startled to find herself discouraging the other woman's help. She had no time for interest in men right now, and even if she did, she surely wouldn't have chosen one like this. Why in the world did she want to be alone with him?

Clay saw her coming. "I can take those and fix it up myself."

"It's no problem, Mr. Cordell," Reina refused. "After all, you did save our lives. It was most unselfish of you, and this is the least I can do to pay you back for your bravery."

"You were the brave one, Sister," Clay told her, watching her every move as she knelt down beside him. It amazed him that she showed no concern over getting her white habit dirty. She seemed only intent on helping him. This generosity of spirit was something he was not accustomed to in women. "Not everyone could have stood up to those men the way you did."

"But you were the one who really saved us. If you hadn't managed to come along when you did, well, who knows what would have happened?" Reina pointed out.

Clay listened to her praise and felt even more guilty. His motives hadn't been unselfish at all. He'd had a reason for being there, and a reason for wanting to save the stage from attack. *Reina Alvarez.*

"I'll have to tear your shirt so I can see what we've got

96

here," Reina told him.

"Why don't I just take it off? That'd probably be the easiest way," he offered, removing the bandana from his arm and then unbuttoning the shirt. That done, he started to strip it off. Until that moment, Clay hadn't realized how bad his arm really felt. He paled a bit and paused in mid-effort.

"Here, Mr. Cordell. Let me help you . . ." Reina had seen his color go slightly ashen and knew he had to be in pain. She tried to remain very business-like and detached as she slipped the garment from his broad shoulders. But when she accidentally touched the hot, hard width of his hair-roughened chest in the process, a surge of excitement shot through Reina unlike anything she'd ever experienced before. She looked up in surprise and once again her eyes met his. Reina colored deeply as Clay gave her a questioning look.

"Sister?" he asked, concerned.

"Can you finish?" she mumbled nervously, quickly diverting her gaze downward away from his. She discovered immediately that she'd made an even bigger mistake for she found herself staring pointblank at his deliciously muscle-sculpted chest. Knowing she couldn't move away without revealing the crazy feelings that were tormenting her, Reina remained as calm as possible as she waited for him to finish removing the shirt.

"Sure," Clay answered, realizing that Sister Mary Regina was probably unused to seeing men's bodies. It troubled him that he'd caused her embarrassment again. Still, being so close to her, he couldn't deny that he was physically attracted to her. It was an attraction, though, he wouldn't act upon. She was a very special woman. He respected her and would not hurt her in any way. "There, all done."

"Thanks. I was afraid that I might hurt you trying to get it off your arm," she lied smoothly as she began to check the gunshot wound.

"You wouldn't have hurt me," he said softly, his words

washing over her in a velvet caress.

Reina paused in her actions. "How can you be so sure?"

"Because I don't think you've ever hurt anyone in your entire life," Clay's voice was suddenly low and deep and slightly husky for he was speaking straight from his heart.

Reina shivered in spite of the heat. "I hope your faith in me is justified."

"It is," Clay responded.

Reina hadn't meant to look up at him again. She'd meant to concentrate only on doctoring his arm, but somehow she found herself almost compelled to glance up. Reina realized instantly that she'd made a serious tactical error as his probing, innately sensual, stormy-gray gaze caught and held hers.

Dazedly, Reina found herself thinking that he had absolutely the most beautiful eyes she'd ever seen. She was held enraptured, a captive of his mesmerizing masculinity. This time she couldn't bring herself to break off the contact, and her heart pounded wildly in her breast as the moment seemed to stretch on indefinitely.

Clay, too, was trapped by the flaring tension between them. She was a woman pledged to God, a woman who devoted her life to helping others, and yet he was sure she was the most beautiful female he'd ever seen. There was no deceit in her manner, no cunning in her soul. Her dark eyes, gazing up at him so trustingly, held him spellbound, and he found himself beguiled by her innocence and gentle openness. Suddenly, Clay wanted more than anything to take her in his arms and kiss the soft sweetness of her mouth.

The blatant, hot desire that surged through him at the imagined embrace, surprised Clay and left him feeling deeply shamed. He grew angry with himself for not being able to control his lusty thoughts. Sister Mary Regina was a woman who spurned worldly goods and carnal behavior, not some whore he could enjoy for an hour and leave without a second thought. She deserved his complete respect and consideration, not his heated musings. He was contrite, and he searched for something to say to break the taut silence that stretched between them.

"How's it look, Sister?" He almost didn't recognize his own voice for it sounded hoarsely disconnected, as if it belonged to someone else.

For an instant, Reina wanted to smile dreamily and tell him that his eyes looked fine, that he had the most gorgeous gray eyes she'd ever seen in her life and that she wanted to spend hours gazing into them. Only his use of "Sister" broke the mood and kept her from forgetting who she was and what she was doing here.

Inwardly, Reina raged at her own stupidity. She stiffened her resolve and turned her full attention to his arm. She was pleased to find that the bullet had passed completely through.

"You're in luck," she told him when she found her voice. "It looks clean. The bullet went through."

"Good. Listen, there's a flask of whiskey in my saddlebags," Clay said, thinking he could certainly use a stiff drink to help ease not only the pain from his arm, but his lecherous yearnings as well.

"Of course, we can use that to sterilize it."

"I wasn't thinking of wasting all of it on the wound, Sister." He grinned at her.

The smile, meant solely for her, left Reina flustered, and she quickly got up. "I'm sorry, I wasn't thinking . . . I'm sure your arm must be hurting you terribly."

Reina hurried to his horse to get the whiskey. She dug through the packed saddlebags and finally got a hand on the slim flask that was practically buried at the bottom. When she pulled it out, though, something else came loose with it and dropped to the ground at her feet.

"I'm sorry," she apologized, embarrassed by her clumsiness. The object looked to be a small, framed picture of some kind, and she bent to pick it up from where it had fallen in the dust.

Reina had had no intention of prying into his personal effects. She had merely planned to put the picture back without comment. But when she found herself staring down at the small portrait of herself her father had commissioned two years before, her heart almost skidded to a halt.

All vestiges of color drained from Reina's face as she stared at her own likeness. She was sure she looked as shocked as she was feeling, and she was glad that she had her back to Clay.

Clay Cordell had a picture of her! There was only one way he could have come into possession of her picture, and that was through her father. Fear shook Reina to her very depths. She swallowed convulsively against the sudden, paralyzing tightness in her throat and fought to keep her hands from shaking uncontrollably. *Dear Lord! What was she going to do now? This man was after her!*

Reina strove for control. She couldn't panic, she just couldn't! Obviously, Cordell hadn't recognized her. Surely, if he had, he would have said something. She'd come too far to let anything stop her now. Drawing a deep breath, she stuffed the picture back into the saddlebag and tied it shut.

"The woman in the picture is very beautiful," Reina complimented herself as she turned back to Clay, a tight rein held on her runaway emotions. She carefully schooled her features into an expression of only mild interest. Relief swept through her when she found that he hadn't even been watching her, but had leaned back against the wheel again and closed his eyes. *Thank heaven he hadn't seen how upset I got!* she thought.

"Yes, she is," Clay answered flatly. *Reina Alvarez.* Just the thought of her sent a shaft of white-hot fury through him. If it hadn't been for that spoiled little witch and her equally arrogant father, he wouldn't be out here in the middle of nowhere, winged in the arm. Instead, he and Dev would have collected their reward for Denton by

100

now and been happily on their way. *Damn her, anyway!*

Reina waited expectantly for him to say more, and she grew irritated when he didn't offer any other information. She was desperate to find out exactly what was going on.

"Is she your fiancée?" Reina asked, forcing herself to act as though nothing unusual had happened as she walked back to him with the flask.

"No," he answered, taking the whiskey when she offered it. "As a matter of fact, Sister, I've never met the woman." Clay wasn't sure if that was a blessing or not as he opened the whiskey and took a deep swig. The burning warmth of it spread through him like a healing balm.

"Why do you have her picture with you then?" Reina tried to come across as just being curious without sounding avid or hungry for details. She didn't want him to suspect her of more than just a passing interest.

"I'm a bounty hunter," he explained. "The girl ran away from home, and her father hired me to bring her back. He gave me the picture to help me identify her when I find her."

"I see." Reina was thrilled that her father hadn't had a newer portrait of her, but she couldn't understand why he hadn't come after her himself. The fact that he'd hired a bounty hunter to track her down, frightened her. She'd never imagined he would resort to anything like this! "Where do you think she's gone?"

"I'm not sure any more," Clay answered. He was glad that he'd been around to save the people on the stage, but it annoyed him to have wasted so much precious time on what had turned out to be nothing but a wild goose chase.

"Any more?" Reina prodded as she knelt down beside him again and poured some water on one of the rags. She began to gently scrub the gore from his arm as she waited for his answer.

"I started looking for her in Monterey, and all indica-

101

tions were that she was on this stage. Obviously, I was wrong." His error in judgment troubled him. He'd thought it would be relatively easy to find the girl. He'd thought it would be over quickly. Now, he was discovering that it wasn't going to be as simple as he'd first imagined. Reina Alvarez was obviously much smarter than either he or her father had given her credit for.

"There were only the five of us on the stage." Reina kept her face averted from his as she continued to cleanse the injury. The attraction she'd felt for him had changed to unholy terror now, for she was afraid he might suddenly recognize her. She prayed desperately that her disguise would hold up under this close scrutiny.

Clay grunted in frustrated acknowledgement. "No one else got on or off?"

"No."

His expression was grim as he reflected on what he had to do next. He had to head for Louisiana and hope against hope that Alvarez's daughter had gone to her friends there as her father had suggested she might. It tore at Clay to think that Dev was going to be stuck in jail for an even longer period of time, but he knew there was nothing else he could do. He had to head back East as soon as he could.

"What will you do next?" Reina asked in a tone that sounded only like she was making small talk to distract him from his pain.

"I've been hired to do a job, and I'll do it. I'll keep searching until I find her." Clay vowed, not revealing anything more as he took another drink.

His words chilled her, and she was suddenly more nervous than she had been before. "You sound like a very determined man."

"I am."

"I'll pray for you, sir," Reina told him seriously. *I'll pray that you never, ever, get any closer to finding Reina Alvarez than you are right now!*

"Thank you, Sister. I need all the help I can get."

"Maybe you're having so much difficulty, Mr. Cordell, because the young woman doesn't want to be found. Maybe she had a good reason for leaving as she did," she subtly defended herself.

"Not this one," Clay answered firmly, without the slightest measure of sympathy or hesitation in his voice. "She's a willful, pampered spoiled brat. She's nothing but a troublemaker."

Reina stiffened imperceptibly at the insult. She wondered how he would feel if he was being forced into a marriage with a woman he couldn't stand. "Really," she replied coolly. "I thought you hadn't met her."

"I haven't, but I know her type of woman. They aren't interested in anyone but themselves," he said.

At his arrogant pronouncement, it took all of Reina's will power not to scrub extra hard on his arm. "Well, I hope everything works out."

"So do I," he agreed. "How's my arm look?"

"It's a relatively clean wound. The bullet passed on through. I'll have you fixed up here in a minute, and you can be on your way," she encouraged, eager to be rid of him.

He nodded and took another quick drink before handing her the flask. "Go ahead and pour some of this on it."

Reina did as she was told, dousing the open wound liberally with the sterilizing whiskey, and she was almost ashamed of how pleased she felt when Clay's jaw tensed against the searing pain. "Sorry . . ." she murmured, biting down on her lip to keep from smiling. *It served him right,* she thought meanly.

"Thanks, Sister," he said through gritted teeth. "It had to be done. Just tie it up tight now, and I'll be fine."

Reina could hardly wait until he was gone, and she made quick work of bandaging his arm. When Ruth and Fred climbed out of the stage, she was glad for the distraction.

"We're ready to roll now," Fred announced.

103

"We're done here, too," Reina said as she finished tying the cloth around his arm.

"Since it's so late, Cordell, why don't you ride with us to the waystation?" Fred invited Clay along. "The least we can do for you is get you a hot meal and a bed for the night."

To Reina's horrified dismay, Clay accepted the offer.

"Sounds good. Thanks," he replied, painfully pulling his shirt back on.

Reina was anxious to stay as far away from him as possible, so she hurriedly got into the stage to devote herself to nursing Poke. Ruth and Melissa joined her there, while Fred retrieved the gold. The two men then loaded the outlaws' bodies onto their horses and tied the mounts to the back of the stage. Clay hitched his horse there, too, and then climbed up to ride on top with Fred.

The last five miles to the waystation seemed endless to Reina. Poke did not regain consciousness, and so she had nothing to distract her from her fears. She hoped the stop would be large enough to give them their own room so she could avoid further contact with Cordell. She knew better than to count on it, though, for the other stations they'd stayed at on the previous nights had been nothing more than one-room cabins that the stationmaster had partitioned off with a blanket to give the women some privacy.

If that turned out to be the case again, Reina wondered how she was going to avoid the bounty hunter without being obvious, until they parted company the following morning. She was still worrying about it when just after sundown they drew to a stop before the small station.

Chapter Eight

It was over an hour later that they all sat around the big rough-hewn table in the waystation. Fred, with Clay's help, had taken care of all that needed to be done, and they were relaxing there now, discussing the holdup and waiting for Hanley, the middle-aged, balding, rather portly station master to finish preparing the dinner. Poke had regained consciousness shortly after their arrival, and he seemed to be doing well. Hanley had given him his own bed there in the single-room cabin, and the old cowboy was sitting up now, propped against the wall eagerly listening to all the details of the day's happenings.

"So you held 'em off, did ya, Sister?" Poke questioned with something akin to delight and pride in her achievement.

"Yes, but it was thanks to your quick thinking and Mr. Cordell's timely arrival that we're all fine tonight," she demurred.

"Did ya have to use the gun?" he asked avidly.

"Yes," Reina admitted reluctantly. "I'm afraid I was forced to shoot, but it wasn't my marksmanship that saved us. It was Mr. Cordell's."

The old cowboy eyed Clay respectfully. "Then I thank you for saving our lives, Cordell. Those were some mean hombres."

"That they were," Clay agreed, glancing over at

Reina. "But Sister Mary Regina deserves more credit than she's willing to take. She's the one who drew the last outlaw out in the open. If she hadn't, I would never have gotten off a clean shot at him."

"She's one special lady," Poke told him knowingly as he regarded her. There was no mistaking the fondness he had for her in his expression.

"She certainly is," Clay agreed, letting the full potency of his silver-eyed gaze rest upon her. Ever since that afternoon when her innocent touch had stirred him so deeply, he'd been battling with himself. Clay had never been so powerfully attracted to any woman before, and the fact that she was unattainable made it even more difficult for him. Watching her now, he thought of how lovely she looked even after the long arduous day they'd just passed. He thought of the spunk and spirit she'd shown facing down the bandits as she'd defended herself and the others, and he knew she was one extraordinary woman.

Reina felt the heat of Cordell's gaze upon her, and though she managed to keep her expression serene, in truth, her nerves were frayed. She'd thought things were difficult maintaining her disguise before Cordell had showed up, but now, here she was, stuck overnight in this isolated cabin with the very man her father had hired to find her!

Reina wanted to run and hide from the bounty hunter's disturbing presence, but there was nowhere to run and certainly nowhere to hide. The small cabin offered no privacy whatsoever. She was trapped for the duration, and her only hope was to brazen it out and pray that in the morning he would ride out of her life forever.

"Here ya go," Hanley announced, distracting Reina from her desperate thoughts, as he set a big kettle of steaming stew in the middle of the table. "Help yourselves."

"Thank you," they responded.

Ruth did the honors, taking up the ladle and dishing out generous portions to everyone. When they had all been served and were about to dig in, Melissa suddenly turned her big-eyed, innocent childish gaze to Reina.

"Sister Mary Regina?" she said her name sweetly.

"Yes, Melissa?" Reina asked.

"Aren't you gonna say Grace tonight?"

Reina almost groaned out loud. She had been so caught up in her worries about Cordell that she'd completely forgotten the prayer over the meal. Melissa had put her on the spot their first night out on the trip, and she'd been stuck saying it every night since.

"Of course, Melissa. I'm sorry," Reina said with a tranquility she was little feeling. "With all the upset, I'd almost forgotten." Ducking her head to hide her embarrassment, she quickly began to pray. "We thank you our heavenly Father for all the blessings you've bestowed upon us this day. We thank you for Poke's health, and we pray that he will continue to improve." Reina knew she had to say something about Cordell, but it irked her tremendously to do it. "We thank you, also, for the intercession of Mr. Cordell, whose unselfish bravery today saved us from certain harm. We pray that you will guide him safely on his way." *Away from me, please God!* she added fervently to herself. "Shelter us all from evil and bless this meal we are about to share. We ask this in the name of the Father, Son and Holy Ghost. Amen."

"Amen," echoed around the table.

"Let's eat, folks!" Hanley encouraged, and they did.

Everyone ate hungrily, but Reina. Cordell was sitting far too close for her to act normally. His presence had been disturbing to her before she'd known who he was, and now that she knew the truth about him, she found him even more so. Reina concentrated on her food, pretending to eat just so she could avoid being drawn into further conversation. The less she said at this point, the better.

"Sister Mary Regina?" Ruth finally spoke up, think-

ing the nun was too quiet and that something might be
bothering her.

"Yes?"

"You're awfully quiet tonight. Are you feeling all
right? Is something wrong?"

"No, not really. I guess I'm just a little tired after the
trauma of the holdup and all . . ."

"I'm sure both you ladies must be, and Melissa, too,"
Fred acknowledged, thinking that the women had held
up very well, considering the circumstances.

"Very," Reina agreed with an honestly weary smile.

"As soon as we get done eating and I get things cleared
away, I'll set up the cabin so you can go on to bed,"
Hanley offered.

"Thank you, sir. I'm sure a good night's rest is all I
need," she responded and then thought, *that, and to wake
up in the morning and find the sun shining, the birds singing and
Clay Cordell already long gone!*

Reina glanced up to find Cordell's fathomless eyes
upon her again. It suddenly seemed as if the cabin was
closing in on her, and she knew she had to escape him, if
even for only a little while. Despite her nervousness, she
managed a small smile. "I think, if you'll excuse me, I'll
just go on outside for a breath of fresh air."

"Sure, ma'am," Hanley assured her. "You'll be safe as
long as you don't wander too far off."

"I won't," Reina promised, overjoyed just to be able to
get away by herself so she could calm down and get
herself back under control.

"If you like," Hanley offered as she started for the
door, "I can heat up some water and you ladies can wash
up tonight."

"Thank you, sir. I know Melissa and I would appreciate it," Ruth answered.

Reina glanced down at her habit then and realized
just how dirty she'd gotten that day. Between the miserable heat, tending Poke's bloody shoulder wound, cower-
ing in the dirt and dressing Cordell's arm, her white

108

habit was filthy. Although at the time, she'd hesitated to take two outfits from the convent, now she was glad that she had. "I guess I'd better take advantage of your kind offer, too, Mr. Hanley. Would it be possible to wash a few things out, too?"

"Of course," he told her. "You go on outside and enjoy your walk, Sister. I'll have it all ready for you when you get back."

"Thank you." Reina retreated from the crowded room, eager to enjoy the peace and quiet of the moonlit California night.

"You be careful out there, Sister. There's all kinds of varmints in the woods this time of night," Poke called after her protectively as she disappeared through the door.

"I will," came her answer. But Reina knew Poke was concerned about the wrong kind of varmints. The only varmint she was worried about was the one who was sitting there at the dinner table staring at her with those damned unnerving gray eyes of his!

Clay watched Reina as she went on outside, then thoughts of Dev, so long denied, surged through him. Clay was glad that he'd been able to help stop the robbery, but he was still angry with himself for the mistake he'd made in chasing after the wrong stage-coach. He wasn't sure how he could have been so wrong, but he had been and now he would have to pay the price.

At the thought, Clay almost laughed out loud in cynicism. He wasn't paying any price! Dev was the one who was paying! He only hoped his friend was holding up well. From the look of things he was going to have to travel all the way back to Louisiana to catch up with the Alvarez girl, and there was no way to do that quickly. It was going to take time, and he prayed that Luis Alvarez would make sure he had enough time to do it.

Hanley put the water on to heat and then, with Fred's help, began to partition the cabin for the women by stringing a line across the room and hanging blankets over it. He fixed it so they had the area closest to the fireplace so they would be more comfortable in the chill of the night. As Hanley helped pour the water for Ruth and Melissa, Clay figured they deserved some privacy while they bathed.

The thought of getting cleaned up before bedtime appealed to Clay, too. So he got some soap and a towel from Hanley, a clean shirt and his shaving gear out of his saddlebags and headed out to the water trough. His arm was stiff and more than a little sore, and it gave him some trouble as he took off his shirt. When he'd discarded the ruined garment, he flexed his shoulders and arms to test the strength of his injured limb. He was relieved to find that he still had full mobility for he couldn't afford to lose any time nursing himself. He had to head straight for New Orleans at first light.

As Clay thought of Louisiana, it was inevitable that memories of his father and Windown would follow. He hadn't been home in years, and he was sorry that this was going to be a trip born of necessity and not a social visit. Clay knew, though, he couldn't concern himself with anything but finding Reina Alvarez. Once that was done and Dev had been freed, then he could think of coming back to Windown. Until then . . .

Clay pushed all regrets aside as he primed the pump. When the icy water finally started to flow, he bent under it, taking care not to get his bandaged arm wet.

Reina had wandered around the station grounds, trying to come to grips with the panic that was threatening to overwhelm her. Over and over she chided herself for her fears. Very logically, she told herself that her secret was safe. If Cordell hadn't recognized her yet, he wasn't going to. But even as she tried to accept that very sane rationale, her instincts refused to allow her to relax. She felt much like an animal hiding in the woods while the predator ranged nearby.

As she paused near a small grove of trees not too far from the house, Reina sighed raggedly and clasped her

110

hands together in an effort to stop them from trembling. She'd lingered outside as long as she could now, and she knew she had to go back inside, appearing calm, even if she didn't feel calm.

Clay had just finished shaving and washing and was drying off when he caught sight of Reina standing alone in the distance. He paused in mid-effort to stare at her, thinking she appeared much like an angel at prayer.

As heavenly as Reina looked, though, Clay was still very much aware of her as a woman. He found her to be everything he'd never thought he'd find in a female. She was a perfect combination of beauty, humility and gentleness of spirit. Yet at the same time, she was so fiercely brave that Clay couldn't imagine her ever running away from anything. Above all else, though, she was a completely honest woman, a woman without guile. Clay wished that he'd had the luck to find her himself before she'd decided to take her vows and enter the convent.

Reina sensed Clay's intense scrutiny even before she knew he was near. She looked up and couldn't stifle a gasp when she spotted him, watching her from where he stood by the watering trough. He was naked to the waist, his sun-bronzed skin glistening wetly in the muted moonlight. It was not the beauty of his powerful body that held her attention, though, but her first glimpse of him, clean-shaven.

In that instant, she realized he was the most magnificent looking man she'd ever seen. Her mouth went dry and her heart lurched madly as she stared at him in fascination. She had thought him attractive before he'd shaved, but now . . .

Reina let her gaze trace his features. Visually, she caressed the hard, lean line of his jaw and the firm, sensual curve of his mouth. Something intense flared deep within her, and she suddenly found herself caught up in a maelstrom of conflicting emotions. She was drawn to Clay physically like a moth to a flame. She

111

wanted him as she'd never wanted another man, and yet in that very attraction was the ultimate danger.

More shaken than she cared to admit, Reina struggled to maintain the fragment of fragile control she'd only so recently acquired. Girding herself, she managed what she hoped was a serene smile and started to walk back toward the cabin.

"Good night, Mr. Cordell," Reina said sweetly as she moved past him, taking care not to look at him.

"Good night, Sister," Clay answered in a husky tone that, unbeknownst to him, sent shivers of awareness coursing through her. He watched Reina go, wondering how it was she managed to stay so tranquil in the face of all of life's ugliness. Clay wished that he had just a little of her inner peace.

Reina's nerves were stretched taut as she entered the station, and she was greatly relieved to find that Hanley had been kind enough to provide for their privacy. It surprised her to find that everyone had retired early, but in a way she was very grateful, for she needed some more time alone to sort out her thoughts.

"There's hot water for you there by the fire," Ruth directed from where she lay on a pallet next to her sleeping daughter.

"Thanks," Reina answered, and she quickly undressed, leaving on only the practical cotton underwear while she washed. At the convent, she had balked at parting with her fancy silk underthings, but Maria had been adamant. Now, Reina was glad she'd listened to her friend, for it would have been difficult to explain to Ruth why she was wearing such fine, lacy undergarments.

Reina was busy scrubbing away the day's dirt and grime when she heard Cordell reenter the cabin. She froze in her actions, much like a deer sensing trouble, and she waited. When she finally heard the sounds of the bounty hunter bedding down for the night, she relaxed and finished her ablutions.

112

Feeling somewhat refreshed, but still a little tense, Reina donned her long nightgown and then believing she was alone, got her brush from her case. She sat on a chair before the low-burning fire, enjoying the luxury of brushing out her hair. It was the first time she'd been able to do it since she'd left Monterey, and it felt wonderful.

Reina let her thoughts drift as she drew the brush over and over again through her thick, ebony mane. She missed her home and the comfortable life she led there, but despite all the hardships she was encountering, she was still firm in her resolve not to go back. She despised Nathan Marlow too much to even consider spending one moment more with him, let alone a lifetime. It occurred to her then, that her father had had better taste in his choice of a bounty hunter than he had in his choice of her betrothed. She wondered resentfully, why, if he'd felt so compelled to choose her husband for her, that he hadn't picked someone like Cordell. Clay Cordell was ten times the man Nathan was, and had her father arranged her betrothal to him, she probably would never have even considered running away. The only place she would have run, she thought wickedly, was straight into his arms. The man was devilishly handsome, and she only regretted that they couldn't have met under different circumstances. Reina gave a delicious chuckle at the direction of her thoughts and then quickly bit down on her lip as she realized how decadent she'd sounded.

Forcing herself back into the role of Sister Mary Regina, Reina abruptly stopped brushing her hair and packed away the brush. She finished getting ready for bed and then snuggled down deep beneath the blanket on her pallet. Soon she would be in New Orleans and everything would be all right. She would be safe there from her father, from Nathan Marlow and from Clay Cordell. As sleep claimed her a short time later, she was only vaguely aware of a deep, soft voice bidding her good night.

Clay was miserable as he lay on his own pallet across the room on the other side of the blanket barrier. In agitation, he wondered if somewhere along the line of his existence he'd unwittingly done some terrible thing and was deserving of this kind of torture. He knew he hadn't lived the life of a saint, but then again, right now, he was beginning to feel like he was in the running for that position.

Clay groaned inwardly as he thought of the innocent, yet totally seductive display he'd just witnessed. The time he'd spent with Frenchie hadn't been nearly this exciting or this tormenting! How was he supposed to know that Sister Mary Regina was going to take her time about retiring? And, if that wasn't bad enough, how was he supposed to know that with the fire going he'd be able to see through the damned blankets?

Clay stared up at the ceiling and asked God in mute appeal why he'd been given this cross to bear. He'd been playing the role of the gentleman, and this was his reward? He'd made it a point to linger outside long after Sister Mary Regina had gone indoors to give her time to get in bed. He'd come in himself then, intending to lie down and go right to sleep, and, instead he'd been subjected to the most tantalizing torture known to man — the sight of a beautiful, but unattainable young woman in all her glory. Her fire-silhouetted image on the blanket had nearly driven him into a frenzy, and when she'd sat down to brush out her hair, he'd almost torn the partition down and grabbed the brush from her hand to finish the job for her.

Clay was perplexed by the power of his reaction to her. It certainly wasn't just because he needed a woman. Frenchie had satisfied that hunger when he'd been in Monterey. No, there was something very different about the way he felt toward this nun, and it was as disturbing as it was powerful.

In a fit of frustration, Clay rolled over, closed his eyes

and pulled his blanket up over his shoulders. As he lay desperately courting oblivion, he found that he was glad he would be riding out on his own in the morning. Knowing how he felt about Sister Mary Regina, Clay knew it was a good thing that he was not making the trip back East on the stage, for he wasn't sure he would be able to control the desire he felt for her. When he finally felt himself drifting off, he whispered a hoarse good night, for he knew that he would be gone in the morning before she awoke and that he would never see her again.

Chapter Nine

It was late afternoon when Philip and Clay mounted the front steps of Windown and entered the house. Clay had been back home for almost a week, and Philip was thoroughly enjoying having him there with him again. They had spent the better part of the day riding the fields and working with their breeding stock, and they were tired but content as they made their way into the study. Clay dropped wearily into one of the leather wingchairs while his father moved to his small liquor cabinet and poured them each a tumbler of his best bourbon. Philip's smile was warm and happy as he handed Clay one of the glasses.

"I can't tell how good it is to have you home again," he told him with heartfelt emotion.

"It's good to be here," Clay agreed, giving a deep, satisfied sigh as he settled back and relaxed. He'd missed his father and Windown more than he cared to admit, and, had circumstances been different, he might have considered staying on for a while. As it was, though, he knew he had to concentrate on his real reason for coming to Louisiana — finding Reina Alvarez. "I'm just sorry that I can't stay longer."

"So am I," his father remarked, knowing it would do no good to say any more on the subject. When Clay had first arrived, he'd confided in him his reason for coming. He'd told him about his friend Dev's arrest and how he'd been forced into taking the job of hunting down the runaway girl. Philip knew how angry and frustrated his son was over the whole situation, and he refused to add to the strain by trying to pressure him into remaining permanently.

"If the Alvarez girl doesn't show up here by the middle of next week, I'll have to head out again." Clay scowled at the thought, aggravated that his discreetly made inquiries about the Delacroix family had turned up nothing. "Damn!" he swore. "If she was heading here to the Delacroix plantation like her father thought, she would have made it by now. But there's no record of her anywhere, not on the steamboat lines or the stage lines or at any of the hotels."

"I know," Philip sympathized. "But maybe you'll find something out Saturday night at the Randolphs' party. The Delacroix family is going to be there."

"I hope so," Clay responded, but he was less than optimistic about his chances. Things had been going so badly for him ever since he'd first started looking for the girl that he was becoming convinced that his luck in resolving this matter was not going to change.

"I'm just sorry that I'm not better acquainted with the Delacroixs. It certainly would have made things a lot easier for you if we had been friendly enough so you could have paid them an unexpected social call. As it is, I've only met them a few times through the years, and those encounters were at large festivities much like the Randolphs' party is going to be. It's really a stroke of luck that they'll be there. Maybe things are finally going to start going your way."

"Maybe," Clay said doubtfully, "but I'm beginning to question her father's idea that she might have come here in the first place. It's kind of hard for me to believe that a young woman of her class and position, someone who's been cosseted and protected all her life, would be capable of traveling across the continent all by herself."

"I understand why you're having doubts, but I wouldn't underestimate the Alvarez girl if I were you," Philip advised sagely. "Desperation can sometimes force people to do things they wouldn't ordinarily do."

"Desperation," Clay gave an arrogant, deriding laugh. "She doesn't know the meaning of the word."

Philip heard the bitterness in his tone and frowned at his lack of compassion. "Don't be too sure about that. You've only heard one side of the story."

"I've heard enough to know that Reina Alvarez is a spoiled, manipulative young woman. She'll do anything she has to to get her own way, and she doesn't care who gets hurt in the process," he answered condemningly and then downed the rest of his drink in one fierce swallow.

"And you also know from your own experience that her father is a bastard who will do whatever is necessary to achieve *his* own ends," he pointed out with maddening logic. "I'd say the girl was well taught."

It surprised Clay to find his father almost defending the girl's actions, and his eyes hardened to silver as he glanced up at him. "Women are all naturally conniving and self-centered. No one had to teach her," he sneered, refusing to believe that Reina Alvarez might have had a very good reason for running away.

"Not all women are like your mother, Clay," Philip chided gently, his expression growing troubled at the bitterness he heard in his son's voice.

Thoughts of the gentle, devoted Sister Mary Regina stirred within him at his father's declaration, but he pushed them away. He wouldn't sully the very special memories he had of her by including her in his overall assessment of the opposite sex.

"You're awfully forgiving considering what she did to you," he countered.

Father and son had never really talked openly about that terrible time in their lives, for it had been much too painful for them. Philip knew that Clay had been deeply hurt by Evaline's betrayal, but he was shocked now to find that it had left such deep, lasting emotional scars on him. He had hoped that during Clay's time away he might have come to grips with the demon of her treachery. It troubled him to find that he hadn't.

"That's all in the past, son. What happened with your mother . . . well, that's one thing. Your dealings with this Alvarez girl are something else."

"Maybe, but first I have to find her before I can start worrying about how I'm going to deal with her." Clay shrugged off his subtle counsel as he got up to refill his glass. He knew better than to trust any woman.

"You will." Philip said with confidence.

"I hope you're right. Dev's life is riding on this, and if I've missed her again . . ."

"Again?"

"I thought I knew exactly where she was when I first left Monterey, but I was wrong." He went on to tell his father all about how he followed the wrong stage and what had happened when he'd caught up with it. "I wasted three days."

"They were hardly wasted days, Clay. You saved the lives of all those innocent people."

"I may have saved them, but I haven't done a damn thing to help Dev."

Philip moved behind him to clamp a warm hand on his shoulder. "Don't worry, son. Everything will work out. You always accomplish everything you set out to do."

Clay took a stout drink of the potent liquor. His father might have unwavering faith in him, but he was filled with his own self-doubts. He could remember all too clearly the time when he had failed, and failed miserably! The similarities between his mother and Reina Alvarez grated on him unmercifully, and as the days went by, his motivation for finding the Alvarez

119

girl and taking her back home to her father was becoming much more personal in nature.

"You're right," Clay replied, just wanting to end the discussion. "It's just a matter of time. Reina Alvarez is bound to show up soon . . ."

Emilie Delacroix, a short, fair-haired young woman, blinked in surprise as a nun answered her knock at the hotel room door. "I'm sorry, Sister," she apologized hastily. "The desk clerk must have given me the wrong room number . . ."

When she started to turn away, Reina reached out and grabbed her by her arm. "Emilie! Wait! It's me!" she exclaimed, delighted to see her old friend.

"Reina?" Emilie stared at her in astonishment. "Good heavens, it is *you* . . ." she muttered in disbelief as she allowed herself to be dragged into the room.

"Yes, it most certainly is me," Reina teased, enjoying her discomfort. Obviously, her disguise was perfect if even Emilie hadn't recognized her.

Emilie was in shock at finding her friend dressed in the flowing white garb and long black veil of a professed sister. Stunned, she remained speechless as she watched Reina close the door.

Never in her whole life would Emilie have dreamed that Reina would enter a convent. Just the idea of it seemed totally at odds with Reina's basic personality. When they'd attended school together, Reina had been the flamboyant, outgoing one. She'd always been the center of attention, and she'd loved it. She was beautiful, rich, and immensely popular. The idea that Reina had given all that up and taken holy, solemn vows left Emilie perplexed. She wondered what had happened in the few years they'd been apart to change her so completely.

"Reina, you never told me . . ." Emilie began, stammering a little in her puzzlement.

For the first time since she'd left Monterey Reina laughed with easy good-humor. "I didn't have time to tell you, Emilie," she started to explain.

"What do you mean, you didn't have time?" Emilie frowned in confusion, puzzled by Reina's whole attitude. She knew nuns spent at least a full year as a novice in the convent before taking their final vows. Surely Reina could have contacted her some time during all those months.

Reina laughed again, feeling very light of spirit now that she considered herself safe. "Emilie, I'm not a nun."

" 'You're not a nun'?" Emilie repeated, her surprise growing deeper.

"I mean this is all an elaborate disguise," she confided.

"A disguise? Why do you need a disguise?" Now Emilie was truly baffled. "And where's your father? Didn't he come with you?" she added cautiously as she began to get the feeling that something very strange was going on here.

"No, he didn't come with me. As far as I know, he's still in California," Reina replied tersely. When she saw her friend's concerned expression, she became more subdued, and her ready smile turned sad. "Sit down on the bed, I've got a lot to tell you."

"I'll just bet you do," Emilie agreed. "I was so excited when I got your note yesterday that you were in town. Mama assumed your father had come with you, and she insisted that I invite both of you to come stay with us for as long as you want."

"I was praying you'd offer," she answered with a teasing grin.

"Of course, we'd offer!"

"I just hope that my being here by myself won't change your mother's mind."

"Don't worry, Reina, if anything, she'll be even more convinced that you should stay with us. But, tell me, what is going on?"

Reina took off the veil as she sat down on the bed next to Emilie. She pulled the pins from her hair and, with a toss of her head, shook her heavy, ebony tresses loose from their confinement. The satiny mane tumbled about her shoulders in curling disarray.

Reina took a deep, steadying breath and then began to explain everything to Emilie. She told her about her father's betrayal in promising her in marriage to a man she couldn't stand and about his cold-bloodedness in hiring the bounty hunter to track her down and bring her back.

Reina did not call Cordell by name out of the fear that by just mentioning him she might somehow conjure him up. It was bad enough that thoughts of the handsome but dangerous gunman haunted her constantly, even in her sleep. She certainly didn't want to talk about him any more than necessary.

"I don't believe any of this . . ."

"I know," Reina groaned. "For a while there, things couldn't have gotten much more complicated."

"I'll bet you were scared to death."

"I was. I didn't relax until he had finally gone, but even then, just knowing that my father was that determined and that desperate . . ."

"Where do you think the bounty hunter went after he left you there at the waystation?"

"I don't know, and I don't care, as long as it's in the opposite direction from me!" Reina declared vehemently.

"I can well imagine, but now that you made it this far, just what do you intend to do next?"

Reina had been struggling with the very same thought. All of the plans she'd made to escape the fate her father had in store for her had ended with her making it safely to Emilie's. She lifted her dark-eyed gaze to her friend's. The uncertainty she was feeling was clearly mirrored there.

"I don't really know . . ." she admitted slowly. "I thought my running away would make my father change his mind. I was hoping that he cared enough about me to come after me himself and that he would tell me that he wasn't going to force me to marry Nathan. But now . . ."

"Do you think he'll suspect that you came here to me?"

"I don't know. Father knows what close friends we are, but I'm not sure whether he thinks I'd be daring enough to make the trip alone. I tried to encourage the bounty hunter to talk about where he was going next, but he wouldn't say a word."

"What do you want to do, Reina? You know you can stay here with me for as long as you want."

Reina took her hand and squeezed it warmly. "Thanks, Emilie."

"You're more than welcome. I know you'd help me if I needed it."

"I would," Reina affirmed. "There's just one thing more I wanted to ask of you though . . ."

"What?"

"I was wondering if you'd mind if I went by another name whenever we're out in public."

"You think you should keep your identity a secret?"

Reina nodded. "I don't think my father's going to give up too easily. He just might send somebody back here to check, and if he does, they'll be searching for Reina Alvarez. If I go by the name Isabel Nuñez, no one will suspect, and we won't really be lying to anyone. Isabel is my middle name and Nuñez was my mother's maiden name."

"All right, Isabel," Emilie said with a conspiratorial grin, amazed to find herself caught up in such intrigue. "But are you going to stay dressed as a nun or did you bring some other clothes with you?"

"There was no time to pack anything . . ." she apologized.

Emilie knew then that they had to do some shopping before she could take her friend home. Her mother was a very strict Catholic and would not approve of Reina's disguise. Emilie started for the door. "You wait here until I get back."

"Where are you going?"

She paused. "I know it's getting late, but I'm going to run out and see if I can find an outfit for you. We'll spend the night here, do more shopping for essentials in the morning, then head home in the afternoon."

"Your mother won't worry?"

"No, my brother, Richard, came with me so I'm well-chaperoned. Besides, I told her when we left that we might have to stay the night in town."

"Emilie . . . wait . . ." Reina quickly dug through her one small valise and pulled out all the money she'd brought with her. "Here, take this." She pressed a goodly amount into her hand.

"Are you sure you can afford this?"

"I didn't have time to worry about packing clothes, but I did bring plenty of money."

"I'll be back as soon as I can," Emilie promised. "And don't worry. Your father will come around. Everything's going to be just fine. You'll see."

They hugged in a warm, spontaneous gesture.

"I hope so, Emilie," she answered. As the door closed behind her, Reina repeated, feeling strangely disquieted, "I really, truly hope so."

The ethereal woman hovered before Clay in the misty semi-darkness. Though she was completely clothed in some unfamiliar, loose, flowing garment, there was something seductively arousing about her. Lithe arms raised to him, beckoning him ever closer.

Clay wanted to go to her. He wanted to hold her. He wanted more than anything to press his lips to hers and seek out the sweet ecstasy he knew would be found in her embrace. For some unknown reason, though, Clay couldn't move or speak. Restrained by an unseen force, he could only look on, desperately wanting, but never having.

The woman called his name, and the sound of her voice, so soft and enthralling, echoed enticingly around Clay, increasing his already fervent ardor. She sounded so familiar to him, and yet . . .

Clay struggled to break free from the invisible bonds that held him, all the while feverishly searching his memory for some clue as to his mystery temptress's name. He knew if he could only call her name, she would come to him. His muscles strained and sweat beaded his brow as he fought against the power that held him immobile. His effort was herculean, but ultimately in vain as she began to move away from him. Her arms were still reaching out for him, and she was still calling to him, but he was helpless to respond. Caught . . . trapped . . . Clay could do no more than watch in mute despair as she was taken from him . . .

The force of the emotions that wracked him in the dream jarred Clay from a sound sleep. Sweat-soaked and breathing raggedly, Clay sat up abruptly in his bed. He stared off into the surrounding darkness, trying to make sense of the chaotic, dream-inspired images that were churning in his mind. Tense but weary, he rubbed a hand over his eyes in an effort to help clear his thoughts, then he swung his long legs over the edge of the bed and sat there for a long quiet moment in the night-shrouded room.

The unknown woman in his dream seemed very real to Clay, but he could put no name to her. She was elusive in his thoughts, teasing the corners of his consciousness with her exciting presence, yet leaving him frustrated in his pursuit of her identity. Clay tried to dismiss his dream temptress as a figment of his imagination for he could not remember ever feeling that strongly about any woman. But as he sat there in the dark, his defenses down, he let his thoughts run wild. The memory of Sister Mary Regina and the night at the waystation came to him. The erotic image of her brushing out her hair as she sat before the fire, surged powerfully through Clay. Just recalling that night aroused him, and with a growl he got up from the bed and pulled on his pants.

Like a caged animal, Clay paced his room. After a restless moment, he paused by the window and brushed back one heavy velvet drape to stare out across the soothing beauty of the moonlit countryside. It troubled him deeply to think that he was perverted enough to dream of Sister Mary Regina as a seductress. He raked a hand nervously through his sleep-tousled hair as he considered this flaw in his character. The sister was the only truly good woman he'd met in his life, and Clay did not want to dwell on that incredibly sensual yet completely innocent encounter. *Hell,* he berated himself angrily, *Sister Mary Regina hadn't been aware of any of it. She was a chaste woman of unimpeachable virtue, and he knew he did her a disservice by even thinking about that night and how beautiful she'd looked . . .*

Clay was a man used to being in control, and it annoyed him that he couldn't completely put Sister Mary Regina out of his mind. Sometimes, he wondered if he ever would. Clay acknowledged that their paths would never cross again, and he found the thought oddly disturbing, although he wasn't sure just why. Too tense to even think about trying to sleep again, he turned away from the window and left the room.

Chapter Ten

Seventeen-year-old, auburn-haired Molly Magee smiled tenderly as she gazed down at her little brother, "Well, Jimmy, do you think you can take care of Ma while I'm gone to work?"

"Of course I can, Molly," the red-haired, freckle-faced eight-year-old declared with fierce pride. "You can trust me."

Though Molly didn't like Jimmy missing school and she had her reservations about leaving him alone with their sick mother, she knew she had no other choice in the matter. She had to go to work. Her job at the Golden Kettle Restaurant was their only source of income right now, and the owner, a big-bodied, mean-spirited woman named Bertha Harvey, wouldn't hesitate to fire her if she dared to miss a day. Molly reached out to give him a loving hug.

"You're a good boy, Jimmy Magee," she told him, ruffling his hair affectionately when she let him go. "Listen, I'm late already, but I promise you I'll be back just as quick as I can."

"I hope Mrs. Harvey doesn't make you stay extra late."

"So do I, sweetie," Molly agreed.

"What should I do for Ma when she wakes up, Molly?"

"Make sure she gets lots to drink and anything else she wants, all right?"

"I'll make sure," he promised.

Molly crossed the room to stand by the small bed where their mother was resting fitfully. Life had not been kind to Eileen Magee. She'd been married and had had Molly by the time she was sixteen. The year after Jimmy had been born, she had followed her husband to the gold fields only to have him get himself shot and killed in a card game shortly after they'd arrived. She had been on her own ever since, making money any way she could to support herself and her two children. It hadn't been easy, especially since she'd refused the easy money to be made through prostitution. Eileen had wanted an honorable way of life, and though she had achieved at least that much, it was that very honorable, hard-working lifestyle that had left her exhausted and too weak to fight off her illness.

Molly studied her mother as she lay, burning up with fever now and realized that she looked far older than her thirty-three years. Her hair, once flaming red, was now dull and streaked with gray. Except for the fever's flush on her sunken cheeks, she was deathly pale. Molly was used to her mother being strong. She'd always bounced back right away from any sickness, but this was the third day she'd been down with the fever, and she was showing no signs of improvement.

"Jimmy, darling, I've got to go. I'm late already," Molly sighed, tearing herself away from the bedside.

"Hurry home . . ." There was a slight tremor in his voice, as if the uncertainty of their situation frightened him, too.

"I will."

Molly gave Jimmy one last hug, then hurried from their small, four room house. It was quite a distance to the Golden Kettle, and she nearly had to run the whole way for fear of Bertha Harvey's considerable wrath.

"You know I don't abide your being late, Molly."

Bertha's snapped greeting welcomed Molly as she came rushing into the kitchen of the restaurant a short time later.

"Yes, ma'am, but my mother's ill and—"

"I have customers who need to be waited on. If you can't do it, I'll find someone else who can!" the gray-haired woman said coldly.

It was exactly what Molly had expected her to say, and yet she still cringed at the threat. "Yes, ma'am."

"You're already late getting the lunches over to the sheriff. Get on that right now."

"Yes, ma'am," Molly replied breathlessly as she hurried around the kitchen gathering what she needed. In a way, she was glad that her first duty of the day would be to take the lunches to the jail. The less time she had to spend in Bertha Harvey's abrasive company, the happier she was, and then there was always the fact that she'd get to see Devlin O'Keefe again . . .

"I want you to deliver the lunches and come straight back. I don't want you lingering over there talking to those prisoners. Do you understand me, Molly?"

Her caustic comment jerked Molly's thoughts away from the young man who'd been arrested for Pedro Santana's murder, but for some reason hadn't gone to trial yet.

"Yes, ma'am, Mrs. Harvey," Molly answered respectfully, "but I really don't think that—"

"I don't pay you to think, Molly. I pay you to work." She silenced any comeback the girl might have had with an icy look. She was a narrow-minded old woman who did not tolerate insolence from her employees.

Molly ducked her head so Bertha wouldn't see the

flash of angry resentment in her green eyes. She remained silent, but she really wanted to argue and tell her that Devlin O'Keefe, with his friendly blue eyes and soft, gentle voice, couldn't possibly be the villain everyone claimed he was. As desperate as Molly was for honest work, though, she knew better than to say anything that might anger her employer.

Hurrying because she wanted to get away from her boss's overbearing nearness, Molly reached for the steaming kettle of stew on the stove without a towel to protect her hand. She gave a small cry of pain as she burned herself. Suddenly letting go of the pot, she spilled some of its contents.

"That was stupid," the older woman ridiculed, not moving to help her. "Now you're going to be later than ever. Clean up that mess and get those pails over to the jail."

Molly fought back tears as she bit her lip in an effort to distract herself from the pain.

"And just remember what I told you, girl," Bertha went on, "I don't want to hear that you were talking with those two. I won't have any sluts working for me."

"I'm no slut!" Molly responded quickly, unable to take any more of her verbal abuse.

"And you'd better keep it that way. Those two prisoners are nothing but cold-blooded murderers, the both of them. Especially that Ace Denton. They're gonna hang him tomorrow, you know."

"I know." Molly shivered involuntarily as she thought of Denton. Where Devlin O'Keefe seemed innocent to her, Ace Denton was just the opposite. There was something about the man that scared her. His eyes were cold and deadly, and she could sense no goodness in him. It was as if all the evil in the world was embodied in him, and she hated even just having to hand him his food through the cell bars.

"Won't be too much longer before the other one's

130

tried and sentenced to hang, too. Although," she mused lightheartedly, "I really shouldn't be complaining about them keeping O'Keefe alive. I'm making good money feeding him."

"They aren't really going to hang him, are they?" Molly spoke up without thought.

Bertha eyed her suspiciously, wondering why it mattered to the girl. "He's guilty. Everybody in town knows it. The sheriff found some evidence linking him to the murder."

"But that doesn't mean he did it," she defended.

"He's the killer, missy. Don't you doubt that for a minute. Sheriff Macauley wouldn't have arrested him if he wasn't sure. It's just a matter of time until he pays his dues like Denton's going to tomorrow." She didn't notice Molly's stricken look as she directed, "Now, just get those meals over there and hurry on back. There's a lot more work here just waiting for you."

Molly finished preparing the hot lunches and then left for the sheriff's office. As she crossed the busy street and headed toward the jail, she questioned her own conviction about O'Keefe's innocence. If everyone in town believed he'd murdered Santana, why didn't she?

Dev lay on the hard, uncomfortable cot in his jail cell, his arms folded beneath his head, staring sightlessly at the ceiling. When he'd first been incarcerated, he'd raged against the injustice of it. But as the long weeks had passed and he realized that he was no longer in command of his own fate, he'd called upon his reserve of patience and control. He would not panic. Only Clay could help him now. Only Clay . . .

Dev thought of the last conversation they'd had before his friend had ridden out of town. Clay had told him how Alvarez had blackmailed him into tracking down his daughter and of how the Californio had promised that nothing would happen to him while he was gone. It had been a relief to know that he wasn't going to be strung up right away for a crime he hadn't committed, but it hadn't really changed anything. He was still locked up in the six by six foot room with no quick hope of getting out. It was only Dev's complete, unshakable confidence in Clay that kept him from losing his sanity. That, and the regular daily visits of Molly Magee, the pretty young woman who brought the meals from the restaurant.

The thought of the lovely Molly stirred a warmth within Dev, and he smiled slightly as he pictured her in his mind. Her hair was a deep, burnished color, not red and not auburn, but somewhere in between. The peaches and cream of her complexion was highlighted by a light sprinkling of freckles across the bridge of her nose. Her eyes were the clearest green. Her figure was slender and still a bit girlish, but with the budding promise of future curves. She was shy, and though he'd made numerous overtures in his most charming manner to try to engage her in conversation, she seldom responded. It troubled him that Molly always tried to keep her eyes averted from his as if she was afraid of something.

Judging the sun's height through the small, barred window in his cell, Dev knew it was almost midday, and Molly would soon be coming with the noon meal. The sound of voices in the outer office alerted Dev to the fact that she had arrived, and he found he was eager just to lay eyes on her again.

Ace Denton, a tall, dark-haired, mean-looking man whose murdering ways were legendary in California, was caged in the cell next to Dev's. He was an ugly man with an even uglier temper, and, unlike Dev, he was not happy about the day being half over. His trial had ended the previous afternoon, and he'd been convicted of his crimes and sentenced to hang. The execution was scheduled for the following morning, and as each hour passed, bringing him closer to meeting his maker, Denton grew more and more nervous and more and more desperate. There was no way he was going to let them hang him! No way . . .

The sound of the girl arriving with their food gave Denton an idea. An evil glimmer shone in his eyes. He knew it would take a daring effort to get free, but he was prepared to pay any price to escape. Feigning indifference to Molly's presence, he waited until the time was right.

"Here's your lunch," Molly announced as she entered the walkway before the two jail cells.

Dev stood to greet her. "What did you bring me this afternoon, Molly?" he asked, giving her his most engaging smile.

"Stew," she answered coolly. She didn't want to be drawn into conversation with him just in case Sheriff Macauley might report it to Bertha Harvey.

"Stew's one of my favorites," Dev responded, taking the lunchpail from her. He lifted the lid to look inside. "It smells wonderful, and it's still hot. Did you make it yourself?"

"No," Molly replied, not looking at him as she moved on toward Denton.

Denton was lingering against the back wall of his cell watching her every move. He knew she was jittery around him and realized that he'd have to move quickly. As she held out the pail for him to take, he stepped forward and grabbed her by the wrist, jerking her forcefully forward.

His action was so unexpected that Molly managed only a shriek as she lost her balance and slammed into the iron bars. She fought Denton automatically, but before she could break free, he turned her around and linked one strong forearm around her neck.

"Denton! What the hell are you doing?" Dev was rigid with fury. If he could have reached him, he would have killed him for putting his hands on Molly, but Denton was standing out of reach near the far side of his cell.

Denton gave a victorious, half-crazed laugh. "This little gal is my ticket outta here, O'Keefe! They ain't hangin' me! Macauley! Get in here! Now!"

"Sheriff!" Molly cried out, her emerald eyes seeming huge in her pale face as fear seized her.

When her terrified gaze met Dev's for just an instant, he knew he could let nothing happen to her. *He had to help her! But how?*

The sheriff came running into the room, gun drawn. "What the. . . ? Denton!" He stopped in his tracks at the sight of the ruthless outlaw holding the young girl in such a painful grip. Ace Denton was a cold-blooded murderer, and Macauley knew he wouldn't hesitate to kill again.

"You just lower that gun, sheriff, or you're going to have a dead woman on your hands," Denton snarled, deliberately tightening his strangling hold on Molly so that she was gasping for air.

"Don't do anything stupid, Denton."

"What have I got to lose, Macauley? You can kill me now or you can kill me tomorrow." The murderer's eyes were wild as he taunted the lawman with the devastating truth.

"What do you want?"

"I want out! Now, you jes' come on over here and unlock the cell door or I swear I'll break her pretty neck."

"Sheriff . . . please . . ." Molly whispered, terror showing plainly on her pretty features.

Macauley knew he had no choice. He couldn't risk Molly's life. His only hope was to somehow trap the outlaw on his way out of the jail.

"All right . . . all right . . ." The sheriff moved toward the cell door and unlocked it. "Now, what?"

"Slide your gun down the hall toward the front office," Denton instructed. When Macauley had done what he was told, the outlaw spoke again, "Now, open the door, leave the key in it and step back."

Again the lawman did as he was told. Slowly, Denton manipulated himself and Molly toward the open door. It was difficult for him to keep a hold on her, but he managed. When he moved out of the cell, he yanked her tightly against his chest.

"Now, get inside, sheriff," he ordered coldly, enjoying the feeling of power that was surging through him.

Dev watched helplessly as Macauley did as he was told. He was growing more and more angry as he watched the killer maneuver the lawman, and his grip tightened unconsciously on the pail of hot stew he still held. When Denton slammed the cell door shut behind the sheriff and locked it, taking the key, Dev knew he was the only one left to save Molly.

"You're free now, Denton, let the girl go."

"No way, Macauley."

"What are you going to do with her?" the sheriff was asking, worriedly.

"I ain't decided yet. But she'll sure be good company wherever I go," he replied, moving down the hall and dragging her along with him. Denton's big mistake was not considering Dev to be a threat. He was so intent on getting away that he started past Dev's cell without thinking.

The only weapon Dev had was the stew, and he knew he had to use it. When Denton moved by, he hurled the pail of hot stew at him. It crashed into the bars near his face and sprayed hot, steaming food all over him. Denton screamed in astonished confusion and pain, and Molly took advantage of the moment to break free.

"The gun, Molly! Get the gun!" Dev shouted, hoping she had enough presence of mind to react quickly.

"Sheriff! Here!" Molly needed no encouragement. She made a mad grab for the gun just as Denton started to recover. She slid the weapon down the hall floor toward Macauley, and he stretched through the bars trying desperately to reach it.

To their horror, Dev was the one who grabbed it. For an instant, time hung suspended. Molly and the sheriff watched in horrified fascination as Dev came up firing.

Denton had been momentarily blinded by the stew, but he recovered quickly and dove for the gun just as Dev pulled the trigger. The bullet struck him squarely, killing him instantly. When he fell dead, an uneasy silence reigned in the jailhouse.

Sheriff Macauley honestly thought O'Keefe was as cold-blooded as Denton. Unmoving, he waited with sickening certainty for Dev to turn the gun on him next. When he didn't, the sheriff was stunned.

"Molly . . ." Dev said her name in a low, non-threatening voice. He could see the fear in her eyes, and he wanted to erase that fear forever. He wanted to show her the kind of man he really was.

"Don't hurt her, O'Keefe . . ." Macauley pleaded, afraid for Molly.

"Molly, get the cell key off Denton and come here," he urged.

Molly was deeply shaken by all that had happened, and her emotions were in turmoil. Devlin had shot and killed the other outlaw. He had saved her from a fate worse than death, but now he controlled the gun. Did that mean he wanted the same thing that Denton had? Was he intent on escaping? Would he try to take her with him, too?

The moment was a tense one, for Molly realized

she had no choice. She couldn't risk angering him. She had to do what he said. Mechanically, she moved to the dead outlaw and got the key. Molly hesitantly approached Dev, fully expecting him to demand that she release him from his cell.

Dev knew both Molly and the sheriff believed him to be a savage murderer, and it was important to him that he prove to them both that they were wrong. As she crossed the few steps that separated them, Dev's eyes sought and held Molly's.

"Are you all right?" Dev asked softly when she drew near.

"Yes." She was so nervous that her reply was little more than a whisper.

"I'm glad." His response drew a surprised look from Molly, and as she stopped directly before him, he reversed his grip on the gun and handed it to her through the bars. "Here, give this to the sheriff after you let him out."

Molly blinked in bewilderment as she stared down at the revolver in her hand. Devlin O'Keefe could have escaped. He could have shot the sheriff and made a run for it, yet he hadn't. He had given her the gun and told her to free the sheriff. It lightened her spirits enormously to find that her instincts had been right about him all along. He wasn't the terrible, amoral killer everyone else thought him to be. Slowly a wide, bright smile lit her face.

Dev was waiting to see what her reaction would be to his gesture, and when she glanced up at him, he knew that he'd accomplished his goal. There in her beautiful green-eyed gaze was all the respect and admiration he'd hoped one day to see. His heart sang at the thought, and he found himself smiling back at her.

A shiver of some unnamed emotion raced through Molly as her eyes met Dev's. Startled by the unexpected strength of the feelings, she tore her gaze from his and rushed off to release the sheriff from Denton's cell.

Macauley was shocked by what had happened, and he breathed an immense sigh of relief at the turn of events. He brought the blanket off the cot with him as he emerged from the cell, and he threw it over the dead man. That done, he put a comforting arm about Molly's shoulders and started to guide her from the scene of the carnage. He stopped before where Dev stood in his cell.

"O'Keefe, that was a mighty decent thing you just did. You saved Molly's life, and we owe you a debt of gratitude for it," he said, self-consciously.

"You don't owe me anything, Macauley. I told you, I'm no murderer," was all Dev replied as he looked him straight in the eye. He knew there was no point in saying anything more.

Macauley studied him for a long moment, wondering if he possibly could have made a mistake in arresting the bounty hunter for Santana's death. Only when he remembered the damning evidence he'd found at the scene of the crime, did he turn away from Dev's unblinking scrutiny.

When the sheriff started to usher Molly away, she balked, turning back to Dev. "Mr. O'Keefe?"

He looked up. "My name is Dev, Molly."

"Dev . . ." She met his gaze openly without hesitation. No longer was she afraid, for she now knew just what kind of man Devlin O'Keefe really was. "Thank you."

It was much later that night, long after the carnage had been cleared away that Sheriff Macauley appeared before Dev's cell.

"O'Keefe."

"Sheriff?" Dev sat up quickly and immediately thought something was wrong, for the lawman's expression was very troubled. "What is it?"

"You still claim you're innocent, but if that's so, how do you explain the evidence I found at Santana's ranch?" He studied his prisoner as he spoke.

It thrilled Dev to think that he might be considering changing his mind about his guilt, and he knew he had to be totally honest with him now.

"I can't explain how the medallions got there, sheriff. I wish I could. None of this makes sense. All I know is, I was never at Santana's ranch, and I didn't kill him."

"Is there anybody around who'd want you out of the way for a while or maybe just plain want you dead? How about your partner?"

"Clay?" Dev was shocked by his suggestion. "No, not Clay, and not anybody else I can think of."

Macauley looked even more troubled after hearing his answer. That afternoon had changed his way of thinking about this young man, and he felt obligated to delve more deeply into the facts as he knew them.

"I see. Well, think on it. If you come up with any ideas, let me know. I'm not adverse to following up on leads, if you think they might mean something."

"I will," Dev promised, but he doubted that he'd think of anything new. He'd already spent endless hours going over what had happened and had turned up nothing. He hoped Clay was having much better luck than he was.

Chapter Eleven

The Randolph party was in full swing. Beautifully gowned women and elegantly dressed men mingled together in the brightly lit ballroom, enjoying the music and partaking of the sumptuous array of food and drink.

In a corner of the room, surrounded by a half-dozen, very handsome, would-be suitors, Reina was in her glory. It had been so long since she'd been able to really enjoy herself that she was exulting in being the center of attention once again.

As Reina sat, drinking champagne and holding court of sorts, she found herself wondering why she'd been so worried about coming here tonight with the Delacroixs. It seemed foolish to her now that just a few hours ago she'd been so consumed by fear of discovery that she'd almost refused to attend. Luckily, good-natured, level-headed Emilie had managed to calm her and convince her that everything would be fine. Reina was glad now that she'd listened to her friend, and she realized that her worries had been nothing more than her overactive imagination running away with her.

"Miss Isabel . . . may I have this dance?" Lucien Picard, a handsome, fair-haired young man of average height, asked just as the music began again.

"Why, yes, Lucien. I'd love to dance with you,"

Reina answered, giving him her most enchanting smile as he took her glass from her and set it aside and then took her hand. He drew her away from her crowd of admirers.

All the other ardent bachelors who'd gathered around stifled groans of defeat and fought down their jealousy as they watched their contemporary escort the beautiful Isabel Nuñez out onto the dance floor and gather her into his arms. Lucien was a known rake, and they felt definitely outclassed in any effort to win her away from him.

Each and every man, though, thought Isabel a stunning woman, and each and every one of them wanted to be the man holding her. Her ebony hair was done up in a tumble of soft curls that begged a man's touch. The pale gold satin, off-the-shoulder ball gown she wore was the perfect foil for her dark beauty. The décolletage was cut low enough to hint at the tempting flesh restrained there, but the deeper gold and cream-colored satin rosette edging added just the right touch of modesty to her sensuous, enticing display. The skirt was full, flaring out from her slender waist, and it swayed gracefully about her as Lucien whirled her about the room. Reina looked the seductive temptress, a woman well-versed in the ways of men, and the men all hoped she'd be in town visiting with the Delacroixs for some time to come.

When the music ended, Emilie appeared at Reina's side and whisked her off to freshen up before another young gallant could take the opportunity to invite her to dance. Lucien watched her go, his gaze hot upon her as he followed her progress from the room. Only when she'd disappeared from sight into the hallway did he move off to mingle with the other available women.

"Well?" Emilie asked, her eyes alight and twinkling as they started side by side up the winding staircase that led to the second floor where several rooms had been set aside just for the ladies.

"Well, what?" Reina countered, struggling to keep from breaking into a smile.

"I hate to be an 'I told you so,' but I told you so. You are having a good time, aren't you?"

"You know I am," she admitted with good grace. "I'm glad you talked me into coming along."

"So am I," Emilie agreed. "It's good to see you relaxed and acting like yourself again. I still don't think I've gotten over finding you in that nun's outfit."

"I wonder if I'll ever get over it . . . any of it."

"Now, Isabel, I thought we made a deal this afternoon. You promised you weren't going to worry tonight. You said you were going to come here and have a good time and forget all about your father."

"I am having a good time. It's just that I still don't know why I was so afraid this afternoon. I don't usually get that upset, but for some reason I was really frightened." Reina shivered a little as she remembered the great sense of impending doom that had gripped her for no apparent reason earlier that day.

"I know," Emilie sympathized. "But it doesn't really matter any more. You're here and everything's fine, just like I told you it would be."

"You're right," Reina dismissed her worries. Tonight, Reina Alvarez didn't exist. Tonight, she was Isabel Nuñez. "Everything is going just fine."

"Well . . . almost just fine," she returned with tart good humor.

"What do you mean?" Reina paused on the step to look questioningly at her friend.

"Do you suppose . . ." Emilie paused for effect, then asked in mock seriousness, "that you could throw a few of your admirers back so that the rest of us, lesser female mortals might have one or two to choose from?"

"Lesser female mortals?" Reina laughed out loud at her friend's wry humor. "Emilie, you look positively wonderful tonight, and you know it! That pink gown suits you perfectly, and your hair is lovely when you wear it down like that."

"Thank you," she chuckled, "now tell all the men!"

Reina sobered for a minute as she touched her arm in a gesture of confidence. "Emilie, you, of all people, should know that men are the very last thing on my mind right now. You can take your pick of them any time you want."

"Well, I have to get their attention first, and that's pretty hard to do considering the competition. If only you'd shown up looking homely we might all have had a better chance," she complained with a smile.

"You're the one who picked out this dress for me, Emilie!" Reina teased, remembering their shopping spree the other day and how Emilie had insisted she buy the golden gown.

"You're right. I've got excellent taste in clothes," Emilie scowled in humorous resentment. "If I'd been thinking straight, though, I would have told you to buy the high-necked, long-sleeved, pea green one with the big, ugly yellow sash and bow."

Both young women broke into easy laughter at the thought of the hideous gown the saleslady had tried to convince them to purchase. They continued on up the sweeping staircase out of sight, unaware of the two tall, attractive men who'd just entered the house and were standing in the foyer below.

Clay was tense with expectation as he entered the Randolph mansion with his father. This was it. Tonight was the night. Tonight, he would find out whether or not he'd wasted his time in coming to Louisiana. Tonight, he hoped he would find Reina Alvarez.

Clay had been thinking about Dev all day, and his nerves were on edge as he followed his father inside. They were greeted immediately by their host and hostess, George Randolph, a robust, gray-haired man of some fifty years, and his lovely wife, Anne, a graceful, blonde ten years his junior.

"Philip! Good to see you again! And Clay! I'm so glad you were able to join us tonight. It's been a long time." George shook hands with his two long-time friends and neighbors.

"That it has, but it's good to be back," Clay responded warmly. He had always liked the Randolphs and had been good friends with their oldest son, David, when he'd lived at home. "Is David here tonight?"

"He most certainly is, and he's been waiting to see you. Take a look in the study, Clay. He's probably in there."

"I will, thanks." He told his father he'd see him later and started off down the hall toward the study to find his old friend, David Randolph, hoping he would be able to introduce him to the Delacroix family as the evening progressed.

It was then as he crossed in front of the winding staircase to the second floor that Clay heard the lilting sound of feminine laughter echoing softly down from above him. He froze in mid-stride. *That voice . . . Something about the one voice was so familiar to him.* He frowned, trying to place it in his memory. *Was it someone from his past or someone he'd met more recently?*

Curious, Clay glanced up quickly, trying to get a look at the woman. But to his annoyance, he only caught a quick glimpse of her back, of dark hair and a golden gown as she disappeared from sight around the curve. Intrigued, he was about to follow her upstairs when David emerged from the study.

"Clay! It's about time you got here!" David called as he hurried forth to welcome him.

The two men had been opposites as boys and little had changed during the intervening years. Clay had always been tall, lean and strikingly handsome, while David had never managed to reach six feet tall, was of average looks and was cursed with the Randolph tendency toward being heavyset. Yet, where Clay had always been so intense about life, David had taken joy just in living. He was as open and honest as Clay was introspective and private. Still, they had been friends as boys, and seeing each other again only reaffirmed that closeness.

They shook hands and then David ushered Clay into the study and pressed a full tumbler of bourbon in his hand. Enveloped in the warmth of David's friendship, Clay took a deep drink of the expensive liquor. For a moment, he almost wished that he could relax and enjoy the evening, maybe even join in the poker game and just let the hours pass sharing good companionship and excellent liquor. But thoughts of Dev, locked up and desperate for his help, refused to let him rest.

Concentrating on the real reason he was there, Clay paid close attention when David introduced him to the men gathered in the smoke-filled room playing cards. He returned their greetings, but it was hard for him to hide the disappointment he'd felt when there wasn't a Delacroix among them. At David's urging, Clay told him of California, yet he carefully avoided any reference to his real occupation and his real reason for being back in Louisiana.

Lucien had been biding his time in the ballroom dancing with all the other available young women while he waited impatiently for Isabel to return.

When he heard that Clay, a friend from their boyhood years, was back, though, he excused himself and immediately sought him out in the study.

"Lucien!" David hailed him as he entered the room. "Clay's back!"

"So I heard! How many years has it been?" Lucien hurried across the room to join them.

"Too many, I'm afraid," Clay answered as they clasped hands. Lucien's reputation with the ladies was legendary. He had already been quite the man-about-town when Clay had left all those years ago, and Clay couldn't resist bringing it up. "Where's your date for the evening or have you broken all their hearts and gotten yourself married?"

"I haven't married yet, Clay," the easy-going Casanova confided. "But, I swear, the woman who could own my heart is in attendance tonight."

Clay and David both erupted into laughter, remembering all the other times Lucien had declared himself madly in love.

"Things certainly haven't changed much," Clay managed, still chuckling.

"This time is different," Lucien declared.

"Oh, really?" David put in with a grin. "And just who is this paragon of virtue? Perhaps Clay and I should have a look at her . . ."

"She is the lovely Miss Nuñez, and I'm declaring her off limits to you two. She's mine."

"Isabel is lovely," David agreed. "But when I saw her earlier, I got the distinct impression that she's not ready to settle down to any one man."

"It is true that she's proving to be quite a challenge," he admitted reluctantly. "She's as elusive as a butterfly."

"Even butterflies can be caught with the right net," David pointed out.

"Who is this Isabel Nuñez? Do I know her?" Clay asked casually, after listening to their good-natured banter. He knew of most of the people in the area and had never heard of a Nuñez family.

"No," David replied. "She's here visiting relatives."

Clay's interest was piqued by that bit of news. A visitor from out of town . . . He knew he had to ask. "Who's she related to?"

"The Delacroixs," Lucien answered.

Clay had to fight to keep his excitement from showing. If Reina Alvarez had been smart enough to escape California without detection, then she'd certainly be smart enough to think of using an alias when she got here to Louisiana. He tried to remain coolly composed as he suggested, "Why don't we go on out to the ballroom so you can introduce me to this girl? She sounds absolutely intriguing."

Lucien protested, "I told you she was mine."

"Only if she agrees, Lucien," David remarked, laughing, thinking that a rivalry between the two men for Isabel Nuñez would certainly liven up the evening.

Neither David nor Lucien noticed the slight hardening of Clay's features as they jokingly sparred over who would win the beautiful, young woman. Nor were they aware of the sudden tautness in Clay's manner as he refilled his glass and followed them from the study.

"Who is *that?*" nineteen-year-old, blond-haired, voluptuous Mirabelle Mosley whispered excitedly to her friend, Rose Jackson, as they stood with several other of the young ladies near the refreshment table.

"Who's who?" Rose was near-sighted, but she refused to wear her spectacles to any social occasion. She knew she was ordinary looking, with her mousy brown hair color and her slim, almost boyish figure, and she had no desire to make herself ap-

147

pear even less attractive. So, nearly blind, if the truth be told, she hadn't even noticed the three men when they'd entered the room.

"Over there!" Mirabelle turned her in the right direction and pointed as discreetly as she could toward Clay. "The man who just came in with Lucien and David."

Rose squinted as she tried to focus on the bachelors. Straining to see, she frowned as she concentrated. When the stranger came into focus, she smiled widely. "I don't know who he is, but he sure is a good-looking devil . . ."

Mirabelle smiled delightedly as she studied the stranger. She decided without a doubt that he was the most fantastic specimen of manhood she'd ever seen. Tall, broad-shouldered and slim-hipped, his dark good looks were accented by his snowy white shirt and cravat and by his expensively cut, perfectly tailored suit. She could hardly wait to dance with him, let alone maneuver him out onto the balcony for a few moments of privacy. But she wasn't sure just how to go about getting an introduction.

"Now, Mirabelle, I know that look . . ." Rose cautioned.

"Oh, hush, Rosie!" she hissed, not taking her eyes off the stranger. "Don't spoil this!"

"Mirabelle!" There was a definite note of warning in her practical friend's tone.

"Rosie, how often does a good-looking man like that come around?"

"Not very often, but you don't want to go making a fool out of yourself."

"Who says I'm going to make a fool out of myself?" Mirabelle defended.

"I do. Don't you remember when—"

"Of course I remember, but this is different." Mirabelle cut Rose off before she could say more.

"It is not!" her friend insisted. "Think about it! The last man you thought was irresistible and chased all over town impressing him with your money and beauty, turned out to be a cad of major proportions! He almost got you to the altar. You can't be so trusting, Mirabelle, or in such a hurry. It's a good thing your father found out about him and how he was only after your dowry before you went through with the wedding."

At the vivid reminder of her last ill-fated excursion on the sea of love, Mirabelle blushed furiously. "I was blinded by love."

"Love, hah," Rose scorned. "You didn't love him. You were blinded by the thought of holy matrimony, and let me tell you, I've got a feeling that it's not as great as everyone lets us think it is."

"You're so cynical, Rosie," she pooh-poohed her friend's arguments.

"Not cynical, just honest. Take your time, Mirabelle. What's your hurry? If you go rushing over there to meet this new man, he'll think you're too aggressive, and it'll end up just like all the other times. Remember Arthur Edison?"

She groaned at the mere mention of the man's name, another one of the men she'd mistakenly thought would be perfect for her.

"Enough, Rosie! You've made your point. I already told you this time will be different," she told her, but even as she spoke the thought of the ripe old age of twenty looming on her personal horizon spurred her on.

"Different?" the other girl spoke up. "How?"

Mirabelle was watching the newcomer across the room and could wait no longer to try to meet him. "Oh, never mind," she dismissed, and she started across the dance floor, leaving her friend standing there, aghast that all her good advice had gone unheeded.

"I can't watch . . ." Rose whispered to herself in humorous agony. Fearful of what her friend might do, she hurried from the ballroom and went upstairs.

When the men discovered that Isabel Nuñez was nowhere to be found, Clay was as disappointed as Lucien, but he kept his feelings hidden behind a mask of congeniality.

"I guess she and Emilie haven't come back downstairs yet," Lucien remarked idly.

Clay stiffened at his words . . . *haven't come back downstairs yet.* He realized then that it had probably been Reina Alvarez he'd heard talking on the steps earlier. Clay wondered why she'd sounded so familiar to him when he had never met her before. There was no way he should have recognized her voice.

Thinking of the golden-gowned woman again, Clay let his gaze sweep the crowded room for her, but to his disappointment his search turned up nothing.

"Look out, gentlemen," Lucien said with a grin.

"For what?" Clay asked, glancing up to see a lovely, blond-haired woman heading their way. For a moment, he feared that Lucien was telling him this was Isabel Nuñez. The momentary rise in his spirits threatened to fall. Reina Alvarez was no blonde.

"Mirabelle's coming." He gave a slight nod in her direction.

"Mirabelle?" Clay was relieved that this wasn't the woman he was searching for.

"Mirabelle Mosley," David replied.

"What about her?" Clay asked his two companions, thinking the woman in the form-fitting, emerald satin gown looked positively luscious.

"She's in the market for a husband, and it looks

like tonight she's got her sights set on you," Lucien answered.

"I'm not the marrying kind," he said firmly.

"Convince Mirabelle, not me," David said.

"Why hasn't one of you obliged her?" Clay was curious, since she was so pretty. "She's easy enough on the eyes."

"She has money, too, but when I marry, I want it to be my idea. I'd like to be the one making the proposal," Lucien said with his usual male arrogance.

"And I'm like you, Clay, I'm not the marrying kind either," David managed before he was forced to play the host and introduce them.

Rose dashed into the sitting room that had been set aside for the ladies to take their rest. When she made out Emilie sitting in a wingchair, she groaned out loud, "You're just not going to believe it!"

"Believe what, Rose?" Emilie asked, looking up from where she sat talking with Reina.

Rose's expression suddenly became reserved when she realized that they were not alone. Emilie hurried to put her at ease, quickly making the introductions.

"Oh, Rose, this is my cousin, Isabel. Isabel, this is Rose Jackson, a very dear friend."

"Hello." The women exchanged greetings.

"You can trust Isabel completely, Rose. I know I do. Now what is it that's got you so excited?"

"It's Mirabelle . . . again," she began to explain, rolling her eyes heavenward.

"Mirabelle?" Emilie had to chuckle. She and Rose had been following the other girl's search for a husband, and she could hardly wait to hear. "What's she up to this time?"

"Well he came into the ballroom with Lucien and

David and . . ."

"He, who?"

"I don't know his name, but he's just about the best looking man I've ever seen."

"You don't know him?"

"No. I've never set eyes on him before tonight, but I sure hope I see him again," Rose sighed, wishing that someday a man like that one would pay her court. Realizing suddenly that she was dreaming, she forced herself to continue, "Anyway, Mirabelle took one look at him and swore he was the one for her."

"Oh, no, not again!"

"Oh, yes, again!"

"What did she do?"

"I don't know for sure. When she started walking over to meet him, I left."

Emilie knew the stranger had to be pretty special to get Mirabelle to go back on the vow she'd made a month ago never to openly pursue another man as long as she lived. Obviously, she'd changed her mind.

"Mirabelle's a beautiful girl, and there's a lot of men who would enjoy her attentions."

"I know, but why can't she wait for them to come after her? Why does she always have to go after them first? You'd think she'd learned her lesson by now."

"I have to admit I'm curious about him. He must be something wonderful if she broke that solemn oath she made to us," Emilie mused.

"He is—tall, dark and handsome with a great physique . . ." Rose affirmed.

"I wonder where he's from . . ."

"I don't know, but I bet by the time the party ends, Mirabelle will."

"Shall we go get a look at him?"

"Why not?" Reina agreed.

152

Reina didn't know why, but as she followed Emilie and Rose downstairs, unbidden thoughts of Clay Cordell assailed her. Logically, she supposed he was on her mind because the man Rose had described sounded so much like him. The bounty hunter *had* been one very attractive man . . .

Reina suddenly scolded herself for her silly romantic notions about Cordell. He'd been a hired gun with a job to do. The only thing he'd been interested in was finding Reina Alvarez and taking her home. Pushing his memory from her, she swept on down the staircase a few steps behind Emilie and Rose.

Reina reached the second step from the bottom just as the music ended. For some reason she couldn't fathom, she paused there and glanced up into the ballroom just then. To her utter horror, across the distance, her eyes met and locked with a pair of chilling silver ones.

Though he'd been giving the impression of having a wonderful time, Clay's mood had been strained as he'd danced with Mirabelle. She was a lovely young woman, but he had no time or interest in a flirtation of any kind. Only Reina Alvarez occupied his thoughts . . . . only Reina.

Clay grew angry every time he thought of the terrible hardships Reina's spoiled little rich girl's antics had caused other people. He knew the woman he sought was nothing more than a self-serving witch, and it was going to do his heart good to turn her over to her father just as soon as possible.

Since he'd become convinced that she might be there at the ball, Clay was filled with a renewed sense of urgency. He wanted this whole ordeal to be over. He wanted to confront his prey and head back to California with her as soon as possible. He had his plan of action ready to be set in motion. All he had to do was locate her.

It happened then, just as the music ended and Clay was escorting Mirabelle from the dance floor. Out of the corner of his eye, he caught a glimpse of gold out in the hall, and he looked up. There, standing several steps up from the bottom of the staircase, her luxurious dark hair piled up on top of her head in a stylish fashion, her shoulders bared in the exquisite golden gown, stood Sister Mary Regina . . .

Chapter Twelve

Clay went completely still, and only his well-honed, rigid self-control kept him from revealing anything in that instant. *Sister Mary Regina?* At first, her name tumbled wildly through his thoughts in questioning disbelief, but he soon sobered. *Sister Mary Regina was here—and she was dressed for the ball.*

Suddenly, with the memory of her voice echoing hauntingly through him, it all became perfectly clear. He'd been royally duped. He'd been made to look the fool. There was no Sister Mary Regina. He'd been right all along. Dear little Miss Alvarez *had* been on the stagecoach, just as he'd believed. Clay would have bet his last dollar right then that she was masquerading tonight as none other than the Delacroixs' cousin Isabel Nuñez just in case her father had sent someone back here looking for her.

Clay was livid, and he tensed in his outrage. He wondered how he could have been so stupid. He berated himself for being taken in by her disguise and for forgetting the ultimate truth he'd learned about women so long ago. There were no sweet, honest, innocent ones. There were no Sister Mary Reginas out there. They were all lying, deceitful bitches—just like his mother! Viciously, he told himself he would never forget again.

"Clay? Is something the matter?" Mirabelle asked sweetly. She was clinging to his arm, and though he showed no outward sign of being upset, the sudden tautening of his muscles beneath her hand had puzzled her.

"Why, no, Mirabelle. There's nothing wrong," Clay lied. He was angry, but very excited at the same time. He realized, though, that he couldn't let Reina know that he'd recognized her. This was no place for a confrontation. He had to let her think that her earlier disguise had fooled him completely. It took a tremendous effort on his part, but Clay managed to keep his expression carefully schooled into one of just passing male appreciation.

For the first time since Mirabelle had approached him, Clay was glad for her presence. She provided the perfect distraction as he fought to curb his turbulent emotions. With an ease born of seeming nonchalance, he turned away from Reina and back to Mirabelle. Giving her an engaging smile, he bent toward her with implied intimacy. "Why don't we have something to drink?"

Yet as Clay led Mirabelle to the refreshment table, playing his role to the hilt, he was filled with anxiety. He wanted to look back and see if Reina was still there. He feared that she might have panicked and run, but he hoped and prayed she hadn't. The next few minutes would tell. If she'd disappeared, he knew he would have to go after her or risk losing her all over again. He remained on edge as he awaited the opportunity to find out.

Reina was poised for flight as she'd watched Clay and waited. *Dear Lord! It was Clay Cordell!* Fear had clutched at her heart as she'd gone suddenly cold. She'd wanted to run, to flee from the terror that

Clay Cordell represented, but his silver eyes had held her pinioned. She'd remained frozen in place, unable to move or speak and barely able to breathe. It had been a climactic moment as his gaze held hers, but then, as quickly as it had happened, it had been over. Clay had turned his back on her and moved off in the opposite direction across the ballroom with the lovely, blond woman holding possessively onto his arm and gazing up at him with open adoration.

Reina began to tremble uncontrollably, and she clutched the banister for support as her knees threatened to buckle. *Clay Cordell was there!* She swallowed nervously as panic pounded through her, and she struggled not to lose control.

A part of Reina wanted to rush from the ball and leave Louisiana, but her more logical side asserted itself. *Yes, Clay Cordell was there,* she told herself, *but so what? He hadn't recognized her!* Surely, knowing how bulldoggedly determined he was to find her, if he'd recognized her either as herself or as Sister Mary Regina, he would have come at her right then. He would never, ever just have walked away.

As blessed sanity reasserted itself, Reina's thundering heart slowed to a more normal pace. Hadn't she suspected that someone might come to Louisiana looking for her? Wasn't that precisely why she'd chosen to use the name Isabel Nuñez? She had to relax.

This wasn't like being on the stagecoach, wearing her nun's habit, being on guard every minute. She had faced her father's hired predator without the benefit of a disguise, and he hadn't known who she was. Her plan had worked out just as she'd hoped it would. Everything was going fine. Clay Cordell would take a look around, decide Reina Alvarez wasn't there and head back to California to tell her

157

father.

Reina wasn't sure whether to laugh or cry as relief flooded through her. The heavy weight of the worry that she'd be found and dragged back home against her will was suddenly lifted from her shoulders. At last, she was truly safe. She had gotten away from Nathan Marlow, and she intended to stay away.

Reina drew a steadying breath and then broke into a wide smile. Now, she could really enjoy the evening. She had something to celebrate. Feeling once more fully in control of her destiny, she descended lightly to the bottom of the staircase to join Emilie and Rose just inside the ballroom doorway.

"Did you see him, Isabel?" Emilie asked excitedly.

"I don't think so, which one is he?"

"Over there," Rose pointed to where Clay was handing Mirabelle a cup of punch and laughing easily at something she said.

Some uncomfortable emotion tugged at Reina as she watched Clay flirting with the pretty, young woman, but she gave what appeared to be a disinterested shrug. "Oh, him . . ."

Reina knew she should look away for fear that Clay might glance up and catch her looking at him, but for some perverse reason she couldn't. It was almost as if she was mesmerized by his overwhelmingly masculine presence. It was hard for Reina to believe that the hard-riding gunslinger who'd saved her life a few weeks before was standing before her now, transformed into an aristocratic, debonair southern gentleman. She found herself wondering about Clay and trying to figure out how he'd managed to ingratiate himself so quickly into Louisiana society.

" 'Oh, him,' she says," Emilie mocked lightly to Rose. "Yes, him!"

"Well, he is very attractive," Reina responded, seeming unconcerned, "but he's not my type."

"What do you mean 'he's not your type'?" Emilie gave her an exasperated look. "He's handsome, and he's obviously single or Mirabelle wouldn't be flirting with him. How could he not be your type or my type or Rose's type?"

Reina was tempted to blurt out the truth, but she restrained herself. This was no time to confide in anybody. She was here in the middle of a ball, and things were fine. Why risk it? The fewer people who knew, the better.

"You know I'm not really interested in men right now, Emilie. Besides, he looks far too intense for me." She shivered at her own words as she thought again of just how determined a man he really was, and grabbed a glass of champagne from a passing servant's tray.

"All right, Reina, I believe you, but are you sure you don't even want an introduction?"

That was the very last thing Reina wanted. She knew it would be far, far better not to tempt fate. Glad to see Lucien and David heading her way, she smiled benignly. "Maybe later." She downed the heady champagne quickly and wished for another.

Within minutes, Reina was once again surrounded by her group of admirers, and she was glad for the distraction.

"I guess with all those admirers, she really doesn't need to worry about one more," Emilie told Rose with a wry grin as they moved off to visit with some other friends.

Reina, meanwhile, was chatting vivaciously with the men around her. All she had to do, she realized, was get through the next few hours without arousing any undue suspicions in Cordell. If she managed that, everything would work out perfectly.

The very idea that she'd faced her worst nightmare and won left Reina feeling ebullient, and as she sipped more of the bubbling wine, she felt almost cocky. Her suitors flowered her with compliments and vied for her attention, and she responded brightly, laughing and flirting outrageously with them all. She felt unthreatened and happy for the first time in weeks.

Clay bided his time, continuing to make conversation with Mirabelle, as he watched and waited for Reina to come into the ballroom. He knew if she didn't show up soon, he was gong to have to go looking for her, and that was something he hadn't wanted to do here tonight.

Clay was greatly pleased and enormously relieved when a few minutes later Reina did enter the room. His ploy had worked! She was convinced that he hadn't recognized her! Clay wanted to laugh out loud as a feeling of power surged through him. He'd turned the tables on her. Now, he was the one holding the upper hand. Now, he was in control.

Clay covertly watched as Reina trifled with the men around her. He could easily understand why the men flocked to her, for outwardly, she was a very beautiful woman. In reality though, he knew she was nothing but a loose-moraled, heartless chameleon of a woman, changing her personality at will to fit in any situation. His acceptance of her duplicity filled him with a terrible, bitter resolve, and it took all of his considerable will-power not to throw caution to the wind and stalk across the room, grab Reina and head straight back to California.

The longer Clay kept watch over his elusive runaway the more furious he became. She might consider herself a good enough actress to alter everyone else's perception of her, but he was wise to her now. She would never fool him again. He knew exactly what kind of woman she was.

A sneer of disgust curved Clay's mouth. For just a split second, Clay's tight control on his emotions weakened, and all the cold, raw anger he was feeling reflected in his eyes.

Mirabelle just happened to look up at him in that moment, and the flicker of emotion she saw there frightened her. "Clay? Are you sure there's not something troubling you?"

At her words, Clay realized what he was doing, and he brought himself back under rigid control. Luckily, the music started up again, and he was given a reprieve from further conversation.

"No, nothing wrong. Would you like to dance?" he invited quickly, wanting to forestall any other questions. At her acceptance, he guided her out onto the dance floor.

Even as Clay squired Mirabelle around the ballroom, his thoughts were on Reina. Soon, it would all be over. Soon he would deliver her to her father, and Dev would be freed.

Clay had the return trip to California all planned. He'd figured out the fastest, safest route back on his long, lonely trek to Louisiana. The only complication he had now was finding a way to get Reina alone. Once he'd accomplished that, it would be a simple matter to spirit her away without raising any immediate suspicions. However, getting her away from everybody else might prove tricky, especially if she suspected he might be setting a trap for her.

Clay knew he had to join the group of idiots who were drooling all over themselves vying for a kind word from Reina and then sweep her off her feet with his charm and good looks. Simple enough, he thought, but in the back of his mind the niggling fear troubled him that he wouldn't be able to get her undivided attention.

Clay didn't like the idea of having to do it, but he realized he had no other choice. He had to act and act fast, and he had to be totally convincing. He would play the ardent lover until he could maneuver Reina alone. Then once he had her in his grasp, he would head for California.

Clay knew it wasn't going to be easy for him to play the lovesick fool when all he felt for the woman was contempt, but since nothing about this job had been easy so far, so why should anything change? At least this time, he was no longer just chasing after blind leads. He had her now. It was just a matter of time.

As soon as he was able without appearing rushed, Clay excused himself from a very disappointed Mirabelle and headed for the study. He was ready to begin his calculated pursuit, but he was in great need of one more stiff bourbon before he began. The study was relatively crowded with card players and onlookers when he entered. Clay didn't notice that his father was among them as he made his way to the liquor cabinet to help himself to the powerful liquor.

"Clay?" Philip saw his son enter the room and knew something was wrong. "What is it? Have you found her?" There was a note of hope in Philip's voice.

Clay had been lost so deep in thought that he was a bit startled to find his father suddenly there beside him.

"Yes, I've found her," he snarled as he took a deep drink of his bourbon.

Philip was taken aback by his vile mood. He'd

expected him to be jubilant. Instead, he could feel the hostility emanating from him.

"Clay?" Philip worried.

He looked up, his icy, determined gaze meeting his father's questioning one. "I've got a job to do, and I'm going to do it."

"Can I help you in any way?"

"No. This is something I have to do alone." At his father's troubled expression, he added, "We'll talk later."

Philip watched in silence as Clay downed the rest of his drink, then refilled the glass and took it with him as he strode purposefully from the room.

Clay's whole manner transformed as he crossed the hall to the ballroom. The anger that was driving him was carefully hidden beneath an outward veneer of cool sophistication. Trying to find David so he could exact the introduction to Isabel he'd been promised, he made his way smoothly through the party-goers, smiling and exchanging greetings. Eventually, Clay spotted David dancing with Reina and Lucien standing alone on the sidelines looking very annoyed. Clay smiled cynically to himself. Reina Alvarez hadn't been satisfied with just capturing Lucien's heart, now she had to have David's, too.

"I take it that's the irresistible Isabel Nuñez dancing with David?" Clay asked Lucien as he came to stand beside him.

"You take it right," Lucien confirmed a bit brusquely.

"She's one lovely woman," he told him. "How did David manage to get her away from you? I thought she was the only one for you."

"We were dancing, and he cut in," Lucien complained. "Some friend . . . he thinks to steal her from me."

"Was Isabel ever yours to steal?"

"I was working on it," Lucien replied with a quick grin.

"How long is she going to be staying?"

"She didn't say, but I would imagine she'll be here for some time yet. She only arrived this week."

Lucien's words gave final confirmation to Clay's suspicions, and he smiled sharkishly, eager to be about his game. "Good. That gives me plenty of time . . ."

Lucien stifled a groan of irritation at the thought of Clay single-mindedly pursuing her. While he'd been away, Lucien had had little real competition for the ladies, but now that he'd returned, things didn't look too promising. Cordell was one of the wealthiest men around. Beating him out for Isabel's hand would not be easy.

When the dance finally ended, David led Reina to where Lucien and Clay stood. David enjoyed aggravating the cocksure ladies' man Lucien, and he thought this would be the perfect time to introduce Isabel to Clay.

Reina had enjoyed her dance with David. She found him a delightful, easy-going companion. She was so caught up in their animated conversation that she didn't notice right away that he was escorting her to Clay.

"Isabel, there's someone here I'd like you to meet," David began as they drew near.

"Oh?" she questioned, looking up just then to find Clay with Lucien and both men watching her approach. Heat flushed through Reina, and then she was filled with an icy dread. Only by pure strength of will did she keep her uneasiness hidden. To the world, she appeared the alluring temptress, enchantingly gorgeous with her ebony tresses done up high on her head and the tops of her creamy breasts swelling oh-so-temptingly above the décolletage of her gown.

Much to Clay's annoyance, as Reina drew near, a flare of unbidden hot desire pulsed through him. It disturbed him to find that he could be attracted to Reina physically while despising her for what she was.

Clay's eyes met hers, and her gaze revealed nothing. He'd expected to see some flicker of emotion there, and he was surprised by her calm. Her consummate acting abilities amazed him. Knowing how good a liar she really was, hardened his resolve all the more. He knew he would never trust anything she said or did again.

"Yes, Isabel, this is Clay Cordell. He's an old family friend. Clay, this is Isabel Nuñez," David made the introductions easily, completely unaware of Reina's quiet desperation.

"Miss Nuñez, it's a pleasure to finally make your acquaintance," Clay returned, bowing slightly in acknowledgment. No one realized just how much he really meant those words.

His deep voice, so well remembered, sent shivers down her spine, and Reina fought to dismiss her reaction, attributing it to her fear.

"Finally, Mr. Cordell?" Reina gave him her most beguiling smile as her eyes met his. When she saw no spark of recognition in the depths of his gaze, a dizzying sense of relief filled her. He didn't even know her up close! Her identity really was safe.

Clay's pulse quickened at her smile, but he ignored it. "Clay, please, Miss Nuñez, and, yes, finally. I've been admiring you from afar for some time," he told her, smirking inwardly in satisfaction at the double meaning of his words.

"I'm flattered, Clay," Reina answered easily, "and please, call me Isabel."

"I'd be honored, Isabel," Clay said her name slowly as if savoring the sound of it.

"You know, David introduced you as an old family friend, but you don't look very old," she told him archly. "Have you known each other for a long time?" Reina was curious about his connections here in Louisiana. It was one thing for her father to send the bounty hunter after her. It was another for him to fit right into plantation society as if he'd been born to it.

"David, Lucien and I all grew up together," Clay offered only sparse information. The less she knew about him, the better he liked it.

"I'm surprised," Reina said, pausing. "My cousin, Emilie Delacroix, was telling me who would be here tonight, but I don't remember her mentioning you." She knew if Emilie had mentioned anyone named Cordell, she certainly wouldn't have come along.

"I've been away for a while, and I'm not personally acquainted with the Delacroix family," Clay answered. "That's a shortcoming of mine I intend to remedy very soon, though."

"Clay's been out west," David spoke up, proud of his friend's daring in leaving home and trying a new way of life.

"Really? Where were you?"

"California mostly."

"How did you find it there? Was it exciting?" Reina asked, wishing more than anything that he'd go back.

"It has its moments," Clay responded dryly. "Where's your home, Isabel?"

"I'm from San Antonio," Reina replied quickly. She'd gone over and over the fake background she and Emilie had created until she knew it by heart.

Another lie, he thought sarcastically, then complimented her through gritted teeth, "I'll bet you broke a lot of hearts when you left. Is there anyone special waiting for you there?"

"No, there's no one back home."

For once Clay recognized that she'd told the truth. She wasn't lying about that. She didn't care about anyone she'd left behind. She cared only about herself.

The music began once more, and Clay knew he had to make his move quickly before Lucien or David or some other young bachelor offered for her. "Isabel, would you care to dance?"

Reina stayed coolly composed as she answered, "Why I'd love to, Clay, thank you."

Chapter Thirteen

The lilting strains of the romantic waltz filled the ballroom as Clay led Reina out onto the dance floor. He was pleased that everything was going so smoothly, and he congratulated himself on his own thespian skills. He had her honestly believing that he didn't recognize her. Clay was confident that if he played it right for the rest of the night he would soon be on his way to California with her in tow.

Clay turned to Reina then, and smiling warmly down at her, took her in his arms ready to guide her into the crowd of dancers. At that first intimate contact of his arm at her waist, a flare of unexpected sensual awareness electrified them both. In a moment of mute surprise, they hesitated, standing perfectly still as they stared at each other in something akin to wonder.

The desire Reina stirred within Clay was potent, but the last thing in the world he wanted to do was get involved with her. The role he'd set out for himself as her hopeful lover was just that . . . a role he was playing, nothing else.

"You're very beautiful, Isabel," he murmured seductively as they began to dance.

"Thank you, Clay," Reina replied, gazing up at him through the pleasant, champagne-induced haze

168

that tingled her senses, mellowing her mood. Dreamily, she thought of that night at the waystation and how magnificent Clay had looked as he'd stood there bare-chested in the moonlight. Her pulse quickened at the memory. She regretted the things that stood between them.

Reina wondered just how different everything might have been had he not been working for her father. Clay was an exciting man who, she knew, could be fiercely brave or kind and gentle as the situation warranted. He was everything she'd ever wanted in a man, and Reina realized with some amazement that if they'd met at any other time for any other reason, she might have fallen in love with him.

"Perhaps fate brought us together," Clay suggested in low tones, drawing her a little closer. But then as a surge of passion swept through him at her nearness, he reprimanded himself firmly. He told himself that he wasn't really enjoying holding her in his arms. He reminded himself, again, that this was his job.

"I'd like to think that," Reina answered, caught up in the perfection of waltzing with him. They moved together in unison, completely attuned to one another, swirling gracefully around the room to the swelling melody as if they were made for each other. Reina was conscious only of Clay's powerful arms about her. She wanted to believe that maybe, just maybe, it had been fate and not her father's devious plan that had brought her to this moment.

They were both lost deep in thought as they continued to dance, wrapped in one another's arms. Clay knew he should concentrate on the reason he was here. He knew he should remember Reina's deceitful ways and Dev's suffering. But his usually sturdy strength of will was weakened by the numerous bourbons he'd had over the course of the evening. Suddenly, the delicate scent that was only Reina, the very feel of her slender, lovely body in his arms and the memory of her combing out her hair before the fire all undermined his iron control. In that heady instant, he became ensnared in the sweet, sweet, magic of the moment.

Clay looked down at Reina to find her dark-eyed, liquid gaze warm upon him. Excitement lurched through him, and he suddenly realized that he wanted this. He wasn't acting anymore. He desired Reina. He had when he'd thought she was a nun, and he did, even more so now that he didn't have to feel guilty about it.

As the music slowed and came to an end, Clay made certain that they were near the ballroom's double french doors that led to the balcony. Then, before Reina could utter a word, he whisked her out into the privacy of the cool, dark night.

Reina was startled by his daring, but she did not resist as he drew her gently, but firmly away from the doors and into the shadowy splendor of the evening.

He gave her a wicked smile as he confided, "I didn't want to risk running into one of the other men. Now that I've finally found you, I don't ever want to lose you—not to David or to Lucien or anyone else."

A thrill of delight coursed through Reina at his words. She was no longer looking for double meanings in his every statement. In her heart, she wanted to believe everything he was saying.

Clay enfolded her in his strong embrace, and she went willingly, eagerly. In the back of Clay's mind, he thought distractedly that she was this way with every man, but his passion was such that he pushed the ugly possibility from him. He wanted only to hold her and kiss her. He didn't want to think . . . not now.

Clay's mouth swooped down to claim hers in a very possessive kiss, and Reina reveled in it. She realized instinctively that this was what she'd wanted ever since they'd met.

Passion erupted between them as their lips met for the first time. Clay crushed her to his chest as he deepened the exchange, parting her lips to seek the honeyed sweetness within.

Clay's kiss was powerful — a man's kiss, and it was unlike anything Reina had ever experienced before. Nathan's embrace had left Reina cold, and the few other men she'd kissed had never managed to stir her in any way. Only Clay with his masterful, persuasive embrace could ignite this deep, burning need within her . . . only Clay. Linking her arms around his neck, she pressed herself even more closely to him as she returned his kiss with flaming fervor. Engulfed by waves of heart-stopping pleasure, Reina wondered if this was love . . .

When they finally broke off, they did not move apart, but remained locked in each other's arms, their eyes closed, trying to understand the wildness of the emotion that had just rocked them. They did not speak. There was no need.

Clay was stunned by his own reaction and by Reina's passionate response. He couldn't really believe what had happened, and he bent to her again, testing, questioning. This time his kiss was gentler, softer. His lips moved over hers with sweet encouragement, and once more hot desire raged through him.

Reina, too, was lost in a maelstrom of sensual excitement. The champagne's effect on her senses left her uninhibited in her response to him. Her obvious excitement encouraged Clay to even greater

boldness. His mouth left hers to seek out the softness of her throat as he lifted his hands to cup the
sides of her breasts through the gown.

Reina's knees grew weak. When his mouth returned to hers, she welcomed him gladly, murmuring to him in a husky, love-laden voice, "Clay, oh,
Clay . . . please . . ." She didn't know what it was
she was begging for, she only knew that she wanted,
no needed, to be nearer to him.

At her urging, any thought Clay had of restraining himself disappeared. Thinking she knew exactly
what she wanted, he began to explore the full,
luscious curves of her breasts, boldly slipping one
hand within her bodice to fondle that silken flesh.

Never before had Reina allowed any man to
touch her so intimately. It was a new experience for
her, and she gasped out loud at the breathtaking
sensation of his hand hot upon her bare skin. With
practiced expertise, Clay sought and found the passion-hardened crest. Reina moaned in sheer ecstasy
as he caressed her. She was on fire for him, lost in
the sensual web he was weaving so expertly around
her.

Only vaguely were they aware of the sounds of
voices coming their way.

"Clay took her out here somewhere . . ." Lucien
was saying impatiently as he and David crossed the
ballroom toward the french doors.

"Don't worry, we'll find them," David answered,
and it was obvious from his tone of voice that he
found the situation quite humorous. "They couldn't
have gone too far . . ."

"Not if we get there soon." Lucien snapped in
return.

Lucien's sarcasm penetrated the mindless pleasure
Clay was finding in Reina's embrace and jarred him
back to the painful reality of knowing who he was

and where he was. Giving a guttural groan of frustration, he broke off the kiss. His breathing was ragged as he struggled to pull himself together, and his thoughts were in chaos. *What the hell was the matter with him? What had he been trying to do?* Reina was his prey. It was his job to capture her and take her home to her father and fiancé, not bed her.

"Clay?" Reina was startled at his pulling away from her. His kisses and caresses had thrilled her, and she didn't understand why he'd stopped. "What is it?"

Clay glanced down at her and was almost unnerved to find her dark-eyed gaze wide and questioning upon him. It continued to amaze him that she could affect this innocent look so convincingly when he knew she was far from naive. He had no doubts about that any more. Hadn't she just been begging him to make love to her? *Hell,* he thought viciously, *he probably could have taken her right there if he hadn't heard Lucien and David coming.* At the thought, a jolt of desire seared him, and he girded himself against it.

Clay's continued silence upset Reina, and she asked worriedly, "Clay . . . have I done something wrong?"

He almost gave a caustic laugh at her query. *Have I done something wrong?* She'd done something wrong, all right. She'd run out on her father and on the man who loved her.

Lying, he answered, "You haven't done anything wrong, Isabel." He moved slightly away from her, grimly reminding himself of the parallel between his mother and Reina. He stiffened at the recognition of his own weakness, and he vowed silently that he would not be caught in any kind of trap of her making. There was no way he was going to allow himself to feel anything for this woman. He knew she was acting. He knew this was all just a game to her. She was only leading him on in hopes of getting him to let his defenses down or to play on his sympathies when he finally did try to take her back.

"Then, why . . . ?" Reina didn't understand why he'd ended their kiss so abruptly.

"I heard someone coming, and I didn't want to cause you any embarrassment."

"Oh . . ." Reina said in soft surprise. She blushed as she realized just how carried away she'd been by his kisses and caresses, and she was glad for the concealing darkness to hide her distress. She was grateful for Clay's presence of mind and for his discretion.

"You're one very special woman, Isabel," Clay said as he lifted one hand to tenderly caress her cheek, playing the lovesick swain.

"I'm glad you think so. I want to be . . . for you . . ." Reina answered, and as she said it, she was startled to find that she honestly meant it. He was the one man who could set her soul aflame, and she wondered if it was possible to fall in love this quickly . . .

Clay listened to her, but heard only lies. With cold viciousness, he wondered how many other men she'd told the same thing to and how many other men had tasted her charms. He hardened his heart against the powerful attraction that threatened his control. He knew what he had to do, and he was going to do it. He was continuing this charade only until he could turn her over to her father and not a minute longer. She meant nothing to him.

"I must see you again, Isabel." Clay pressed ardently, for he was sure that once David and Lucien located them, he wouldn't get another moment alone with her for the rest of the night. He needed to see her again so he could set his plan in action. There were arrangements that had to be made, and people who had to be contacted. . . .

"I'd like that. . . ."

"Are you free tomorrow? We could go on a picnic, and I could show you Windown."

"Yes, yes, tomorrow would be wonderful." Reina was dazed. Everything seemed to be happening too quickly. A part of her warned that it was dangerous to have anything more to do with this man, that she had already been far too reckless, that she should be cautious and evasively refuse to see him again. But her heart overruled her sensibilities.

To Reina's way of thinking, there was no danger. Clay didn't know who she was, and he was attracted to her as a woman, not as Reina Alvarez. The thought thrilled her, and she could hardly wait for the next day. She wanted to be with him, to be held in his arms and . . .

At her acceptance, Clay's spirits soared. He had done it! Tomorrow everything would fall into place! Tomorrow he would be on his way back to Monterey to free Dev.

Realizing that he had to keep up his pretense, Clay smiled tenderly, gently framed her face with his hands and kissed her one, last, fleeting time. It was a simple kiss, a mere grazing of their lips, but he found it so intoxicating that he drew away, unsettled. Clay had had a tight rein on his emotions and hadn't expected to feel anything.

Reina was moved by Clay's tenderness and caught up in the thrilling thought that he cared for her and wanted her. She suddenly felt the need to confess everything to him, to be fully open and honest with him.

"Clay, I—" she began, but just when she would have told him the truth, Lucien and David came upon them.

"Here you are." David's mood was jolly. He had stalled Lucien as long as he could before finally agreeing to come looking for Clay and Isabel.

"We were wondering where you'd gone," Lucien sounded almost sullen.

"We just came outside for a while to enjoy the night air, but we're just about ready to go back in."

"Good," Lucien agreed, quickly moving to insinuate himself between Clay and Reina. He offered her his arm. "I'd like to finish our dance without interruptions this time, if it's at all possible."

Trapped because she could not refuse without insulting him, Reina agreed and allowed Lucien to escort her back inside. She managed one last glance back at Clay where he still stood in the shadows. Their gazes locked briefly until the other man's conversation forced her to look away.

Clay scowled as he watched her disappear indoors with Lucien. He wondered why he felt suddenly driven to go after her. He'd gotten what he'd needed from her—a promise to meet him tomorrow. Why should he care what she did the rest of the night?

"Clay? Are you coming?" David asked as he waited for him near the french doors.

"Yes, right now."

"Isabel's some woman, isn't she?"

"That she is," he agreed. Though he hated to admit it or give her credit for anything, there was much more to Reina than just her exquisite looks.

"Are you going to give Lucien a run for his money with her?"

"Well, we've already made plans to picnic tomorrow. Who knows what will happen after that? Let's go get a drink, what do you say?"

They entered the house and as they made their way through the ballroom toward the study, Clay saw Reina on the dance floor with Lucien. He told himself that he didn't care that she was in his arms, laughing and obviously having a good time. But as he watched them, an emotion he'd never felt before gnawed at him. He was glad when he and David reached the hall and moved out of sight, and he knew a bourbon was going to taste real good right then.

"I can't believe it, Reina!" Emilie said with open delight as they sat together later that night in Reina's room sharing tales of the party. "Clay Cordell really asked you to go on a picnic with him tomorrow?"

"Yes," she answered excitedly, almost ready to count the hours until they'd be together again. "Oh, Emilie, he was so wonderful . . ."

"It's not fair! Here, Rose and I tried all night long to get an introduction and we never could, and you didn't even want to meet him, and you're the one who ends up seeing him again!" Emilie raged on good-naturedly against the injustices of romance.

"I know," she mused. "Clay seemed to think that it was fate that brought us together."

"Fate or the Randolphs," her friend remarked with a grin. "Well, at least, I'll get to meet him tomorrow when he comes for you."

"He told me as we were leaving the party that he'd probably arrive a little before noon. He wants to show me around their plantation."

"Windown is beautiful. The Cordells breed the finest horseflesh in the state, and do they have money!" Emilie's tone gave testimony to the Cordells' considerable fortune. Then, ever the romantic, she fantasized wildly, "I've got it!"

"Got what?"

177

"The solution to all your problems!"

"Oh, really," Reina chuckled.

"Really! You should elope with Clay! That way you'd never again have to worry about your father or Nathan Marlow."

Reina's eyes sparkled with merriment, though in her heart she couldn't deny that she found the thought of being married to Clay quite a pleasant prospect. "That's not a bad idea, Emilie, but he has to ask first."

"Who knows? Maybe he will."

"Well, if he does, I just might take him up on it!"

They laughed together in easy camaraderie and then fell to discussing the rest of the evening.

"I have to be honest about this and tell you that it doesn't sit well with me," Philip said as he spoke with Clay much later that night in the study at Windown.

"And it doesn't sit well with me that Dev's locked up in a damned jail cell in Monterey!" Clay ground out.

Philip didn't respond. He knew there was nothing he could say that would change his son's mind about what he had to do.

"I'll be leaving tomorrow," Clay finally spoke again.

"Do you know when you'll be back?" Philip changed the subject, wanting to avoid any further controversy on this, their last night together.

Clay appreciated him not talking about Reina and the job he had to do. He softened toward him, visibly relaxing a bit. "I can't be sure. I promise you, though, I'll try to return as quickly as I can."

Philip managed a bittersweet smile as he regarded his offspring. He was proud of Clay. He had grown into a fine, strong man. "I can't ask for more than that. But when you do come back, you have to do one thing for me."

"What?"

"Bring Dev with you."

Clay smiled easily. "I will."

"I'm going on up to bed now. It's been a long day."

"I'll be up for a little while longer. There are still a few things I have to take care of tonight." Clay declined to detail any more of his plans for he didn't want to involve his father.

"I'll see you at breakfast then."

When Philip had gone, Clay sat down at the desk and drew out pen and paper. A little while later he summoned Jacob, one of the servants who had been with the family for years and who he knew to be completely trustworthy.

"Yes, Mr. Clay?"

"I have an errand for you to run, Jacob. I need for you to go to New Orleans," Clay told him.

"Right now? At this time of night?" He was surprised by the unorthodox request.

"That's right. It's important. Now, listen—" Clay quickly explained exactly what he needed for him to do. He then handed him two envelopes, one with a letter and the other bulging with cash. "Think you can handle this?"

"Yes, sir. I'll do just like you told me to, Mr. Clay. I'll make sure everything is all ready for you when you get there."

"Good. I'm counting on you."

Clay watched as Jacob left the house, then returned to the desk to write the other note he needed. That done, he folded the missive and tucked it safely in his pocket. Clay knew that there was only one more thing he needed. Leaving the

179

study, he unlocked the closet where his father kept his medicinal supplies and took the bottle of laudanum he found there.

Clay reviewed his plan several times in his mind and could find no fatal flaw as he headed upstairs to his bedroom. He was sure he had covered everything. With any luck at all, by this time tomorrow he would be out of New Orleans and on his way to California. Clay's mood was determined, but excited, and though he was going to try to get some rest, he doubted that he would sleep at all that night. He was too close to his goal. He was too close to success.

Chapter Fourteen

"You look lovely today, Isabel," Clay complimented Reina as he drove their carriage over the back roads to Windown.

"Thank you," Reina replied, smiling at him as she smoothed the full skirt of her pale blue daygown. She was glad that he'd noticed for today, for the first time in her life, she'd deliberately dressed just to please a man.

Before Clay, Reina had never cared enough about any man to want to do anything special just for him. Oh, she always wanted to look her best, but she'd dressed to suit herself. However, Clay had changed all that. Reina wanted to please him. She had chosen this particular dress, because, sedate though it was, the style flattered her. The form-fitting bodice was demurely cut, yet hinted at her very feminine curves beneath. It enticed while revealing nothing. It was a gown designed with men in mind. She had also worn her hair down for him today, pulling it back from her face with only a simple ribbon and then letting the thick, ebony tresses tumble casually about her shoulders. Her suitors back home had always loved it when she wore her hair unbound, and she hoped Clay would react the same way, too.

"It's not too much farther," he was saying, "just around the next bend."

"Oh, good. I haven't been on a picnic in ages. I'm really looking forward to this," she told him.

"So am I," Clay responded with deep meaning.

"Do you take time for picnics very often?" Reina asked.

"Hardly ever. In fact, I really can't tell you the last time I did."

"Good," she teased, "then today will be special for both of us."

"It most certainly will," he agreed, turning the carriage onto a narrow, slightly overgrown side road. They drove on only a short distance before he reined in at a small grassy clearing framed by ancient oak trees. "What do you think?"

"It's perfect," she said, looking around at the lush greenery of the Louisiana countryside. It was far different from her California home, but beautiful in its own right.

"Let me help you down," Clay offered, taking her hand and assisting her in her descent. "Now, I'll get the basket, and you can carry the blanket."

He handed her the folded cover and then led the way to the shade of one of the spreading oaks.

"How's this?" he asked, setting the basket down and taking the blanket from her.

"Wonderful," Reina replied as she watched him unfold the cover and spread it upon the soft grass. He looked so very, irresistibly male in the dark, slim-fitting pants and a white shirt he wore that her heart thudded wildly in her breast. She realized then that the suspicion she'd had during the long, sleepless hours of the night just past had been true. She had fallen in love with him.

Reina knew it was illogical. Clay was the man who'd been hired to make sure she showed up for the horrible wedding her father had planned for her. But even as she acknowledged that it was irrational to feel this way, she also knew that he was the man who'd haunted her dreams for weeks now. In the beginning, right after they'd parted company in California, she'd thought she would forget him. It hadn't happened, and having tasted of his passion last night, she knew she never would.

Though there was a risk involved, Reina planned to pick up where she left off last night, and tell Clay the truth about everything just as soon as she could. She knew it would be difficult, but she didn't care. Today, she intended to clear up the many lies that lay between them. Their relationship could not be based on deception.

It was a happy determination that filled Reina. She remembered how she'd been so instinctively drawn to Clay the first time they'd met, and now she understood why. Somehow from the very beginning, she'd sensed he was the man for her. All she had to do now, she realized, was convince him of that.

Clay was feeling confident as he finished arranging the blanket. His plan was going perfectly. It wouldn't be long now! Just a few more minutes and —

Clay glanced up at Reina just then from where he knelt on the cover, and the sight of her looking so absolutely breathtaking sent a shaft of unwanted desire racing through him. He wanted to pull her down on the blanket with him and make mad, passionate love to her right then and there. He wanted to —

With rigid control, Clay managed to subdue his wayward passion. He told himself sternly that it didn't matter if Reina looked like an innocent angel today. It was all an elaborate ruse. She was no more a sweet innocent than she'd been a nun on the stage in California!

Clay girded himself for the upcoming scene with her. He would play his role, but he would not forget why he was here! He would not allow this purely animal attraction he felt for her to detract him from his purpose! He smiled at her and held out his hand, inviting her to join him on the blanket. He was more than pleased when she didn't hesitate to sit beside him.

"I've been waiting for this moment since last night," she told him, meaning every word of it.

Reina sounded so believable that Clay wondered how she'd ever become so accomplished at her acting. He realized with some disgust that he might have fallen for her lies had he not known the truth.

"I've been waiting for this moment, too," he returned, keeping his tone serious. "I think I have been all of my life." *Or at least it seemed like a lifetime since he and Dev were together last.*

Reina's breath caught in her throat at his declaration. She couldn't believe how lucky she was. Clay did want her! He did care! She had to tell him—

Reina hesitated. The moment was so perfect that she didn't want to ruin what promised to be a perfect day. The weather was glorious, the delicate scent of flowers perfumed the air, Clay was here. Right now, she needed nothing else. There would be plenty of time later to confess, maybe after they'd eaten.

"Then the waiting's over now for both of us." Her words were a whisper. Feeling almost magnetically drawn to Clay, she leaned toward him.

Clay shifted toward her just enough to meet her in a single, gentle kiss. He didn't try to touch her or try to deepen the embrace, yet even so, hot excitement radiated through him. Instead of thrilling to his own reaction, he was annoyed by it. He pulled back first, schooling his expression into one of tenderness and affection.

"Hungry?" he asked with a slight smile as he opened the basket.

"Starving," Reina replied, craving more than just sustenance for the body. She was starving for Clay . . . for his touch and his kiss. She felt oddly bereft that he'd drawn away from her so quickly.

"So am I," he echoed.

Clay began laying out the feast the cook had prepared for them on the blanket before them — a big, thick chunk of cheese, crusty french bread, golden butter and crisp fried chicken. He set aside the plates and utensils, and then withdrew two crystal glasses and the bottle of wine he'd chosen personally for the occasion.

"Would you like some wine?" he offered, praying desperately that she wouldn't refuse.

"Yes, please," she quickly agreed.

At her acceptance, he casually uncorked the bottle and poured her a glass, though there was nothing casual about his intent. He handed her a glass, then poured one for himself.

"A toast . . . to us." Clay lifted his glass to her.

"To us," Reina repeated, her heart swelling with joy.

"May we always remember the first time we met." Clay finished, knowing full well that he would never, ever forget Sister Mary Regina. None of his bitterness of the memory showed in his eyes, though. He was acting like a man deliriously in love.

Reina found the last of his toast a bit odd since she believed they'd only met the night before. She rationalized, though, that maybe Clay thought last night had been extra special since he'd won her away from all the other men who'd been pursuing her.

"And may we always remember today," she breathed taking a sip of the fine vintage.

You'll remember today, all right, Clay thought with vicious sarcasm. He gave the appearance of taking a small drink of the wine before setting his glass aside. It pleased him that she was drinking deeply of the wine.

"More?" He invited, picking up the wine bottle.

"Yes, it's delicious." She enjoyed wine and thought this one quite good.

When Reina held her near-empty glass out to him, he added to it. Their hands accidentally touched, and all concept of time evaporated as their eyes met. The moment seemed to last an eternity.

Clay could not believe the feverish need that threatened to overpower him. He tried to deny it, but his body rebelled against his mind's dictates. He told himself angrily that it was only physical desire he felt for her. He told himself that despite the romantic setting he still had a firm grip on things. He was a man who prided himself on being in control, and he would not allow Reina to break that mastery.

Desire pulsed through Reina, too. She took another deep drink from her glass, but her eyes never left his.

"The wine really is wonderful, Clay."

"I'm glad you like it. I took particular care selecting it. I wanted something just for today . . . something memorable."

"This whole day is special."

"I'm glad you think so. It is for me, too," Clay said with a smile as, again, he added more of his select vintage to her glass. "I want everything to go perfectly."

"Well, it's been perfect so far, and I can't imagine anything that could possibly ruin the rest of the day for us."

"I think we'll both remember today for a long time to come. I know I will." Clay's baser instincts urged him relentlessly to take her in his arms and kiss her again, but he fought against it and busied himself fixing them plates of food. He handed Reina her plate, piled high with a sampling of every good thing. They ate slowly, enjoying the simple yet delicious fare. Reina finished her wine and willingly accepted Clay's offer of another refill. She noticed that he had not drunk any more of his own.

"You aren't drinking much wine," she remarked, feeling delightfully relaxed. "You do like it, don't you? You didn't just bring it along for me, did you?"

"I have to admit that I did choose that particular bottle for you. I wanted you to have the very best this afternoon. And, as far as me not drinking much, I don't need any help feeling good right now, I feel heady enough just being with you."

Reina gazed up at him rapturously, thinking him the most handsome, most thoughtful, most exciting man she'd ever met. The guilt she'd been experiencing over keeping her secret from him faded as she was filled with a pleasantly drowsy sensation. All that mattered was that she was there with Clay, alone in the countryside.

The memory of the ardent kisses they'd shared the night before came to her, and she was feeling so wonderful and so perfect that she found it easy to ignore the last clinging fragments of her inhibitions. She was with the man she loved.

"Clay—" Reina's voice sounded strangely distant to her, and had she not been feeling so delightfully happy, she would have worried. Right then, though, it didn't seem very important. She was afire with the need to be held by him. She desperately wanted him to kiss her. "Kiss me."

At Reina's unexpected invitation, Clay's desire for her flamed even hotter. But knowing her for the liar that she was, he firmly believed her display of wanting him was just a put-on. He thought she might eventually try to use his passion as a tool against him, and he was not going to let that happen. He would play along with her. He would match her lies with lies of his own, but only for as long as he had to. Taking her in his arms as an ardent lover should, he claimed her lips in a commanding kiss.

Reina was enthralled that he hadn't thought her too brazen. She melted eagerly against him. *This was what she'd wanted . . . this was what she'd been longing for.*

Clay's mouth moved hungrily over hers, his tongue seeking and dueling with hers in an intimate dance of love. She returned his fervent ardor without reserve. Her hands restlessly touching him, exploring the broad width of his chest and the strength of his powerful shoulders. She wanted to get close to him, closer than she'd ever been to anyone before.

Reina's wanton, unbridled response excited Clay even against his will. She was like a fire in his blood, yet he struggled against surrendering to the need to cast fate to the wind and slake his passion for her. *Her kisses really meant nothing to him,* he told himself angrily. *Her touch did not thrill him. This was his job. He had to be convincing.*

Yet, even as Clay tried to persuade himself that that was all true, he was being swept away by a force of emotions he didn't understand. Rational thought deserted him completely at the feel of her body close to his. No matter how much he'd tried to deny it, he did want her. God, how he wanted her! Consumed by his driving need, he began to caress her.

Reina was feeling lightheaded and dizzy, and she attributed it all to Clay's exhilarating kisses. Every nerve in her body was tingling in anticipation. When he finally sought the soft roundness of her breast, a moan of pure ecstasy escaped her. Overnight, she'd pondered the intimacies she'd allowed him and how she'd been so excited by his touch. Reina had found it difficult to believe that anything could have really felt that exquisite. She'd thought that maybe she'd made it all up, imagined it all. Now, however, she knew her memory hadn't been faulty. Clay's caress was intoxicating. Why, even now, the joy of it was so great, she felt as if she might faint.

At the sound of her pleasure, Clay shifted them both down onto the blanket. Reina thought it was heaven to lie next to him and to have him stretched out full length beside her. His kisses deepened, becoming even more fervid as he began to undo the buttons on her bodice. She shivered in anticipation of his touch, and when he parted the fabric, she cried out softly to him of her eagerness.

His breathing ragged, his face flushed with excitement, Clay stared down at the beauty of Reina's bared breasts. His passion for her raged at a fever pitch. He was like a man possessed as he moved to press hot, stirring kisses to her lips, throat and then lower to the creamy mounds of her breasts.

At the caress of his lips upon her bosom, Reina arched upward in surprise. The touch of his hand had been wonderful. The touch of his mouth was pure bliss. Reina was on fire with yearning, yet she couldn't think any more. Her thoughts were a confusing jumble. Only Clay was reality . . . only Clay.

Clay continued to arouse her with practiced expertise. When she began to move restlessly beneath his caresses, he moved up over her and sought her lips in a devouring kiss.

Breathlessly, Reina returned it full measure. She found she suddenly wanted to give him as much pleasure as he was giving her. In the way of innocents because she wasn't sure exactly what to do, she just tried to imitate his caresses. She thought it odd that her arms felt so heavy and awkward as she lifted them to him, but she was too enthralled by the erotic sensations that were throbbing through her to worry over much.

Clay began to caress her again, exploring the taut peaks and silken valleys of her breasts. Brushing aside her skirts and underthings, he sought that which made her woman. Frightened, Reina initially shied from this boldness.

"Easy, love . . . easy . . . I won't hurt you," he promised.

Her heart swelled as she heard him call her "love." She believed him. She believed he would never hurt her. She trusted him and wanted him. When he touched her so intimately again, she did not resist.

"Clay . . . there's something—" she started to confess all, but his lips sought hers again, and it was momentarily forgotten.

His passion was surging. His need was hot and real.

"Clay . . . oh, Clay," she cried as his touch created sensations within her that she'd never experienced before.

He had been intent on making love to Reina until the sound of her calling his name jolted him from his sensual reverie and chilled him to his heart. *Think! Remember!* his conscience screamed. *Was it worth risking Dev's safety for one quick moment of sensual pleasure?* For that's all this was—a flash of passion and desire, nothing else. His body throbbed with need, but he ignored it. Angry, and wanting to let her know her little charade was over, he rose above her.

"Isabel . . ." Clay began.

She tried to focus on him, knowing that she had something important to tell him, but she found herself befuddled. It seemed as if reality was slipping away from her. She suddenly felt very sleepy. She was having trouble keeping her eyes open, and when the fight became too much to continue she let them drift closed. The last words she heard as she drifted off were . . .

"Isabel," he repeated, "*if I were a religious man, I'd swear I'd been blessed in finding you. You really must be a godsend.*"

Clay paused, waiting and watching. He'd expected her to react in some way to his words, but when Reina went limp in his arms, he was not disappointed. He smiled sharkishly, pleased that at last, the laudanum had done its work.

Clay took a deep, steadying breath, then shifted away from her. He quickly straightened her clothes, and it was an exercise in self-discipline to rebutton the bodice of her dress. Reina was lovely. It would be a hard man who could refuse her, but he considered himself a hard man. A little frustrated right now, but hard.

He carried Reina to the carriage, then made short work of cleaning up the area. He kept only the wine bottle with them. A short time later, he reached the rendezvous point he'd set up with Calvin and Jefferson, two of his father's servants. He was glad to find that they were there right on time just as he'd instructed.

"Did you hear from Jacob?"

"Yes, sir. He sent word that the name of the boat you're wanting is the *Crosswinds*."

"Good," Clay answered. As he'd arranged with them earlier that morning, they switched vehicles. He and Reina were now riding in the privacy of an enclosed coach with Calvin driving.

Both Hal and Jefferson exchanged worried looks as Clay placed an unconscious Reina in the carriage. They had had no idea that their special meeting with him had anything to do with stealing a woman, and they wondered why someone like Mr. Clay would have to resort to such tactics. Still, he had sworn them to secrecy that morning when he'd asked for their help, and they knew they would never breathe a word of what happened here today, even though they thought it mighty strange.

At Clay's instruction, Jefferson took the carriage that had been used for the picnic and headed off to the Delacroix house to deliver the letter to Emilie that Clay had penned the night before.

"Where we going, Mr. Clay?" Calvin asked after Jefferson had driven off.

"New Orleans, Calvin, and be quick about it. There's not a lot of time."

As the carriage moved off at a good clip, Clay settled back in the plush confines to consider his next move. Everything had to go exactly as he'd planned or he might find himself in big trouble. It wouldn't look very good in town if he was forced to carry a screaming, battling Reina up the gangplank to the *Crosswinds*. They had to reach the boat before she awoke from her slumber. He could only hope that she'd imbibed enough of the drugged wine.

Clay glanced over at her where she was braced awkwardly against the side of the carriage. He thought she looked miserably uncomfortable. For some unknown reason, he found himself changing seats to sit beside her. With care, Clay gently drew her across his lap. He held her there, cradled against him as they raced through the afternoon on the first leg of their desperate return journey to California.

Chapter Fifteen

Reina felt as if she was spiraling upward from the bottom of a deep, deep pool. She could hear, but the sounds were garbled and seemed strangely foreign to her. She struggled to open her eyes, but her eyelids were too heavy. She tried to think of the reason why she was so tired, but she couldn't remember much of anything. Her thoughts were blurred and vaguely disconnected.

Reina attempted to move, then grew frightened when she discovered she had little control over her body. Her arms were like leaden weights at her sides. She wanted to call out for help, but could find no words to use. Tossing fitfully on the bed, she groaned in abject misery, wondering what was wrong.

Suddenly out of nowhere, strong, protective arms were around her lifting her up, pressing a cup to her lips.

"Drink, Reina. Take a deep drink," a deep, familiar voice encouraged.

Reina knew she should recognize that voice, but every time she was about to remember the man's identity, it slipped elusively away from her. The man had told her to drink from the cup he was offering her, so she obediently took a big swallow. It surprised Reina that the liquid he was offering her was wine.

"Good," the mystery man praised. "Try another."

She took another sip at his urging.

"It's a shame that you're not always this submissive," the voice said.

The man laid her back down on what she guessed was a bed, for it was soft beneath her. A comforting warmth stole over her, and reality slowly vanished. Reina was quietly unconcerned as she felt herself floating away.

Reina opened her eyes, then quickly closed them again as a wave of nausea turned her stomach. She felt so ill that she remained completely still while she took a deep breath.

"Emilie?" Reina called out her friend's name and was startled to find that her voice was hoarse almost to the point of being a rasping whisper. When there was no response to her call, she figured that her friend probably hadn't heard her. Surely, Emilie was close by.

"Emilie?" Reina tried again, a little louder this time. When she heard the scrape of a chair on the floor, she relaxed a little, feeling somewhat better, knowing her friend was there. "I don't know what's wrong with me, but—"

With an effort, Reina had finally managed to open her eyes again just as she started to speak. At the sight of Clay, not Emilie, sitting beside the bed, she stopped in mid-sentence.

"Clay?" she asked in bewilderment, wondering what he was doing there in her bedroom. Her gaze swept quickly around the room, and she realized with some shock that nothing was familiar to her. It was not her bedroom. But if it was not her room, then whose was it? Where was she? Her thoughts were in turmoil as she tried to remember—tried to think.

"Glad to see that you're finally back among the living," Clay drawled as he flashed her a wide smile. He'd been sitting there at her bedside for the better part of a day just waiting for her to come around. He was glad to see that the drug had finally worn off, but he was not looking forward to the explosion of wrath he knew was about to take place.

"What happened?" Hazy memories of the picnic were spinning through her mind. "Did I get sick on our outing? Where am I?"

"You're on a boat," came his answer.

Reina was perplexed by his reply. Why would she be on a boat? Her head was pounding, and the more she tried to figure things out, the more confusing everything became. When she tried to lift one hand to rub her aching brow, she discovered to her horror that her arms were tied to the bed at her sides. It was then that everything became perfectly clear to her. It was over . . . *he knew! Clay knew the truth!*

"You know . . ." she whispered.

"Oh, yes, Reina. *I know,*" he snarled. "I knew the minute I saw you at the Randolphs'."

She almost groaned out loud in mortification. Completely humiliated, she wondered how she could have been so stupid as to believe that he really hadn't recognized her! How naive and gullible she'd been! "But you acted as if—"

"I *acted,* Reina, and I learned from watching a master performer—you. You really should think about giving lessons, you know," he complimented her snidely. "I was completely fooled back on the stagecoach. Wonderful disguise—Sister Mary Regina. You had me believing you were a pure, chaste young woman who'd devoted her life to doing good works and serving God. Goes to show just how wrong you can be about people sometimes."

Reina remembered then the very last thing she'd heard him say right before she'd lost consciousness. *"If I were a religious man, I'd swear I'd been blessed in finding you. You really must be a godsend."* She was mortified. She'd been such a fool! She should have run that night at the Randolphs' as her instincts had told her to. She should never have stayed and tried to brazen it out. Never!

"Why didn't you just drag me off that first night and be done with it? Why did you play along with me?" She was humiliated. She'd fancied herself in love with him and had thought he was falling in love with her. How could she have been so mistaken?

Clay gave a derisive laugh. "Just how far do you think I would have gotten if I'd tried to carry you off? No, no, it was far better to carry you off quietly, than to carry you off fighting and screaming. You were very quiet when I brought you on board, Reina, you were sleeping in my arms just like a baby."

"The wine!" she gasped in outraged horror. "No wonder you wouldn't drink any of it!" She recalled his statement about choosing the wine "just for her" and she remembered how special she'd felt knowing he'd been so thoughtful. Now, all she felt was sick. *Lies . . . What she'd thought had been the beginning of a beautiful love had all been lies.*

"Yes, this has turned out to be a most interesting job," he mused. "My plan worked quite well, don't you think?"

Clay sounded so smugly secure that all Reina wanted to do was hit him. Had she been untied, she would have done it. She flushed scarlet as she

197

thought of how simple she'd made everything for him—never telling Emilie that he was her father's hired gun and then by stupidly agreeing to go on a picnic with him. She'd thought herself in love, but he'd never really wanted her at all. He'd only been doing his job! Pain stabbed at her heart.

Reina blanched as she realized that her worst fears had come to pass. Clay had found her; Clay had trapped her; Clay was taking her back against her will!

"Untie me!" she demanded, growing more furious with each and every passing minute. She wasn't sure if she was angrier with him or herself.

"Not yet," he said simply, annoying her even further.

"Not yet?" she echoed outraged. "Why not? We're on a boat, out in the middle of God knows where! What do you expect me to do? Jump overboard and swim back to shore?"

"I wouldn't put anything past you at this point, Reina, and I'm not going to let you go until I'm sure you won't cause any trouble. Right now, we're in the Gulf about six or seven hours from port, heading full steam for the Isthmus of Panama," he went on coolly, leaning back in the chair and folding his arms across his chest in a very self-confident gesture. "You're on your way home. It's my job to make sure you get there."

Reina's thoughts turned chaotic as she stared at him. For an instant tears burned her eyes, but she fought them back. She couldn't go back and marry Nathan! She just couldn't! The thought that she might break down and cry angered her even more, and she began to fight against her bonds.

"Let me up!" she snapped.

"As soon as you admit defeat and agree not to make any trouble for the rest of the trip, we'll talk about untying you."

"I hate you, Clay Cordell!" Her dark eyes flashed defiantly at him. "I'll never stop trying to get away!"

"That's your choice, and that's exactly why you're tied down. It won't inconvenience me in the least to keep you flat on your back for the rest of the voyage. In fact, it might prove interesting. You certainly were willing enough on the picnic . . ."

"You . . . !"

"Pleasant as it was at the time," Clay went on easily, "I knew you were only acting. I never believed you for a minute."

He'd thought she'd been pretending the whole time they'd been together. Reina was devastated. "But I believed you."

She sounded so sincere that for a moment Clay was almost convinced. At the last second, though, he remembered just who he was dealing with, and he gave a derisive laugh. "Sure you did, Reina," he drawled disparagingly. "Is this some new act now? How many other lies do you want to tell me?"

Reina's spirit stiffened under the cruel onslaught of his reply. "You'll never know!"

"That's exactly why I want your word that you're going to behave yourself before I let you up. Not that I mind keeping you like this, but it might prove a bit awkward, if the captain starts wondering why you never leave our cabin."

"You're a vile, disgusting man!"

Clay shrugged off her words as if her opinion of him mattered little to him. "I'm a determined man, Miss Alvarez. Surely, you knew that a long time ago."

Fear frissoned through Reina as she tried to think. "What about Emilie? She's going to be worried about me. I'll bet the whole Delacroix family is out looking for me right now!"

199

"I doubt it," he answered, apparently unconcerned that a posse of Delacroixs could be scouring the area looking for her.

"Why?" Reina barely whispered, knowing that somehow he'd covered that possibility, too.

"Because Emilie got a wonderful letter from us telling her how happy we were and how we were running off together."

"You didn't . . . ?"

"I most certainly did."

"But you don't know that she believed you!" Reina was grasping desperately for straws.

Even as she said it, though, Reina realized that Emilie probably would have believed it. After all, hadn't she teasingly told her to elope with Clay if the opportunity arose? Reina could have kicked herself for having gone along with her ridiculous suggestion at the time. If she'd balked at the idea, then Emilie might have suspected that something was wrong. Right now, her friend probably thought she was blissfully happy.

"She believed me, Reina," he stated matter-of-factly. "In fact, Emilie was quite pleased to send on a small trunk of your clothes."

"When she finds out the truth, they'll come after me!" she cried, feeling his trap closing around her.

"So what if they do? Let them look," he drawled sarcastically. "Even if they do try to come after you, they'll be too late. We have such a good head start on them that we'll be back to California and your father before they can possibly catch up."

"Why, you . . ." Reina glared at him. Seeing him through different eyes now, she couldn't imagine how she'd ever thought him so wonderful. His dark good looks seemed positively diabolical to her.

Clay cocked one eyebrow at her mockingly. "Yes?"

Furious, Reina looked away from him. She was

shaking with anger for she knew he was enjoying this. She fell silent, knowing the only way to save herself was to bring her feelings under control as best she could and take a logical approach to her situation. She wouldn't think about how Clay had outsmarted her. She wouldn't think about how embarrassed she was over having thought herself in love with Clay. That had been a terrible mistake that would never be repeated. She had learned her lesson. Never again would she allow her senses to overrule her judgment.

That decided, Reina knew she had to take first things first. She had to do something to save herself from a fate worse than death—marriage to Nathan Marlow. Maybe, she reasoned, since Clay was a bounty hunter, money would be the one thing he would understand. In desperation, she tried the only argument she thought might work.

"Look, why don't we make a bargain?" Reina finally asked.

He regarded her levelly, his eyes cold and wary. Knowing her as well as he did, he hadn't thought that she'd give up easily without a fight. He'd been expecting this, and he was anticipating much, much more. "What kind of bargain?"

"I've got money. How much is my father paying you? I'll double it. Just let me go."

Clay realized that he should have known she'd want to talk about money, only money didn't even enter into this.

"Sorry," his refusal was curt. Dev was the only reason he'd come after her, and Dev was the only reason he was taking her back.

"Sorry?" Reina was livid. "You're a bounty hunter, aren't you? You'd do anything for the right price, wouldn't you?"

His gaze turned an icy silver as a muscle tensed

201

in his jaw. "It's true that every man has his price. Mine just happens to be more than you can afford."

His snide comment enraged Reina. She started to struggle again against the bonds that held her. "Let me go! Let me up! I swear I'll scream if you don't!"

Clay casually reached for the bandana on the small table beside him. "This would make a perfect gag. Don't force me to use it."

Reina blanched at his threat, physically shrinking back away from him. "You wouldn't dare—"

"I'd dare a lot, Reina. You, of all people, should know that by now."

"Let me up! Let me out of here! I'm going to tell the captain of this ship that you kidnapped me and brought on board against my will!" she seethed through gritted teeth.

"I don't think so." Clay cut her off.

"And why not?" Reina challenged angrily, beyond fear.

"Because, for one thing, he's not going to believe you. You see, when I carried you aboard yesterday, you were sleeping contentedly in my arms. I told the captain that we were married—newlyweds, in fact, and that's why you were so exhausted." Clay paused in satisfaction as she gasped in outrage.

"How could you!"

"It was easy. But now, if you go to the captain and tell him this whole other story . . ." Clay lifted his shoulders in an expressive gesture. "Well, he may believe you, but he'll also remember that we spent the night here in this cabin . . . sleeping together in the same bed."

"Why you no-good, low-down . . ." she stormed and then looked suddenly stricken. "You didn't. . . ? You wouldn't have. . . ?"

"Make love to you while you were sleeping?" Clay asked candidly, reading her thoughts. "No, Reina, I didn't lay a hand on you. As you very well know, I don't have to drug women to make them want me."

Reina thought him hateful for reminding her of her weakness! "You're a foul man, Clay Cordell! You can't keep me tied up here for the whole voyage! I'm going to get out of here and when I do, I'm going to tell the captain the truth!" she threatened, not thinking of the consequences that would result from such an action on her part.

At her continued defiance even in the face of undeniable defeat, Clay erupted in anger. "If you want the man to think you're nothing more than a slut, Reina, you go right ahead and tell him everything!" Clay ground out savagely. "You can even have me arrested if you want to. Then you'll be all on your own out here in the middle of the Gulf with only the captain's good graces to rely on for your protection. He might be a good, honest man, and then again he might not."

"What are you saying?" Reina was stricken by his insinuations.

"I'm saying that as long as you're under my protection, you'll be safe. Nothing will happen to you. It's my job to make certain that you're returned to your father unharmed, and I fully intend to fulfill my obligation to him. But if you have me locked up . . ." He looked her straight in the eye as he went on, "That leaves you alone and helpless. There isn't much sweeter to a man at sea than an unprotected, beautiful young woman. The captain would probably use you first, then, once he's had his fill of you, he'd share you with the other crew members."

Reina swallowed convulsively at the ugly tale he was spinning, but she said nothing.

Clay could tell by her strained expression that he'd made his point. He only hoped she was smart enough to believe him. "The evening meal is due to be served soon. It would be nice to be accompanied by *my wife.*"

"I'm not going anywhere with you, Clay Cordell!" Reina still refused stubbornly.

Clay laughed at her. "Ah, but I'm afraid you are, Reina—all the way to California. Now, what's it gong to be? Do I leave you here, tied and gagged, until I get back or do you come along quietly and play the part of my adoring little wife?"

"Never!"

"That may very well be, but as good an actress as you are, you shouldn't have any trouble hiding your true feelings and convincing everyone on board that we've just wed and are madly in love."

"Go to hell!"

"It's your decision then," Clay said almost regretfully as he quickly, effectively gagged her. "It's a shame you're still feeling so indisposed, my darling *wife.* I'll give the captain your regrets and tell him that you'll be joining him just as soon as you're feeling less indisposed."

Clay checked her bonds once more to make certain she couldn't escape while he was gone. Certain that she wouldn't be able to work herself free, he then took care of freshening up himself for dinner. He ignored the wild-eyed, desperate, hate-filled looks she was shooting at him. As he started for the cabin door a few minutes later, Clay turned back to her one last time.

"There's still time for you to reconsider and join your husband for dinner."

Beneath the gag, she screeched her fury and anger at him, but Clay only laughed again and reached for the doorknob.

"I see you still haven't had a change of heart. Well, I'll see you a little later. I hope you'll be feeling more amenable when I return."

Reina had never known such blind fury as she watched the cabin door close silently behind Clay. All the love she'd once thought she'd felt for him had now turned to hate, and oh, how she hated him! The arrogance of him! The unmitigated gall! Tears threatened again, but she refused to give in to them. She was no weepy female! She was stronger than that.

Reina's heart was filled with a burning desire to teach Clay Cordell a lesson. He wanted to play tough, and two could play that game. If he'd thought her "performances" were good before, he could just wait and see what she was going to do next! She'd give the outward appearance of going along with him, but in the end she was the one who was going to win. She was not going to allow him to take her back to her father and Nathan Marlow.

Reina willed herself to relax and to quit fighting the ropes. Now was the time to plot what she was going to do. She knew it wasn't going to be easy, but somehow, someway she was going to escape from Clay before they got to California.

It was dark by the time Clay returned to their cabin carrying a tray laden with food. Upon entering, he lit a lamp and found Reina awake, watching him.

"Good evening, my darling wife," he taunted as he set the tray aside. "I've brought you a little something to eat. Hope you're feeling hungry."

Under the stifling gag, Reina told Clay what he could do with the food.

"The captain sends his regards," he went on, "and hopes that you'll be feeling much better tomorrow.

He's looking forward to meeting you."

Clay went to her then and removed the gag. The dinner he'd brought her smelled wonderful, but she wasn't about to let him know that she was starving. She wasn't about to accept any offer of kindness from this man.

"Well, the captain will just have to wait, won't he?" she countered, not yet willing to concede to his blackmail.

"That's up to you," he answered and then surprised her by releasing her arms.

"You're letting me up?"

"I thought you might want to eat."

"I don't want anything from you!"

Clay ignored her and continued, "And I'm sure you'll want to take care of your needs and change into a nightgown."

"I'll sleep in my clothes," she declared firmly as she got up. Rubbing her sore wrists, she went into the small convenience room to tend to her private matters. That done, she had no choice but to rejoin her captor.

"Sure you don't want to eat? The meal was delicious," he offered again, removing the towel that covered the tray to reveal the tantalizing food there. "There's chicken and rice and—"

"I'm not hungry," Reina cut him off, trying to ignore the mouth-watering scent.

"Seems a pity to waste such good food, but if you're not hungry," Clay shrugged. "You might as well go ahead and change then. You're going to be mighty uncomfortable sleeping in that." He began to move about the cabin taking off his own clothes.

"I'll be fine," she replied tersely, trying not to watch him as he stripped down to only his pants.

He turned to face her and gestured toward the bed. "Lie down. I want to know exactly where you are when I turn off this lamp."

Reina did as she was told, even though it went against her grain. She lay there stiffly, anticipating him tying her arms once more. The cabin was engulfed in deep darkness when he put out the light. She was tense as he stretched out beside her on the bed. To her relief, he made no move to restrain her again.

"I know what you're thinking, Reina, and no, I'm not going to tie you tonight. Just keep in mind that I'm a very light sleeper. You'll pay the price if I catch you trying to get away from me. Do you understand?"

With his cold declaration, Clay snatched what would have been a moment of profound relief from her.

"Yes," she answered sullenly.

"Good. Now go to sleep."

Reina would have liked nothing better than to drop off into a deep slumber, but it was not to be. Clay's nearness left her on edge. Seeing him only half-dressed had reminded her of the time at the waystation, and in spite of her avowals of hatred for him, she'd felt an unwanted stirring of passion. Reina knew that was something she would not allow herself. But here he was, lying so close beside her. She could actually feel the heat of his body even though they were not touching. She wondered as the hours passed with miserable slowness if the night would ever end. It was the wee hours of the morning before she finally managed to fall asleep.

Clay had been exhausted as he'd stretched out beside Reina. He'd had little rest since their picnic, and he was sorely in need of a good night's sleep. Even so, he knew he could not relax his guard. He'd caught her and now he had to hang onto her. Folding his arms beneath his head, he lay on his back next to her, trying to ignore the memories of the last time they'd lain together. Sometime well after midnight, Clay finally drifted off. His last thought as sleep claimed him was of Reina and if it was always going to be this hard for him to fall asleep with her at his side.

Chapter Sixteen

Clay awoke just after daybreak, startled to find that he'd actually been sound asleep. His first thought after his head cleared of the cobwebs of slumber was of Reina, and he quickly sat up to check whether she'd fled during the time he'd been asleep. He heaved a huge sigh of relief to find her slumbering peacefully beside him on the bed.

Clay studied Reina as she slept on, unaware of his scrutiny. She looked beautiful with her lush, dark hair unbound and loose about her shoulders. Her cheeks were sleep-flushed, and her mouth looked soft and vulnerable. The curve of her breasts rose and fell in steady rhythm with her even breathing. She looked innocent.

"Damn," he muttered as he reacted to that innocence. He struggled to resist the compelling temptation to reach out and caress her. She might look sweetly innocent while she was sleeping, but he knew better. Reina was a woman who used her feminine wiles and physical attributes to her advantage. She was so good at it that she'd almost made him forget himself twice. He had himself under rigid control now, though, and was positive it wouldn't happen again.

Clay wondered what Reina was going to try next. Knowing how cunning and manipulative she could be, he didn't expect her to return with him without a fight. But he was ready for her.

Keeping her tethered to the bed for the rest of the voyage was not an idle threat to Clay. He wasn't about to let her destroy his only chance to rescue Dev. In silence, Clay once again cursed her father for his devious plot in getting him involved.

While he sat there, naked to the waist, watching Reina, her eyes suddenly opened, and she looked straight at him. He found himself staring, mesmerized, into the brown velvet of her gaze. Clay marvelled at the total guilelessness of Reina's expression, and he wondered how she could assume this innocent act of hers so immediately upon waking. He'd expected to see hatred and resentment for him on her unguarded features. It irritated him that she could appear so blameless, and it annoyed him further that he allowed it to bother him.

In the softness that comes with first waking, Reina stared at Clay for a long, quiet moment. She wondered if it would do any good at all to try to explain her situation to him . . . to tell him why she'd run away and try to sway him over to her side. She was almost ready to try to reason with him, when his distant regard suddenly turned openly hostile. Reina realized then that there was no use. If he wouldn't take her money, he certainly wouldn't care what her real reasons had been for running away. He was her father's mindless henchman. He wouldn't listen. Reina's anger with him returned, and with it, her iron-willed determination to escape him.

"You look lovely in the morning," Clay said in a low, almost seductive voice, before adding his hateful commentary. "I'm sure your fiancé is going to enjoy waking up beside you every day!"

"I don't have a fiancé!" she countered sharply, sitting up and turning her back on him. While she gave the appearance of being angry, on the inside she was cringing at the thought of ever being in bed with Nathan.

"Oh, yes, you do, and according to your father, he's anxiously anticipating your upcoming nuptials," Clay taunted. "With any luck, we'll be there in plenty of time for the wedding."

Reina refused to be baited into an argument. She wanted to turn on Clay and throw it up to him that they still had a long way to go to California, but she held herself back, for she sensed his ability to do even worse things than tie her to the bed to achieve his ends. She would play his game by his rules. If he thought she'd been acting before, now he was really going to see a masterful performance.

"It looks at this point as if I have no choice," she finally said, hoping she sounded resigned to her fate.

"Oh, you have choices all right, Reina, but not about making the trip. You're going. You can, however, choose how you care to spend the time involved. You can pass the entire voyage locked here in our cabin or you can make things easy on yourself and go along with the story I told the captain." He saw her stiffen as he spoke. "It's all up to you."

Turning to face him, Reina paused. He'd left her no choice, no choice at all. Her expression was a curious mixture of anger and an almost haunted desperation as she stared at him.

Clay was surprised that he felt a twinge of conscience, and he quickly put it from him. Her feelings were of no importance to him. "Well?"

"All right," she finally responded. "I'll go along with you."

Her acquiescence left Clay suspicious. "You realize what this will entail? You know you've got to play the part of my new bride."

Reina glared at him. "Oh, I'll play the part of your adoring little wife when we're in public, Clay, but that's all it will be—an act! The charade ends the minute we step back through that door."

He gave her a mocking look and said pointedly, "I don't remember asking you to do more than that."

At his sarcasm, heat crept into her cheeks. Not wanting him to see her embarrassment, she mumbled, "Good." Then she got up and started rummaging through the small trunk she recognized as her own. "If you don't mind, I do have to change clothes."

"My, my, such modesty in my new bride after we've just spent the night sleeping in the same bed." Clay got up and leisurely began to pull on his clothes.

Reina wished she could throw something at him and wipe that arrogant, superior smirk off his face.

"I'll be waiting for you on deck," Clay told her coldly. "Don't be too long or I'll come looking for you."

It was a threat Reina knew he'd keep, so she said nothing as he left the cabin. The minute he shut the door behind him, though, she picked up her hairbrush and threw it furiously at the closed portal. It bounced off the door and clattered harmlessly to the floor while she continued to seethe in frustration.

It was much later in the day when Reina stood at the rail of the ship, enjoying the feel of the wind whipping around her as they sped ever southward. After being cooped up in the cabin for so many hours, just being out-of-doors was wonderful. The warmth of the late afternoon sun combined with the fresh air buoyed her spirits considerably. She didn't doubt for a moment that she was going to find a way to rid herself of the obnoxious, tenacious Clay Cordell.

Reina knew she couldn't go to the captain. Not that he didn't appear to be a nice man. She'd met him earlier in the day when they'd first come up on deck, and he'd seemed decent enough. It was just that what Clay had said was true. Her reputation would be thoroughly compromised if she tried to tell anyone on board the truth about her situation.

Coming up with a whole new way to escape her captor's clutches was proving a challenge, considering where they were, but she already had another idea. There were a few days left before they reached Panama and made port. She had that much time to put her new plan into action. She would start tonight, at dinner. It just might work.

Clay was standing across the deck talking with the captain while he kept a careful watch over his bride.

"Lovely young woman, your missus," Captain Gibson, a barrel-chested, full-bearded, gray-haired, mountain of a man, observed as he regarded Reina's trim figure with open male appreciation.

"Thank you. I think so, too." Clay realized his words were true. He did think her beautiful, and he was touched with the kind of pride a husband might have. It annoyed him.

"Are you two heading for the gold fields like everyone else?" Gibson pried.

"No. My wife is from California. Her family is there."

"I'm looking forward to our dining together this evening and getting to know her better. She looks like quite a charming lady," the captain said, his gaze still resting on Reina, for she was by far the most attractive female on the boat.

The ship's master's appreciative gaze was beginning to stir an emotion in Clay he would never recognize—jealousy. It struck a raw nerve, and he grew tense and uncomfortable as they continued to talk. He noticed a handsome young man join Reina at the rail, and he thought the fair-haired youth far too attentive where she was concerned. He didn't like it one bit, and in spite of himself, he scowled blackly.

"Excuse me, Captain Gibson. I think I shall see to my wife," Clay bit out tersely, striding straight across the deck to where Reina was chatting with the young man.

Gibson watched him go, and he chuckled to himself. *Cordell's one jealous man, and I got a feeling that that pretty, little bride of his is going to run him ragged. She's a beauty, and men are drawn to her like a magnet. He's going to be one busy man if he thinks he can keep them away from her and keep her all to himself.*

Clay's features were like carved granite when he stopped by her side, interrupting her lighthearted repartee with the gallant, would-be suitor. He told himself that the only reason he was angry was because he thought she might be up to something. Why else?

"Darling," he stressed the word as he took possessive hold of her arm. "Are you going to introduce me to your friend?"

"Of course," Reina said tautly, "Michael Webster, this is my husband, Clay Cordell. Clay, this is Michael Webster. Michael's going to California, too."

Clay bristled. Considering that she'd just met the young fellow, he thought she was being much too familiar in addressing him by his first name. "How nice for you, Mr. Webster."

"Yes, it should be exciting. I've heard a lot about California. I'm really looking forward to it," Michael reported cheerfully, ignorant of the dangerous undercurrent that lurked just beneath Clay's civilized veneer.

"Reina, don't you think it's time we went below?" Clay turned away from the young man, in an attempt to cut him dead, but Reina wouldn't allow it.

"I'd really rather not just yet, sweetheart," she emphasized the endearment. "It's such a beautiful day out, and you know how much I hated being forced to stay in our cabin when I was feeling so ill before." She faced him fully, meeting his glowering silver stare without flinching.

"You did say you wanted to rest up before dinner, though, didn't you?" he came back at her, not giving her an easy out.

Reina's eyes flashed fire, and she refused to be coerced into going along with him. "I really feel quite fine, dear, but if you want to go back to the cabin for a while, go right ahead."

Clay was about to erupt. He'd never had a woman so openly defy him before. "I really would prefer you come with me, darling. I'm sure we'll see Mr. Webster later at dinner." He tightened his hold on her arm in a subtly threatening gesture that only she was aware of.

Reina knew she'd pushed him as far as she dared for right now. Smiling at the unsuspecting Michael, she turned the full power of her potent female charm on him. "My husband needs me, Michael. If you'll excuse me 'til later?"

"Yes, ma'am," Michael responded, beaming.

"We will be seeing you at dinner tonight, won't we?" She made sure to include her husband in her question.

"You surely will, Mrs. Cordell," he promised eagerly.

She gave him a gracious nod as Clay led her away. They appeared the perfect couple as he es-

215

corted her below, and more than a few eyes followed their progress with silent approval.

Clay didn't speak again until they reached the privacy of their cabin. Only then did he allow himself to explode. "What the hell did you think you were doing out there?" he demanded.

"I was having a simple conversation with a very nice, very *lonely,* young man," Reina explained simply. She was pleased that she could stay so remarkably calm on the surface, while deep inside she wanted to rage at him that it was none of his business what she did or who she did it with.

"I don't care how lonely young Webster is. I don't care if the man doesn't have a friend in the world!" Clay ground out. "It's going to stop, and it's going to stop now."

Reina regarded him from beneath lowered lashes. If she hadn't known better, she might have thought him jealous, but that couldn't be. If there was one thing Clay Cordell wasn't, that was jealous of her.

"I agreed to go along with your little charade of pretending to be married, but that's all I agreed to!"

"You're supposed to be acting like a married woman."

"I didn't know that married women weren't allowed to have conversations with other passengers," Reina challenged.

"Not with single men. I've seen you work your wiles on men. An innocent like Webster would be putty in your hands. I want you to stay away from him. Leave him alone."

Reina wondered how he could have come to have such a low opinion of her. He didn't really know her. It enraged her that Clay thought her decadent enough to try to seduce the youth. The only thing she wanted from Michael Webster was his help in escaping, if the opportunity ever arose.

"There's a big difference between you and Michael Webster, Clay. He's—"

"You're right," he cut her off in mid-statement. "There's a damn big difference. He's a boy still wet behind the ears, and I'm a man. You'd do well to remember that."

"I was about to say," Reina continued with precision, ignoring him. "There's a big difference, Clay. Michael Webster is a gentleman."

"I'll tell you what," Clay said smoothly when she'd finished. "I'll act like the gentleman you say I'm not, if you'll act like a lady."

Clay's barbed comment left Reina seething, but she held herself in check. This was not the time or place to push him further right now. She had to wait, bide her time.

"I never forget that I'm a lady, although you seem to have," she replied with dignity.

"I never knew it to forget it," Clay countered hatefully.

Reina wished their stateroom was ten times bigger so she could get away from him and his overbearing ways for a while. But she knew there was little hope of any real privacy for her between here and California. If anything, it seemed that Clay was even more determined than ever not to let her out of his sight.

Reina pretended as though nothing he'd said had bothered her in the least, and she went on about the business of getting ready for dinner. She drew the one nice evening gown Emilie had packed out of the trunk and smoothing the wrinkles from it, she spread it out on her half of the bed. It was a teal blue gown that, while not as dramatic or as eye-catching as her gold gown, certainly paid full tribute to her loveliness.

Clay took the seat near the bed and sat there watching her as she moved calmly and efficiently about the cabin laying out her clothes for the evening. His expression was closed to her, and she never knew of the tumultuous emotions stirring within him. He was trying to figure out why he'd gotten so angry over the incident on deck, and he couldn't quite put his finger on it. He only knew that from now on he was going to keep Reina with him. He was sure his chances of getting her back to California would be much better as long as he carefully monitored everything she did.

With still over an hour to go before the evening meal would be served, Clay found that he was growing more and more restless in his self-imposed surveillance of Reina. In the confined space of the cabin, he was becoming more and more conscious of her. The trimness of her figure and the gentle sway of her hips as she moved about the room all heightened his perception of her as a woman, and that was something he was trying to forget.

When Reina dabbed a touch of her favorite perfume at her wrists and throat, Clay stifled a groan. The scent she used was special, a delicate, spicy, floral perfume that seemed to have been made only for her, and it was a heady scent and very potent to his senses. The elusive fragrance would always remind him of their passionate encounter at the Randolphs', and much to his regret, it would always have the power to stir him. He tore his gaze away from her and tried to think of something else less disturbing.

Reina wanted to finish getting ready for dinner, but the only things she had left to do were her more private, more feminine duties. Since Clay had cruelly accused her of not being a lady, she was determined to show him just how modest she could be.

"Clay . . ."

"What?" he sounded particularly surly.

"I'd appreciate it if you'd leave the cabin for a

while. I have a few personal things I have to do, and I'd like some time alone."

"Sorry," his answer was flat and unyielding. "I'm staying."

Reina couldn't believe he was refusing to go.

"Clay, be reasonable," she argued. "Why would you want to stay in here and watch me get ready? Surely, there's something else you could be doing."

"Actually, there really isn't. Keeping tabs on you is my most important duty, Reina."

"But I need some privacy," she protested.

"You just go ahead and do what you have to do. I'll stand here at the window out of your way."

"You . . ."

"Yes, my dear?" he taunted, then went on. "If we're playing husband and wife, it wouldn't look too good if every time you have to change clothes you make me leave the room."

"If anyone asked, you could just tell them I'm the bashful type."

Clay gave a jeering laugh. "I don't mind a half-truth now and then, but after everybody saw you in action with Webster this afternoon, I doubt that tale would hold up for long."

Reina gave him a chilling look, but it didn't bother Clay in the least that she was angry. It wasn't his job to please her. It was his job to get her home to her father in one piece.

"I'm afraid, whether you like it or not, you're stuck in enforced intimacy with me all the way to Monterey." He smiled.

Reina managed to hold back the shriek of fury that threatened. She stood there, her expression calm, waiting. When he didn't move right away, she demanded, "Well?"

Clay's grin turned mocking at her unspoken yielding. Feeling quietly victorious, he moved to the small window to look out at the sea. To his absolute delight, he found he could see her reflection quite clearly in the glass as she stood at the foot of the bed staring at him resentfully.

"It's safe now, Reina. I can't see a thing," he lied.

"Thank you," she muttered irritably as she started to unbutton her dress.

"You're welcome. You know, I certainly wouldn't want to offend your delicate sensibilities by seeing you undressed, although, it certainly would be anti-climactic. I mean I have already seen you in a certain state of deshabille."

"It's very crude of you to bring that up," Reina said icily.

"Crude? It was a rather pleasant experience at the time," he chuckled at the annoyance in her tone.

"Why don't you just forget that it ever happened? We both know it didn't mean anything. It was a mistake that'll never be repeated."

"You're right that it didn't mean anything," he agreed with her assessment thoughtfully. "But don't think it happened by mistake, Reina. I was determined to get you alone, and I picked what seemed to be the easiest way to do it."

Reina was glad that Clay couldn't see her, because she flushed painfully at his revelation. It was obvious that he'd thought her less than virtuous from the very beginning, and she hadn't helped matters any by almost giving herself to him completely. He'd been totally blind to the fact that she'd been in danger of falling madly in love with him. He'd thought that she'd been acting through the whole thing, teasing and taunting him just as he'd been teasing and taunting her.

The knowledge was painful, but Reina was glad for it. As long as he continued to believe that she'd been just playing a role, she would be saved from any further humiliation at his hands. It would never do for Clay to find out that she really had felt something for him, if only for a little while.

"How fortunate that I made it so easy for you." The sarcasm was evident in her voice.

"If that hadn't worked, there would have been other times and other places. Rest assured, Reina, I'd have found a way," Clay answered with confidence. "I wasn't about to let you get away from me a second time."

Reina smiled to herself as she began to disrobe. Clay was feeling quite superior right now, but if she had anything to say about it, his mood wasn't going to last very long. Soon there *would be* a second escape! All they had to do was make landfall. Once the ship made port, she'd be gone, and this time she'd make sure he would never be able to find her!

As Reina undressed, dreaming of her triumphant getaway, she was completely unaware of Clay watching her every move. He had begun this folly, thinking the trick on Reina. But as his desire for her stirred unbidden, he realized too late that he was the one who would suffer from his ploy. Cursing himself for his stupidity, he fought against the longing that filled him. In misery, he recognized that it was going to be one very long night.

Chapter Seventeen

Reina was still angry as Clay escorted her to the ship's sumptuous dining room a short time later. His dictatorial demand that she not speak to Michael Webster any more had left her silently fuming. She'd hoped Michael would prove to be the one ally she needed in this ordeal, and she wasn't about to change her plans just because Clay thought she wasn't acting like a married woman.

Anyway, she thought fiercely as they swept into the richly, wood-panelled room, *just who did Clay think he was, trying to tell her what to do?* Stubborn and headstrong as she was, Reina was determined to pay him back. Even if she only made his life miserable for a little while, it would well be worth it. Feeling very daring, she lifted her chin in an unconscious gesture of confidence and girded herself for the evening to come. They had been invited to dine with the captain; Reina couldn't have been more delighted to see that Michael Webster was also seated at their table.

As Clay led her across the room, Michael saw them coming and immediately got to his feet. He rushed forward from the table to welcome her, his expression eager. To Clay's way of thinking he looked almost puppyish, and when Reina greeted him openly and warmly, he tensed.

Reina had never dreamed everything would work out so perfectly, and she smiled brightly as Michael rushed to her side.

"Mrs. Cordell, I'm so glad we've been seated at the same table." Michael had seen her smile, was sure it was just for him. If possible, he fell even more deeply under her spell. He was unaware of anything, save Reina's presence in the room. She was an angel, a goddess.

"So am I, Michael," Reina responded and she meant it.

"I was wanting to talk to you some more after our time on the deck, and this is going to be perfect."

"Yes, it will be," she agreed, totally ignoring Clay standing by her side.

Clay was seething. The boy was practically drooling all over her right here in front of everybody! He didn't like the way Webster eyed her so hungrily or the way he hung on her every word. Clay wanted to grab him by the scruff of the neck and shake some sense into him, but he knew this was neither the time or the place. Although it wasn't easy, with a concerted effort, he managed to control himself.

"Perhaps we should go on and sit down?" Clay prodded tersely as he spied the captain looking their way.

"Oh, yes . . ." Webster was a bit shaken by the realization that he'd been so oblivious to everything and everyone but Mrs. Cordell. "Sorry. Evening, Cordell."

"Good evening, Webster." Clay's was a strained civilized greeting. He led the way to where Gibson awaited them, drawing Reina along with him in a possessive move that left the youth alone to follow.

223

Captain Gibson had been watching the exchange, enjoying it in his own dry-humored way. The Cordell woman was a looker, and though Webster was a handsome enough boy, he stood no chance at all in competition with her husband. Cordell was a full-blooded male, a man's man. It was easy to see just by his stance and actions that he would tolerate no interference with his wife. Gibson hoped the youth caught on before any trouble broke out between them. In any kind of fight, the kid wouldn't last a minute against the husband. He rose to greet the three of them as they came forward.

"Good evening, Mrs. Cordell, Mr. Cordell. Ma'am, if I may be so bold, you are a lovely sight tonight," Gibson complimented in a booming voice. "You grace my ship with your beauty."

"Why, captain, you're too kind," Reina replied sweetly, turning on her charm. She was very much aware of Clay's glowering presence beside her, but she was not going to allow him to intimidate her in any way.

"I'm not being kind, my dear," he countered. "I'm a New England Yankee, through and through. I make it a practice to only speak the truth, and this evening, you are a vision to behold."

"And I agree, Mrs. Cordell!" Webster put in hastily, enraptured as he hurried forth to pull out the chair next to his for her.

"Well, thank you, both." Reina smiled graciously.

Clay, having no choice in the matter, directed Reina to the chair Webster held out.

Reina could sense that he was annoyed, and she was glad as she sat down gracefully, bestowing glowing smiles on both the other men. *Let Clay be irritated!* she thought with glee. *What did she care?* He meant nothing to her. He was her captor, her unwanted guardian, her miserable jailer. Every minute she was forced to endure his domination. His cocksure attitude annoyed her so much that she was eager to prod him here in public. She wanted to let him know in no uncertain terms that he could not tell her what to do.

Clay was fully and completely frustrated. He couldn't remember the last time he'd encountered so much trouble doing something so simple. All he had to do was get Reina back to California. After seeing her lift her chin in that subtly defiant move, he'd known for sure that he was going to be in for a rough night. She was a willful wench, and he was going to have a devil of a time controlling her. *Hell*, Clay thought in misery, *bringing in Ace Denton had been child's play compared to this.*

Clay ignored the compliments the men were heaping on Reina as he sat down to her left. He didn't care for the seating arrangements, but there was nothing he could do about it without coming across as either jealous or foolish. Still, it was much too intimate, as far as he was concerned. Clay would have preferred a massive, eight-foot-long plank table like the crew used in the galley with Reina at one end and Webster at the other, rather than this rather private setting.

As soon as everyone was comfortably seated, Michael immediately engaged Reina in conversation, and she responded without reserve, just as Clay feared she would. He realized then the mistake he'd made in trying to force her to behave. As self-centered and stubborn as she was, he should have known that she would react exactly the opposite of how he'd wanted her to act. He cursed himself for being so short-sighted, but at the time, his temper was flaring.

As the two of them talked on, their light, easy-going, unconcerned comments began to grate on

225

Clay's nerves. He drank his glass of wine, then had another. When Gibson asked him a few questions in an attempt to begin a discussion of their own, Clay's answers were abrupt and discouraged any further talk. He refilled his glass and told himself that he didn't want to talk because he didn't want to be distracted from Reina. He had to keep track of what she was doing.

Clay glanced at Webster and saw that the youth was completely taken with her. He was listening raptly to her every word, his eyes upon her adoringly. His gaze swung to Reina then, and he saw that she was looking at him quite fondly.

Anger seared Clay. *Reina was having one helluva good time at his expense!* He knew she was using Webster just to make him mad, and he didn't dare give her the satisfaction of knowing she was succeeding. She was too quick and too bright to give her an inch. His baser desires urged him to grab Reina by the arm and haul her back down to their cabin. He wanted to lock her away there, safe from the young man's avid gaze. Instead, he was forced by circumstances to sit there beside Reina, acting as if her openly flirtatious ways were harmless . . . just an everyday occurrence that he tolerated because he loved her.

The meal began. Course after course of delicious food was placed before them, but the business of eating did not deter Michael Webster from trying to dominate Reina's attention. He bombarded her with questions, and she blatantly encouraged him with quick answers and friendly smiles. Michael was enthralled. He had never met a woman as sophisticated and beautiful as Reina Cordell. He thought her about the most wonderful woman he'd ever known, and he hated the fact that she was married. Michael wondered if Cordell knew what a lucky man he was to have her for his very own.

Clay ate what was placed before him, but it was all tasteless to him. He just wished the damned dinner would be over.

Gibson could see that Webster was enamored with the beauteous Mrs. Cordell. He could also see that her husband was not at all happy with the way she and the young man were carrying on. Remembering the incident on deck that afternoon, he decided to try to defuse the situation himself.

"Mrs. Cordell," Gibson interrupted them smoothly, "I understand that you have family in California?" He garnered an irritated glance from Michael for cutting in on their conversation, but he didn't care.

Reina wanted to deny her father's very existence, but for the sake of outward harmony, went along. "Why, yes, I do. My father's ranch — Rancho Alvarez is just outside of Monterey. It's quite a showplace He's very proud of it." Bitterly, she believed that he loved the ranch far more than he loved her.

"That is a beautiful area," the captain agreed.

"I was telling Captain Gibson this afternoon, how eager you are to return home," Clay explained tightly.

"Oh, yes. I'm definitely looking forward to our making landfall." Reina meant every word. "How much longer will it be?"

"For us, barring bad weather, we'll be at sea at least five more days," Gibson answered.

Five more days, Reina groaned mentally.

"After that," the captain was saying, "you still have to cross the Isthmus and then take another vessel up the west coast."

"It sounds like it'll be an eternity before I see my father again." Reina's emotions were torn at the thought. She'd had a close relationship with her

227

father all her life, and it hurt to think that had all changed. She wished things could be as they used to be, but she wondered if that would ever be possible again. Nathan Marlow stood between them now.

Smitten as he was, Michael wanted only to please her. Trying to brighten her day, he didn't think about how his idea would sound to her husband.

"I'll be glad to help you pass the time," Michael offered quickly, dreaming of spending endless wonderful hours in her company, escorting her around the deck, listening to her delightful laugh. She was such an excellent conversationalist and so lovely to look upon that he thought it heaven just to be with her.

Reina was a bit surprised by his suggestion, but was not about to discourage him. She accepted graciously, "Why, that's very kind of you, Michael . . ."

Reina's ploy stoked Clay's blazing fury to even greater heights. Wanting to put the young interloper in his place once and for all, Clay slipped an arm possessively across the back of Reina's chair. His gaze was steely as it met Michael's across the table.

"The lady does have a husband, Webster," he said in a flat, but dangerous voice.

Michael flushed as he realized how forward he'd been. "Sorry, Cordell . . . I . . . um . . ."

"It's all right, Michael. I'm sure Clay understands you were just being nice." Reina spoke up in his defense, her dark gaze gleaming with challenge as she met Clay's.

The heat of Clay's anger burned in his eyes and in every muscle in his body. Had Reina known him better, she would have realized just how dangerous a line she was treading. Clay Cordell was the type of man who could be pushed only so far. Reina, however, was unaware that she'd just reached the point of no return.

Furious with her, Clay leaned closer. In an exaggerated whisper, he said, "It was nice of Webster to be thoughtful, love. But if you find the trip boring, my darling bride, I can think of many more *enjoyable* ways to pass the time than by walking the deck or making idle conversation. I'm sure you know what I mean." He lifted one curl from her shoulder and rubbed it between his fingers in a sensual gesture that declared his private ownership to those looking on.

Though to the world Clay appeared the adoring, doting husband, Reina heard the ice in his tone and saw the flintiness in his eyes. A tingle of fear threatened, but she ignored it. Let him be angry! She didn't care. He was not going to intimidate her. He deserved every bit of this and much, much more.

"Oh, I'm not bored in the least, Clay, darling," Reina returned, "It's just, you know how anxious I am to be home with my father, and sometimes the time does pass so slowly. You know how miserable I was when I was indisposed and couldn't leave the cabin . . ."

Clay responded through gritted teeth, "Oh, yes, I know very well how miserable you were and how very anxious you are to go home to your father."

"Have you been away from home long, Mrs. Cordell?" Gibson asked.

"Far too long, Captain," Clay answered for Reina. "Her father's missed her greatly and is most eager to have her back."

"There's nothing quite like a loving family waiting for you at home," the captain agreed.

Reina wanted to shout at the good captain that she didn't want to go back, that the loving home

229

she'd grown up in didn't seem to exist any more! She wanted to cry out that Rancho Alvarez must mean more to her father than she did, for he hadn't even bothered to come after her. He'd sent Clay in his stead. But she remained quiet.

"Do you come from a large family, Mrs. Cordell?" Michael asked, having recovered from Clay's curt remark.

"No, my family's quite small, really," she declined to be more specific, not really wanting to talk about her father. "What about you, Michael?"

Encouraged, Michael launched into a long dissertation about his oversized family.

Clay saw red as Reina turned more fully in her chair to face Webster. She made it plain that she was giving him her undivided attention and she smiled warmly as she encouraged him to talk about himself.

"That's quite a large brood you come from," Reina told him. "It must be nice having so many brothers and sisters."

Clay wondered in irritation what it mattered to her what size family the boy had. He couldn't care less if Webster had thirty sisters and four hundred brothers! Wanting to distract Reina from the avid young man, he commented, "I know we haven't talked much about having a family, love, but perhaps one day soon we'll be having our own baby. I'm particularly fond of children and would have no objection to quite a few, if you're so inclined."

Reina had been caught by surprise by his comments, and she took them as snide. She turned a fiery regard on him. "I do want children some day, but I don't think I'm ready just yet."

"We mustn't keep your father waiting too long. You know, we're his only hope for grandchildren since your sister entered the convent."

Her gaze hardened at his taunt. "That's very true, darling," she stressed the endearment. "Mary Regina definitely won't be having any children." She deliberately turned back to Michael. "Tell me more about your family, Michael. Were they upset when you left home?"

He shrugged. "I'll miss them a lot, but we need the money. I'm never going to have a chance to get rich back there, so this is about my only hope to really make it big. I'll start sending money back to help out just as soon as I can start making some."

"That's very noble of you," Reina was honestly impressed with his sincerity and his determination to make good. She didn't know if he'd find gold or not, but she hoped he found some way to make his fortune when he got to California.

Clay sat there, barely able to contain his irritation as the boy seemed to swell with pride over Reina's praise. It aggravated Clay that she was making him out to be some kind of a knight in shining armor and it annoyed him greatly that Webster was believing it. He seemed to be hanging on her every word, gazing at her with stars in his eyes, and his precious bride was enjoying every minute of it and not discouraging him in any way. Clay's annoyance was rapidly threatening to turn to full-blown anger at her playing him for a fool here in public. As soon as he could manage it, he was going to drag her out of there and set her straight about a few things.

"I've always envied you men," Reina said honestly.

"Why?" Michael asked.

"Well, you wanted to take a big chance and go to California, so you are. That's exciting. You're free to do what you want. Now, take my husband and me, for example. Our life's really quite dull and very restricted. There's little excitement." Rena said

231

with hidden delight.

Clay tensed at her implied insult. "I didn't know it was excitement you wanted, darling." Reina glanced at him, and she saw the unspoken threat in the depths of his gaze.

"Every woman wants some excitement in her life. She also longs for the power to make choices for herself," she said pointedly, her eyes holding his momentarily.

"I don't understand," Michael put in, decidedly confused. "I thought women wanted to be protected and cared for."

Reina almost groaned, thinking of how her father had always told her that he would take care of her and see that she was protected. He'd lied. She'd been helpless before the power of his authority over her.

"They do to a certain extent," Reina began, "but they want to have a voice in their own destinies. Our opinions are never asked. Sometimes, we aren't even consulted about matters that deal directly with our very lives. You see, we're not free to make our own decisions the way you men are. Why, first we're dominated by our fathers, who give us absolutely no voice in matters directly concerning us and our welfare. Then, when we marry, we're forced to be completely submissive to our husband's wishes, no matter what."

Clay reacted angrily to her words, his eyes narrowing dangerously as he took her hand and brought her attention back to him. There was a smile on his handsome face, but it was a cold one.

"But, darling, you're giving everyone the wrong impression," Clay protested in a mild tone that belied his mood. "It's not that way between us. Force has never been a part of our relationship." *Yet,* he added in his mind. Then, sounding as if he

232

was teasing, he went on, "Now that I know you feel this way, though, I promise that we'll discuss everything you want to discuss from now on, including which of my wishes you don't want to submit to." He gave her a knowing look. "Although, I never knew you to be so shy about such things before . . ."

Reina felt the heat of a blush sting her cheeks as mortification washed over her. She wondered how Clay dared to say those things, but even as her fury grew, she knew how he dared. He had her trapped, and he knew it. She longed to strike out at him, but she couldn't. *Some day, Clay Cordell!* she swore to herself. *Some day!*

Seeing how upset Reina became, Michael was embarrassed for her. He wished he could defend her honor in some fashion, but he knew he had no right to say anything. He wondered why she had married such a man in the first place.

"It really surprises me to find you feel this way, Reina," Clay continued almost philosophically. He'd found his excuse for getting out of there, and he was fully intending to use it. "Maybe, dear wife, we need to discuss this at greater length, in private — if we're going to remain so happily married."

Reina stifled a gasp of indignation as Clay stood up and drew her to her feet with him.

"Captain, Mr. Webster, if you'll excuse us?" Clay was coolly precise as he made their excuses.

"Of course, Mr. Cordell," Gibson answered, his eyes alight with admiration for him. He'd been wondering just how long Cordell would stand for his wife's unusual friendship with Webster. He was pleased to find that the other man was a lot like himself — a strong believer in the old school that women needed a firm hand to keep them in line. The captain was certain that the Cordell marriage would be a good, long and happy one.

"Good night, Mrs. Cordell," Michael said softly, miserable that the evening was coming to an end so soon.

"Good night, Michael. Perhaps I'll see you tomorrow on deck."

"That'd be wonderful!" He brightened almost immediately.

"And Captain Gibson, thank you for dinner. It was a splendid meal," Reina told him graciously.

"Thank you, ma'am."

"Gentlemen." Clay gave a brief nod of dismissal and led Reina from the dining room.

Chapter Eighteen

Reina carried herself with regal dignity as Clay ushered her out of the dining room into the passageway. She kept her head held high as he practically dragged her along to their cabin. His grip on her arm was almost painful, but Reina was not about to let him know it hurt. She had too much pride for that. As they reached their stateroom, Clay opened the door and stood back to let her go in first. When she defied him, refusing to go obediently, she tested his temper even further.

"Get in there," he seethed in a low, dangerous voice.

Reina was furious. She heard the threat in his tone, but refused to heed it. She would not show any fear before him. Chin up, she marched inside. She lit a lamp as Clay followed her inside. Once the door was closed, she whirled around, attacking him full-force before he could say a word.

"How dare you, Clay Cordell!" she snarled, her eyes flashing fire.

"Shut up, Reina, before you push me too far," Clay returned ominously.

"Push you too far?" she raged. "You've pushed me too far! How could you embarrass me that way? How could you say those things in front of Michael!"

Her throwing Michael up to him at that moment broke the last thread of tenuous control Clay had over his wrath. He had not intended to get physical with her, but all rational thought fled. Grabbing her by the arms, he hauled her bodily up against him.

"Michael . . . what the hell do I care what Michael Webster thinks about anything?" he ground out savagely. "There's only one thing that's important to me! There's only one thing I care about!"

"Oh, yes. I know all about what's important to you!" she taunted. "Money is what you care about . . . only money!" She fought to get free of him, struggling against his hold, as she threw the words at him in a verbal slap. "You don't care about honor and decency! You're an amoral bastard!"

Clay gave a vicious chuckle as he worked to control her. "And you're such a model of virtue?" he demeaned, thinking of her betrayal of her fiancé and the misery she'd caused her father. "I pity your father, and I pity the man who wants you. You're a lying, deceitful, self-centered, little coward. At least, I keep my word."

"Your word?" she seethed, pounding on his chest with her fists. "Your word isn't worth the breath it's spoken with! You'd probably double-cross your own mother if you thought you'd profit by it!"

Her statement just stoked the flame of his own fury that much hotter. Releasing her arms and quickly seizing her wrists to stop her from hitting him. With one easy move, he'd twisted her arms behind her back, effectively subduing her, and yanked her tight against his chest.

"You might as well give it up, Reina. You've lost."

"I concede nothing," she declared arrogantly. She glared up at him, her features flushed from the exertion of her fight.

Clay shrugged. "It doesn't make any difference to

236

me whether you do or not. All I care about is the job I was hired to do. I'm taking you back to your father, with or without your cooperation."

"You can try," she challenged, still trying hard to break away.

As Clay stared down at her, he couldn't stop the reluctant admiration he was feeling. If nothing else, she was a fighter. Even against such overwhelming odds, she refused to surrender to the inevitable.

"It's not a matter of trying. I'll do it," he said with finality.

"Oh, you. . . !" She gave a tremendous jerk, trying to break away once and for all.

The effort didn't surprise Clay in the least, and he reacted accordingly, yanking her back even closer. All too late, he realized his mistake. She slammed against him, her slender curves pressed far too intimately against him. He could feel every inch of her body as he held her pinioned there. He froze, suddenly, achingly aware of her as a woman.

"Let me go!" She writhed ineffectually, trying to get free, but her actions only stirred his tight-reined ardor all the more.

At the silken feel of her in his arms, his fury waned. His concern for Dev faded. His emotions were in turmoil, and his silver eyes darkened as heat surged through him. He wanted Reina! He had since the first moment he'd laid eyes on her, and that desire had only grown with time. Watching her dress earlier had only teased his senses. Touching her now was more than he could bear.

Reina seemed to sense a sudden change in him and she looked up. She gasped at the intensity she saw in his gaze. "Let me go, Clay!"

"I can't," he groaned, not thinking of escape. "Not now. Not when I've finally found you . . ."

Reina tensed at the naked desire reflected in the stormy gray depths.

"No, Clay . . ." she began to protest, but she had no time to say more as Clay's mouth descended to hers, claiming her lips in a demanding exchange.

Reina began to fight again. She didn't want this. She didn't want him! But as his mouth moved persuasively over hers, her struggles weakened. This was no longer Clay, her captor, but Clay, the man . . . the man she'd thought she'd loved only a short time before.

"Don't . . ." she whispered in hoarse protest when his mouth left hers, but he ignored her.

When he bent to seek the sweetness of her throat, a small whimper escaped her. She shivered at the ecstasy of his touch. When he released her hands, she pushed ineffectually against his chest for a moment. But that resistance ended completely as he caressed the full mound of her breast. Passion long-denied exploded within her. With a groan of surrender, she ceased her struggle and melted willingly against the hard wall of his chest.

Anger and some other equally powerful emotion mixed together in a tempest of excitement. They were caught up in a maelstrom of need.

Clay kissed her once more, deepening the kiss this time. They drank of each other, tasting of the wine of their desire. They had refused to recognize it for too long. They had fought it for too long. Their consuming passion could no longer be held back, no longer be denied.

Breathlessly, they clung together. They refused to think about what was happening between them. There was no time for logic. There was time only to feel, to react, to give in to the rampant need that burned hotly within them both and which they were both finally acknowledging.

Reina groaned softly in anticipation as his lips left hers to explore the hollow of her throat once more, seeking out that sensitive pulse point. Clay lifted her easily into his arms, kissing her passionately as he laid her upon the bed. He moved to lie beside her, and in that instant, their gazes locked.

It would have been the time to put a stop to the madness that was engulfing them. It would have been the time to throw accusations at one another and break apart in brittle hatred, but it did not happen. Instead, Clay bent to her with loving intent, his lips brushing hers with short, tender-soft kisses until Reina reached up and drew him down to her for a full, flaming exchange, murmuring his name in almost exquisite agony as she did so.

"Clay . . ."

"Ah . . . Reina," came his answer, and her name was a moan of pure desire.

He moved over her, settling his weight upon her, and she welcomed him with open arms. Reina knew this was what she'd always wanted, ever since that day on the stage . . . ever since that night at the waystation.

Clay worked the buttons at her bodice, freeing her breasts to his ardent caresses, and she was enraptured. As he shifted lower to press hot, wet kisses to that silken flesh, she held him close, savoring his practiced touch.

A yearning grew deep within the womanly heart of her, and Reina knew it was a need only Clay could satisfy. She wanted him desperately. No other man had ever stirred such wild, wonderful emotions within her. It was almost as if she couldn't get close enough to him, as if she couldn't get enough of his kisses or touch. She never wanted this to end.

He rose above her to capture her lips once more. This time it was a tender kiss, but a kiss that held such promise, Reina felt dizzy from the power of it.

"I want you, Reina," he declared in a love-husky voice. "I want you more than I've ever wanted any woman."

"I want you, too," she whispered, drawing him back for another kiss. She didn't want to talk. She only wanted Clay, and the joy that would come from knowing him fully.

At her invitation, Clay could wait no longer. Impatiently, he began to strip away the gown and underclothing that she'd just so carefully donned a few short hours before. He remembered watching her reflection in the cabin window, and the heat of the memory fueled his passion to even greater heights.

When he moved over her again and kissed her, Reina was ready. It felt right . . . so right — the crush of her full breasts against the fine, soft fabric of his shirt, the shock of his belt buckle, cold against her belly, the long, lean length of his muscle-hardened thighs against her soft, unclad ones.

Clay caressed her silken limbs, his hands never resting as they traced pattern after arousing pattern across her satiny skin. He cupped her breasts, laving them with kisses, then moved lower to tease the slender curve of her waist. He shifted up to kiss her again as he stroked her velvety thighs, urging them apart. He explored the heat and desire nestled between them, his caresses seeking the dark, sweet entrance to her love.

Reina arched upward in surprise at his boldness, but almost immediately relaxed at his murmured urging. He began a rhythmic massage then that transported her and left her enthralled and almost mindless in her pleasure.

"Clay . . . oh Clay . . ." Reina found herself moving with him, matching his caress.

He quickened his touch. He wanted to please Reina, to show her the delight that could be found when passion was sated. Throbbing desire pulsed deep within her and seemed to gain strength as his ardent caress became more and more arousing. It

seeme
bod

he coaxed
e was startled
wing caresses
more. It sur-
now that she
o easily and
had pleased
oloring the
with her
er to his
d at her
ne pride.
an could
good to
as he

re spi-
onger
g his
n to
an
nd
he
g

ding a response from her experienced before. When more with hungry kisses, for the heart-stopping ex- in her.

ms as ecstasy raced hands clutched at him, wave after wave of pure . His name escaped her wonder as she was swept e of love. When the last had died, Reina lay weakly, lay's now-cradling embrace. at her, his gray eyes stormy ions neither could begin to un- nordinately proud that he'd given had never known a woman so touch, and he never wanted to let

he whispered.

s flew open at the sound of his voice, pression was soft and unguarded. She her eyes drifted shut as he bent to kiss more.

ever of Clay's own, barely-controlled desire ll demanding release.

need you," he said slowly in between, passion- drugging kisses.

Reina could feel the hard, proud heat of him pressing urgently against her through his clothing. She wanted to know the perfection of loving him, of joining with him, of knowing him as only a woman can know a man. "Yes, yes . . . please . . ."

Her encouragement sent his senses soaring, and he left her only long enough to shed his clothing. Joining her back on the bed, Reina gasped at the feel of his hot male body next to hers.

"Clay . . . I . . ."

"Hush, just let me love you," before kissing her again.

Reina had felt so languid that sh when Clay's fervent kisses and kn stirred the fire of her passion once prised her, but it also thrilled her to k could respond to Clay so fully and s cause the same reaction in him.

Wanting to please him as much as he her, she began to return his touch, ex vast, muscle-sculpted width of his chest own arousing caresses then moving low waist and stomach. When Clay groane sensual ploy, Reina knew a burst of femini She had never realized what power a wom exert over a man, and it made her feel know that she could arouse him the same could her.

Reina's innocent brazenness sent Clay's desi ralling out of control, and he could wait no to sample of her love. He rose above her, fittin body intimately to hers.

Her eyes widened at the sensation, so foreig her femininity, yet somehow so perfect. She had understanding of what went on between a man a woman, but knew little beside the basic facts. T reality of his masculinity was much more excitin than anything she'd ever dreamed. She tensed, wai ing for whatever was to come next.

Clay did not press his possession of her at that moment, though, for he felt her go tense in expectation. Her action surprised him a bit, because he thought her a woman well-versed in the ways of men.

"Easy . . ." he told her.

He began kissing her and caressing her again until he felt the anxiety ebb from her slender form. Then with the utmost of care, he lifted her hips to receive him and, positioning himself, surged forward to enter her completely and fully.

The fact of her virginity became known to Clay only as he breached that slight barrier of her innocence. It shocked him, even as it shamed him. He stopped, holding himself rigidly still, even though his body demanded satisfaction, now that it was buried in the sweet-heat of hers.

"Reina . . ." he rasped.

Clay tried to hold back, but his passion was too strong to be long denied. His sensibilities were brushed aside when he found he could no longer hold himself in abeyance. He wanted her . . . needed her . . . couldn't wait another moment to have her.

He began to move, tenderly at first, gently plumbing the depths of her womanhood. Reina was quiescent initially, but as he continued to kiss and fondle her, her desire sparked again. She was soon meeting him in that most sensual and natural of rhythms.

At her response, Clay quickened his pace, needing to reach that pinnacle of passion's dream and wanting to take her along with him. They moved together in love's melody, surging and ebbing, giving and taking, until the rainbow of desire's storm burst upon them, showering them in the thrilling ecstasy of excitement's perfect completion.

Clay and Reina lay wrapped in each other's arms, their bodies still locked together. Neither wanted to move or speak. They wanted to cling to the peace-filled comfort of passion's aftermath. It was a time for tender caresses. A time for gentle quiet.

Clay's thoughts were completely befuddled as he held Reina close. Never in his life had he known such ecstasy. The touch of her, the scent of her, the glory of having her completely had touched him as he'd never been touched before. He closed his eyes, not wanting to think about it too deeply. It felt too perfect holding her close.

Reina rested in the circle of his arms, her head nestled on the broad width of his shoulder. Her thoughts were pleasantly distracted and far from the painful reality she would soon have to face. She didn't want to dwell on anything except the contentment she was feeling at lying in his protective embrace. A serene drowsiness soothed her, and she drew a deep breath, then gave herself over to the blissful oblivion of sleep.

Reina woke slowly, opening her eyes to the brilliant sunlight streaming through the window. Morning . . . She was just starting to stretch and roll over when the passionate memory of the night just passed jumped into her drowsy thoughts. Clay! Dear God, what had she done? She stopped all motion and turned slightly to glance at him.

The sight of her captor slumbering peacefully by her side, looking extraordinarily handsome, unnerved her. He appeared much younger in his sleep, the hard edge to his features easing, the errant lock of dark hair that fell across his forehead giving him an almost boyish look. A part of Reina wanted to reach out and brush his hair back off his face, but wisely she refrained. She didn't want him to wake up just yet. She was too confused . . . too troubled. She had to sort out her thoughts and come to grips with what had happened.

Her gaze drifted lower, visually caressing his wide, powerful shoulders and his strong, furred chest. A slightly self-conscious blush pinkened her cheeks as she remembered how wonderful it had felt to be held close against him and how erotic the crisp hair on his chest had felt against the sensitive peaks of her breasts.

Reina's glance shifted even farther down the fascinating length of him. She marvelled at how lean Clay was, for there wasn't an ounce of extra flesh on him. He was solid, rock-hard muscle. She found it particularly enticing that the hair covering his chest and stomach tantalizingly narrowed just past his waist. Her view of him was restricted from there, because the blanket was wound around his lower body.

It was then Reina recalled that they had fallen asleep naked in each other's arms. Some time during the night then, he must have roused himself enough to draw the covers over them both. An odd feeling of tenderness filled her at the thought of his action, and her thoughts grew even more confused.

This was Clay Cordell—her father's henchman . . . her nemesis . . . and now her lover. Reina wasn't sure what she felt for him. She only knew that the moment he touched her, she melted to his will. There was something about him, something so compelling that she couldn't refuse him and, in fact, didn't want to.

Reina wondered what he was feeling. She wondered if what had happened between them had been as special for him as it was for her. She felt almost certain that it had been. Their lovemaking had been beautiful. She could think of no words wonderful enough to describe it.

A smile curved her lips. Certainly, this had changed everything between them. She suddenly wanted to talk to him about it, to discuss her feelings with him. She looked up, hoping to find him awake. She was delighted to find that he was, his silver gaze resting upon her with a piercing intensity she could almost feel.

Clay watched her in silence. He wanted to trust her. He longed to think that he could. Last night had been more exciting than he'd ever dreamed it could be, but the lesson he'd learned early in life, even now, colored his thinking. He was cautious, judging her smile by his memories, and, in that judgment, concluding that it was all an act. A voice warned him that she couldn't be believed, that she would do whatever she could to achieve her own ends. He listened to her, his heart and mind already set against her.

"Clay . . ." she began hesitantly, "We have to talk. What happened last night . . ."

"Was special?" Clay offered guardedly

"Oh, yes," she said. "It was wonderful, and it changes so much between us."

When Clay had come awake to find Reina studying him intently, he'd wished for just an instant that things could be different between them, but then when she'd started talking and telling her lies, reality had set in. Her innocently offered words and sweet smile jarred him, for he knew from past experience that she didn't mean any of it. He kept his expression inscrutable as he'd listened to her, and then he asked in a particularly harsh voice, "Tell me, Reina, exactly what does it change?"

She blinked in surprise at his coldness, but her smile never wavered. "Why, everything," she said.

His eyes were totally devoid of any warmth as he continued sarcastically, "I don't think so."

"What?"

"Look, Reina, it's not going to work. I've seen how women like you operate."

"Women like me?" she repeated in innocence.

Clay gave a snort of disbelief at her pretense, and he climbed out of bed. His motions were quick and sure as he pulled on his pants. "Save it. Don't waste your time thinking that you're going to convince me you gave yourself to me last night out of any great emotion. I wouldn't believe it. I know how women use their bodies to manipulate men. If you think

246

you can use your beautiful body to get me to set you free, you're wrong. You're going home to your father."

His cold, brutal statements killed any more tender emotion she'd harbored toward him, and she berated herself for having thought things might have changed. How could she ever have forgotten that only hostility and mistrust existed between them! How could she have given herself to him that way! The fire of her fury and the power of her hatred for him glowed heatedly in her dark eyes.

"Why would I want to convince you it was a love match? There was certainly no love involved in it for me," she belittled sharply.

Her words reinforced what he'd believed from the start. It had all been an act.

"Then we both know what it was all about," Clay said coolly, shrugging on his shirt and buttoning it. He saw the fire of her hatred in her expression and knew then he'd been right all along.

"You're a predator, Clay Cordell," she charged, the anger and hurt she was feeling driving her to strike out at him. "You were sent to find me and take me back home, not take advantage of me at a time when I was helpless and unprotected!"

Her words stung. She had been a virgin. Any further guilt he might have felt was dismissed though, for he remembered that she wanted him just as much as he had wanted her. Clay gave a terse laugh. "Helpless and unprotected? You? I've never known a woman more capable of taking care of herself."

"Damn you! I hope you rot in hell!" Reina hissed.

"You aren't the first to wish that upon me, and I'm sure you won't be the last," he pointed out with a slight, mocking smile.

Tears of frustration burned her eyes, but Reina

247

fought them back. She would not let him see how he'd hurt her. She would never let him know that his cold rejection this morning was even more painful to her than her father's betrayal. She left the bed, grabbing the blanket as she went. Keeping her back to him, she wrapped it firmly around her, and without looking back, she moved stiffly away to stare out the window.

In her most icy tone, she said slowly, "Stay away from me from now on. Don't you ever touch me again!"

"You don't have to worry, Reina. What happened last night won't be repeated." He waited for a minute staring at her rigid back, then finished dressing and strode from the cabin, closing the door firmly behind him.

Chapter Nineteen

"Señor Luis!" Carlos, the six-year-old son of one of the house maids, came charging full speed into the stable in search of the ranch owner.

"He's here, Carlos!" Vicente, the head stable man, shouted from where he and his boss were standing near the rear of the building discussing business. "What is so important that you must interrupt us?" he scolded as the child came running up to them.

"My mother sent me!" the boy replied in a breathless pant, the exertion of racing all the way there having left him gasping for air. He totally ignored the stablehand then and turned to the real boss. "Señor Luis, you must come up to the main house at once!" He took Luis' hand and tugged nervously.

"Whoa, Carlos." Luis resisted the boy's effort to drag him off without an explanation. "Can't you see that I'm busy right now with Vicente? Just what is it that you feel requires my immediate attention?"

"My mother said to find you and bring you right away! She said to tell you that he was there!" Carlos blurted out.

"Who is there?" he asked, excitement gripping him as he imagined it was Cordell returning with Reina or at least word of her whereabouts.

"An American!"

The boy's words confirmed his high hopes, and he smiled widely in triumph. Reina would be home soon. He just knew it. Things were going to work out after all.

"Thank you, Carlos," Luis said happily. "Run along back up to the house and tell your mother that I will be there right away."

"Yes, sir." Grinning, knowing that he'd done well in delivering the message, he darted off in the direction of the house.

"Señor? All is well?" Vicente noticed his boss's happiness and was pleased for his mood had been particularly black lately.

"All is very well," Luis answered, his tone pleased. "I will be back later to finish our discussion."

"Yes, sir."

The distance to the house had never seemed so long to Luis as he hurried on up the path to meet with Cordell. He had known the man would show up sooner or later, he had just hoped it would be sooner. It had been well over a month ago when they'd last spoken, and he'd been waiting impatiently ever since for word from the bounty hunter about his missing daughter.

The weeks since they'd parted had been difficult for him. He'd been forced to lie to Nathan about Reina's whereabouts, telling him that she'd gone to visit an aunt who lived south of San Diego. He'd accepted the story at face value at the time, but as the days had turned into weeks, Luis had wondered just how much longer he would continue to believe it. But now, that Cordell was back, his worries were over, providing, of course, that he'd located Reina.

Reina . . . thoughts of her left Luis troubled and unsure. He loved her so, but was furious with her for her disobedience. She had never caused him this kind of aggravation before, and he wondered what had gotten into her. Surely, she wasn't really this upset about marrying Marlow. The man was handsome, rich and had all the right connections. Luis could see absolutely no reason why she would object.

Still, Reina was his only daughter. When they spoke again, he would give her a chance to explain herself. The niggling fear that he might never see her again, that she might have come to some harm during her flight, stirred in his thoughts, but he pushed it away, refusing to think about the possibility. She meant too much to him to even consider such a terrible thing. No, Luis told himself, Reina was alive and well and if she wasn't here now, she soon would be. Cordell was supposedly the best. He would bring her back.

Entering the main house through the kitchen, Luis paused only long enough to wash. That done, he went forth to the main parlor where his guest awaited him. He was about to call out with pleasure to Cordell, when his black-eyed gaze fell on none other than Nathan Marlow. He felt a terrible sinking feeling in the pit of his stomach at the sight of the American for he knew he had to stall him again. He said a silent, violent curse as he strode forward, and he tried to ignore the sudden cold sweat that dampened his forehead.

"Nathan!" Luis called out in a jovial tone as he extended his hand. "What a pleasant surprise!"

Nathan rose from where he'd been sitting to return his future father-in-law's greeting. "Luis, it's good to see you again." They clasped hands.

Luis offered refreshments, but Nathan refused, preferring to get straight to the point. They sat down together.

"What brings you to Rancho Alvarez today?" Luis sounded calm.

"What do you think?" he returned with a slight

251

smile. "I've come to see Reina."

"Oh . . . Reina . . ." her father's tone reflected only disappointment and not the heart-stopping fear that really gripped him.

"She has returned, hasn't she?" Nathan pressed.

"I'm sorry to say, she has not."

"But she was supposed to be back two days ago," he complained. "I waited the extra day to give her time to rest from the trip."

"That was very thoughtful of you, and I know I told you originally that she would only be gone a few weeks. But she sent word just yesterday that she wanted to spend a little more time with her aunt."

Nathan's eyes narrowed as he regarded the old Californio. "There isn't a problem, is there, Luis?"

"No," he protested quickly, "there's no problem. What could be wrong?" He played innocent, glancing at the younger man questioningly, as if completely surprised by the suggestion.

Nathan studied him for a moment, then asked, "She will be back soon, won't she? I miss her, and there are a lot of things I want to discuss with her about the wedding."

"You needn't worry, Nathan. My daughter will be back home before you know it. She just wanted to spend some extra days with her aunt now, because once she's a married woman with the complete responsibility of running a household, she won't be able to get away for any great length of time."

"Ah, I see," he agreed. "Perhaps this time apart will help us to realize just how much we really care about each other."

"Oh, yes, I'm sure it will do that," Luis said, feeling cornered. *Where was Reina? And just as important, where was Cordell?*

"You know, I'm looking forward to the wedding. It should prove to be the social event of the season."

"I'm certain of it," he responded. "My daughter

will be the most beautiful bride Monterey has ever seen."

"There's no doubt about that," Nathan remarked as he got to his feet ready to leave. "Please, send my best to her and let her know that I'm eagerly awaiting her return."

He stood to usher him from the room. "I shall. I only regret that you made the trip all the way out here for nothing. Are you sure you won't stay and partake of my hospitality for the night? It is a long journey back to town."

"I appreciate the offer, Luis, but I have pressing business in Monterey. Had my intended returned, I could have justified the dalliance. But, since she is still out of town, I'd better get back to my work."

"I understand, of course. I'll let my daughter know of your visit, and as soon as I receive word of the exact date of her return, I'll notify you."

"Good. Until later . . ."

Once more they shook hands and bid each other good-bye. Luis felt only relief as he watched him ride off down the main drive. He couldn't believe that he had made it successfully through the conversation and that he had managed to put Nathan off for at least another few weeks. Luis drew a deep breath, and once Nathan was out of sight, he went back inside and downed a straight double shot of his finest, most potent whiskey.

As Nathan headed back to town, he was lost in thought. He had picked up on the old man's anxiety and couldn't help but wonder if his would-be bride was giving him trouble about their marriage. He found the thought oddly exciting. He was truly going to enjoy taming Reina Alvarez.

He had no fear that she would not show up for the wedding for he credited Luis with the ability to control his strong-willed daughter. He was fully confident that the wedding would take place as planned. What did it matter if she wasn't around right now? He had Lilly, and she was all the woman he'd ever really need.

Charley Stevens, a lean, dark-haired, wild-eyed young man sat in the back of the Golden Horseshoe Saloon in Monterey drinking and playing cards with his two friends, blond, buck-toothed Bucky Porter and skinny, red-haired, hot-headed Rex Jones. Though Charley, the leader of the small group, gave the appearance of being in a mellow mood, he was really very worried. Nothing seemed to be going right lately, and it was making him very nervous.

Weeks ago when Sheriff Macauley had arrested Devlin O'Keefe for Santana's murder, Charley and his companions had been thrilled. It had left them off the hook, free and clear. But now things had turned decidedly sour. Though it appeared to be such an open and shut case, the sheriff was stalling about going to trial, and that didn't sit well with Charley. He couldn't understand why Macauley had any doubts, and he certainly didn't want the lawman digging around too much for fear of what he might find out.

Charley took a deep drink of his beer, knowing that he had to do something. He couldn't risk the investigation being reopened. He had to protect himself. He had to make sure that O'Keefe took the blame and paid the price for Santana's murder.

"Ya know, boys, I think it's time we took matters into our own hands," Charley said calculatingly to his two companions.

"You talkin' about this Santana thing?" Rex asked nervously.

"It's been dragging on for too damned long," Charley swore in agitation. "O'Keefe should have been hung by now."

"What d'ya want us to do?" the drunken Bucky asked, anxious to do anything that would cover up their involvement in the crime.

"Well, first we're gonna need some help. We can't do this alone . . . we'd look suspicious." He sat back giving the impression of being quite relaxed and then slowly began to talk in a loud voice that was guaranteed to stir up trouble. "Does everybody in here know that that Dev O'Keefe fella who killed Santana, is still sittin' over there pretty as you please in the jail getting the royal treatment, while ol' Pedro is rotting in his grave!"

Understanding his role, Rex picked up on what his friend was doing. He demanded angrily, "You mean to tell me there ain't no plans to try him yet?"

"Yep," Bucky answered playing along, "and it's a damned shame, too. The man's guilty as hell!"

A murmur of interest rippled through the crowd in the bar.

"I know it," Charley agreed, seeing that people were starting to listen and deliberately heating up the arguments. "I thought they had him good, but I guess not."

"They found enough damned evidence to arrest him, but now it ain't enough to convict him?" Rex went on in irritated disbelief, trying to provoke people.

"They found some evidence all right, but I guess for some reason the sheriff still ain't sure," Bucky complained.

"Ain't sure? How much more sure do they gotta be?" Charley hollered, slamming his now-empty beer mug down on the table top. "I know what the evidence was. I heard tell they found something personal of O'Keefe's out there at the murder site, and they found a big roll of money he can't account for in his saddlebags."

"He's guilty all right!" Rex declared.

A chorus of "Yeahs" came from the bar as the crowd began to be swayed. Charley was pleased for this was just what he'd wanted.

"Sounds guilty to me, but maybe we just got ourselves a coward for a sheriff. Maybe Macauley's afraid for some reason." Charley raised his voice again as he made his comments.

"Yeah! What the hell else could he be waiting for? Pedro Santana was our friend!" Rex argued.

"Yeah! Everybody liked Pedro!" Bucky echoed. "Yet his killer is still sitting there in jail!"

The men at the bar were getting more and more caught up in the argument. They, too, had been wondering what the delay was in prosecuting O'Keefe. Sentiment was definitely running in Charley's favor. Their expressions were turning hostile, and their murmurings were growing stronger.

Now Charley saw his chance. "I say we settle this ourselves! I say we go over to the jail and do the sheriff's job for him since it's obvious that he's too afraid to do it himself!"

A rousing shout of agreement came from the crowd, and the atmosphere turned decidedly ugly. They began milling around excitedly, talking about the savageness of Santana's murder and how justice needed to be wrought swiftly.

"Everybody here knew Pedro. How can we just sit by and act like nothing's happened? O'Keefe killed him, sure as hell. The man's guilty! He should pay for his crime!" Charley incited.

"What are we waiting for?" Bucky cried out.

"Let's do it!" Charley came aggressively to his feet. "Come on!"

"They're right! We been waiting too long!" Someone at the bar called out. "Let's go!"

Standing at the end of the bar near the back of the saloon, Wily Andrews, a grizzled old-timer, was sipping a whiskey and listening to the talk. As the crowd began to grow openly hostile toward the sheriff, he started to get nervous. Lynch mobs weren't pretty things. Innocent people got hurt. To his way of thinking, the crowd was beginning to sound dangerous. When Wily heard somebody yell that they ought to take care of the sheriff's business for him if he was too scared to do it himself, he knew he had to move. As quietly as he could, he crept out the back of the bar and ran for the jail.

"Evening, Molly," Sheriff Macauley said as the young woman entered the office with Dev's dinner pail.

"Evening, sheriff," Molly replied. Her tone was a little subdued this evening, but Macauley didn't notice.

"O'Keefe must be hungry tonight. He's been watching for you for the last half hour."

The news pleased her, and she smiled slightly at the thought. "I guess I'd better hurry on back and give him his dinner then." She had more than one reason for rushing this night.

Macauley waved her on into the back room and turned his attention once more to the papers spread out before him on his desk. Since Denton's thwarted escape attempt, he'd come to trust and respect O'Keefe. He did not fear for Molly's safety as she disappeared into the cell block for he knew how the prisoner felt about the young woman. It had been evident in his behavior the day of Denton's death and during her daily visits since.

Macauley let his thoughts drift to his prisoner then, and the terrible future that he faced. The sheriff knew he would soon have to go to trial with his case against O'Keefe, and that was bothering him. He could tell just from the general feeling in town that Dev's conviction was almost assured. But ever since Ace Denton's death, he had become convinced that Dev was not Santana's murderer. The man seemed a decent sort. He was not the kind of man who would cold-bloodedly back-shoot a stranger.

Macauley attributed his success as a lawman from being one who followed his hunches, and for that reason, he'd hesitated to press Dev's prosecution yet. He kept hoping that something would turn up to exonerate the young man. He kept hoping his friend, Cordell, would come back with something that would prove his innocence. He didn't know what had happened to the other bounty hunter, but he wished he would show up soon.

The sheriff sighed in frustration. He knew he couldn't wait too much longer without people getting suspicious of his motive. A gut feeling that the man was innocent wouldn't sway a jury or prove powerful evidence in a court of law. Forcing his thoughts away from an increasingly difficult situation, he turned his attention back to his work.

Molly entered the quiet of the cell area to find Dev stretched out on his bunk.

"The sheriff tells me you're hungry," Molly said, giving him a small smile.

"I'm starving, Molly. What did you bring tonight?" Dev smiled brilliantly at her, bounding up from his bed, delighted to see her. She was the one thing in his otherwise long and torturous days that made life worth living. If it hadn't been for her, Dev wasn't sure he could have kept up hope.

Molly told him quickly what was on the menu for him that night, and as she spoke, he noticed immediately that she was not her usual cheerful self. He sensed that there was something bothering her, and he wondered what it could be and if he could help.

"Is something wrong?" Dev cut in, his expression serious as he studied her, waiting for an answer.

"No, nothing . . ." she replied far too quickly, looking away from him and rousing his suspicions even more.

"What do you mean 'nothing'?" he chided gently. "There's something troubling you, I can see it in your eyes and in your smile. Tell me about it. Maybe I can help."

Molly had always thought that she was pretty good at hiding her emotions, and she wondered how Dev had become so attuned to her moods. Certainly, no one else had noticed that she was worried and unhappy.

"I don't know . . ." She thought of her mother, growing weaker and weaker as the illness continued to ravage her.

"What is it?" The iron bars that separated them were the only things that prevented Dev from taking her in his arms. He ached to hold her and ease her fears, and he cursed the law that caged him like an animal.

"It's my mother . . ." Molly admitted softly.

"She's not any better?" She had told him the day before that her mother was ill, but it had only been a single remark made in passing.

"She's worse," she agonized. "I didn't want to come to work and leave my little brother, Jimmy, alone with her tonight, but I knew Mrs. Harvey would fire me if I didn't show up."

"What about the doctor? Has he seen her? Can't he help?"

"Mother said I shouldn't call him. We still owe him money from when Jimmy was sick the last time, and she refuses to take charity," Molly confessed miserably. "I keep hoping she'll get better, but she's getting so weak. The fever hasn't let up at all, and I'm starting to get scared . . ."

Tears sparkled in her emerald eyes as she feared that her mother might not recover. Dev could no longer resist reaching out to her. He took her hand through the bars and drew her closer.

"She'll be all right, Molly," he encouraged. He longed to comfort her and reassure her, but realized there was precious little he could say or do that would help. If Clay had been in town, he would have been able to enlist his friend's aid for her, but trapped as he was all alone here in Monterey, he was helpless.

At Dev's gentle touch, Molly lifted her glistening gaze to his. "I hope you're right. I don't know what I'd do without her."

"It'll be fine. You'll see."

"I'd like to believe you . . ." Molly gave him a tremulous, watery smile as their eyes locked in silent understanding. Her heart lurched as she saw the gentleness and tenderness mirrored in the depths of his blue eyes.

Dev saw the hope warring with the despair in her gaze and had a sudden idea. He was almost positive that his own days were numbered, and since he was unable to help her himself, he thought maybe his money could do for her what he couldn't. *He'd certainly have no use for it where he was going,* he thought wryly, *and if it could do some good here . . . now . . .*

"Sheriff!? Could you come here a second?" he called out.

Macauley heard his call. Molly moved away from Dev as the sheriff entered the room.

"What is it?" he asked, wondering what was wrong and why the girl looked so sad.

"You've got the reward money for Denton, right?"

"Yes," he answered.

"Well, half of it's legally mine, and I want you to give my share to Molly."

"What?"

"Look, you and I both know I won't be using it any time soon, so just give her my half," Dev directed. "Her mother's ill and needs a doctor. I want to help pay for it."

"You're sure you want to do this?"

"Positive." He glanced over at Molly and saw her look of wonder.

It took Macauley only a minute to get half the money out of the locked drawer in his desk where he'd been holding it for Cordell. He returned to the cell area and handed it over to her in front of Dev.

"I . . . I can't take this from you . . ." Molly was stunned, and she looked from the money in her hand to the man behind the bars. Her heart swelled with emotion at his generosity. She'd never known anyone who was this kind or this wonderful.

"Of course you can. I just wish I could do more for you," Dev told her in a tone that was gentle, yet brooked no argument.

At what he'd just witnessed, Macauley's belief in Dev's innocence grew even stronger. Giving the girl the money was not the act of a murdering criminal.

"Dev . . . thank you." Her eyes were shining as she gazed up at him.

There was no time for them to say more as they heard someone come racing into the office, banging the door open and then slamming it forcefully shut.

"Sheriff Macauley!" the man yelled.

"What is it?" Macauley heard the very real fear in the man's voice and hurried out front to see what was going on. "Is there trouble somewhere?"

"There's gonna be trouble, all right, and it's gonna be right here!"

"What are you talking about?" the sheriff demanded, wanting the facts.

"I'm talking about vigilantes!"

"Vigilantes?" He went a little pale at the thought.

"Yep. They're over at the saloon gettin' all riled up 'cause O'Keefe there ain't been hung yet. They're plannin' on comin' here and doin' it themselves! You gotta do something and fast!"

"Son of a . . ." Macauley strode to the gun cabinet to get his rifles. He wished his deputy, Carter, was there, but he'd sent him out of town on business for the next two days. It was going to be just him against the mob. "Here." He held out a rifle toward Wily, but the old man refused, backing nervously away.

"No, sir. I ain't gonna try to stop 'em. I just did my part. I warned you ahead of time. That's all I want to do with it. What you do from here is your business."

He ran quickly from the office and disappeared into the night, leaving Macauley all alone to face the raging mob.

Chapter Twenty

Macauley hesitated only an instant, then quickly pulled down the shades and locked the door. He knew he would have little chance of stopping a vigilante mob should they storm the office, yet he knew he couldn't let them have O'Keefe. He had to do something to protect him. His conviction about his innocence urging him on, he grabbed up the keys and ran back to the cells.

"Molly, I'm going to need your help," he said solemnly, his expression grave as he started to unlock Dev's cell door.

"What's happening?" she asked. The sudden change in his manner made her nervous. Something had to be wrong.

"It looks like some of the hotheads down at the saloon are thinking about taking the law into their own hands."

"You mean. . . ?"

"A lynch mob," he stated flatly, "and according to my informant, they're on the way here now."

"No!" she gasped, looking over at Dev, her eyes wide with fright. She'd heard about these kind of things and the violence that resulted. She couldn't bear to think of him facing such a fate.

Dev had been holding onto the bars as he listened, and his grip tightened so much at the sheriff's news that his knuckles showed white. He'd expected the end to come one of these days, but he hadn't thought it would be tonight.

"Listen, Molly, I want you to sneak out the back and take O'Keefe with you. Hide him out somewhere safe until I come for him."

"Macauley, I don't want her involved in this," Dev protested. "It's too damned dangerous. She might—"

"Shut up, O'Keefe. You're in my charge, and your safety is my concern," the sheriff cut him off sharply, then turned back to the girl. "Molly, if you don't take him, I can't guarantee he'll be alive in the morning."

"It's that serious?" she asked.

"It's that serious. Will you do it? Can I trust you?" Macauley studied her face, trying to read her expression.

Molly glanced at Dev where he stood caged like a wild animal. She knew he would stand no chance of survival should the mob get past the sheriff. She wondered if she could trust him, and she needed no more than a fraction of a second to make up her mind. Dev needed her help. Could she do less than her best for him after he'd done so much for her?

"Yes, I'll do it. What exactly do you want me to do?"

"Go out through the alley with him and keep him hidden until everything settles down. Can you handle that?"

"I can do it," she declared determinedly.

The sheriff turned his piercing gaze on his prisoner as he finished unlocking the door. "What about you, O'Keefe? Can I trust you or will you run first time you get the chance?"

"I'm not going to run," Dev answered, looking him straight in the eye.

Macauley gave a terse nod and waited no longer in throwing the door wide, freeing him. In the distance, they could hear the discontented rumble of the oncoming mob of drunks, and suddenly there was a loud pounding on the front door.

"Get out of here, quick, before they come around back!"

Molly looked up at Dev, seeing him for the first time without the barrier of the bars between them. He happened to meet her gaze, and they stared at each other for a moment in silent understanding before she held out her hand to him. He enfolded her soft, small hand in his big hard, calloused one.

The sheriff went ahead of them and opened the back door. "Molly, girl, you be careful!"

"You, too, Sheriff!" she whispered as she drew Dev out of the jail and into the dark alleyway. She was still clutching the money he'd given her in her free hand.

"Thanks, Macauley," Dev told him.

Macauley watched them slip away into the protective shadows of the night, then closed and barred the door. Extinguishing all the lights inside, he prepared to face the angry crowd of drunks bent on their own brand of justice.

The passageway was pitch black as Molly and Dev ran, hand in hand, from the jail. She was familiar with the area and made certain that they headed in the opposite direction of the oncoming mob. Dev kept close behind her. The sound of the crowd faded a bit as they neared a cross street, but neither of them were ready to relax just yet. Molly slowed her pace and moved forward cautiously to peek down the street.

"Oh, no!" she gasped.

"What is it?" Dev stiffened, fearing a confrontation when he had no weapon with which to defend themselves.

"There's someone coming," Molly said in a hushed agonized tone.

"Damn!" he whispered, thinking they were about to be caught and wanting her to get away safely. "Molly, you go on. Get out of here. I can find a way out by myself."

She smiled at the realization that he would worry about her before himself. It made it clear to her that she had made the right decision. Her judgment reaffirmed, it was still up to her to save him now.

Molly did some fast thinking, and she surprised Dev completely when she grabbed him with a strength she didn't know she was capable of and threw her arms around his neck. Before he could say a word, she kissed him passionately. In that moment a couple walked by the alleyway's opening. Molly had seen the women of the night plying their trade this way on numerous occasions and hoped that the passersby would believe her act.

The man and woman were not part of the vigilantes, but merely a lady and gentleman out for an evening stroll. They caught sight of the two of them, saw the money clutched in her hand and gasped in dismay as they hurried on about their own business.

The kiss had been meant to be a deterrent to their being discovered. Molly figured no one would ever suspect that Devlin O'Keefe was the man out back kissing a girl. She thought it would be the perfect ruse just in case the oncomers had been part of the vigilante group.

Molly had never kissed a man this way before, and she certainly didn't expect it to mean anything. It was a total shock to her then, when the touch of Dev's mouth on hers sent her senses soaring. The danger of the moment, coupled with the pure, unadulterated hunger of his kiss stole her breath and left her weak and pliant in his arms.

Dev was caught completely by surprise by Molly's shrewd move, and he meant to tell her that it was a brilliant ploy on her part. He would have too, except that he was stunned by the ferocity of the embrace. It was supposed to be fake. It was supposed to fool those around them into thinking that they were making illicit love in a back alley. But there was nothing scurrilous about the emotions that were surging through him.

This was what he'd been dreaming about during the past days. Yet, even in his tender imaginings, he had never come close to the glorious reality of having Molly in his arms. Her kiss was the most wonderful thing he'd ever experienced. Dev knew without a shadow of a doubt as their lips met again and again in tender exploration, that she was the one woman in the world for him. He knew this at the same time he knew he could not take advantage of her gentle honesty. He had nothing to offer her, no future to promise her. He had nothing . . . not even his freedom.

Dev vowed there in the darkness of that alley, that somehow he would prove his innocence and be vindicated. He had to prove to Molly that he couldn't be guilty of such a terrible thing. He wanted her complete trust.

When the couple had moved on, Dev and Molly broke apart, staring at each other in wonder in the deeply shadowed night. It was Molly who came to her senses first as the roar of the mob echoed strangely through the passageway. The realization of the danger Dev was in, plus the fact that his very life hung in the balance, jarred her into action.

"Come on! We've got to hurry!" Tearing her gaze from his, she grabbed his hand again and led him out into the open.

They moved off quietly down the now-deserted street making sure to keep their pace normal and unrushed so they would draw no attention to themselves. They were tense and on edge as they crossed the street the jail was on, and both were horrified when they looked down the block and saw a crowd of about twenty-five drunken rowdies milling angrily around in front of the jailhouse. They couldn't see Sheriff Macauley anywhere, but they knew he was there somewhere, holding the line, giving them the precious time they needed to get away.

As slowly as they were walking, it took Molly and Dev some time to get to her home. When they finally arrived, she rushed him immediately inside and locked the door behind them. Her face was pale and her hands shaking as she stared at Dev across the main room.

"We made it," he said in a low voice. "Molly, you risked your life for me. I'm grateful."

"You risked your life for me . . . or have you forgotten?" she said clearly, her eyes sparkling with the pride she felt at having been able to help him. She had so little else in her life that she needed that sense of pride.

"No, I hadn't forgotten," Dev told her. "But you didn't have to do this. You could have left me there. You didn't have to endanger yourself."

"I couldn't have left you to the mercy of that mob! They might have killed you!"

Dev's eyes met and held hers. "It might have been better for you, Molly, if you hadn't gotten involved."

"No," she whispered, "I don't believe that." She gazed up at him, wishing things could have been different, easier, but she knew this was no fairy tale. She was no princess, and Dev was no prince here to rescue her on his white charger. This was Dev, an accused murderer, whose safety depended on her ability to keep him hidden in her house until the sheriff could come for him. He had come to mean too much to her. She loved him. Despite the fact that everyone else thought him guilty, she knew in her heart that he was no cold-blooded killer.

The magnetism between them was nearly overpowering and just as they would have moved together, Jimmy came out of her mother's bedroom.

"Molly?" he said her name questioningly as he glanced from his sister to the strange man standing in the middle of the room. "What are you doing home?"

"Jimmy . . ." she said his name almost as if she was surprised to see him there. Then she regained control. "This is a friend of mine who's coming to stay with us for a while. Dev, this is my brother, Jimmy."

"Hello, Jimmy. Do you mind if I bunk here a day or so?" Dev was aware of the boy's intense scrutiny, and he smiled. It pleased him to find that the boy was protective of his sister.

Jimmy blinked. It was the first time anyone had ever addressed him as if he were the man of the house. His self-esteem rose a notch, and he returned Dev's smile tentatively. "No . . . It's all right, if Molly wants you to." He was puzzled by his presence, but trusted his sister's judgment. It wasn't like her to bring just anybody home. "Molly, Mother—"

Molly's whole focus changed immediately. Secure that Dev was relatively safe now, she turned her thoughts to her mother again. "How is she?"

"I don't know."

"Dev, wait out here. I've got to see how she is," Molly said as she disappeared into the bedroom with Jimmy following her.

Left alone, Dev looked around. There were a table and three chairs in the small kitchen area and only a few pieces of threadbare furniture in what was considered the sitting room. Two other bedrooms, besides the mother's, opened off that main room, and they were both just as spartanly furnished, too. Though the family had few belongings, what they had they took care of, and they kept the house impeccably clean. Dev was impressed.

Meanwhile, Molly and Jimmy moved to stand beside their mother's bed.

"How's she been?" she asked him nervously as she knelt down beside the bed and touched her mother's forehead to find she was burning up.

"She's been real quiet," he said worriedly. He struggled manfully not to cry. "I'm scared."

"Don't worry, everything's gonna be fine. I want you to run out and get the doctor."

"The doctor? How are we gonna pay for it?" Jimmy asked, surprised by her command. "You know what Mother said. She said we owed him too much already."

"I know, but Dev's helping us. He's going to pay for the doctor."

"He is?" That elevated Dev to a new plane in his thinking. No one had ever helped them out before, except the doctor, and his mother was too proud to let them take any more charity from him.

"He is, but, Jimmy, there's something you have to do for us . . . for me."

"What?"

"We can't tell anyone that Dev's staying here."

Her brother frowned. He wasn't used to being secretive about things. "How come?"

"Can you just trust me for now, and I promise I'll explain everything to you later?"

"Sure," he said seriously, "we've always been able to trust each other, haven't we?"

"You've grown up a lot," she said quietly. "Our father would be proud of you."

Jimmy was uncomfortable with an emotion he didn't understand. "If nobody's supposed to know, where's he gonna be when I come back with the doctor?"

"We'll think of something. Just remember, no one, absolutely no one, can know he's here. Promise?"

"All right, I promise."

Molly gave him a quick hug. "Now, run get the doctor. I'll be waiting right here for you."

"What about work? Don't you have to go back?"

"I will, but I'll go after the doctor leaves. Right now, mother's more important."

Jimmy was relieved to turn the burden of concern over to Molly again, and he rushed off to get the physician.

After the boy had left the house, Dev waited for Molly to come back out. When she didn't appear right away, he went to stand in the bedroom doorway where the door was slightly ajar. He could see her bending over her mother's inert form as she bathed her face with a damp cloth.

"Molly?" he said her name softly, not wanting to risk disturbing the ill woman. "Can I help you?"

"No, I was just trying to make her more comfortable," Molly answered, dampening the cloth once more and then wringing it out before she placed it on her mother's forehead. That done, she got slowly to her feet and went to join Dev. "We've got to find you a place to hide before the doctor gets here."

"Just tell me what you want me to do."

"You'll . . . you'll have to stay in my bedroom." The strain of the entire situation was beginning to reflect in the haunted shadows of her eyes.

"There's no telling how soon Jimmy will get back. It might be five minutes or it might be two hours. We can't take any chances."

Dev could plainly see the fear in her expression, and a great sense of protectiveness filled him. He wished there was some way he could ease her plight. Without really thinking about it, following his instincts only, he reached out for her and took her in his arms. For a moment her body was stiff as she fought the tears. But she had ached too long, and Dev had touched that vulnerable spot with his tenderness and understanding. He cradled her near as she wept, realizing how right it seemed to be holding her this way. The soft womanliness of her body fit naturally against the hard male contours of his own.

"You're so very special, Molly . . ." Dev said in a husky voice. He lifted his hands to frame her face and tilted it up to him, and Molly suddenly felt special . . . and warm . . . and . . .

Molly felt like swaying against him. He was so warm and tender and caring. She had never known anyone like him in her life. The thought that she might soon lose him, filled her eyes with tears.

Dev saw the shimmer of tears in her gaze and gave a guttural groan. "Ah, Molly, I want so badly to make everything right for you." Then, unable to resist any more, he kissed her. It was a loving kiss filled with passion and promise.

Molly was the one to break off the embrace. She was afraid that at any moment they might be interrupted and Dev might be caught. "You have to hide. You know what will happen if they find out you're here."

Her concern for him eased the ache Dev felt when she moved deliberately away. Dev gave her a crooked grin, touched her cheek in a gentle caress and without another word walked into her room and closed the door. Molly was frightened of an emotion she didn't know or understand. It grew like a tidal wave, overpowering her thoughts until she sighed in confusion.

Lying on the bed with his arms folded behind his head, Dev listened to the sound of her retreating footsteps as she hurried back to tend to her mother. As he remained hidden, he prayed that the doctor would come soon and that everything would be fine, if not for him, then for sweet, gentle Molly.

Sheriff Macauley stood alone in front of his office, ready to face down the crowd of drunken men heading his way. He stood tall and immovable, the shotgun he carried held across his chest.

As they drew near enough he spoke, "You'll all have to go on home. There will be no vigilante justice in my town."

"We ain't goin' nowhere!" Rex hollered. "We've come for O'Keefe. We want to see real justice done!"

"O'Keefe's in my custody. He'll stand trial when the time is right. That's when justice will be done," Macauley replied, as if he was unperturbed.

"That ain't good enough!" Bucky yelled. "We know he's guilty! Let's hang the bastard!"

"Yeah!" Bloodlust was running high in the crowd, and they started to surge forward.

Macauley wasn't about to give ground or be overrun. The sharp click of the gun hammers sounded as he lowered the barrel of the shotgun to aim at the first approaching man. The action brought the lead man and the crowd behind him to a halt.

"I said, O'Keefe's in my custody, and he's going to stay that way!"

"How long you plannin' on keepin' him in your custody? Santana's cold and rottin' in his grave, and that bastard is still sitting pretty in jail!" Charley said in a loud voice, wanting to keep the crowd fired up.

"Shut up and go home!" Macauley threatened. "Move along! I don't want any trouble with any of you."

"We don't want any trouble with you either, Sheriff, so just hand O'Keefe over and then we will move along."

"Get out of here, all of you. I don't want to have to shoot, but I will."

"The sheriff ain't gonna hand him over, so let's just take him ourselves!" someone cried, and again they moved forward.

Macauley fired one barrel into the air. "Next man who moves is dead," he declared in a murderous tone, pointing the gun directly at the leaders of the crowd. Look," he continued, "I hope you think this prisoner is worth dying over, because if you try to break in my jail, one of you sure as hell is gonna die."

"You can't kill us all!" Rex snarled.

"No," the sheriff said calmly, "but the first man gets a load in the stomach. Think about it."

Rex was no hero and neither was any other man in the crowd. Enthusiasm for a hanging was fading before the sheriff's steady gaze, and even steadier shotgun.

"What'll it be?" Macauley pressed, and he was immensely relieved when the mob began to break up and drift away.

Charley was furious, but knew he could do nothing more right now without being too conspicuous. He headed back to the saloon with Rex and Bucky.

"Somebody must have warned him we were coming," Charley seethed. "How else could he have been ready and waiting for us?"

"Yeah, but who?"

"I don't know, but I intend to find out," he vowed as they reentered the bar.

Doctor Lyle Rivers, a portly gentleman with a trim, gray beard and mustache, responded right away to the urgent knock at his door. He was surprised to find little Jimmy Magee standing there.

"Why, Jimmy, good to see you again," he greeted him warmly. He liked the Magee family, thought them good, honest people, though they were having a rough time of it right now.

"Dr. Rivers, you gotta come with me!" he cried. He'd managed to contain his worry up until now, but he was desperate to get home as quickly as he could.

"What is it? What's happened?"

"It's my mother, sir. She's real sick. Will you come, now? Right away?"

"It's that serious?"

"Yes, sir. She's been sick for days now with a fever and all, and she's not getting any better. Molly's got money to pay you this time, so you don't have to worry," he added, not wanting him to think that they'd be asking for charity.

The physician gave him a tender look for he knew how important it was to this family to pay their own way and not be indebted to anyone. "That's never been a problem, Jimmy. Don't worry about it." He hurried to get his bag. "Let's go, shall we?"

The boy broke into a bright smile as he accompanied him on the long trek back home.

"Sorry it took us so long, Molly, but there was a lot of trouble at the jail," Jimmy told his sister as soon as they reached the house.

Their walk back from the doctor's office had taken them past the jail. They'd witnessed the whole dangerous scene that had transpired there, and the doctor had stopped to speak with Macauley about what had happened.

"Trouble?" She questioned hoping her fear didn't show. "What happened?"

"Some hotheads and a crowd of would-be vigilantes tried to overrun the jail and hang the prisoner. I feel sorry for whoever started it," Dr. Rivers informed her. "The sheriff is not the forgiving sort. He won't rest until he catches him."

"That's terrible, but thank heavens nothing serious happened. Sheriff Macauley is a good man."

"He certainly is, and he's a smart man, too. He told me that he'd found out about the trouble ahead of time and had already moved that O'Keefe fellow out of the jail to safety. There was no hanging tonight."

"Good," Molly tried to sound surprised and relieved.

"You take the food over to the jail from the restaurant, don't you?" Rivers asked astutely.

"Yes, and I've come to know the man quite well over these weeks. He seems nice enough. I wonder where the sheriff hid him out."

"Nobody knows, and Macauley isn't saying, which may very well be for the best, all things considered. Now, let's see about your mother. Your brother, here, tells me she's been sick for a few days now."

"Yes, sir." Molly led the learned man back into her mother's bedroom.

After checking Eileen Magee completely, Dr. Rivers drew Molly out of the room, leaving Jimmy to tend to her. He handed Molly some packets of medicine.

"Mix this with hot tea and see that she takes at least a good drink of it four times a day. If you can manage it, have her take more. If there's no improvement by tomorrow night, send for me again. Hopefully, though, this will do it."

"Yes, Dr. Rivers, thank you," Molly promised. "And here's your money."

"Now, Molly, you'd best keep that. You might need it."

"We owe you so much. I insist you at least let us pay on our back bill," Molly smiled, "that you so kindly never mention. Please, Dr. Rivers," she added, "let me pay a little."

"All right, child, all right." He took the money reluctantly. "I hope your mother's better by tomorrow. This medicine should do it."

"Thank you," she said simply.

When the physician had gone from the house, Molly quickly called Dev. "It's safe now, you can come out."

"I thought he was never going to get here, and then I thought he was never going to leave."

"Me, too," Molly agreed. "But thank goodness he did come. Did you hear everything he said?"

"Yes," Dev said, frowning. "I'm worried about Macauley. What if they come back? He's in danger, and he's going through all of this just because of me."

"It's his job, Dev," Molly insisted, not wanting him to feel guilty.

"It's not his job to defend an accused murderer from a mob of wild drunks."

"It most certainly is. You haven't been convicted of anything! You aren't guilty of any crime!" she defended him passionately.

Dev looked up at her, surprised by the vehemence in her tone. "You sound like you mean that."

Molly blushed vividly, then confessed, "I do mean it. You didn't kill Santana. I'd bet my life on it."

Her professed faith in him warmed him. He would need the memory of that warmth when he had to leave. "You're right, Molly. I didn't kill Santana, but outside of Clay, you're the only one who believes me."

"I think you might be wrong there. I don't think Sheriff Macauley would have allowed you to go with me like he did, if he didn't trust you."

"That's true enough, but I've got to have some kind of proof, something that will convince a jury."

"It'll turn up, you just have to have faith," Molly lifted glowing eyes to his.

"Faith . . ." Dev repeated slowly. "Sometimes it seems so difficult to keep hoping . . ."

"I know, but just remember, I believe in you and so does your friend Clay. I'll never let you down, and neither will he, if he's half the man you say he is," Molly promised fervently.

"Clay is, but I hope you're right," Dev sighed, not sure whether to be elated or despairing. "He's been gone a long time."

"Molly . . ." Jimmy's plaintive call summoned her from the other room.

"I have to see to my mother," she apologized, sorry that she had to end the intimate moment with Dev. "We'll talk more later on."

"Don't worry," he gave her a bittersweet smile. "I'll be right here waiting for you."

Their gazes locked for a long heart-stopping moment, and then she tore herself away to see what Jimmy wanted.

Chapter Twenty-one

Bertha Harvey pinned Molly with a glacial glare as she returned to the restaurant some time later. "Where have you been? You've left here over two hours ago, and I ain't seen or heard from you since!"

Molly had practiced her story for her boss all the way there, and she was ready to face her with her version of what had happened. "There was trouble at the jail while I was there. Didn't you hear about it?"

"Trouble?" Bertha's eyes lit up at the thought of some excitement in town. "What kind of trouble?" Business at the restaurant had been slow, and she hadn't heard a thing about what was going on.

"There was a vigilante mob, trying to get to the prisoner."

"Did they?" Bertha asked avidly. She'd been waiting ages now for a hanging.

"No," she said, not wanting to explain any more than she had to.

"What about the prisoner?"

"I guess he's all right, I really don't know."

"What do you mean?"

"Evidently, the sheriff suspected something might happen, and he moved O'Keefe somewhere for safe-keeping."

"Did you find out where he moved him to?" Bertha pressed aggressively.

Molly was growing nervous under her demanding questioning. "No, he didn't say."

"Did you ask?"

"No," Molly answered, wondering at her point. Why did she care about where the prisoner was?"

"I thought so," Bertha sneered. "What use are you, girl? Aren't you even the least bit concerned about the business we're going to lose?"

"The business?" She was astounded at her train of thought.

"Yes! If O'Keefe's been moved out of the jail permanently, they won't be needing us to bring the meals over any more. We'll be losing some good, easy money there." In disgust the older woman turned away.

"You're talking about money when a man's life is at stake!" Molly couldn't stop herself from protesting Bertha's callousness.

The old woman shot her a frosty glare and snapped, "I care about money. I don't care about O'Keefe. Anyone with half a brain knows the man's a murdering thief!"

"He hasn't had a trial yet," Molly defended.

"That's just a formality. The man's as good as hung," Bertha announced with conviction. "I'll tell you one thing, Molly, I'll just bet those vigilantes don't give up. If they were as angry as you say they were, they might just keep looking until they find him and when they do—"

Molly couldn't suppress the shiver that wracked her as she imagined a gang of wild, vicious men dragging Dev bodily from her home. "The sheriff will protect him," she countered.

"One man can't stop a whole town," her boss said nastily and then turned and left the room.

Molly felt frozen inside as she watched her go.

She wondered if what she'd said was true. If the vigilantes didn't give up and kept searching for Dev, how would she ever be able to keep him safe? She couldn't let anything happen to him, but what good would she be in trying to protect him? She didn't even own a gun!

The thought of Dev being killed wrenched at Molly. Knowing she would be fired if she left early, she continued to work, but all her thoughts were focused on getting home as quickly as she could to make sure he was still there and still safe. She knew his survival depended on her, and it was a heavy responsibility to bear. Tomorrow, she decided, she would go talk to the sheriff. If he wanted her to keep him at her home, she would, but she was going to ask him for a gun, just in case.

Dev was nervous as he paced the front room of Molly's home in agitation. Jimmy had been watching over his mother ever since Molly had left the house to return to her much-needed job, so he'd been left alone with his thoughts, and he was finding that they were not pretty as the hours dragged by.

Dev was worried, deeply so, but it was concern for Molly that filled him, not for himself. He knew his presence in her home was putting her in jeopardy. The idea that he might ultimately be responsible for her being hurt in some way troubled him. He wanted to protect Molly, not place her at risk. He wanted to take care of her, not rely on her to protect him.

Again, the helplessness of his situation infuriated Dev. He was used to dealing with problems and dangers head on. He wasn't used to hiding out and slinking around like a thief in the night. He almost laughed at his unwitting analogy, but the comparison was too bitterly real.

Dev paused in the middle of the small room and sighed. It had been hard being cooped up in the jail cell, but it was even more difficult confining himself willingly to Molly's house. Still, though the door was locked from the inside and there was no one to prevent him from walking out, he knew he wouldn't leave. Too much depended on him staying where he was.

Molly had told him to use her bed for the night, and though he wasn't the least bit ready to sleep, he decided to lie down for a while. When she'd first offered him her bed, he'd argued with her, telling her that he'd be glad to sleep on the floor. She'd been adamant, though, telling him that Jimmy's bed was big enough for the two of them and that it would probably only be for this one night.

Dev stretched out on the softness of her small single bed, relishing its comfort after the long weeks of sleeping on the cot in jail. The pillow and covers held the faintest trace of Molly's own sweet scent, and just being that close to her filled him with warmth and a strange sense of well-being. He lay on his back and stared at the ceiling, remembering the way Molly had moved around both rooms before she'd left, making sure that all the curtains were tightly closed and how she'd told him to stay hidden in here should anyone unexpectedly show up at the door. It had been years since anyone had cared about him that way, fussing over him and worrying about him, and Dev found that he liked it very much.

Dev's thoughts drifted as he lay there. He thanked God silently for Macauley's quick thinking in getting him out of the jail. He liked Macauley as much as he could under the circumstances, and he wished him no ill.

There was the chilling possibility that the vigilantes might keep looking for him. There was also the chance that their activities might have stirred sentiment about him to a fever pitch and force the sheriff to go to trial before Clay could return.

Dev grimaced at the thought of going to trial. He knew he had no defense to offer, no proof that he'd never been to Santana's ranch in his life. There was only his word on it, and, considering the general opinion of him in town, his word of honor didn't mean much. He knew he had to accept that the threat of his hanging was very real, yet he railed against the injustice of it all. He had found the one woman he could love, but until this was cleared up, if it was ever cleared up, he could never let anything come of his feelings for her. Lost deep in his despair, he was unaware that Jimmy had emerged from the bedroom and was standing in the doorway, watching him.

"How's your mother?" Dev asked, concerned that she might have worsened and that he needed his help. "Do you need any help?"

"She's sleeping," Jimmy answered as he continued to study him, his expression curious. "You're him, aren't you?"

"Him, who?" Dev was surprised to find the youth there with him.

"The man from the jail, the man they were wanting to hang . . . O'Keefe."

Dev returned the youngster's regard in silence for a moment, then answered with the truth. "Yes, I am."

Jimmy nodded knowingly, seeming far older than his eight years. "I kinda figured you were. I knew Molly had to have a real good reason to make you hide like that."

"I appreciate you not saying anything."

The boy shrugged. "I promised Molly, I wouldn't." He paused, then asked boldly. "Why'd you kill Santana?"

Dev's spirits sank. *Did everybody believe him guilty?* "I didn't kill him," he replied quietly, "but everyone seems to think I did."

"Why?"

"The sheriff found a part from my silver belt at Santana's ranch and that supposedly linked me to the crime. Truth is, though, I've never been to Santana's ranch, and I didn't shoot him. I don't know how that evidence got there."

"What are you going to do about it?"

"There's not much I can do. I've got a friend named Clay who's trying to help get me free, but for the time being, all I can do is sit and wait and hope that a trial will prove me out."

"Molly must think you're innocent or she would never have brought you home with her," he stated bluntly.

"I'm glad she has faith in me. What about you, Jimmy? What do you think?"

Jimmy was thoughtful for a moment, then spoke with a child's clear and uncluttered honesty. "If Molly says you're innocent, then I guess I think you are, too. You're not going to try to run away or anything, are you?"

"No, I'm not going to run. If I ran, people would really think I was guilty," Dev said fiercely. He wanted his freedom, but not at the expense of his reputation. He did not want to go through life a wanted man.

Jimmy listened attentively, judging the man not by an adult's logical standards but by a child's standards of the heart. Dev was nothing like what he thought a killer would be. He looked him in the eye and talked to him man to man. He was nice, and he was certainly brave if he wasn't going to try to escape like a regular bad guy would. Jimmy was convinced.

"Don't worry," the boy assured him. "I won't tell anybody you're here. I promised Molly, and I never break promises."

Having straightened things out in his own mind, Jimmy returned to his mother's side.

It was late when Molly finally finished work. Bertha had been particularly mean and demanding, and Molly had had to work twice as hard just to stay even with her vicious, nitpicking ways. She was exhausted as she made the trek to the small house, but she knew the night was far from over. She still had her mother to worry about. She was torn between the fear that she was worse and the hope that she was better. That, along with her concern about Dev, was taking its toll.

Molly had told Jimmy to lock the door from the inside when she'd left, and she was pleased to find that it was still firmly barred when she returned. She knocked lightly.

"Jimmy . . . it's me, Molly." She called out very softly, not wanting to disturb her mother, should she be sleeping. After only a moment, Molly heard the lock turn. When the door swung slowly open, she found herself face to face with Dev.

Molly was startled by the surge of heartfelt love that rocketed through her at the sight of him. He looked so tall, powerful, and handsome that her breath caught in her throat. She wondered distractedly how it was that he'd come to mean so much to her in such a short period of time.

Dev was glad that she was back. He didn't realize just how much he'd missed her until he saw her again. Stepping quickly aside to allow her to enter, he breathed her name in an almost aching sigh, "Molly . . ."

Mesmerized by his nearness, Molly had to force

herself to action. Giving herself a mental shake, she hurried inside and shut and locked the door behind her. Trying to maintain her equilibrium, she diverted her own attention, asking, "Did everything go all right? How's my mother?"

"Everything's been quiet. Jimmy's stayed in with your mother all evening. I offered to relieve him several times, but he wanted to be with her. Last time I checked, she was resting peacefully."

"Thank goodness. I've been so worried about her . . . and about you."

"You have?"

"Yes." Ever since Bertha had remarked about Dev being strung up, Molly had been tormented by the thought. She knew without a doubt that Dev was a good, decent man. He had come to mean a great deal to her, and she couldn't bear the thought of anything ever happening to him.

Their eyes locked, and Dev saw in the depths of her gaze all the turbulent emotions she was feeling for him. There was a hungry desperation to the moment as they stood there in silence. But Dev put an end to it, letting his gaze slide away from hers, breaking that intimate contact.

The misery of his situation was almost too much for him to bear. Not too long before, his life with Clay had ambled on in relative contentment. He hadn't needed anyone or anything. Then this trouble over Santana had engulfed him, and he'd been trapped. Only Molly's presence had gotten him through the last long days and nights. He'd come to love her even before he'd laid a hand on her.

Now, though, he was afraid of what her contact with him would do to her. He had nothing to give her—nothing, not even his good name. He had to put an end to this madness before it got started. He had to keep his distance from her for fear that he wouldn't be able to control his own volatile emotions. He wanted her. He ached to hold her close, kiss her and keep that look in her eyes. He knew it would be so easy, too, for she was a warm, loving and giving person. Yet he knew it was impossible.

Dev suddenly had to get away. She was much too wonderful, and he needed her too badly. He moved away from her and didn't stop until he was at the door, one hand resting on the knob. He paused as he glanced back over his shoulder.

"I need to go outside for a while."

Molly was stunned by the sudden change in Dev. Just moments before they had almost embraced, and now he was being cold and elusive. "All right," she answered, not knowing what else to say.

"And Molly . . ."

"Yes?"

He could see the confusion and hurt in her expression, but he thought it was far better that he stop what was happening between them now. "I just want you to know that I'm grateful for everything you've done for me. You've given me far too much already." With that, he opened the door and left the house.

There had been something so grim and so final about his words that they chilled Molly. She stared after him in dismay, realizing that it wasn't his gratitude she wanted. She wanted his love.

Charley, Rex, and Bucky all sat at a table in the Golden Horseshoe trying to figure out who had gone ahead to warn the sheriff that they were coming. Charley's mean-eyed gaze surveyed the men at the bar as he wondered which one had ruined his plan to kill O'Keefe.

"Who didn't go along with us?" Charley asked, unable to pick the one man who might have betrayed them.

"I'm not sure." Bucky was indecisive. "I thought most everybody joined us."

"What about that old coot there in the back?" Rex pointed to where Wily stood at the end of the bar. "I remember seeing him when we were first startin' to talk it up, but I didn't see him anywhere in the crowd."

Charley's eyes narrowed as he studied the old man. Almost as if he'd felt his gaze upon him, Wily looked up in his direction. For just an instant, they glared at each other, staring each other down. Wily's expression was tinged with defiance, and he didn't flinch before Charley's intimidating look.

All three men read Wily's expression correctly and exchanged knowing looks.

"It was him, all right," Bucky spoke up.

"If the sheriff talks to that old man, he's gonna find out everything that went on in here tonight," Charley said slowly, calculating his next move.

"Then get rid of him," Bucky suggested casually.

"Yeah, why don't you just shoot the old geezer and be done with it?" Rex suggested with drunken casualness. "There wouldn't be anybody missin' him, that's for sure."

"What are you two, idiots? All I'd need is another body to worry about," Charley growled at his companions, not believing their stupidity. "His kind's weak and scares real easy. It won't take much to chase him off. Watch . . ."

Charley slid his chair back noisily from the table. Taking his beer with him, he stalked toward Wily.

Wily watched him approach and knew he faced danger. As Charley drew closer, he directed his attention back to his tumbler of whiskey in hopes that the trouble would just pass him by. But it was not to be.

"Old man," he called out to him derogatorily.

Wily looked up again, his expression wary and

frightened. "You want somethin'?"

"Yeah. I want to know where you were tonight during all the excitement?"

"I don't believe in all that rabble-rousin' foolishness. I got out of the way," he responded, downing the rest of his drink with a shaking hand, then pushing the glass forward toward the barkeep for a refill.

"I'll just bet you did. Well, you know what? Me and the boys were just talkin', and we got a feelin' that somebody went to the sheriff and told him that were were comin' to string O'Keefe up. What do you think about that?"

"I don't think nothing about it. Why're you tellin' me this?"

"I was just thinkin'." Charley lowered his tone as he braced one elbow against the bar next to Wily and leaned real close.

"You were, eh?" Wily didn't look up. He kept his gaze focused on his glass. He wanted to tell him that the thought of him thinking was an amazing thing, but he knew better. His life wouldn't be worth a plug nickel if he pushed this man too far.

"Yeah, old man, I was, and I came to the conclusion that you might have been the one who told the sheriff what we were plannin'. You know, if that's the case, it might be real healthy for you to make yourself scarce, maybe even get out of town. You understand me?"

Wily wanted to face him down, but he didn't. Years ago, he might have been fast enough on the draw to beat him, but these days he was just too blamed old. This Stevens fella was a cold one. He could feel it, and he wasn't about to rile him up any more than he already had. "I hear ya."

"Good." Charley turned and walked back to his own table, his stride confident and cocky.

Wily remained at the bar, shaken by his unspoken threat.

The barkeep leaned close to give him some sage advice. "If I were you, I'd do what he says. That man is one mean hombre."

Wily finished off the refill the bartender had given him and then quickly departed the saloon. He never glanced back in Charley's direction.

Charley was smug as he rejoined his friends. "Didn't I tell you the man was a coward? I'm a good judge of a man's character," he bragged.

"Except for Santana," Rex added, and he was rewarded with a vicious look.

"I thought the bastard would just give us the money without much of a fuss. I sure as hell didn't think I was going to have to shoot him, but he made me mad." Charley scowled as he remembered his encounter with the rancher.

"So what are we going to do now?" Bucky asked.

"Nothing," came his curt reply. He was still annoyed that his plan had been thwarted. "There ain't a damned thing we can do, now that the sheriff's expecting trouble. We'll just have to sit tight and hope O'Keefe is found guilty."

"And if he ain't? What if they let him go and start lookin' again?" Bucky asked fearfully.

"We'll worry about that later."

Sheriff Macauley was sitting slumped at his desk, his loaded shotgun laid out ready before him, a single, low-burning lamp turning the darkness of the office to a semi-gloom. Though he was physically weary, there was nothing slow or tired about his thoughts as he contemplated the events of the evening. He'd been running this town for years now, and had never had anything like this happen before.

This unexpected frenzy to see O'Keefe hang didn't make much sense to him. O'Keefe had been locked up for weeks now, and there had hardly been a word said. Then all of a sudden tonight, the public was worked up about it and wanted to see immediate justice done.

Macauley wondered what the reasons were behind this avid interest. He had a nagging feeling that there was something more to this than just an angry mob of citizens out for vigilante justice, that there was someone out there who, for some as yet unknown reason, wanted O'Keefe dead. Since he always followed his instincts, he knew this bore looking into. He had a suspicion that if he found out who'd started it all, he might uncover a connection to Santana's real murderer.

Macauley tried to remember if there had been an instigator in the crowd, but no one person stood out in his mind. Certainly when he'd backed them down, no one had come forth and tried to rally them against him. He knew there had to be somebody behind it all, though, and he made a mental note to locate Wily in the morning and find out from him exactly who had been stirring things up in the saloon.

Chapter Twenty-two

"Jimmy, I'm going to go outside for a few minutes. I'll be right back," Molly told him softly as he kept the vigil in the chair at their mother's bedside.

"All right," he answered sleepily. "I'll keep watch."

Molly smiled softly at his determination to stay awake. He was tired, but he was also as stubborn as they came. He had no intention of going to bed yet. He wanted to remain right where he was, just in case their mother awoke and needed anything.

Confident that he would be fine, Molly left the house, then paused outside the door for a moment, trying to guess where Dev might have gone. He'd left her over an hour ago, and as time had passed she'd grown concerned about him. The possibility that he might have fled didn't even occur to her. She knew he would never do that. Finding no clue as to the direction he'd gone, she wandered down the path that led past their small tumbledown barn and on to the small pond beyond.

It was late, and the moon was high in the night sky, casting everything in silvered relief. Molly couldn't see Dev anywhere around, but the irregular sound of something like pebbles being thrown into the water drew her on. As she moved down the bank, she caught sight of him sitting on a rock there gazing out across the moon-dappled pond.

The harsh shadows of the moonlight cast sharp lines and angles to his face, giving him a very lonely, forlorn look as he aimlessly tossed one small stone after another. Her heart contracted in sympathy at the pain she saw etched in his features. She wanted to go to him and embrace him. She wanted to reassure him and tell him that everything would be all right, but remembering his coolness when he'd left her earlier, she hesitated to be so bold.

"Dev?" she said his name gently.

Dev glanced up to see Molly standing there in the moon's glow. He'd done nothing but think about her since he'd left the house, and it seemed almost too good to be true that she was actually there. Gilded as she was by the pale light, she looked more lovely than ever, with her hair streaming down around her shoulders in soft, loose curls. He had to fight down the urge to cast aside the handful of rocks he was holding and rush to take her in his arms. It took an effort, but he managed to stay where he was.

"Molly." His voice was husky as his gaze devoured her. He wanted to remember for all time just how beautiful she looked right now. "Why did you come? Is something wrong?"

"You tell me," Molly prodded. She wanted him to open up to her, to share all that was troubling him. She wanted to help if she could.

"Nothing's wrong," he lied. Resisting the temptation to love her, he tore his gaze away from her and looked out across the placid waters.

"Are you sure?" she asked again, taking a step closer to rest a hand on his shoulder.

Her gentle touch ignited Dev's passion, and his anger. He didn't know how one simple touch could arouse him so, but it did. He wanted her! God, how he wanted her! He'd been sitting here dreaming of nothing else, and yet he knew it could never be. He cursed the hand fate had dealt him as he came abruptly to his feet, shrugging away from her hand.

"Hell, Molly, everything's wrong! But there's nothing we can do to change anything," he told her, raking a hand through his hair in a nervous, weary gesture.

"We can talk about it. Maybe that will help."

"Talking about it won't do any good. Nothing will," he said bitterly.

Molly could see the agony he was in, and she ached for him. She could no longer stop herself from reaching out. She needed to comfort him. Without thought, she went to him and wrapped her arms around him, resting her head against his chest. The beat of his thundering heart beneath her cheek sounded strong and sure, and a soft sigh escaped her.

"Let me try, Dev."

Her offer was a mesmerizing enchantment in the midst of his torment. She lifted her head to gaze up at him, and her eyes were shining with the love she felt. Dev had managed not to react to her embrace until he made the mistake of looking down at her. His control snapped as he saw her expression. He groaned in abject misery as he surrendered to his need to kiss her once more.

"Ah . . . Molly . . ."

It was a kiss for all time as his warring emotions drove him to new heights of passion and pain. He wanted her, but couldn't have her. She was offering him the heaven he'd longed for all his life, and yet he couldn't take it. He tightened his embrace, crushing her to him.

Molly clung to him, feeling and sharing his desperation. She loved him completely and only wanted to please him. When his lips left hers for a moment, she whispered, "Dev . . . I love you so . . ."

Her words jarred him to the depths of his soul. He continued to hold her close for a moment, then took her by the arms and stepped back away from her. "No, Molly."

"No?" She was puzzled. "Dev?"

"Molly, you don't mean that. You can't mean that," he argued, releasing her abruptly.

"But I do," she insisted.

Dev's mouth twisted as the hopelessness of his situation haunted him again, and he turned his back on her, walking down to the water. "I won't let you," he declared, as if such things could be dictated.

"What do you mean you won't let me?" She stared after him in disbelief.

"It's impossible, Molly. I can't give you anything. I can't even promise you tomorrow!" Dev found that his hands were shaking as he argued with her, denying himself that which he desired most.

She understood what he was thinking, but she refused to be so easily dismissed. "I don't care about any of that! I love you!"

"You don't even know me."

"Oh, I know you, all right, Dev O'Keefe. You're a fine, honest, wonderful man. You're no killer. The truth is going to come out. You'll see." She followed him, coming to stand right behind him.

At her declaration, Dev faced her, his impotent fury fueling his words. "What if you're wrong? What if the truth never comes out? What if they find me guilty, and I hang? It could happen, Molly. Believe me, it could happen."

"It won't." Her faith that everything would turn out right did not waver.

"But it might," he repeated. "Don't you see that it's better for you if this stops right here, right now."

"I can't stop how I feel. I'm in love with you. That's never going to change."

"I won't do this to you, Molly. I want to protect you. I don't want you to be hurt."

The thought that he was protecting her was noble, but she didn't want protection from him. She wanted his love. "What about what I want, Dev?" she challenged.

"Molly, you just don't understand."

"Oh, yes, I do. You're the one who doesn't understand, Dev. Love me, please, love me." She didn't give him any further chance to respond, but went to him, looping her arms around his neck and drawing him down for a flaming kiss.

As their lips met, Dev uttered a moan of defeat. Enfolding her in his embrace, he brought her fully against him. She held tightly to him as she eagerly demonstrated in the kiss just how much he meant to her. His denied passion blazed hotly, and his body burned for her.

This was Dev's wildest desire come true—kissing Molly in the moonlight, and for a time he was caught up in the splendor of it. Framing her face with his hands, he drew back to gaze down at her, seeing the happiness and adoration sparkling in her eyes.

"Molly," he growled her name in a hoarse, agonized whisper as he bent to kiss her again, his mouth covering hers this time in a slow, possessive exchange.

Without ending the kiss, they sank down together to the softness of the grassy bank. Their lips met, parted and cherished. Each kiss was more precious than the last as they celebrated the glory of the moment.

Dev knew he should stop, but somehow he couldn't bring himself to. He needed this . . . needed it desperately. Molly wanted it, too. She had somehow always known that they were perfect for each other, and she thrilled to his every kiss.

When he began to caress her, softly and tenderly at first, she whimpered in ecstasy. She was enraptured as he pressed hot kisses to her throat, and when he began to work the buttons of her bodice, she waited in breathless expectation. That sweet flesh bared to his questing touch, he moved lower. As his lips sought the swell of her breasts above her chemise, she cried out his name in rapturous delight.

The sound of her voice jolted through him, and Dev realized just what he was doing. A shudder wracked his body as he fought to bring his rampant desires under control. This was exactly what he hadn't wanted to happen! He raged at himself for his weakness, and he vowed then and there never to allow it to happen again. He rolled slightly away from her to pull himself together.

Molly had been blissfully unaware of anything except Dev and the wonder of his touch. When he stopped so suddenly, and shifted away, she was heartbroken.

"Dev?"

"Don't say a word, Molly. Just don't say a word." The tautness of his voice silenced her.

The coolness of the night air on her partially exposed breasts, chilled her as much as his words did, and she shivered. She watched in silence as he got up. He stood over her for a moment, staring down at her, and she would never know that the image of her lying there with her hair spread out on the lush grass, her bodice partially undone and her lips swollen from his passionate kisses, would be the memory that would stay with him forever and give him many a restless, sleepless night.

With an iron-will that surprised even him, Dev said slowly, "I won't let this happen, Molly. I respect you, and I care about you too much. Wait for a man who can give you what you need—a family and a future. I'm not that man."

He strode off quickly toward the house, knowing that if he'd lingered another minute, he wouldn't have been able to hold himself away from her. He drew a long, tortured breath as he moved through the darkness, and he wondered why his eyes were burning. By the time he reached the door, he'd managed to pull himself together, and he let himself in quietly.

"Jimmy, it's me. I'm back," Dev said softly, thinking the boy would be wondering who had come in. But as he walked past Molly's mother's room, he saw that the boy had fallen sound asleep in the ladderback chair beside the bed. He smiled thinking of the boy's diligence in staying by her side in spite of being tired.

Feeling tense and very barren inside, he wandered to the fireplace, and stood looking down at the hearth. He thought the cold, dead ashes there greatly resembled his emotional state right now — barren and lifeless. A short time before a fire had been burning within him, now it had been brutally smothered, all its brightness and light extinguished forever. He remained there, staring sightlessly at the fireplace, his thoughts as dark as the soot that stained the walls.

Moments later, he heard the door open behind him, and he knew without looking that Molly had returned. He wanted to face her and tell her that he was sorry. He wanted to make endless love to her and never leave her. But he knew it could never be, so he stayed where he was.

Molly entered the room to find Dev standing at the fireplace with his back to her. She noticed how he stiffened slightly when she came in, and a great sorrow filled her. Without speaking, she went toward her mother's room to check.

"Jimmy's asleep," Dev spoke as she would have

298

gone in.

"I'd better wake him and get him in bed then," she said, intending to rouse him and have him switch rooms.

"Wait, don't wake him, Molly. Let me help," he offered. "Do you mind if I go in?"

"No." She was surprised by his offer.

She watched from the bedroom doorway as Dev crossed the room and carefully lifted Jimmy into his arms without waking him or disturbing her mother. Carrying him like a baby, he took him on into his own bedroom. Dev lay the soundly sleeping eight-year-old upon his bed and drew the covers up over him.

Molly saw the infinite gentleness in Dev's manner, and the unbidden thought came to her that he would make a wonderful father. It touched her deeply, and she said a silent, fervent prayer that nothing would happen to this man. He was too good, too special, and she loved him so.

"You can have my room for your own while you're here, Dev. I'll share with Jimmy," she told him when he emerged from Jimmy's bedroom.

"Are you sure?" He hadn't minded hiding there during the day, but he hated the thought of her being put out of her own bed because of him.

"I'm sure. I'll be able to hear Mother better if I sleep in here."

He agreed reluctantly. "I just hope I don't have to impose on you too much longer."

"Dev," Molly said his name sharply to get him to look directly at her for he'd been avoiding doing it ever since she'd returned. "You're not imposing. I was happy to help you. I'm glad that I did."

They both said good night then and parted, bedding down in separate rooms even though in their hearts neither of them wanted to.

Later as Dev tried to fall asleep, he was tormented by the knowledge that he was lying in Molly's bed. He could smell the faint sweet scent of her on the sheets, and he uttered a groan of frustration as his body ignored his logic and responded to the delicate fragrance. He rolled over, trying to force himself to rest, but it only got worse for him as every time he closed his eyes the vision of her lying on the grassy bank tortured him in a most agonizing way. Memories of the heart-stopping power of her kiss and the exquisite feel of her satiny skin beneath his hands taunted him endlessly. Tossing and turning, he sought escape through sleep, but the long hours stretched dark and desolate ahead of him. When sleep finally claimed him, it was not the blissful oblivion he'd hoped for, but a turbulent rest filled with twisted images of angry mobs, gallows and death. Only as morning neared, did Molly slip into his dreams. Dev quieted, enjoying, at least in his sleep, the joy of the way things might have been.

Molly had trouble falling asleep, too. The memory of Dev's kisses and caresses, followed by his rejection left her feeling strangely restless and empty. She knew that he'd meant it when he'd said there could be nothing between them, and she knew that the threat of his hanging was very real. But she was not one to give up easily. She would be patient and hope for the best. She did love him, and she fully intended for them to be together. Holding that hope in her heart, she finally drifted off to sleep and dreams of Dev.

"Molly! Hurry!"

Jimmy's call startled her from a deep sleep, and she rushed from the bedroom to see what was wrong. Dev had heard him, too, and hurried from the bed. They came face to face, Molly clad only in

300

her floor-length gown and Dev wearing just his pants.

Dev saw her sleep-flushed cheeks and the demure style of her nightgown that emphasized her innocence and thought she was the most beautiful woman in the world. Molly saw the wide strength of his chest and the powerful, corded muscles of his shoulders and arms and knew he was the most virile man she'd ever seen. A shock of sensual awareness shook them both, but they had little time to think about it.

"What is it?" he asked, forcing himself to get tough. There might be trouble on his account, and he had to be ready. He had to be thinking sharply.

It took Molly only an instant to realize her brother had called her from their mother's room.

"It's Mother," she muttered nervously, then hurried in to see how she was.

"Molly," Eileen Magee managed a weak smile as she saw her daughter coming toward her, and she lifted a hand toward her in welcome.

"She's better!" Jimmy declared, his eyes alight with relief and love for his mother.

"How do you feel?" she asked tenderly, thrilled to see a look of sanity in her eyes as she dropped to her knees next to the bed and took her mother's hand.

"Awful, but judging from your reaction, I must be better than I was," she said, sounding tired. "Have I been sick very long?"

"A few days. We were worried, but the doctor came last night and left some medicine. It looks like it's working."

"You had the doctor in?" Eileen looked worried for she knew they had no money. "But I told you—"

"Don't worry, Dr. Rivers was wonderful and very understanding. Everything's going to be fine," she told her earnestly.

She nodded slowly, then frowned slightly. "Did I hear a man's voice in the other room?"

"Oh," Molly knew she had to think quickly. "Yes. That was Dev."

"Dev?" Eileen gave her daughter a questioning look.

"Sheriff Macauley sent him. A prisoner got out of jail, and the sheriff thought there might be some trouble. He sent Dev here to make sure things are all right." Molly was very much conscious of Jimmy's eyes upon her as she related the story, but she didn't flinch as she told only part of the truth. There was no point in upsetting her too much right now. She would tell her the whole story when she was feeling stronger.

"Oh," she sighed heavily. "There's no danger, is there?"

"Not with Dev here. I'm sure it will all be straightened out real soon."

Eileen thought it a bit strange that Sheriff Macauley would send someone out to their home in particular, but she said nothing more. She was too exhausted right now to worry about it. Molly seemed to have everything under control, and she'd always been a good girl.

"Are you tired? Do you want to rest some more?"

"I think I'd better," she agreed.

"Let me get you one more dose of your medicine, and then you can sleep."

Leaving Jimmy there merrily chatting away, Molly went to mix the potion the doctor had left. She found Dev waiting anxiously for her return.

"How is she?" Dev's concern was evident in the seriousness of his expression. He'd had no idea whether Jimmy's urgent call had been one of horror or one of happiness.

"She's awake, and she seems to be getting better, finally," Molly said smiling.

"I'm happy for you, Molly," he told her honestly, ignoring the compelling urge he felt to hug her.

"It's all because of you and your help paying the doctor," she responded.

"It was only money, Molly. I don't take any of the credit for her recovery." Dev denied any heroic claim. He had only wanted to help Molly any way he could.

"If it hadn't been for you, who knows how she would have been this morning," Molly looked up at Dev, her eyes shining with love for him.

He felt a constriction in his chest. "I'm glad I was able to do it for you," he answered, growing uncomfortable with the emotions that were plaguing him.

"She heard your voice and asked about you," she told him as she moved off to get the medicine.

"What did you tell her?"

"The truth, or at least part of it. I told her you were sent out here from the sheriff's office."

"That's all?"

"For now. I'll tell her the rest tomorrow, when she's stronger."

He nodded, wondering silently how the older woman was going to react to his presence in her home.

Molly sensed his unease. "Don't worry, she'll understand. Now, I'd better get back in there with this." She held up the medicine for him to see.

"If you need anything, if I can do anything for you, I'll be right here."

She gave him a bright smile as she returned to her mother, and Dev went back into her room and settled on the bed, to wait and see what the rest of the day would bring.

Chapter Twenty-three

Macauley strode into the Golden Horseshoe shortly before noon the following day. He knew it was too early for the place to be crowded, and that was fine with him. He was looking for Wily, and he wanted to talk with him in private.

"Mornin', Sheriff," Abel, the bartender, called out from where he stood behind the bar. He'd been expecting the lawman to pay him a visit, and he'd been worrying about what to tell him, should he ask about last night. "What can I do for you?"

"I'm looking for Wily Andrews. Is he around?"

"Nope, not this morning."

"He was here last night, though, right?"

"Yes, sir, but he left some time after midnight. I haven't seen him since."

Macauley nodded as he let his gaze sweep the room. "Tell me, Abel, what went on in here last night?"

Abel didn't want to get in trouble with the sheriff, but then again he didn't want Stevens and his friends mad at him either. He knew how mean those three could be, and he had no intention of having them come in here and bust up his place. Besides, he justified what he was about to say, what did it matter anyway? No one had been hurt or killed. The prisoner was still safe. Everything had turned out fine. The furor had died down, and life was back to normal.

Abel tried to sound casual as he answered, "Well, a bunch of the boys got drunk, and one thing led to another, I guess."

"How'd it all get started? Who got them all riled up?"

"I don't rightly know that there was any one man who started it," he replied. "I went in the backroom for a few minutes to get something, and when I came back out the whole place was in an uproar. They were all talking hot and heavy about 'seeing justice done.'"

Macauley's look was knowing. "You don't remember anybody in particular making the most noise?"

"No, I sure don't, sheriff. But I'll be glad to ask around for you and see what I can find out," he offered, knowing damn good and well that he wasn't going to tell him a thing.

"You do that, Abel, and if Wily comes in before I get a chance to talk to him, tell him that I want to see him over at the jail."

"Yes, sir."

The sheriff left the saloon, even more convinced than ever that something was going on. He knew Wily was the key to everything, so he headed for the boarding house where he knew the old man kept a room. Mrs. Johnson, the gray-haired, heavy-set widow-woman who ran it, was happy to help, and she guided him upstairs to his room.

"I don't know if he's still sleeping or not. I didn't hear him come in last night, but that's not unusual, he's always very late. He does love his liquor," she told him primly, as if not approving of her boarder's drinking habits.

"Here we are," she said good-naturedly as she knocked at the door. "Wily? The sheriff's here to see you." When there was no reply, she looked puzzled.

305

"My, now that's strange." She knocked again, and when once more there was no answer, she looked questioningly at Macauley. "Shall I open it for you?"

"Yes, please. I won't disturb anything. Let's just make sure he's all right." He had a sickening feeling that the old man might be lying in there dead, murdered for telling him about the lynch mob, and if he was . . .

Mrs. Johnson fumbled with her ring of keys and then finding the right one, opened the door for the sheriff.

Macauley entered slowly, looking carefully around. He wasn't sure whether it was a relief or an aggravation to find that Wily and most of his things were gone.

"My, now that's strange," the landlady said in confusion.

"What is?"

"Well, Wily just paid me last week for the whole month. It isn't like him to just take off like this — and without a word."

Macauley quickly thanked her for her time. "If you hear from him, let me know."

"Oh, I will, Sheriff, you can be sure of it."

Blocked in his attempt to find Wily and with him the truth, he headed back for the office in frustration.

The news of the vigilante attack reached Rancho Alvarez quickly, along with a rumor being spread by the owner of one of the restaurants in town that Devlin O'Keefe had disappeared from the jail. The minute Luis heard about it he dropped what he was doing and raced into Monterey to find out the truth.

The stories alarmed and angered Luis for he couldn't afford to have anything happen to O'Keefe.

306

Santana had been a mildly popular man in town, but hardly the kind of citizen whose murder would inspire such an outraged show of devotion. He himself had only used the idea of a mob as a threat to blackmail Cordell into taking up the hunt for Reina. He had never believed that it might really happen.

Luis was worried as he stormed into the sheriff's office. If O'Keefe had had the misfortune to fall prey to a mob of law-abiding citizens, he was afraid Cordell would make him answer for his fate. The sight of the lawman sitting calmly at his desk reassured him somewhat. Surely, if his prisoner had been strung up, Macauley wouldn't be so at ease.

"What the hell is going on, Macauley?" Luis demanded haughtily as he marched up to the desk and glared down at him.

"I'm not sure I know what you mean, Alvarez," the sheriff replied coolly.

"I want to know what happened here yesterday."

"I'm not so sure that's any of your business," he said caustically.

"As a concerned citizen, it most certainly is my business. There were all kinds of terrible rumors reaching the ranch, and I want to know the truth. Where's O'Keefe? Did they get to him and lynch him?"

"Since when are you so interested in what happens to O'Keefe?" Macauley asked, his eyes narrowing as he studied the old Californio, wondering at his concern.

"Santana was a friend of mine," Luis said, stiffening at the implied insult. "I want to know what's happened to the man who was accused of his murder!"

"O'Keefe's not here," he answered bluntly.

Luis stared aghast at Sheriff Macauley. "Then it's true . . ."

"What's true? What have you heard?"

"That vigilantes stormed the jail and O'Keefe disappeared."

"That's the way it happened, to a point," the lawman snapped at the meddlesome rancher.

"The vigilantes didn't hang him, did they?" he voiced his greatest concern.

"No, but that's why I moved him out of here. I want to keep him safe. There's no guarantee those damned fools won't try again, although I'm hoping they're smart enough not to."

"Where is he?"

"You may be one of Monterey's leading, upstanding citizens, Alvarez, but that doesn't mean I have to tell you anything. Just suffice it to say, that O'Keefe is safe for now. There isn't going to be any mob justice in my town."

"You're certain he's protected?" Luis pressed.

The sheriff gave him a strange look. One minute it seemed the old rancher wanted the prisoner dead for his misdeeds, and the next he sounded thoroughly worried that something might happen to him.

"He's protected, Alvarez."

Maintaining his regal bearing, Luis dictated, "Just make sure he stays that way until the trial."

"That's my job," Macauley answered in a level tone, though he would have liked to have thrown him right out of his office.

As Luis turned to leave, he passed Molly on her way in. Sensing the tension, she glanced nervously between them. She waited until Luis had stepped outside and then shut the door behind her.

"Is everything all right?" Molly asked.

"I should be the one asking you that question." The sheriff's mood lightened to see that the young girl was well. He'd been concerned about her all morning, but didn't want to make a point of going out to her house and drawing suspicion down on her. "How did it go? Did you have any trouble?"

She quickly told him about their trek through town last night. "So far, everything's fine. What do you want me to do now?"

"O'Keefe hasn't given you any trouble or tried to escape, has he?" Macauley had to know.

"No. Dev won't try to escape. He's innocent, sheriff. He has no reason to run," she said firmly.

The lawman was surprised and a little pleased by her ardent defense of O'Keefe. He was glad that he was not the only one who saw the good in the man. "Can you keep him at your house for a while? It's about the safest place I can think of."

Molly had been hoping he would suggest that. She had been miserable at the thought of Dev being locked up in that cell again. She answered quickly, without hesitation. "Yes. No one ever comes to see us. There's just my mother, my brother and me."

"That's good, but how is your mother feeling?"

"Better."

"I'm glad to hear that. Now, listen, I don't want to bring O'Keefe back here to the jail until I've caught up with the ones responsible for the trouble last night."

"Do you really think you'll be able to find them?"

"Oh, I'll find them all right," Macauley answered firmly.

"I hope you do, and right away before they do something else crazy."

"I'm working on it, Molly, and maybe once I locate the troublemakers, I might have some real good news for O'Keefe."

Her expression brightened. "You mean you think there's more to this than just a bunch of drunks?"

"I'm not sure yet, but as soon as I work it out, I'll let you know. Don't say anything to him, though. I wouldn't want to get his hopes up, just in case I'm wrong."

"You aren't wrong, Sheriff, and we both know it." She was serious as she met his gaze. "Dev didn't kill anybody."

"I hope I can prove it. Until then, let's leave things as they are. You go on about your regular daily routine. Don't come back here unless it's an emergency. I don't want anyone putting two and two together and figuring out where he is. All right?"

"Yes, sir."

"Good girl. As soon as I learn anything, I'll be in touch. Until then, tell O'Keefe to lay low."

"I will," she promised and her mood was more confident than it had been in days as she left the jail. She was thrilled to know that the sheriff might be onto something, and she was also pleased that Dev would be staying on with her. At least, they would be together for a little while longer.

Dev had been nearly driven out of his mind by his enforced inactivity of the past weeks, and it seemed even worse to him now that he was there at the house. He wanted to get outside, to breathe some fresh air, even to do some kind of work. He was tired of just lying around, letting time go by.

When Molly left to see the sheriff and then go on to work, he decided to take a walk out back. He had seen the ramshackle barn the night before and wondered how bad it really was. He was not unused to hard manual labor, and the thought of fixing it up for Molly appealed to him. He wanted to give her something back for all she'd given him.

Since Jimmy was busy with his mother in her room, Dev went on outside. He was glad that Molly lived so far on the outskirts of town. It made it easier for him to move around without being seen. He took care to watch, though, checking thoroughly before he emerged in the daylight.

The heat of the sun's brilliant rays warmed him as he walked down the path, and he surveyed the old building inside and out with a jaundiced eye. It was in poor condition, but it could be fixed with minimal materials and a lot of elbow grease.

Without another thought, Dev started to work on the inside, shoveling it out first, then sweeping and then making what repairs he could with the few old tools he found there. He labored non-stop for the better part of an hour, working up a sweat and finally shedding his shirt. He kept at it, enjoying the physical exertion involved and the quick passage of time. When he finally took a breather, he stared around himself at what he'd accomplished and felt a contentment he hadn't known in years. There was a certain peace about the work, about doing this for Molly.

At the thought of precious Molly, Dev forced himself to get back at it. A long, hard day's work and total exhaustion would surely afford him a good night's rest tonight.

Jimmy was worried as he searched the house for some sign of Dev. When his mother had decided to take a nap, he'd come out of her room to talk to him for a while and could find no trace of him anywhere.

Disappointment filled the boy as he suspected the worst—that Dev had run away. It upset him to think that he'd do that. He had trusted him, just as Molly had, but it looked like the man had only been waiting for Molly to go so he could flee himself.

Jimmy was busy debating whether or not he should leave his mother alone and go tell the sheriff that his prisoner had gone, when he glanced out the window that overlooked the path and barn. He almost did a double-take as he realized someone was down there cleaning it out. His spirits surged as he saw Dev appear in the barn door for a minute and then go back inside. His faith in him restored, Jimmy charged from the house to see what he was doing.

"Dev!" he shouted.

Dev heard him coming and went out to meet him, wiping the dirt from his hands on his pants.

"What are you doing down here? I was looking for you everywhere," Jimmy asked breathlessly when he reached him.

"Why? Do you need me up at the house?" he questioned him, thinking something was wrong.

Jimmy had the grace to look shamefaced. "No," he muttered, looking at the ground, feeling mortified.

"Jim, what is it?" Dev, seeing that something was really troubling him, put a hand on his shoulder in a friendly gesture.

It was the first time anyone had addressed him as "Jim," and it made him feel more grown up. Still, he was ashamed that he'd thought Dev had escaped, and he was reluctant to look him in the eye.

"Come on, you can tell me. What's bothering you?" he encouraged.

"I'm sorry, Dev," Jimmy began slowly for he didn't want to confess that he'd doubted him.

"Sorry? For what?"

"Well, when you weren't up at the house, I was scared that you'd run off. I'm sorry. I should have known better," he told him fiercely.

Dev couldn't suppress a smile as he studied the boy. "You know, Jim, it takes quite a man to admit when he's wrong."

"It does?" He brightened considerably.

"It does," he confirmed, his deep, caring voice soothing the youth's fears. "It also takes a man not to run from trouble, but to face it squarely and deal with it."

"That's why you're never going to run away, right, Dev?"

"That's right, I'm not running," he stated, leading the way farther down the path to the pond to sit with Jimmy and take a break for a while.

"How come?" the boy wondered out loud. "I mean, it would be so easy for you to go and then you'd be safe. You wouldn't have to worry about the trial or anything."

Dev dropped down on the grass and the boy followed suit.

"You're wrong about that. I would have to worry. I'd be a wanted man. I'd be hunted wherever I went. I'd never be able to look myself in the mirror again, either. A man's got to have his self-respect and good name above all else. People won't like you, if you don't like yourself."

Jimmy's father had died when he was just a toddler, and since then he'd had little real contact with men. He was relishing this time with Dev, listening to his every word as gospel. He seemed so big and smart. Jimmy could understand why Molly liked him so much.

"Well, I like you, Dev, a whole lot, and so does Molly."

"I'm glad. I like you, too."

"Enough to stay forever?" he asked, innocent hope showing in his face.

Dev didn't want to bring up the pain he knew would come, so he avoided answering directly and responded, "For as long as I can, Jim."

"Good."

For just a fleeting moment, Dev let himself imagine what it would be like to stay here forever. The daydream was blissful as he pictured them all laughing and working and loving together. He knew with some hard work and a little money this place of theirs could be shined up and turned into a real nice home. If he added some fence they could even run a few head of cattle and some horses. But reality had a way of ruining Dev's dreams, and he pushed the fantasy aside. He scolded himself silently for even allowing himself to think about it. He knew what the future held for him, and it was not a happily ever after ending with Molly by his side.

"What do you say, we get back to work?" Dev invited. "Do you know how to hammer nails or use a saw?"

"No," Jimmy admitted.

"Well, come on then, it's time you learned." With an arm draped around the boy's slender shoulders, the two of them headed back to the barn.

Wily glanced nervously back over his shoulder for what must have been the hundredth time that day, as he continued his ride out of Monterey to the shack he kept in the hills. Though he'd done what Stevens had told him to, leaving town as fast as he could last night, he still didn't trust the man, and he feared for his life.

Wily didn't know why Stevens and his friends had been so intent on hanging O'Keefe the night before or why they were so worried about the sheriff now, but he figured it had to be pretty important for them to threaten him that way. He'd considered going to the sheriff and telling him about it, but the sheriff couldn't protect him all the time, and he was not eager to die.

Wily always considered himself, above all else, a practical person, so he'd high-tailed it out of town. He planned to stay away for at least a few weeks until all the trouble was over. Only when he was sure it was safe, would he willingly return to Monterey. Until then, he would hide out at the cabin and try to enjoy himself. He patted his saddlebags affectionately for he'd brought two bottles of whiskey with him, and he figured they were guaranteed to be his closest companions during the long days to come.

Though Luis' concern about O'Keefe's safety had been temporarily set to rest, he was still a troubled man as he rode up the drive to his home. Worrisome thoughts of Reina plagued him. The days since she'd disappeared had turned to weeks, and now the weeks threatened to turn to months and still there had been no word. He wondered desperately whether Cordell had managed to find her yet, and he hoped that he had.

The anger Luis had originally felt over Reina's defection was being tempered now by his growing anxiety over her personal safety. As he imagined her in some kind of life-threatening danger, his hands tightened involuntarily on the reins, and his horse shied at the unexpected pressure. If anything bad had happened to Reina he would never forgive himself. He loved her. She was his only child, and he only wanted what was best for her.

Luis supposed it was a good thing that he hadn't heard from Cordell. No news was good news, and he could console himself with the fact that at least as far as he knew, right now, Reina was safe. He would try to be patient, though it was growing more and more difficult, and perhaps, if he prayed just a little harder, his prayers would be answered and she would return home soon.

Chapter Twenty-four

Reina appeared as tranquil and serene as the turquoise sea this late morning hour as she stood at the rail staring out across its untamed beauty, but in reality it was a very deceptive comparison. While the waters might be calm, there was nothing calm about Reina. Only a few hours before at breakfast the captain had announced that they would be making landfall in Panama the following day, and now she was frantically trying to plot an escape that would free her from Clay Cordell once and for all.

Clay. The mere thought of the man was enough to infuriate her. He controlled her destiny completely, and she despised him for it. Yet, even as she'd claimed to hate him, he'd had only to touch her that fateful night, and her body had betrayed her, surrendering willingly to his sensual mastery.

The discovery of that vulnerability had left her shaken. Of all the men in the world, why did this man — her father's henchman — have to be the one to set her soul aflame? Why couldn't she have felt this way about Nathan? If she had, none of this would ever have happened. As it was, though, she had only one alternative, and that was to escape.

"Where are your thoughts, Reina?"

Clay's voice came close behind her, and she actually shook with the awareness it ignited in her. He joined her at the rail, and his unexpected presence startled her. Agitated, she glanced up at him, and for just a fleeting instant their eyes met. He caught a glimpse of some emotion he couldn't readily identify in her gaze, but she quickly shuttered it from him.

Clay gave a low chuckle as he slipped an arm about her shoulders in what appeared to all around them to be a gesture of protective affection between husband and wife. "Just the look on your face is enough to give you away, but you can forget running away. The only place you're going is Monterey with me."

She wanted to jerk free of his touch. She wanted to tell him that in one more day when they got to Panama, she'd be gone. But instead, she gave him a cool smile.

"If you say so, Clay," she replied all too agreeably, while silently she bristled over his arrogant assumption that she wouldn't be able to get away from him. She planned on showing him and showing him good.

"I say so," he said with a confident grin, giving her a little squeeze and then letting her go. He knew this sweet, submissive routine of hers was nothing more than a ruse. "It's almost time for the noon meal. Are you ready to go below?"

Reina wanted to slap that self-satisfied smile right off his face. She wanted to get away from him, not go down to the dining room with him and appear to be his loving wife.

"I'm more tired than hungry," she answered, and it was not an untruth.

She'd gotten precious little sleep these last few nights for she'd been forced to continue to share the bed with him. At first, she'd demanded that he

317

sleep in the chair or take another cabin, but he'd only mocked her. She'd flushed in furious anger when he'd told her that she had nothing to worry about, that he had no intention of doing anything other than sleep in the bed. Despite the fact that he'd kept to his word and had not tried to touch her again, just lying beside him in the darkness had left her nerves stretched taut. Each night she'd lain awake for hours before finally succumbing to a fitful rest.

"I think I'll go back to the cabin and rest for a while. You go on and eat."

Clay studied her for a moment, seeing for the first time the dark, shadow of weariness in her eyes. He felt a touch of guilt he had to do battle with. "Shall I escort you below?" He started to take her arm, but she moved away from him.

"I'll be fine, unless you're worried that I'm going to jump ship and swim to shore."

"It has crossed my mind a time or two," he responded and when she gave him a quick look, he just gave her another taunting smile. "I'll see you later."

As Reina hurried away, she could feel Clay watching her, and she was glad when she entered the companionway and moved out of sight. It felt good to be free of his oppressive presence if only for a little while. To her surprise, she came face to face with Michael.

"Mrs. Cordell, hello," the young man blustered, thrilled to see her. Since the scene at dinner the other night, he hadn't had the chance to talk with her again, and he'd missed her.

"Michael, it's so nice to see you," she greeted him warmly.

"It's good to see you, too, ma'am," he told her, meaning it with all his heart. He thought she was wonderful.

Reina was well aware of his feelings, and she also knew that he was her one hope for help in escaping. She didn't like the idea of using him for her own purpose, but realized there was no other way.

"Michael, I was wondering if there's somewhere we might talk — privately."

"Privately?" He was astounded by her suggestion. But to him, the thought of a few minutes alone with her was well worth risking the other man's ire. "Well, um, I share my cabin with three other men, so I don't know where we could go."

Reina glanced around and then touched his arm in a gesture that hinted at intimacy. She drew him along to the end of the corridor where there was a small alcove out of sight from anyone in the companionway. Unaware that anyone was aware of their presence.

"My husband's gone to eat, so we should be able to manage a short time to ourselves."

"Yes, ma'am."

"Michael, there's something important — a favor, I have to ask of you."

Michael was hooked. He couldn't believe it! Reina Cordell wanted something from him. His heart was pounding. Though he knew there might be danger involved since she was a married woman, his deeply ingrained chivalry wouldn't allow retreat.

"Of course," he agreed quickly.

Reina could sense his excited anticipation, and as much as it pained her, she knew she would have no problem bending him to her will. Michael was a nice man, the type of man who, unlike Clay, would respond to the plea for help of a woman in trouble. All she had to do was convince him that Clay was treating her wrong. Once she managed that, she was sure he would help her escape his abuse.

"Michael . . ." she spoke hesitantly, wanting him to believe her uncertainty, her fear and helplessness.

"What is it you wanted, Mrs. Cordell?" Michael led eagerly. "What can I do to help you?"

"It's . . . it's my husband . . ." Reina said in a choked voice.

"Your husband? What about him?" he asked gently, a great feeling of protectiveness filling him. She was so lovely and so very feminine. He wanted to help her in any way he could.

"Oh, it's so hard to talk about, but I knew you were the one person I could be honest with . . . the one person on this ship I could ask to help me." She lifted her gaze to his imploringly.

"Of course I'll help you. But how? What do you want me to do?"

"I have to escape," Reina answered quickly.

"Escape?" he repeated, his eyes rounding slightly at the thought. "You want to escape from your husband? I thought you two were newly married."

"It's true we haven't been together long," she said softly.

"Don't you love him?"

"No, how could I, when he's so cruel and heartless?!" Thinking of the misery that would be hers once Clay took her back to marry Nathan, tears welled up in her eyes. She used them to her advantage.

"He treats you badly?" Michael was astonished and swelled with indignation at the thought.

"It's terrible. He's so abusive . . . but only when no one else will see . . . You must help me, Michael. There's no one else I can turn to."

"Tell me what you want me to do," the young man said ardently. It outraged him to think that her husband might harm her in some way, and he was ready to do whatever she asked without question.

"I want to run away from him when we get to Panama. Will you help me do that?"

"Yes," he vowed gallantly, feeling a rush of masculine pride at his ability to come to her rescue.

"Oh, Michael, I always knew you were someone special."

The young man beamed at her praise. He felt like a knight in shining armor. He wanted, was eager, to do battle for her. "What do you want me to do?"

Reina quickly explained her plan to sneak off the boat and get a horse before Clay could miss her. Michael listened and knew he couldn't let her go alone.

"I'll leave the boat first and arrange for the horses," he said firmly.

"Horses?"

"It wouldn't be safe for you to go alone. I'll go with you."

"Do you think that's wise? My husband—"

"Won't be able to find us, so we'll be fine."

"Thank you, Michael. I don't know what I would have done without you." Reina wasn't comfortable with the idea of him going along with her, but could see no way around it right now.

"It's an honor to be of service to you," he swore earnestly, taking her hand in his and gazing, lovestruck, into her eyes.

"I'd better be getting to my cabin now."

"Yes, yes, of course." Michael offered her his arm and accompanied her to her cabin. He paused outside her stateroom door, gazing down at her.

"Until tomorrow. . . ?"

"Yes, Michael . . ."

He lifted her hand to his lips, then stayed right there until she'd gone inside. Michael's head was in the clouds as he turned and started back up on deck. He was startled when the man stepped out in front of him, cutting off his path, and he stopped in his tracks, puzzled. He looked up, frowning, to find himself staring into a pair of the fiercest, coldest, steel-gray eyes he'd ever seen.

Michael stiffened, his eyes widening as he recognized him. "Cordell . . ." he croaked.

"Hello, Webster," he said coolly, menacingly, his gaze never leaving the younger man's face.

"Hello." There was something so threatening about Cordell's stance, something so dangerous, that Michael suddenly realized he knew everything. He began to tremble.

Clay studied him for a long minute, letting him sweat beneath his ominous scrutiny.

"Webster," he finally began, breaking the taut silence that had stretched between them, "if you go near my wife again, you're a dead man."

Seeing the pure, unadulterated promise of pain in his deadly regard, Michael blanched.

"Do you understand me?" Clay pressed.

Michael nodded, swallowing nervously. He wished he was brave enough to stand up to him, but he wasn't. He might be infatuated with Cordell's wife, but he wasn't stupid.

"Let me hear you say it out loud, Webster. Do you understand me?"

Struck silent by his threat, he could only whisper the words in a hoarse, frightened voice. "Yes, sir."

"Good, I'm glad we understand each other." Clay smiled wolfishly as he stepped aside.

Michael found he was shaking uncontrollably. He didn't say another word, but took the opportunity to escape his sinister presence at a dead run. He didn't know where he was going, and he didn't care. He just wanted to get as far away from Clay Cordell as he could, fast.

Clay watched him go, then started off toward his and Reina's stateroom. He was cool and calculating as he thought of what he would do next. He'd taken care of Webster, and now it was time to set Reina straight. He'd stopped this plan before she could move on it, and he would stop any other scheme she concocted.

The door was locked when Clay reached the cabin, and he knocked lightly as he called out. "Reina, it's me. Open the door." His command was cool and controlled just as he believed himself to be. He prided himself on the fact that he'd kept himself under tight control during these past few days. It galled him that he'd given in to his weakness for her that night, and he fully intended that it would never happen again. He knew what kind of woman she was. Her actions with Webster just reinforced his opinion.

Reina had not expected him to return this quickly, and hearing him at the door now annoyed her. She had hoped that he would stay away for a while so she would have some time to finish figuring out her plan. Still, in spite of her irritation, she was in a very good mood as she moved to open the door for she believed that by some time the next day she would be rid of Clay forever.

"Thank you, my darling bride," Clay drawled as he stepped into the room and closed it firmly behind him.

"I'm not your darling anything!" she snapped back. They were in their stateroom now, and there was no need for all the sweetness and light he insisted upon when they were out in public.

"Well, well, well," he said slowly. "I'm certainly glad to see that the change in you wasn't lasting."

"What change?" Something about his tone cautioned Reina, and she cast him a curious glance.

323

"Why the teary-eyed, helpless female who just poured her heart out to Webster," Clay hit her hard with the knowledge that he knew about her plans.

"You heard . . ." she whispered, horrified that she'd been discovered. She wondered miserably if she would ever be able to get away from this man.

"Everything, my dear, and you needn't count on his help any more. I straightened him out about a few things."

"Why, you!" Reina's eyes blazed with fury as she took a menacing step toward him. Michael had been her one hope, her only ally, and now . . .

"That's more like it," he gave a sarcastic laugh as he studied her, watching how her breasts were heaving in indignation and how her cheeks were burning in proof of her anger. He remembered another time when she'd been breathless, and a jolt of desire shot through him. "You know you really are the consummate actress, Reina. You might have tricked the boy that easily, but I would never have been fooled by your weak little woman routine. I know you better."

"You don't know me, Clay Cordell. You don't know anything about me!" she told him, her ire evident in the taut line of her body.

"I know all I need to know. There's nothing helpless or delicate about you. You're nothing but a conniving, deceitful, little . . ."

Reina had had enough, and she exploded in outrage. Clay never had time to finish his sentence as she slapped him full force. The sound of her hand connecting with the leanness of his cheek resounded through the room.

Her action shocked Clay, and he reacted instinctively, grabbing her by her arms and jerking her off her feet as he hauled her up against him. He glared down at her, his gray eyes stormy with the power of the emotions that were raging through him. With one hand he held her bound, with the other he gripped her chin and forced her to look up at him. Reina tried to fight against his hold, but his fingers bit painfully into her flesh, refusing to yield.

"I've warned you about pushing me, Reina," he said slowly, his threat implied and understood. "I'm not a fool like Webster."

"Michael's no fool! Michael's—"

Clay pulled her even closer. "Michael's an idiot. He couldn't hold a woman like you, but I can . . . and I will."

Reina stared up at him, her expression mutinous even as she faced the truth of her defeat. Frustration welled up inside her. Was there no way she could outsmart this man? Was there no way to escape him? Tears of fury burned in her eyes, and she tried again to jerk free of his paralyzing hold, but he refused to release her.

Clay wanted to prove to her, once and for all, that he was not a man to be trifled with. He was bending to her, meaning to kiss her, meaning to prove his point when he saw the unshed tears shimmering in her eyes. Suddenly some emotion more powerful than any he'd ever known before stormed his senses. Without conscious thought he eased pressure of his restraining grip, no longer holding her prisoner, but cradling her against him, his hand no longer gripping her chin, but tilting her face to his. Desire swept through him with the force of a raging torrent as he lowered his head to hers.

Reina watched as passion darkened his expression. She began to tremble as he bent to her. Her heart lurched in a breathtaking acknowledgment that despite everything she felt about this man, she wanted his kiss. There was one brief moment when she would have fought against him, but then his lips met hers and it was too late.

With gentle ferocity, Clay's mouth moved over Reina's, and a firestorm of desire flared to life. Hands that had moments before fought against him, surrendered, sweeping upward to encircle his neck and draw him ever closer, ever nearer. He groaned as her action brought her fully and willingly against him. Sliding his own hands down her back to her hips, he pressed her tightly to the heat of his need. She gasped at the sensation, moving her hips instinctively against him in nature's rhythm.

When Clay lifted her up into his arms to lay her upon the bed, Reina murmured not a protest. She was lost in the fiery splendor of his embrace, caught up in the hot power of this thing that existed between them, that they could neither name or resist.

Long forgotten was the argument that had led to this explosion of long-denied desire. Long forgotten was Reina's need to survive, her need to flee. Feverish with excitement, there was only a man and a woman, clutching at a moment of ecstasy in a world ugly with too many half-truths.

Garments were stripped as steamy passions demanded fulfillment. Bare flesh on bare flesh, they came together. Differences celebrated now. Hard male dominating and, yet even as he conquered, surrendering to the softness of the female. Woman giving of herself completely, and in that giving, claiming without demanding, the very soul of the man. It was a union borne of volcanic passion that erupted into the red-hot lava flow of love. Their desires exploded into brilliance and bound them together in the fever of oneness. Sated as never before, they drifted mindlessly in the heated tempest's aftermath.

Reina was first to realize the gravity of what she'd allowed to happen, and shame overwhelmed her. He had bragged that he could handle her, and he had. It infuriated her that she had made it so easy for him. Needing to get away from him, she drew back out of his embrace.

"Reina?" Clay could see the hostility reflected in her eyes, and he was careful that no trace of emotion showed in his own.

"You certainly proved you're a man of your word." Rancor sharpened her voice as she moved from the bed, clutching a cover to her.

"Reina . . . I . . ." For a moment he almost told her that it hadn't been a power struggle, that it had been something else he didn't understand, but she didn't give him a chance to speak.

Feeling cornered and trapped, knowing this man's power over her was complete, she struck out at him in the only way she could. "You can drug me and tie me to the bed. You can drag me bodily back to my father against my will. You can even make me respond to you physically, but that's all it is — a physical response! You may possess my body, but you'll never possess me. Never!"

Clay bristled at her words, but was determined not to let her know. He shrugged carelessly as he got up. "For some men, that's enough."

He watched as his words hit home, and she turned pale. Casually, he began to dress as she looked on in helpless fury. Without a backward glance, he quit the cabin, leaving her staring after him, more frightened than she'd ever been before.

Chapter Twenty-five

Michael stood at the bar in the men's lounge and ordered another shot of the barkeep's less than mellow whiskey. Since his humiliating confrontation with Cordell the day before, he'd been slinking around the boat like a whipped dog. For the briefest period of time, he'd fancied himself a knight in armor rescuing a lady in distress, and yet when he'd been threatened, he'd backed down like a coward.

He hadn't meant to dwell on it, but the more he thought about it, the more upset he became. He felt guilty. There was no doubt about it. And he felt worried. When Reina hadn't shown up for dinner last night he'd feared that her husband had confronted her, too, and possibly harmed her in some way. Only catching a glimpse of her looking as lovely as ever this morning on deck with her husband had relieved his attack of conscience, but he still harbored the feeling that he should do something to help her.

As Michael drained the last of the biting liquor from the glass, he glanced idly around the room and noticed for the first time the young boy of about fourteen or fifteen busily straightening things up. He frowned thoughtfully as he studied the youngster, a short, thin, almost wiry youth, and an outrageous idea came to him. Knowing time was growing short, he approached him.

A short time later Michael stood on deck keeping watch for Clay Cordell, a bundle tucked securely under his arm. He knew his plan was risky, but he had to chance it. He would never be able to look himself in the mirror again, if he didn't at least make the attempt.

When at long last Cordell emerged, alone, from belowdecks, Michael made his move. Without hesitation, he hurried off to find Reina. It was absolutely important that he speak to her before her husband returned and found them together. He rushed to her stateroom as fast as humanly possible and, after one last, furtive look around, knocked on the door.

"Mrs. Cordell? It's me, Michael," he called out in a hushed tone, not wanting anyone else to be aware of his presence.

"Michael?" Reina was surprised. Hope buoyed in her heart that maybe he hadn't been scared off by Clay's intimidating tactics. She quickly opened the door to him.

Michael still thought she was the prettiest woman he'd ever seen, but he had no wish to suffer another encounter with her husband. He had to hurry.

"Mrs. Cordell . . . I, um . . . I'm sorry I won't be able to help you more, but I got these for you," he said quickly as he shoved the big bundle into her hands. He glanced nervously over his shoulder for fear that her husband might have materialized out of thin air.

"What is it?" she asked, having no idea what it was he'd just handed her.

"Clothes . . . boy's clothes. I thought you might

be able to use them. Look, I have to go. I'm sorry I can't do more . . ." With that he was gone at an almost run. He disappeared from sight without another word.

Reina stared after him for a minute, then closed the door again. She shook out the pants, loose-fitting top and nearly crushed straw hat, and as she did, a slow smile lit her face. By now, Reina considered herself a master of disguise, and her confidence surged. She'd fooled Clay into thinking she was a nun, certainly it would be easier to act out the part of a boy. Everyone would have noticed her had she tried to sneak away in her ordinary clothing, but dressed as a boy, she would be able to slip off the ship and onto the docks unnoticed.

Feeling once more in control of her life, her disposition greatly improved. They were to arrive in Chagres some time that afternoon and leave the boat then. They wouldn't be using the bed again, so she hid the clothes under the rumpled covers, knowing they would be safe there.

There was a lightness to her step as she left the stateroom a short time later. It was a struggle for her to make sure the excitement she was feeling didn't show in her expression or her manner. She knew she had to do it, though, for her whole future depended on it. Clay might think he'd outsmarted her, but he had another think coming. This time she was going to show him, but good.

The town of Chagres on Panama's east coast was a hot, insect-infested, muddy town, but several hours later when Reina caught her first glimpse of it as they made landfall, it looked like paradise. Her exhilaration grew. This was it! The moment she'd

330

been waiting for ever since Clay had dragged her off from Louisiana. The time had finally come. Now, she would take her big chance.

She didn't notice the squalor of her surroundings. She didn't think that it might be dangerous to make the escape here. All she could think about was the glory of getting away from Clay and fleeing from the awful, threatening horror of marriage to Nathan.

"We'll have to spend the night here in town, so I'll be going ashore as soon as possible to find a room for the night. I want you to stay on the ship until I get back," Clay instructed, breaking into her reverie with his orders and directions that she had absolutely no intention of following.

"Whatever you say," Reina answered, just wishing he would go ahead and go. She had a lot to do and couldn't start until he'd left the ship.

He glanced at her and, noting the stubborn set of her chin, he knew she was planning something. Skilled bounty hunter that he was, though, he'd already anticipated her next move.

"The captain and his men will look out for you while I'm gone. Chagres is a dangerous place even at the best of times," he warned. He told himself that his need to caution her came strictly from his duty to her father, that she was his responsibility. Yet, he knew it was much more than that, and he hoped she had sense enough to listen to him and not try anything stupid.

"It hardly looks it," she remarked, not prone to believe anything he had to say.

"Looks can be deceiving, as you should well know," Clay countered, an image of Sister Mary Regina dancing through his thoughts. He pushed the memory out of his mind.

331

Captain Gibson just happened to join them then. "You can go ashore now, if you're ready."

"Fine. Thank you, Captain. Reina, I'll be back as soon as I can."

"I'm counting on it," she replied sweetly, solely for the captain's benefit. "I can hardly wait to be on land again."

Gibson stayed with her until Clay had left the ship, and then he offered, "Shall I walk you back to your stateroom?"

"That would be wonderful, sir. I do have some last minute things to see to."

As he escorted her below, she complimented him on the voyage and thanked him for getting them to their destination safely.

"It's been our pleasure to have you aboard, ma'am," he told her. "You're the loveliest lady to grace our ship in a long time."

"You're too kind, Captain Gibson."

"Those who really know me, seldom say that," he said with a smile. "I make it a point to only speak the truth, Mrs. Cordell."

They stopped before her cabin door, and he waited as she unlocked it.

"In case we don't get the opportunity to speak again, I hope the rest of your trip home is as safe as our voyage. I also extend to you my best wishes for your future. Your husband's a good man, and it's obvious that he loves you very much. I hope you two have a long and happy life together."

"Thank you," she murmured, wondering what the man would think if he knew the truth.

"If you find that you need anything before you disembark, please just let me know."

"I will."

He bid her good-bye, and she went into the room

and locked the door behind her. She leaned back against the closed portal and sagged in joyous relief. She was alone, at long last! Immediately, she set to the task of transforming herself.

Moments later Reina stood before the small mirror surveying her outfit. She thought she looked like a boy in the baggy clothes and sandals, but she couldn't be sure until she'd stuffed all her hair up under the hat. With swift, sure motions, she did just that and then regarded herself critically. A smile lit her face as she adjusted the brim, pulling it down low over her face as she'd seen the natives wear theirs to protect them from the sun. Only she would know it was a disguise. She took a quick look out the stateroom door and seeing no one around, made her great escape.

Reina walked across the deck and was thrilled no one paid her any mind. She headed down the gangplank expecting at any minute for someone to call out to her to stop, but no one did. She couldn't believe her luck when her feet finally touched terra firma. It took all of her will-power not to break into a run. A furtive glance around revealed no sign of Clay, so she headed for a small group of boys lingering nearby. She hoped one of them would be able to tell her where to find a horse.

Knowing that this was the first time Reina would have the chance to escape him, Clay wasted no time in town. As soon as he'd booked the hotel room, he started straight back to the waterfront. Thoughts of the night just passed and the passion that had exploded between them haunted him as he made his way through Chagres, and he was aggravated that he couldn't just forget last night had ever happened.

It irritated him that he'd been unable to stop from making love to her after that first kiss, and he wondered where his much vaunted self-discipline had been when he'd lost himself in the heat of his desire for her.

Clay knew he had no business getting involved with Reina, and as much as he would have loved to deny it, he was in danger of becoming involved. His actions last night had shown him just how weak he could be around her. It was a weakness he planned never to give in to again. He refused to be caught like his father. He had learned from him. He would be strong.

As he neared the ship, the raucous sound of several youths arguing among themselves, interrupted his train of thought. His first inclination was to ignore them after a cursory glance in their direction, but for some unknown reason, something about them drew his attention back. He stopped to listen.

"I'll get the horse for you," a tall, skinny, ominous-looking, dark-haired youth named Rafael was offering, "but first let me see the color of your money, gringo."

"I will get the horse," a shorter native boy interrupted in a more commanding tone.

"Shut up, Chico, I saw him first. I will do it," the first boy countered, drawing himself up to his full height in an intimidating move.

"Hey, I know of the perfect horse for you," the third youth spoke up. "Let me get it for you."

"I've got the money," she said impatiently, "and I don't care which one of you gets me a horse, just get it!"

"Pay me, then I will get the horse," Rafael demanded, bullying up to Reina.

She stood her ground, glaring up at him as the youth towered over her. "Bring me the horse, and then I'll pay you," she returned, trying to sound as fearless as she possibly could. "Only a fool would pay you now."

"And you're no fool?" Rafael smiled wickedly as he moved menacingly closer. He figured it would be a very simple thing to take this boy's money. After all, there were three of them and only one of him.

Reina took a slight step backward at the implied physical threat.

Clay had remained stock still as he'd listened to the conversation. He recognized the "boy" as Reina the moment she'd opened her mouth, and he'd suddenly become explosively angry. Damn her! Hadn't he warned her how dangerous Chagres could be?

The moment Rafael made his ominous move, Clay reacted. His expression was thunderous as he stormed toward them. Without preamble, he grabbed Reina by the upper arm and dragged her out of harm's way. She uttered a startled cry, then began to sputter in a rage as she saw it was him. Her stomach gave a sickening lurch as she realized that she'd been found out. She tried to pull free, but he held her fast as he faced down the boys.

"You're right, amigo. This boy's no fool. He has friends — mean friends," Clay was saying.

"He wanted us to get him a horse."

"I know what he wanted, and from now on, I'll take care of his traveling needs," he ground out savagely, his expression murderous.

They had seen that look in the eyes of men before, and they knew what it meant.

"Whatever you say, hombre." They backed up nervously and then raced away.

Clay didn't wait to see where they went. Keeping a firm grip on his captive hellion, he took a step in the direction of town.

Reina, however, had other ideas. She couldn't believe he'd shown up, right then, when she was about to get her horse and get away! She dug in her heels, resisting his pull with all her might.

"I'm not going anywhere with you!"

"Like hell, you're not!" he fumed in a low voice. "Don't open your mouth again or I swear I'll throw you over my shoulder and carry you off! I warned you, Reina!"

Reina stopped struggling, but she let him feel her reluctance as he led her off. She had expected him to take her back on board so she could change clothes and was surprised when he didn't. She hung back the entire distance into town, and, when he led her up the steps of one of the better looking, though a far cry from sumptuous, hotels, she tried to bolt. Clay's hand tightened on her with bruising force, and the look he shot her convinced her that his earlier threat still held.

He dragged her through the small lobby, completely ignoring the amused, interested stares of the other guests and then hauled her behind him up the stairs to the single room he'd rented for the night. When he'd unlocked and pushed the door wide, he shoved her roughly through in front of him. The room was sparsely furnished with only a bed and single dresser, but Reina didn't even notice as Clay slammed the door behind him. The sound of the lock turning sent a shiver of fear through her.

"What the hell did you think you were doing?" His face was a glowering mask of fury as he jerked her around to face him.

"What do you think?" Reina challenged defiantly,

tearing her arm free of him.

"Don't you realize what might have happened to you?"

"Yes," she challenged with a lift of her chin, "I might have gotten away from you! My disguise was certainly clever enough!" She was proud of what she'd almost accomplished, and she wasn't going to let him browbeat her.

"Your disguise." Clay spat, his hand snaking out to rip the hat from her head and throw it aside.

Reina's ebony hair tumbled down freely about her shoulders. "Was perfect!" she finished sharply for him. "If only those boys hadn't been so stupid . . ."

"You're the one who was stupid!" he cut in. "You could have been killed!"

"I could have been free!" she argued heatedly. "Free of you and free of Nathan!"

"You're never going to be free of me," Clay snarled, his anger growing unbounded over her continued refusal to listen to reason. "Not until I deliver you to your father. Now, get out of those ridiculous clothes."

"I will not," she defied him.

"Oh, yes, you will. You told me once not too long ago that you were a lady. I expect you to dress like one." He stepped toward her, and she backed away. He was relentless in his pursuit, trapping her between the bed and the wall.

Pushed to the limit, enraged and feeling more than helpless, she hissed, "I don't care what you expect or want!"

"I know. You don't care about anybody or anything except yourself," Clay said viciously. "Now get undressed."

"No!" Reina's back was to the wall. There was nowhere left to run. Still, she met his gaze boldly,

337

refusing to give in.

"I've had enough of your disguises, Reina. Are you going to take it off or am I?"

"You just try!"

It was all the challenge Clay needed right then. Never in his life had he met anyone who could rouse such near violent emotions within him. Seeing her being threatened by those boys had enraged him, and now her stubbornness filled him with a driving need to show her just who was in charge here—again. Provoked beyond reason, he reached out for her shirt.

"Don't touch me!" Reina ordered, trying to avoid his hands.

Clay was not to be deterred, however, and he got hold of the shirt anyway. He pulled it roughly over her head leaving her naked to the waist as she stood before him. He crushed it in his hands, then cast it aside in disgust. She wrapped her arms around herself in a modest gesture, shielding her breasts from view. Her protective action touched a chord of response within Clay, but her next words jarred him again.

"There! Are you satisfied?"

"The pants next, Reina."

"No."

Demons he didn't understand and didn't want to understand drove him on, he said nothing more, but reached out and untied the narrow cord that served as a belt. The loose-fitting pants dropped away. Reina did not cower away from him now, but met his gaze daringly.

The sight of her standing there completely vulnerable, yet at the same time, proud and unflinching, moved Clay deeply. He had won this battle, but at what price? His victory over her had been a physical one again. He had forced her to his will. He remembered her words from the night before, and though he knew it was true, he couldn't stop his own desire for her. He wanted her. His body was on fire with the need to have her again.

"There'll be no more disguises, Reina. The games are over."

Reina saw it in his eyes—the flaring passion that neither one of them could control, and she began to tremble. Her instincts for survival screamed to her to flee before she lost herself in his arms again.

There was nowhere for her to go, though, as Clay loomed before her, the single, biggest threat to her existence. She hated everything he stood for, yet there was something so utterly irresistible about him that she could refuse him nothing. When his hands closed over her shoulders, she held herself rigid, refusing to give in immediately, trying to fight with all her might the raging inferno of madness that swept through her at his touch.

And madness it was, as he had his way with her. Their joining was cataclysmic. Each caress followed by another more demanding one. Each kiss more desperate than the last. Anger transformed to desire. Desire to ecstasy's passion.

Clay's clothes were discarded in haste as the fury of their need urged them to hurry . . . hurry before reality intruded. As excitement took them to the heights, the very pinnacle of breathless delight, all else was forgotten. They were no longer adversaries, but nameless lovers without past or future. They were no longer hunter and quarry, but two souls bound by something so powerful, they were frightened by the immensity of it, and so, denied its existence.

Clay's obligations drove him. His heart was still

cold and wary of this thing called love.

Reina, too, was disbelieving. She felt uncertain that this physical need she had only for him could be more than just that. She thought his desire for her was only a means of coercion, that he really felt nothing for her. Hadn't he said as much?

But even as their emotions roiled in confusion, they were swept up in sea of rapture. All rational thought was lost as their bodies united in perfect oneness. There was only feeling and touching and love's bliss in its wake.

As quickly as it had happened, it was over, and Reina could not bring herself to look at Clay. She rolled away from his intoxicating nearness, needing time to pull herself together. *This has to end!* she raged at herself. She couldn't allow this to go on. She rose from the bed and wrapped a blanket around her.

"Do you know what you've done to me?" she asked, frantic for answers to questions she didn't even know.

Clay had been too bewildered by what had happened to move or to think—until she spoke.

"What are you talking about?" The mellow mood that had held him evaporated before the coldness of her question. He glanced over at her and saw the misery and torment mirrored in her eyes.

"You were sent to find me and bring me back to my father. You were hired to protect me during that journey." She gave a brittle laugh. "But it seems you're the only one I need protection from."

Her words were like lashes from a whip, cutting him to shreds, tearing into his soul.

"I can't fight you," she said. "You're stronger than I am. I can't escape you. You block my every move. What do you want from me?"

340

When he didn't respond, she went on.

"Leave me alone, Clay. Just stay away from me."

Her words of the night before echoed painfully through him again. *He might possess her body, but he'd never possess her.* He dressed, feeling strangely bereft. He gathered her boys' clothes and started to the door.

"I'm taking these with me. I need to be sure you won't leave the room while I'm gone. As soon as I see that the rest of our things are unloaded from the boat, I'll be back."

Reina did not look up. She was sitting on the side of the bed with her back to him, and she stayed that way until long after he'd gone. Only then did she give vent to her tears.

Chapter Twenty-six

Macauley's hopes were guarded as he urged his mount to the top of the low rise and reined in. He knew he was taking a long shot in coming here, but if a man's life was saved because of it, it would be worth the time lost. Turning his gaze below to the dilapidated cabin that stood there in the small clearing, the sheriff experienced a surge of satisfaction as he recognized the hobbled horse contentedly cropping grass in front of the shack. It was Wily's.

"Damn!" he muttered to himself as the pride he'd felt about his hunch being right, faded. Irritation and impatience with himself replaced the smugness. He'd known that Wily owned some land up here in the hills, and it annoyed him that he hadn't immediately figured out that this was where he'd gone.

Putting his heels to his horse, Macauley headed down the narrow rocky path that led to the small house. Never one to ride into possible trouble unarmed, he let one hand rest on his sidearm, just in case. He'd seen too many men gunned down during his years as a lawman to take any chances.

"Yo! Wily! You in there?" he shouted out as he drew to a halt out front.

"Who's callin' me?" Wily asked drunkenly as he

stumbled to the door and, leaning against the door-jamb, looked out. "Sheriff!" he gasped in stunned recognition.

"Yeah, it's me, Wily. You alone?"

"Why? What d'ya want?" the old man demanded suspiciously, stiffening as Macauley dismounted and approached him.

"I just want to talk, that's all." The sheriff could see that he was really jittery and upset, so he tried to calm him. "I just need the answers to a few questions, and then I'll be on my way."

Wily tilted his bottle of whiskey to his lips and took a deep drink. Wiping his mouth on the back of his arm, he eyed the lawman for a minute. "What kinda questions?"

"Can I come in? We can sit and talk about it."

Cornered, he knew he had no choice. "I suppose." He went back inside, moving unsteadily, and Macauley followed him.

The interior of the shack was in worse shape than the outside. Dirt and dust were everywhere. One window had been broken out and not replaced. The fireplace looked like it hadn't been used for years, and what furniture there was was in an advanced state of disrepair—the single, narrow bed sagging and dirty-looking, the table and two chairs looking downright rickety.

"Come here often?" he asked conversationally.

"No" was his only reply.

"How come you decided to come up here now?"

Wily eyed him nervously as he slumped down in one of the chairs. "I needed to get away for a while."

"Any particular reason?" he asked as he sat down opposite him.

"Why're you askin' me all this? You didn't ride all the way up here just to see how I was doin'."

"You're right, Wily. I need to talk to you. You're the only one who can help me."

"What d'ya mean? Help you with what?"

Macauley decided to get straight to the point. "I want to know why you left town so suddenly."

The old man puffed up with indignation, not wanting him to know of his cowardice. "I didn't leave suddenly. I just decided it was time to check on the cabin, is all."

"Right after you'd paid Mrs. Johnson a month's rent?"

Wily colored at having been caught, and he took another big swig. He wished with all his heart the sheriff would just go away. He had enough trouble already. He didn't want to make it worse.

"What happened, Wily? What happened that night at the saloon? Who started all the talk about hanging O'Keefe?"

His eyes were shifty as he sought some way of escaping telling him the truth.

"Wily," Macauley pressed urgently, "if you're worried something's going to happen to you, I promise, I'll do everything I can to keep you safe. A man's life is at stake here—an innocent man."

"Well, I ain't guilty of nothin' either!" he exploded. "What if I end up dead?"

"You won't if you tell me everything, right now. Let me help you. It's my job to handle this."

"It was Stevens! Charley Stevens! He's the one who started it all that night. He's the one who wanted to string up O'Keefe. He was rantin' and ravin' real good, and the rest of 'em were just all drunk and went along with his rabblerousin'."

"Go on."

Wily needed reinforcement and once again took a slug of liquor. "He was mad later on that night back

344

at the saloon. I don't know why he wanted O'Keefe to hang so bad. Hell, I didn't even know that he and Santana were that good friends."

"They weren't. Not that I know of," Macauley said tersely, angrily. Charley Stevens . . . it fit. He knew the young man was no good, but he'd never caught him at anything before. He'd arrest him for disturbing the peace as soon as he got back to town and take him in, but he still didn't have any direct proof of him being involved in Santana's murder. "Go on, what happened next?" he asked, hoping that he might know something more.

"Well, anyway, he was sittin' there and saw me at the bar. I guess he figured out that I was the one who warned you. He told me to get outta town, so I did. He's a mean cuss, and I didn't want nothin' to do with him."

"Why would he want you to get out of town?"

"I didn't ask." He gave him an incredulous look. "I just left."

He nodded in understanding. "Do you want to come back with me now?"

"Now?" The old man's eyes widened at the thought. "No. I think I'll stay right here for a while."

"You can rest easy, Wily. I'm going to get to the bottom of this."

"I hope so, Sheriff."

Macauley mounted up and started straight back for Monterey. It was a long, tiring ride. He knew he should probably spend the night and give his horse time to rest, but he felt this was too important. He wanted to get his hands on Stevens while he could.

All the way back to town, he pondered the pieces of the puzzle that was Santana's death. The rancher had been shot in the back and robbed. O'Keefe's medallions had been found out there, and a large

345

sum of money had been found in his belongings. After weeks of having the bounty hunter in custody, Stevens riles up a mob and tries to get him lynched. Why? It couldn't have been out of moral outrage. Stevens and Santana barely knew each other. There was more to it, and he was determined to find that last, missing piece that would answer all the questions that were plaguing him. When he picked him up in town and brought him in, he was going to make him sweat for a while. Then maybe, just maybe, he'd get the answers he was looking for.

For a moment, the possibility that O'Keefe really was guilty occurred to him. He wondered if he could be wrong in his judgment of the man, but remembering Denton's escape attempt and how O'Keefe hadn't tried to run even now, he knew he was right. O'Keefe was innocent. He just had to find the man who wasn't.

"Charley, ain't you getting nervous about it? I mean the word's out that Sheriff Macauley's trying to find the man who started all the trouble the other night," Bucky asked a bit excitedly as he chugged another beer.

"Hell no, I ain't nervous. Why should I be nervous? There wasn't no violence or bloodshed," Charley swore easily as he studied his cards with care. The three of them had been drinking and playing poker at the Golden Horseshoe for the better part of the evening. Their general mood had been good up until Bucky had started to talk about the ill-fated lynch mob.

"But the sheriff's a stubborn man," Rex warned. "He ain't gonna quit lookin'."

"Let him look," Charley said tersely.

346

"What if someone tells him it was you?"

"And just who's gonna talk? Wily was the only stupid, weak one around. Everybody else is smart enough to keep their mouths shut."

"Guess you're right," his companions agreed, relaxing a bit.

"Damn right, I am. There ain't nobody gonna tell the sheriff, unless one of you is thinkin' about it."

"Hell, no!" they quickly denied.

"That's good, 'cause you two know what'll happen if either one of you does, don't you?" He looked up from his cards, his gaze cold and threatening.

Rex and Bucky nodded, thoroughly intimidated. The day he'd bushwhacked Santana, they had been along. He'd made it clear, then and there, that they were just as guilty of murder as he was, even though he did the shooting. If he was turned in, he'd vowed that he would make sure they were arrested, too. They believed him.

"We ain't about to talk, Charley. You know us better than that. We're just afraid somebody else might say somethin'."

"Well, if they were going to, they would have done it by now, wouldn't they?" he asked sarcastically. "Don't worry. Things'll be fine. All we gotta do is sit tight."

It was midnight when Sheriff Macauley entered the Golden Horseshoe. He was tired from riding all day, but he didn't care. He was too intent on what he had to do. His expression was as deadly serious as the shotgun he carried.

"Evenin', Sheriff," Abel called out.

"Abel," Macauley nodded in his direction, his gaze focused on his prey where he was playing cards near

347

the back of the saloon.

"You expectin' trouble?"

"Not if I can help it," he answered, moving slowly in Charley's direction.

Charley had seen Macauley enter the bar and wondered what he was up to. He didn't start to worry until the lawman looked to be making his way deliberately toward him. He glanced around, judging his distance to the back door, but knew immediately that he had no hope of making it out. Deputy Carter had just come in that way and was standing sentinel there, watching him. Realizing there was nothing he could do right now, he slumped back in his chair as if he hadn't a care in the world and picked up his drink.

"Charley Stevens, I'd like to talk to you over at the jailhouse," Macauley stated in a friendly tone, as he came to stand a few feet away from their table.

"Oh? What about?" He cast the lawman a sidelong glance as if his presence was unimportant.

"You tell me," the sheriff returned. "Come on. Let's go. Put your gun up on the table real easylike." He had the scattergun pointed directly at his chest.

"All right, Sheriff, but I don't know what this is all about, or why you need all the guns," he pleaded innocently. "Me and the boys here were just having a friendly little game of chance."

"Don't try to humor me, boy, I'm dead serious about this. Now, shut up and move, Stevens," he ordered a little more brusquely. "And don't try anything funny or ol' Carter there might just have to shoot you . . . that's if I miss."

Charley did as he was told, not wanting to irritate the sheriff while he was holding the shotgun on him. "Whatever you say, Sheriff. You're the boss."

"You're damned right I am," Macauley said angrily. "Now, move it."

Charley was forced to lead the way out of the Golden Horseshoe with the sheriff following right behind him. Carter paused only long enough to pick up his gun from the table, and then he went after them. When they reached the jail, they put Charley directly in a cell and locked the door.

"I don't understand any of this, Sheriff Macauley. Why did you arrest me? What have I done?"

"Right now the charges are disturbing the peace. If I think of anything else, I'll let you know."

"What? When was I supposed to have done that? I've been playing cards all night, ask anybody at the saloon!" Charley was just barely keeping a hold on his temper.

"How about the other night, Stevens, when you tried to overrun my jail?" Macauley snarled.

"I don't know what you're talking about," he responded stubbornly.

"I know you're the one who fired them all up, and I'm gonna see that you pay a nice price for that and a few other things."

"Whoever told you that is lying, Sheriff!" he argued hotly.

"Well, now, we'll just see, won't we?" He walked away without looking back, ignoring the man's howls of indignation.

Meanwhile, back in the saloon, Bucky and Rex were very worried.

"What are we gonna do?" Bucky asked worriedly. "He arrested him!"

"There's nothing we can do."

"We have to do something!" he demanded. "Charley's been arrested, and you and I both know why! That means they'll be coming after us, too!"

349

"You don't know that," Rex was trying not to get frightened, but he had a feeling Bucky was right. Hadn't Charley just warned them minutes before what would happen to them if he was arrested?

"I do know that!" he insisted as he leaned across the table toward his companion. "Look, he just told us he wouldn't let us get away if he was taken in! You know we're next!"

Rex was nervous. He didn't mind a little excitement now and then, but he had never really been in trouble with the law before. The thought of spending years behind bars just because of Charley didn't sit well with him.

"Well?" Bucky forced the issue.

"You're right," he finally admitted, scared and shaking. "We didn't shoot Santana. Charley did. I ain't takin' the blame for him."

"We gotta talk to the sheriff now, before Charley does." Bucky was convinced that they had to come clean to save themselves. He glanced at Rex, hoping he would go along with him. Even if he didn't, though, Bucky knew he would do it on his own.

"All right, let's go see him," he consented. "Charley ain't the forgivin' type. Even if he does get back out, he ain't gonna believe it wasn't us who turned him in."

"I know."

They fell silent, finishing off the last of their drinks for courage, then got to their feet. They were frightened and unsure as they left the saloon, but they knew they had no other choice. They refused to be dragged down with Charley.

They went straight to the jail, but hesitated outside for fear that Charley might overhear them. Tapping on the window, the two men motioned for the sheriff to come out.

350

"Carter," Macauley called his deputy who was in back with the prisoner.

"Yeah, what d'ya need?"

"I'll be out front for a while. Seems I got somebody who wants to talk in private." He didn't know what was going on, but he intended to find out. He felt good about arresting Stevens, for he'd found that his gun was the same caliber as the one that had been used to kill Santana.

Macauley was cautious as he emerged from the jailhouse. He carried the shotgun with him as he went to meet with Stevens's two friends.

"You gentlemen wanting something?"

"We need to talk to you, Sheriff. It's real important. I think you'll want to hear what we have to say."

Macauley studied them silently for a minute and, reading the terror in their eyes, knew this might be the break he'd been waiting for. "Who are you? What are your names?"

"I'm Bucky—Bucky Porter," he answered quickly, skittishly.

"And I'm Rex Jones."

"Well now, what can I do for you?" he asked, eyeing them suspiciously as he maneuvered himself into a position that, if the need arose, he'd be able to get off a clear shot at them. He didn't put it past them that they just might try to break their friend out.

"We got somethin' to tell you," Bucky began anxiously.

"Like what?"

"Like we didn't have nothing to do with shooting Santana! No matter what Charley says!" he blurted out.

"It wasn't us, Sheriff! We didn't do it!" Rex added.

Macauley couldn't believe his ears. Excitement burst through him, but he contained it. He kept his expression emotionless as he regarded these two. They obviously thought Stevens had told him something, and they wanted him to know their version of what had happened. He allowed himself a small smile. One thing about killers, they generally weren't too bright, and many of them were just plain stupid.

"Why don't you tell me your story, and we'll see?" he led the conversation.

"All right . . ." Bucky stepped farther back into the shadows and Rex moved with him. "We were out riding, and we came to Santana's ranch. He was alone, and we knew he had some money."

"One thing led to another, and he ordered us off his property," Rex went on. "Charley got mad and shot him down like a dog when he was walking away from us. We took the money and split it up. Charley got the biggest part 'cause he did the shootin', but he told us if he was ever arrested that he'd see that we got blamed, too."

"I see," the sheriff replied, nodding. He needed more information, and so he asked, "How does O'Keefe figure in all this? Was he with you?"

"O'Keefe?" Bucky looked puzzled. "No, we don't know the man. I don't know how he even got involved in this, but he ain't the one who killed Santana. It was Charley."

"So Stevens riled up the crowd over at the saloon thinking to get O'Keefe hung, so nobody would be asking any more questions about Santana's death?"

"That's about it," Bucky confirmed.

"Right. He was gettin' worried, 'cause you hadn't hung O'Keefe yet. He was wantin' to help things along a bit," Rex added.

Macauley was thrilled to hear this and proud that

his instincts had been correct. He still didn't know how O'Keefe's medallions had gotten out to Santana's ranch or where the money in his saddlebags had come from, and it didn't matter any more. He had the real killer locked up all nice and tight in his jail. It had been a very rewarding 24 hours, and well worth the ride out to see Wily. He'd have to remember to reward the old man when he came back to town.

"Will you two be willing to testify in court to this?" he pressed, wanting to be sure of his case.

"What would happen to us?" Rex balked.

"Nothing. I'll see to it. We'll keep Stevens locked up until the trial, so you won't have to worry about him. As far as a hanging goes, you can be sure there'll be one soon, but it won't be O'Keefe's."

"Then you ain't arresting us?"

"No, just stick around. Stay in town so I can find you if I need you."

"We got rooms over at the hotel."

"All right. Don't get any ideas about leaving, boys. I need your testimony, and I'll track you to hell and back if you try to get away."

"Yes, sir. Don't worry. We'll stay put."

"I'll be speaking to you soon."

Bucky and Rex rushed off, disappearing into the shadows of the alley. Macauley watched them go, his smile broadening. O'Keefe was innocent. He'd been right all along.

contamination electrifying the bath . . . She was a
once . . . She could lead them into lies . . . [illegible] the
wife
[illegible] below her [illegible] [illegible]

Chapter Twenty-seven

It was near dark, but Dev lingered on in the barn not yet willing to go back inside. He'd had enough of being walled up. He needed open spaces and fresh air. He paused in the last of the failing light and surveyed his handiwork, noting with pride how much he'd accomplished in the short time he'd been working. The old building would never be a showplace, but it was sturdy enough now to withstand use. He could easily visualize some healthy breeding stock taking up residence here, a growing herd of cattle out in the field beyond and maybe even a dog or two running around the place. He'd always wanted a dog of his own for some reason, he mused distractedly.

When Dev realized the direction of his thoughts, he sighed dispiritedly. He didn't know why he kept daydreaming about a future that was forbidden to him. It only made it that much more painful to accept the reality of his situation when he kept fantasizing about a life of loving Molly, of taking care of her and her family.

Thoughts of the Magees would not be so easily put away from him, though. He'd become inordinately fond of Jimmy, having worked side by side with him in cleaning up the barn. He was a good, quick-learning, intelligent boy, and Dev knew he could go far in life if he got the chance. He'd met Molly's mother the day before when she'd finally felt good enough to venture from her sick bed. The woman was as kind and gentle and fair-minded as her daughter. He'd been grateful when, even after Molly had told her the complete truth, she'd accepted his presence without question. And then there was Molly . . . always nearby, always smiling, always enchantingly lovely.

Ah, Molly . . . Despite his mood, he smiled bittersweetly into the gloom that was slowly surrounding him as the sun sank lower in the western sky. She was the brightness in his existence. Her faith in him never wavered. If anything, her belief in his innocence had only grown more strong with each passing day, and it amazed him. She never doubted he could eventually be released. She kept reassuring him, telling him that the sheriff believed in him, too, and that he would soon be free.

Dev wished he shared her conviction that everything would turn out all right, but too many times in his life he'd seen the cruel twists that fate could play on you. He wanted to believe that he would get out of this mess unscathed, his reputation intact. He wanted to believe that he could have a future with her, that they could marry, have children and grow old together. But the harsh realist he'd become through the years refused to allow him that dream.

He loved Molly more than he'd ever loved anyone, but with that love came a deep abiding respect and caring. He refused to be a source of hurt for her. He didn't want to cause her any pain. So, since that first night here at her house, he'd held himself slightly aloof from her, even though the longing he had for her in his own heart gnawed at him endlessly.

Dev wondered how much longer this could go on. Surely, he mused in frustration, purgatory couldn't be any worse. He was surrounded by a loving family, but he could never be a part of it. If only things had been different. But they weren't, he warned himself sternly. He was an accused murderer. His future looked less than bleak. Short of Clay showing up with some wonderful new shred of evidence, he didn't see how any of this was going to change.

The sound of footsteps outside alerted him, and because of the ever growing darkness he couldn't see who was coming. Though he'd been safe so far, he never let his guard down; just one mistake could prove fatal. He was about to dive behind one of the walled stalls when he heard Molly softly call out his name. He relaxed and went to meet her as she came through the ramshackle door.

"Dev? I didn't know how much longer you were going to work, but dinner's ready up at the house." She stopped just inside the doorway to look around for him.

He feasted his eyes on her, the beauty of her burnished hair as it tumbled about her shoulders, the gentle curves of her slender figure. He ached to sweep her up in a lover's embrace, to hold her and kiss her for all eternity, but he didn't. Mentally, he chided himself for even thinking such thoughts.

"Here, Molly."

Molly's heart was pounding when she spotted him in the shadowy interior. He came walking toward her, his stride confident and easy and so manly. His shirt was unbuttoned and hanging open to the

356

waist, revealing just a teasing view of his broad chest, and his bearded jaw, unshaven since he'd come to stay with them, made him seem a bit untamed, yet even more masculine, if that was possible.

She hurried forward, eager to be with him again. It had only been a matter of hours since she'd last seen him, but it seemed like days. The time at the restaurant was miserable for her now that she knew Dev was here. She always hurried straight back home as soon as she could.

"I've fixed something good tonight, since it's my only night off from the restaurant," she told him cheerfully, giving him her brightest smile. She was tempted to throw herself into his arms, but she held back.

"Your meals are always good, Molly."

She glowed under his praise. "Thanks, but tonight is special. We've got chicken and dumplings, and I even made a pie. Are you finished working here?"

"Yeah, it's getting too dark to do any more."

"Let's go on up to the house then. Jimmy can hardly wait to attack the pie."

Dev chuckled as they left the barn and started up the path. "I imagine he's got quite an appetite. I worked him hard today."

"I really appreciate you being so nice to him. Not many men would take the time." She cast him a sidelong glance.

"Jimmy's a good boy. I like him, and I enjoy being around him."

"He really likes you, too."

As they neared the water pump about half-way up to the house, he paused. "I'm pretty dirty. I'd better get washed up before I go in. You can go on

357

in, if you want to."

"No, that's all right. Go ahead, I'll wait for you."

Dev quickly stripped off his shirt and started to work the pump. The muscles in his arms and across his back flexed with the action, and Molly found herself standing watching him, mesmerized. The moon was out, sculpting his chest and shoulders in silver as he began to wash, and she was nearly overwhelmed by the crazy desire to caress that powerful sleekness.

Her pulse quickened at the thought of touching him, and her mouth went dry. She actually felt herself blushing, and she was glad that the cover of the night hid her discomfort from Dev. She had never thought a man could be beautiful, but he'd changed that. She thought him the most glorious man God had ever created. She had not forgotten the heated embraces they'd shared that first night. It had been heavenly, and she longed to know the ecstasy of his kiss and touch again.

"How's your mother feeling tonight?" he asked as he finished washing and was slipping his shirt back on. He turned to face her, fighting with himself not to notice how desirable she was or to think about how much he wanted to kiss her. He forced himself to concentrate on buttoning his buttons, but even that dredged up memories of when he'd unbuttoned Molly's buttons . . . Dev stifled a groan as he brought his errant thoughts under rigid control.

An odd disappointment filled Molly at his question, but she didn't let it show. She kept her voice light and happy as she answered him, "She's much better. Another day or two of rest, and I think she'll probably be fine."

As much as Dev tried to avoid it, their gazes met and locked as they stood there. A force more powerful than the both of them drew them magnetically toward each other. In another minute they would have embraced, but a heavy footfall and the sound of a twig snapping somewhere on the far side of the house broke them apart.

They knew immediately that it was not Jimmy for it was just not in his nature to move quietly. Unable to think of anyone else who would have a reason to be out there snooping around, Dev grabbed her hand and they ran silently back to the barn, seeking a hiding place there until they could see who was coming. The tension that had enveloped them changed quickly from sensual awareness to fear.

"Stay down and be quiet," he warned.

"Why? What are you going to do?"

"I'm going to find out who's out there, that's what I'm going to do."

"Oh, no, you're not!" Molly argued in a heated whisper. "That's all we'd need is for somebody to see you. You stay right here, and you keep down and be quiet. I'm the one with a reason for being here, and I'm the one going out there to look."

Without giving him a chance to respond, she hurried away from him. Dev cursed under his breath, feeling once more totally and completely helpless. He knew she was right, but it didn't make it any less emasculating to have to hide in a damned barn while the woman he loved risked her life for him. Jarred by the thought of her possibly being in danger, he threw all common sense to the wind and crept from his hiding place. He kept her slender form in sight as he moved soundlessly from the barn.

Molly was scared, but she didn't show it as she walked out of the barn and up toward the house.

When she saw a man coming toward her, she stopped, startled and more than a little scared.

"This is private property! Who are you? What are you doing out here?" She tried to sound as indignant as possible.

"Molly?"

The sound of Sheriff Macauley's voice drained all the fear right out of her, and she sagged weakly as relief surged through her.

"Oh, it's you, Sheriff . . ." she answered. "Thank God."

"It's me, all right," he replied good-naturedly. "Sorry I gave you a fright, but your brother told me you and O'Keefe were out here somewhere. Is he around? I need to talk with him."

"He's waiting inside the barn."

"No, I'm not," Dev interrupted, appearing at the sheriff's side. He had managed to stay in the shadows and slip around to the side of her to make sure she was safe. He wasn't about to let anything happen to her.

"Dev! I told you to stay inside!"

He ignored her protest as he faced the lawman. "What is it, Sheriff? Has something happened?"

"Yes, something has, O'Keefe."

The sheriff sounded so sober and serious that Dev automatically assumed the worst—that he had come to tell him that he was taking him back to jail and that his trial would start soon. For a split second, he thought about running, but just as quickly as it came, he discarded the idea. He was not guilty, and he was certainly no coward. If he could do nothing else, he would act like a man and keep Molly's respect.

"I see . . ." Dev said slowly, resigning himself to his doom, accepting the unacceptable. "Well, let's go then . . ." He wanted to get away from Molly. He didn't want her to know how badly this was tearing him up inside. He didn't want her to see him at his lowest.

"Go?"

"Back to jail. That is why you came, isn't it? To take me back?"

"I think you're jumping to conclusions, boy," Macauley told him, and for the first time Molly and Dev could hear a lightness in his tone.

"What are you talking about, Sheriff?" Molly grabbed the lawman's arm in an excited hold at the thought that his news might not be all bad. She looked up at him questioningly, hopefully.

"I'm talking about the fact that O'Keefe here's a free man as of right now."

"What?" Molly and Dev exclaimed in astonished unison.

"Earlier tonight I arrested Charley Stevens, and I've now charged him with gunning down Santana in cold blood."

"You did?" she cried in happiness.

But Dev was not so easily convinced. He couldn't believe his good fortune. "But what about all the evidence pointing at me?"

"I can only figure that Stevens planted it himself, trying to frame you," he answered, "but really, O'Keefe, what does it matter as long as you're a free man again?"

"You're right, Sheriff. Nothing else matters. Nothing else at all!" Dev was so stunned that he was hardly able to think. He had never really expected things to work out right, and now that they had, he was at a loss. Molly, however, was thrilled, and she threw herself into his arms, hugging him tightly.

"I told you everything would work out! I told you

so!" she cried in delight.

Dev hugged her back, swinging her around in a full circle of celebration and then gave her a quick, excited kiss as the sheriff looked on, quite pleased with himself.

"Why don't you come back to the office with me now and pick up your things? After that, you'll be free to go," Macauley suggested, smiling at their happiness. Watching the way Molly looked at him, he had a good feeling about these two. He hoped everything worked out for them for they certainly deserved it.

"Fine," Dev agreed, still a little in shock. "I'll be back just as soon as I can, Molly."

"I'll be right here waiting for you, Dev," she promised, hardly able to contain her excitement.

He gave her one last, enthusiastic kiss then joined the sheriff for the walk back to the jail. Molly walked with them as far as the house, then remained outside watching as they moved off toward the jail. Tears traced damply down her cheeks, but she wasn't even aware of them. She was only aware of the deep, abiding joy that filled her. Dev was free! It had happened so suddenly, and yet it couldn't have come soon enough for her. She believed with all her heart that he should never have been locked up in the first place.

As Dev and Sheriff Macauley disappeared out of sight, Molly went inside to tell her mother and Jimmy the good news. When she had, Jimmy erupted in whoops of happiness.

"Oh, boy! Now Dev doesn't have to hide any more when we go outside to work on the barn!"

"Well, now Jimmy, I doubt that Dev will be working on the barn any more," Eileen cautioned. She knew how fond her son was of the young man,

362

but she also knew that Dev had a life of his own to live.

"Sure he will, Mother," Jimmy argued. "We still have lots to do."

Her mother's words of warning struck Molly hard, and her heart skipped a painful beat at the very real possibility that Dev might leave. She hadn't thought beyond Dev's being found innocent and being freed. She hadn't considered that he might return to his old way of life, hunting down criminals all over the country with his friend Clay.

"He'll be back, won't he, Molly?" Jimmy asked plaintively as he, too, was filled with the sudden fear that he might be losing his good friend.

"He told me he would be, and he's a man of his word," she answered confidently.

"He's gonna stay, isn't he?" he pressed, wanting to be reassured.

"I hope so, Jimmy."

Eileen heard the worry in her tone, and her gaze sharpened as she regarded her daughter. "You've come to care for this young man, haven't you, Molly?"

"Oh, yes, Mother." Molly gave her mother a small, tremulous, teary-eyed smile. "I more than care for him. I love him."

"Then you're crying because you're happy?" she questioned astutely. She'd always been able to read her daughter's feelings, and she had a feeling that Molly was not crying out of joy.

Molly looked quickly away.

"What is it? What's bothering you?"

Wringing her hands nervously, she went to stare out the window into the darkness of the night. "I'm not sure. It's just that when you said he wouldn't be working on the barn any more, it suddenly dawned

363

on me that he might leave." She spun around to face her. "I always knew he was innocent. I wanted him to be free. I prayed for it! But I'd never thought past that. I don't want to lose him."

"How does he feel about you?"

"I don't know . . . I'm not sure."

"He's never said anything?"

"He wouldn't. Not before. He said he wouldn't let me be hurt that way." She shrugged. "He said he cared about me and respected me, but now . . ."

Eileen got up and went to hug her daughter. She had always liked Dev, but now she felt an even greater admiration for him. It had been a very chivalrous thing he'd done in the way he'd treated Molly, and she thought a lot of him because of it. She only hoped that now that he was free, that caring would become something deeper. She hoped he would see what a treasure her daughter really was.

"Sometimes, darling, you just have to wait and see what happens. If Dev said he was coming back, he will. When he does, you'll be seeing him for the first time as a free man. Maybe things will change, but maybe the change will be for the better."

"I hope so," she answered, and at her mother's urging, they set about having their dinner before it got cold.

"Got any future plans?" Macauley was asking Dev as they strolled through town.

Dev gave a weary laugh. "If you'd asked me that an hour ago, I would have told you no. I didn't think I had much of a future, short of a hangman's noose. Now, though . . ." He paused, allowing himself to visualize once more, the dream he'd been

364

longing and hoping to share with Molly. "Now, I know what I want to do with my life."

He said it with such passion, that the sheriff glanced at him curiously. "Oh? What?"

"I'm going to propose to Molly. If she'll have me, I'll marry her tomorrow! Hell, if she'll have me, I'll marry her tonight," he said with a chuckle.

The sheriff smiled knowingly. "I was hoping you'd say that. She's a fine young woman, and the two of you will do well together."

"I hope so."

"What are you planning on doing for a living? You going to keep working with Cordell?"

"I hadn't really thought about it," he remarked. "Why do you ask?"

"Well, I've got an offer I'd like to make you."

"What kind of offer?"

"A job offer. I could use another good deputy, and I think you'd be perfect. You've got the experience. You know how to handle a gun, and you're an honest and fair man."

Dev felt honored at this assessment of his character. "Thank you."

"No need for thanks, I'm only telling the truth. I like you, O'Keefe, and I think we could work well together." Macauley stopped as they came to stand in front of the office. "What do you say?"

Dev couldn't believe that everything was happening so fast. One minute, he'd been a prisoner with a rope practically around his neck. And, the next, he was being offered a job as a deputy sheriff here in the very town that had locked him up. He gave a rueful shake of his head as he thought about it.

"How long do I have to make up my mind?" he asked. He knew the job would give him the security he would need if Molly accepted his proposal.

There was no way he could spend his time chasing around the countryside with Clay if he and Molly were married. He'd have a home and a ready-made family to care for.

"As long as you want. The job's yours if and when you want it," he promised as they went inside.

Dev knew he had to talk to Molly first, before he could decide anything. Then, too, there was Clay to consider. He wondered suddenly where his friend was and how soon he'd be back. He wished he was here to celebrate his release with him.

Deputy Carter was sitting at the desk as they entered. When he saw Dev, he stood up and offered him his hand. "Sorry about all the trouble, O'Keefe."

"So am I. I'm just glad everything's been resolved," he responded, shaking his hand in friendship.

"Here you are." The sheriff handed him his gunbelt, saddlebags and the rest of his things.

"Thanks." Dev quickly strapped his gunbelt on, and he enjoyed the heavy feel of it against his thigh.

"And here's your money." Macauley handed him the money he knew was his and the extra cash that did not belong to him.

"This isn't mine, sheriff," he said, holding the money back out to him. "I don't know how it got in with my things, but it doesn't belong to me."

"It's not Santana's either, his money has already all been accounted for."

"Does he have a widow? You could give this to her."

"No. He lived alone, and we don't know of any living relatives. Keep it, O'Keefe. After what you've been through, you've earned it."

366

Dev didn't like taking money that didn't belong to him, but if there was no one else to claim it, there wasn't much else he could do. "If you're sure . . ."

"I'm sure," Macauley insisted. "It'll be a good nest egg for you and Molly."

He looked up at the lawman and smiled. "Thanks."

"Your horse is in the stable down the street. You can get him any time you want."

"All right."

"Think about my offer, will you?" the lawman urged.

"I will," Dev promised.

"I'll be waiting to hear from you," he told him as he walked him to the door, a hand resting on his shoulder.

"I'll let you know just as soon as I have Molly's answer." Dev strode from the jail a free man. He paused in the street to take a deep, cleansing breath, then moved off down to the stable to get his mount. After that, it would definitely be time to see Molly.

Chapter Twenty-eight

Dev felt like a green, callow youth as he rode the distance back to Molly's. His stomach was in knots, and, had he not had such a firm grip on his reins, his hands would have been shaking. He thought it strange that he could track down outlaws and shoot it out with them without flinching, that he could contemplate his own hanging all those weeks and face his own mortality without terror, but just the thought of telling Molly he loved her rendered him nearly useless.

He was happy, there was no doubt about that. His life was perfect right now . . . or at least it would be soon . . . once Molly said "yes" to his proposal of marriage. But he was scared. The horrible, terrible possibility that she might turn him down haunted him.

As Dev caught sight of the Magee house just a little way down the street from him, he almost wheeled his horse around and took off. Only the sarcastic urging of some inner voice tauntingly calling him a coward kept him going forward.

It wasn't that he was a coward exactly, Dev rationalized to himself, alternating between excited anticipation and something he refused to identify as fear. It was just that he had never asked a woman to marry him before, and he wasn't sure exactly how to go about it. If he did it wrong, and she said no . . . Well, he couldn't even bear to think about that right now.

To settle his nerves, he remembered that Molly had declared her love for him. He hung on to that encouraging thought as he reined in before the house.

The special dinner Molly had so carefully prepared was eaten in relative silence. Though Eileen tried to make conversation, neither Molly nor Jimmy was in the mood to talk. Eventually, she gave up trying.

As they began to clear away the dishes, Jimmy heard the sound of a horse outside.

"He's here!" he shouted excitedly, almost dropping the load of plates he was carrying.

He dumped the dishes near the sink and raced to the front door to throw it wide. The sight of Dev on horseback sent his spirits soaring. He charged forward to greet him with youthful exuberance.

"Dev! I knew you'd come back! I knew you would!"

Jimmy nearly tackled Dev when he dismounted. He threw his arms about his waist and hugged him tight. For a minute, he kept his face against Dev's chest because he didn't want him to see the tears that were burning in his eyes.

"Whoa, there, Jim," he said as he gave a warm laugh at the rousing welcome. He tousled his hair affectionately as he held him back away from him to get a look at him. "Where did you get the idea I wouldn't be back?"

The boy gazed up at him, his expression worshipful. "Mother said that you didn't have a reason to come back to us any more now that you were free. I was just afraid you wouldn't. Molly and me, we were worried about it." He glanced toward the house where his sister was standing in the doorway.

Dev looked up with him and saw Molly there. Her slender body was silhouetted by the light behind her. Her whole manner was tense, poised and watchful.

"Well, this time your mother was wrong, Jim. I do have a reason for coming back."

"You do?"

"Yes, more than one, in fact," he reassured the boy.

"Are you going to stay?"

His earnestness surprised Dev. He wanted to tell Jimmy that there was nothing he wanted more in the world than to live with them, but he knew he had to talk to Molly first. "I'm not sure."

Molly heard his answer, and the hope she'd been feeling died. She believed Dev had only returned to thank them and to say good-bye.

Dev started to walk toward Molly, keeping an arm around Jimmy's shoulders. "Molly."

"Hello, Dev," she said, her voice almost a whisper.

She sounded so forlorn that he gave her a curious look. When he'd left her she'd been as excited as he'd been, but he realized that something must have happened while he was gone. Without hesitation, he held his hand out to her, knowing he had to set things straight right away.

"Let's go for a walk, Molly, just you and me," he invited.

She took his hand without hesitation and let him draw her down to his side. Dev was aware of the coldness of her small hand as he held it in his, and he wondered why she seemed so nervous.

"Hello, Dev, and congratulations," Eileen called as she came to the door to greet him. "I'm glad things have worked out right for you."

"Thank you, ma'am."

"Jimmy, you come on inside now," she told her son, wanting to give Dev some time alone with Molly.

Jimmy looked up to Dev, hoping that he would ask him to stay, but he gave him a shake of his head.

"You go on in like your mother says," he told him. "I need to talk to your sister for a while."

"Will you come back inside when you're done?"

"Sure."

At his promise, the youth did as he'd been told. He entered the house and shut the door behind him.

When the front door closed, Molly and Dev were engulfed in the darkness of the night with only the moon to light their way. They stood there for a moment in total silence. Both of them were a little hesitant and unsure, but for completely different reasons. Neither of them knew quite what to say first.

Molly trembled as she imagined that this was the last time they would be together. She feared he was only here to say his farewells before resuming his life as a bounty hunter. The thought of never seeing him again upset her, and she fought hard to control her emotions.

Dev felt Molly shiver slightly, and he looked down at her to see the uncertainty in her expression. It hurt him to think that she could be that unsure of him, but then he realized that he'd never given her anything solid to believe in. He had always held himself deliberately aloof from her and had tried desperately not to care about her or her family. He'd failed miserably, of course, but Molly didn't know that. Evidently, she'd believed his act completely. He knew then that right now, he had to prove to her he loved her.

"Let's walk down to the pond, all right? I think there are a few things that need to be said between us."

"All right." She nodded in agreement. As they started to walk down the path, memories of that last time they'd been at the pond swept through her. She wondered miserably if Dev would kiss her good-bye before he left.

They had walked nearly to the barn before Dev finally spoke up.

"Did you really think I would just leave and never come back?" he asked huskily.

"I wasn't sure," Molly replied with painful honesty, gazing up at his moonlit profile as they walked through the night. He looked so handsome, and remembering his kiss, her heart fluttered wildly in her breast.

"Why?"

She gave a little shrug. "Everything's changed now. I mean, there was no real reason for you to return here any more. You're free to go. You have your job as a bounty hunter and your friend Clay . . ."

"I am a free man now, but I never said I wanted to leave," he told her gently.

"You don't?"

"No, or at least right now, I don't think so. But you tell me whether I should leave or not, Molly. The sheriff's just offered me a job as a deputy, working for him. Should I take it? Should I plan to spend the rest of my life here in Monterey?"

"I can't tell you how to live your life, Dev. It's a decision only you can make."

"Oh, no," he countered. "It's our decision."

They started walking again, moving past the barn and on down to the gentle, grassy slope of the bank.

"Ours?" His statement was such a surprise, that Molly stopped to look up at him.

"Ours," he repeated firmly. "The pay's decent and steady. Enough to support a family on, I think."

"A family?"

They stopped near the water's edge much where they'd stood the other night. The whole scene had a dream-like feeling to it. The moon, the stars, the gentle night breeze and the soft lapping of the water at the bank. It was romantic and wonderful, and Dev only hoped everything turned out the way his dreams usually had—happily.

Dev faced Molly, his expression growing serious as he struggled to find the words. In desperation, he finally decided just to tell her the truth and be done with it. The suspense was driving him crazy. He had to know if she would marry him. He wouldn't be able to relax until he knew.

"Molly . . ." He paused, then forged ahead. "Molly, I love you."

His words were a heart-sent caress, but at first, she didn't quite believe it. *Dev loved her?*

Dev wasn't sure if her silence was good or bad. He lifted one hand to caress her cheek.

"I love you, Molly." Said the second time, his words were almost a groan. "It seems like I have forever."

"But you were always so cold . . . so distant . . ."

373

"Not all the time," he reminded her, giving her a lop-sided, self-deprecating grin. "I'm sorry if I hurt you, but I had to be strong . . . for both our sakes. I thought I was going to die. I didn't want to drag you down with me. I'll make it up to you now, if you'll let me. I love you, and I don't ever want to leave you again."

"Oh, Dev . . ." she sighed ecstatically. "I never thought I'd hear you say that. I love you. I love you with all my heart."

No more needed to be said then, as Dev bent to Molly and claimed her lips in a passionate kiss of promise. He had denied himself for so long that the embrace was exquisite agony for him. It felt so good and so right. She was so wonderful. He knew there was no place else on earth he would rather be than there with her. When the kiss had ended and they broke apart, they stared at each other in a fever of sensual understanding.

The kiss had told him all he needed to know, and Dev delayed no longer. Emboldened, he asked the question that had been tormenting him.

"Marry me, Molly . . ." he urged. "Let me make a life for us. Let me love you like I've wanted to for so long."

It had been wondrous enough that he'd told her he loved her, and now he wanted to marry her. It was all she'd ever hoped for, all she'd ever dreamed of.

"Yes, Dev. Oh, yes!" she cried in delight as she clung to him.

"You will? You really will?" Dev was amazed that his luck could have changed so dramatically within the space of just a few hours. That morning, he'd been nearly certain that he would hang, and now his every wish in life had been fulfilled.

"There's nothing else I would rather be than Mrs. Devlin O'Keefe," Molly vowed, linking her arms around his neck and kissing him soundly.

Standing in the quiet of the night, their arms wrapped around each other, they were lost in a haze of rapturous contentment. Their lips met and parted, savoring the taste of one another. It was a tender moment, a foreshadow of the years of loving to come.

"How soon?" Dev asked hoarsely, breaking the sensual mood. His need for her was threatening to overpower his common sense, and he knew he had to be sensible. They weren't married yet.

"How soon, what?" Molly blinked, trying to focus on something besides the glorious feelings that were sweeping over her. Just a short time before she'd feared never to see him again, and now he wanted to marry her . . . to make her his wife.

"The wedding," he answered, pressing a gentle kiss to her forehead, then one to the softness of her cheek, and then settling on the sweetness of her mouth once more.

Shivers of delight coursed through Molly at his tender ministrations.

"The wedding," she rhapsodized, her expression decidedly dreamy. "Whenever you want."

Dev kissed her again, unable to resist, then said distractedly, "I suppose I should wait until Clay gets back."

"I guess that would be best," she agreed slowly. "When is he due to return?"

"I don't know. He was hired to find somebody and bring them home. As soon as he does that, he'll be back."

"Will it be much longer?" Molly wondered, her fingers innocently tangling in the hair at the back of his neck where it grew over his shirt collar.

Dev knew she wasn't being deliberately provocative, but at her simple touch, the heat within him was building to a fever pitch. He wanted her. He had for weeks now. It had been difficult enough not making love to her when he'd been a prisoner, but now that he was free and the future was theirs for the taking, he was finding it next to impossible to control himself. She was all woman, warm and willing, and he loved her.

"God, I hope not," he growled as he pulled her close and kissed her deeply.

Molly melted against him. This was heaven for her. Her prayers had been answered. Dev loved her, and they were going to make a life together.

Caught up in the splendor of their embrace, Dev never wanted it to end. His lips plundered hers, teasingly arousing her to heights of desire she'd never experienced before. The raging emotions he'd created within her, left her feeling weak and pliant to his will. She wanted him, and she wanted to please him. They dropped down to the grassy bank, their bodies pressed hotly together. Their hands moved restlessly over each other as they strained closer, anxious for complete intimacy.

For Molly, it would have been enthralling to share his love fully, but Dev was not about to let that happen. He could feel the eagerness in her. He could sense that she was his for the taking, but he would not do it. He held her trust, and he would keep that trust. He would do what was right for the both of them.

"Molly . . . we can't do this. Not yet." Dev protested painfully. His body clamored for him to satisfy his desires, but his heart and mind cried out for him to wait.

"But Dev, it feels so good to be with you this way," she argued in a love-laden voice.

"That's the point, sweetheart," he began to explain as he stopped kissing and caressing her, but continued to hold her close. "It feels too damned good."

"I don't understand," she said in confusion.

"I know, and that's part of the trouble, too."

"I don't mean to be troublesome to you."

She sounded so regretful, that he had to laugh. "You should always be this troublesome to me."

He gave her a quick kiss, then released her and rolled away. Getting to his feet, he held his hand out to her to help her up. Molly took it reluctantly for she was still puzzled by his words. Her thoughts and feelings were confused by the mesmerizing power of his passion.

"Your mother and Jimmy are waiting for us at the house. Think we'd better go back up?" he reminded her.

"Oh," Molly gulped, a little embarrassed at having forgotten everything but the magic of being near Dev. "I forgot."

"I almost did, too, love," he admitted, chagrined. "But I bet your mother hasn't."

"We'd better hurry back."

Hand in hand, conspirators in love, they rushed back up the walk. The night wind carried the sounds of their private sighs and their soft words of promise and devotion. They paused by the water pump to share one last kiss before facing her family.

It was then, lost in the headiness of Molly's embrace under the canopy of silver moon and twinkling stars, that Dev knew he couldn't wait for Clay's return. He'd been looking all his life for this kind of love, and he didn't want to wait any longer to claim Molly for his very own.

377

As much as Clay's friendship meant to him, Dev knew he didn't want to spend the rest of life days like a tumbleweed, riding aimlessly about the countryside, without roots or binding ties. He wanted a family, a wife and children. He would marry Molly just as soon as they could arrange it, and he would tell Sheriff Macauley that he had hired himself a new deputy.

Dev felt a twinge of guilt about making plans without telling Clay, but his need to marry Molly overshadowed any doubts he might have. He believed in his heart that ultimately, his friend would understand.

"Molly . . ."

"Um?" she responded, her eyes still closed as she relished his nearness.

"Molly, I don't want to wait for Clay."

At this, her eyes flew open as she gazed up at him, both startled and pleased.

"I've waited too long for you already."

Molly was thrilled. When he moved to kiss her once more before returning to the house, she met him hungrily in that torrid exchange.

"Let's go tell your mother," Dev said in a strangled voice as they moved apart.

Breathless, her cheeks flushed with passion, Molly took Dev's hand and they went to plan their future.

The lamp glowed golden, gilding the lovers in a soft, gentle light that matched their mood. Lying together in a loving embrace, Dev and Molly rested, sated from the wonder of their first joining.

For Dev, making love to Molly had been the most exciting thing he'd ever done in his life. As he held her close, cherishing the tenderness of the moment, he stared down at the gold band on her left hand. He couldn't imagine life getting any better than this. Molly was his, and they had their entire lives ahead of them to spend loving each other.

In peaceful contentment, Molly lay fully against him, her head resting on his shoulder. She had never known that making love could be so perfect. She smiled as she remembered the surprise she'd felt at her initiation to love's ways, and then the joy that had been hers when she'd become one with him. Dev was her husband . . . the man she loved.

"What are you smiling about?" he asked in a love-husky voice as he pressed a kiss to her forehead.

Molly nestled closer as she replied, "I was just thinking about you."

"I'm glad I make you smile."

"Oh, you do more than make me smile, Devlin O'Keefe," she answered as she rose up on one elbow to gaze down at him. He looked so handsome, that her heart ached. She was glad this man was hers, and she knew she would never let him go. Leaning forward, her breasts crushed sweetly against his chest, Molly gave him a quick kiss.

"I do?"

There was a twinkle of devilment in her eyes as she shifted her weight up on top of him and began pressing little kisses to his jaw, then down his neck and across his chest. She moved slowly lower until she had Dev practically squirming with impatience.

"Molly, don't, love," he protested in a guttural growl.

"Don't?" She raised up, wondering why he wanted her to stop. When he'd kissed her in that same fashion earlier, she'd been in heaven. She'd thought it would affect him the same way, too.

"No, darling, don't tease me like this."

"I'm not teasing," she told him with a slow, dangerous smile.

"You don't understand, love. We can't . . . at least, not any more tonight," Dev said seriously. He assumed that since he'd just breached her innocence, it might cause her discomfort if he tried to make love to her again.

"Why not?" Molly was completely naive about such things and, so, was naturally curious.

"Because, it'll hurt," he explained as best he could. He'd never talked to a woman openly about these things before, and he wasn't quite sure he was expressing it right.

"I'm sorry . . ." She was suddenly remorseful. "I had no idea it hurt you . . ."

Dev was overcome by a feeling of deep tenderness at her innocence, and he laughed gently to himself as he thought of how wonderful she was. She actually thought that making love again would hurt *him*, she wasn't even thinking about herself.

"No, no, no," he teased with infinite affection, slipping one hand up to tangle in the sleekness of her hair, then pulling her down for an adoring kiss. "Not me, darling. Being with you is pure heaven for me. It's you I'm worried about. You just made love for the first time, and your body's not accustomed to it. You'll be sore tomorrow."

Molly blushed a little as she realized how dumb she must have sounded to him, but he read her thoughts easily.

"Don't be ashamed of your innocence, Molly," he soothed. "It's something you should be very proud of. It means a lot to me to know that I'm your first lover."

"You'll be my only lover, too," she declared

fiercely, her eyes darkening with passion's intent as she met his lips again, this time in a slow, arousing exploration.

"Molly, we shouldn't."

"Dev, we should. What I'm feeling for you now is more important than anything else. This is our wedding night. I want it to be perfect."

His every protective argument refuted, Dev gave up the noble fight and surrendered to the desire he'd been trying to deny. Crushing her against him, his mouth sought hers. He began to caress her, tracing hypnotizing patterns down her silken length from the soft, swelling sides of her breasts to the gentle curves of her hips.

Molly moved restlessly against him as his knowing touch sparked her desire to a full flame. She could feel the heat of his manhood pressing hot and hard against her thigh, and it pleased her to know that he was as easily aroused as she was by their play.

Dev rolled with Molly, bringing her beneath him. He drew back to stare down at her for a moment, and then began to trail kisses down her throat to the curve of her neck. She gasped as he moved even lower, seeking out the peaks and valleys of her breasts. She clutched him nearer as his lips moved over her satiny flesh. His mouth closed over one taut, sensitive peak just as his hand sought the juncture of her thighs in an intimate caress.

Molly felt her control drifting away as he massaged her in a thrilling rhythm. She arched against his hand, enthralled by his practiced touch. Dev could tell that she was near the peak of ecstasy, and he moved over her, slipping between her thighs and positioning himself to claim her for his own.

"Yes, Dev . . . Please hurry, I want you so," she

said in a hushed voice.

Dev slid forward, piercing the center of her love, making her his. He had been slow and careful the first time they'd made love, teaching her, taking her along with him to the heights of satisfaction. This time, however, her aggressiveness had driven him wild. It excited him that she wanted him, and he couldn't hold himself back. Swept on by rapture's promise, he thrust deep within her, seeking the glory he knew would be theirs.

Molly had been an avid student of love earlier, and she remembered his tutelage now, putting into practice all that he'd shown her. She met his rhythm without hesitation, welcoming the brand of his body upon hers. They moved as one, eagerly seeking the glory of union and the enchantment that came with desire's crest.

Ecstasy built within them, lifting them higher and higher until it exploded in a million glowing sparks of passion. Soul-stirring in its intensity, their mutual pinnacle took them to the heavens and beyond, before allowing them to fall softly back to reality.

Sated, enraptured, the lovers lay locked together, neither willing to move apart. They nestled close, captivated by what was happening between them.

Molly lay with her head on his chest, listening to the steady thunder of his heartbeat as it slowed to a more normal pace. Dev held her near, cherishing the softness of her slender body against him. He marvelled at this thing called holy matrimony that had made them one in the eyes of God and man. It was right that it be so . . . it was perfect. They were meant to be together for all time, and he never wanted it to end.

Chapter Twenty-nine

"Shall we go?" Clay invited, offering her his arm after they'd descended from the train in Panama City.

"I don't suppose it would do any good to say no, would it?" Reina shot him a red-hot glare.

"None whatsoever," he replied tersely. "It's all but over now. Why don't you just admit it and give it up?"

Her expression was grim as she realized that time was running out. If Clay managed to get them on a ship to California, and then her doom would be insured, her fate would be sealed. Until that happened, though, she still held out hope.

"You'd like that, wouldn't you?"

"I don't like any of this, Reina. If I'd had my way, I wouldn't have come after you in the first place. I'm just glad we're almost through. I will be one happy man when I deliver you to your father." Clay was brusque as he answered, the curtness of his tone hiding his own confusion. He didn't understand what he was feeling right now, and he didn't want to. He had a job to do. He had to take Reina home. Period.

Yet, whenever Clay thought about turning her

over to her father so she could wed another man, he grew annoyed. He told himself that she didn't mean anything to him, that she was a woman just like his mother and for that very reason he couldn't let her mean anything to him. But still, the fact remained that he had only to kiss her or touch her to lose all semblance of self-control and that bothered him deeply. It was totally uncharacteristic for him to be so lacking in constraint.

For some reason Reina didn't understand, his declaration that he couldn't wait to be rid of her hurt. "Well, if you didn't want to come after me, why did you?" she challenged. "You could have just refused."

She hated him, she knew she did, and she despised herself for the weakness she had for him! Last night had been miserable for her when he'd proven to her again just how powerless she was against him. He only had to touch her, and her resolve to fight him disappeared.

"Your father can be a very persuasive man sometimes," Clay said with a harsh laugh, and he wondered again for what must have been the thousandth time if Dev was safe as Luis had promised he'd be.

"He is a master at getting people to do exactly what he wants, one way or the other," she remarked with her own bitter sadness, thinking of how his machinations had led to her current predicament.

"And his daughter grew up to be just like him," he observed sarcastically.

"That's not true!" she argued. "If I was, I wouldn't be in this fix right now."

"Oh, it's true, Reina. Just think about it. You convinced someone to help you disguise yourself as a nun. You convinced Emilie to lie for you, and you worked your wiles upon Webster so he'd help you with your grandiose plan of escape. You're your father's daughter, all right."

The comparison was a cutting one. One she didn't want to believe. She didn't want to think of herself as a manipulative, devious person. It wasn't true! Not at all! She accompanied him the rest of the way to the hotel in complete silence, troubled by the fact that he thought of her that way and not understanding why it bothered her.

As they entered the lobby and approached the desk, Clay knew what he had to do. He could not spend another night sharing the same bed with Reina. He'd gotten no rest at all the night before in Chagres when he'd returned to their room. He'd lain wide awake by her side all night long, remembering the desire that had overwhelmed them both earlier that day and wondering at its force. It was true that he needed to keep a close watch over her, but he also needed to get some sleep.

Reina, too, had been thinking about the previous night when she'd cried herself into an exhausted sleep. She put a firm, restraining hand on Clay's arm as they neared the desk, stopping him. He looked over at her, his expression curious. This was the first time she'd willingly touched him all day.

"I want separate rooms," she demanded haughtily. "There's no longer any reason to keep up the charade of marriage, since no one knows us here."

Clay's regard turned cool as he listened to her, and then he shrugged as if it was of little importance to him. He turned to the clerk and ordered, "I'd like two connecting rooms, please."

"Yes, sir," he answered respectfully, turning the registration book for him to sign.

It annoyed her that their rooms were adjoining,

385

but she rejoiced in the thought that at least she would have some privacy tonight and a small chance of escape.

Clay inquired about ships departing for California, and the clerk informed him that there was a ship leaving the following afternoon and that the last he'd heard, there were still vacancies. When he offered to get the tickets for them, Clay accepted, giving him the money for the fares and telling him that he would pick them up for them later when they came down for dinner.

"Miss Alvarez, Mr. Cordell . . . enjoy your stay."

They thanked him and, taking their keys, started upstairs. Clay unlocked Reina's room first and went in. This hotel was a vast improvement over the one in Chagres. The bedroom was spacious, very clean and quite comfortably furnished. Reina was more than pleased with her accommodations for it was located very close to the top of the stairs. All she had to do was figure out a way to sneak out without him catching her. Once she made it downstairs to the lobby, it would be simple to lose herself in the crowded town and in the process lose Clay.

Clay was paying little attention to Reina as he opened the connecting door and went into his own room. It was almost identical to hers, and he was satisfied. He strode to the window and brushed the curtain aside. The view was not the best, just what must have been the roof of the side porch and a patio below. He let the curtain drop back down and went to check on Reina.

"Are you hungry?" he asked.

"No, not at all. I'd really just like to have some privacy and rest for a while."

He regarded her suspiciously, his gaze searching her lovely features for some sign of guile. When he could detect nothing, he agreed to leave her alone. "All right. I'll be next door."

"Fine." She could hardly wait for him to get out. When he'd passed through the connecting door once more, she shut it firmly behind him. She would have locked it, too, but she discovered that he'd taken all the keys with him. To her dismay, a second later she heard the lock on her bedroom door turn from the outside. She ran to it, twisting the doorknob in an effort to make it open, but it was securely locked. In a fit of frustration, she called him every vile name she could think of, muttering under her breath about the legitimacy of his birth. The man was impossible!

Clay heard her try the door and called out to her with a low chuckle, "Enjoy your rest. We'll have a late dinner." He returned to his own room and stretched out on the bed to relax for a while.

Reina heard the satisfaction in his voice, and she stormed to the window, looking for another avenue of escape. To her complete and utter disappointment, it was a straight drop to the ground, a full two stories. Thwarted, she sat down on the side of her bed to think.

For weeks now, she had managed to keep thoughts of Nathan at bay, but trapped as she was, with nothing else to distract her, images of him flooded her mind. She remembered his kiss and touch, and she couldn't stop the quiver of revulsion that wracked her at the memory. She wondered how she would ever be able to bear his children if she couldn't even tolerate being near him.

Reina just knew that the rest of her life would be a living hell if she didn't find a way out of this mess. Again she paced to the window, searching for some way out. She'd been a tomboy in her youth and was not afraid to take a chance if it meant freedom. Even so, there was nothing even remotely close by that she could climb down. She was stuck.

There was absolutely nothing else she could do right now, so Reina lay down fully dressed and pulled the covers over her. She was tired, but she was also keyed up and really didn't expect to fall asleep. She only intended to rest for a while.

It was dark when Clay awoke to the sound of music coming from the patio below. It surprised him to find that he'd slept so soundly, and he was a little groggy when he sat up. After a moment, he left the bed and strode to the window to see what all the noise was about. There seemed to be a celebration of some kind going on, for bright, color-ful hanging lamps illuminated the patio, musicians were playing lively, festive tunes and the people seemed lighthearted and carefree as they mingled and danced. It looked like it might be a good party, but he couldn't think of that. He had Reina to worry about.

At the thought of her, he immediately worried that he might have been so deeply asleep that she had managed to slip away without disturbing him. Needing to check and make sure she was still there, he hurriedly lit a lamp and opened the connecting door. Lamp in hand, he moved quietly into her room and was both relieved and pleased to find her sleeping peacefully in her bed.

Clay stared down at her in the dark, studying her, committing her beauty to his memory—her dark hair, flawless complexion, the soft curve of her mouth that just seemed to beg to be kissed. Heat stirred within him, but he fought it down. Still, his

388

gaze would not be torn away.

He remembered the time when he'd thought her to be Sister Mary Regina and how he'd wished he'd found her before she'd taken her vows. That wish had come true for him. He had found her, and she hadn't been a nun. Reluctantly, he admitted to himself that she had been a virgin, not the wanton he'd suspected her of being, and that he'd taken her innocence.

Reminding himself of her actions, Clay tried to tell himself that it didn't matter. He told himself that though she might look like an angel while she was sleeping, when she was awake she was much closer to being the opposite.

He was tempted to wake her, but didn't. He decided to let her rest, instead. Backing from her room, he closed the connecting door, satisfied that locking the hall doors from the outside was sufficient to keep her safely captive.

Clay took a few minutes to get cleaned up, then left his room, making sure to lock his door, too. He wanted to insure that she would be there when he returned. His hunger driving him, he went downstairs to get something to eat.

Reina waited, eyes closed, until she heard the connecting door shut. Wanting to be completely safe, she hesitated longer, listening to every sound, trying to judge just where Clay was. The sound of the music kept her from being certain about his moves, but she was almost positive that the footsteps she heard in the hall were his.

Time was of the essence, so she got up without delay. It was dark, but that was fine with her. She went to the door to his room and pressed her ear against it, hoping to hear if he was still in the other room moving around. When only the vibrant strains of the music came to her, she knew she had to try. The worst that could happen would be that he would still be there, and if he was, she would tell him that she'd just waked up and was ready to eat.

With utmost caution, Reina turned the knob, and she was thrilled when it moved. An inch at a time, she drew the door slowly open. There was a lamp burning low on the nightstand, and to her complete delight, there was no sign of Clay anywhere. He was gone! She was alone!

Unable to restrain herself, she bolted for his hall door. Her moment of excitement was short-lived. It ended abruptly in defeat when she discovered that he'd outsmarted her again. He'd locked his own door from the outside, too!

Reina was so furious she was tempted to start banging on the door and screaming that she'd been kidnapped. Cool liar that Clay was, though, she was certain he would come up with a very believable tale to tell whoever came to her rescue. He'd probably tell whoever tried that she was his crazy cousin or something, she thought angrily, and that he needed to keep her locked up for her own safekeeping.

Stalking around his room, she felt almost crazy. This was it . . . her last chance. She had to do something! Though she was short-tempered and about to scream in frustration, the sound of music and laughter below drew her to Clay's window. As she brushed the curtain back and saw the porch roof right outside, a slow, conspiratory smile curved her lips. She was going to make it after all!

Reina rushed back to her own room to get the

small purse that held her money, and she stuffed it in the pocket of her dress. Afraid that Clay might return at any second, she ran back and unlocked the window. Bundling her skirts up, she climbed out onto the roof.

Reina stayed down low as she moved carefully toward the most secluded side. She breathed a huge sigh of relief when she saw the drain pipe attached to the corner there. Encouraged because everyone on the patio was too busy enjoying themselves to look up, she daringly hiked her skirts, got a firm grip on the pipe and maneuvered herself over the edge of the roof.

Mickey Barton, a short, wiry, ugly little man, was standing back against the building with his friend Leo Collier, drinking a cheap whiskey and watching all the dancing and celebrating, when he saw her. At first, he couldn't believe his eyes, and he blinked twice just to make sure. Once he was sure he wasn't dreaming, he stood, staring in astonishment at the sight of a pretty young woman, climbing off the porch roof onto the drain pipe.

"Leo! Look!" He grabbed his companion's arm and pointed in the right direction.

"What the. . . ?" Leo turned and didn't say a word as they exchanged shocked looks. They automatically assumed that she was not the most virtuous of women if she was sneaking out of some man's room, and they rushed over to the drain to watch her descent.

Reina was feeling confident. She was making great progress. She was better than half-way down when it happened. One of the brackets holding the pipe let loose, and she lost her hold and started to fall.

Leo, a tall, bearded, bad-smelling man of massive

proportions just happened to be in the right place at the right time, and Reina tumbled like a gift from the gods right into his big, brawny arms.

"Whoa, there little senorita, where ya goin' in such a hurry?" Leo was laughing as he held her deftly.

Reina didn't know if she was more embarrassed or angry. Would anything in her life ever go right again? It took her only a second to recover. She was grateful she hadn't landed on the hard ground, but she was not at all thrilled to find herself in the clutches of this stranger.

"Thank you for helping me," she said sweetly, "but could you put me down now?"

Leo didn't budge. He wasn't about to let go of her yet. "Tell me your name first, *chica,*" he cajoled, keeping a firm grip on his prize. Mickey was looking on avidly.

Reina's temper was frayed, but she managed to sound calm. "My name's Isabel."

"That's a right pretty name for a right pretty lady," he said, but instead of releasing her, he just let her legs down and kept her crushed against him. "Where were you going, sneaking out like that?"

Reina tried to pull away, but his hands were biting into her flesh, bruising her as he held her with an almost brutal force. Realizing that there was little she could do right except play along, she figured she would try to keep them happy by dancing and talking with them. Then when they got drunk, she'd be able to get away from them. It had never occurred to her that they might turn mean and nasty or that they could very easily overpower her and do whatever they wanted to with her.

"Why, I heard all the music and laughter and wanted to join the party," she said lightly, gazing up

392

at him with a rapt expression that Clay would have immediately recognized as trouble.

Leo and Mickey thought she was probably lying, but they didn't really care.

"Well, let's go," Leo said, still keeping her firmly at his side.

Reina was wild to get free of his grip, yet she bided her time, waiting for the opportunity she was sure would eventually come.

"What're your names?" she asked, wanting them to believe she was interested in them.

"I'm Leo," he told her proudly. He was fool enough to think she really cared.

"And I'm Mickey," he joined in, refusing to be left out.

"Well, Leo and Mickey, do you want to dance? I just love to dance," she cooed.

The thought of spending the evening with a beautiful woman excited them both. They assumed she was a whore out for a good time, and they meant to oblige. It didn't occur to them that she was dressed like a lady. It didn't matter. They merely thought that their luck was finally changing for the better. It had been quite a while since they'd been with a woman, and they didn't mind sharing her between them at all.

"We sure do like to dance!" Mickey boomed.

"I'm first," Leo insisted, almost dragging her to the dance area. "C'mon! This one is a real good tune!"

Reina had no choice but to go along as he took her in his arms and started to cavort about the floor. Leo, she discovered, was not graceful, was not coordinated and was definitely not a dancer. But what he lacked in talent, he made up for with enthusiasm. She was jerked, yanked, stepped on, whirled, spun and otherwise abused as Leo had his fun. Her hair had been done up sedately when she'd started down the drain pipe, but now it hung down around her shoulders, torn loose from her pins by her partner's gusto.

When the music ended she thought she'd be given a reprieve to catch her breath, but to her misery, Mickey claimed her for his turn. The musicians played another tune with a fast beat, and the short man danced her eagerly around the patio.

In comparison of the two, if there could be a comparison, Leo was by far the better dancer. Short as Mickey was, his eye level was at her bosom, and he let her know in no uncertain terms just how much he enjoyed the view. His hands were never still even in the midst of the crowd.

"I really need a drink, Mickey," she told him when the song was over, willing to do almost anything not to have to suffer another dance with him.

"Whatever you want, sweetheart," he answered, hurrying off to get her a drink.

Before she could say another word, Leo grabbed her wrist and tugged her with him out on the dance floor again. The music was decidedly slower this time, and he held her as close as he could. He'd had another whiskey while he'd watched her dance with Mickey, and he was now feeling no pain. He'd seen how his friend had pawed her, and he'd grown aroused thinking of what a great night this was going to be. He ground his hips against hers letting her know what was on his mind, unaware that she was growing more and more panicky with every passing minute.

Reina was wondering frantically if she'd fallen from Clay's trap into an even far more dangerous one. She tried to block Leo's gropings, but met with little success. When he started thrusting himself against her hips right there in front of everybody, she tried to pull free of his arms, disgusted.

"Stop!" she insisted, hating the feel of his hands on her body even through her clothing.

Leo laughed loudly, telling her over the noisy music, "C'mon, relax, you know you love it! All you girls do!"

"I'm no whore . . ." she hissed, trying to fight him now as she felt the threat implied in the tightening of his arms around her.

Again he laughed, then pulled her even closer. "Of course you're not."

"It's true!" She repeated, deliberately stomping on his booted foot, but he took no notice.

"Sure it is," he coddled her. "You want to drink instead of dance?"

He leaned back slightly to look down at her, and she noticed his eyes were hot with desire for her. Just being this near to him left her feeling dirty and soiled.

"Yes," she lied, grasping at any excuse to get out of his despicable hold. She was still firmly convinced that, as drunk as these two men were, she'd be able to get away from them. All she had to do was play her cards right and wait for a minute when they were distracted so she could slip away and disappear into the night.

Leo led her to a rather secluded table near the back of the patio, and Mickey joined them there with a round of drinks.

"Tell us, *chica*, how long have you been here in Panama City?" Mickey asked, his eyes riveted on her bodice.

"Not long," Reina answered, uncomfortable beneath his hungry eyes. She knew her dress was very demure and that the bodice was definitely all buttoned up, but he still continued to stare at her lecherously as if she was naked. "What about you?"

"We're just passin' through on our way to California. There's still money to be made out there, and we're gonna get our share of it."

She pretended to sip the cheap whiskey they had bought her as she listened. Leo, however, noticed right away that she wasn't really drinking it.

"Hey, how come you ain't drinkin'?" he demanded. "You said you'd rather drink. Then drink."

"I am. It's just that this is strong, and I can't drink it fast." She forced herself to take a sip of the awful liquor.

The men were pleased when she did, and they sat back, savoring the thought of taking her up to the privacy of their room at the saloon down the street. By the time they'd finished their whiskeys, the anticipation they'd been feeling had changed from mild excitement to a burning need. They knew they couldn't wait any longer. Exchanging knowing looks, the two men stood up.

"Let's go," Leo urged.

"Go?" in her naivete, Reina didn't understand.

"C'mon, don't play dumb. We got a room at the saloon down the street a ways, and we'll pay you whatever you want."

Reina's heart plunged as ice-cold fear filled her. "I'm not going anywhere with you. I told you before, I wasn't a—"

"Just shut up and let's go. We've been nice. We've been showin' you a good time. Hell, we even bought you a drink," Mickey said in a low, vicious voice.

Leo grabbed her arm and hauled her up out of the chair. "If you're thinking that you can do better than us, you're wrong."

Reina realized all too late that she'd been wrong in comparing them to Clay. They were nothing like him. Clay might have forced her to go along with him, but he would never have hurt her physically. Yet, there could be no doubt about the very real threat of injury in Leo's unmerciful grip. She swallowed nervously, her eyes darting around in search of help, but there were no familiar faces in the crowd of revelers.

"I won't go with you! I won't!" she cried, struggling to get free.

Mickey moved to her other side and took her other arm in a savage hold. "We're gonna pay you. Why don't you just stop fussin' and walk along with us real quiet-like?"

"No! Let me go, now!"

"Shut up, woman," Leo seethed. He was hot for her, and he did not mean to be denied.

"I won't . . . I . . ."

"Oh, yes, you will." They were trying to make her walk away from the table like nothing was wrong.

Reina was fighting against them with all her might, but it was a losing battle. She realized now how stupid she'd been to leave the safety and protection of their hotel rooms. Clay was nowhere around, and even if he did go back there and discover she was missing, he wouldn't have the slightest idea where to start looking for her.

Reina wondered desperately where Clay was, and she found herself wishing, to her own amazement, that he would show up and save her from these two. Wish though she might, she realized horribly that there would truly be no escaping her fate this time and that she had nobody to blame but herself.

"Please don't do this to me! I'm not what you

think I am—really—" she was telling them desperately.

"Look, *chica,* we're gonna have our own little party back at our room. You'll enjoy yourself. Don't worry. We'll have a lot of fun, just the three of us," Mickey said as he kept trying to urge her into the shadows from the patio.

"I don't think so."

The firm command of the deep, deadly voice cut through the rutting heat that was inspiring the two men. They stopped dead in their tracks as they came face to face with Clay and the very lethal looking pistol he was holding, aimed directly at them.

Chapter Thirty

"She's ours," Leo declared possessively.

"She's goin' with us," Mickey agreed.

"Clay . . . Thank God, I . . ." As perverse as it sounded, Reina had never been more happy to see anyone in her entire life as she was to see him at that minute. Had she been able to, she would have thrown herself in his arms and hugged him for dear life. She tried to twist away from the man once more, but still they would not let her go.

"Well, boys, it doesn't appear to me like the lady wants to go with you," Clay cut her off, ignoring the pleading look in her eyes as he concentrated solely on her companions.

"Sure she does! She told us she wanted to join the party. That's why she was climbin' down off the porch roof."

"Climbing down off the porch roof?" Clay sounded almost casual as he said it, but his gaze flicked to Reina, searing her for an instant before turning back on her pair of amorous companions.

"Yeah. She wanted to have some fun, and we're gonna show her some. Right now," Mickey announced.

"Like I said, I don't think she's of a mind to leave

the party just yet. I think she wants to stay here
. . . with me." With deadly purpose to emphasize
his point, he cocked his gun.

At the sound, both Leo's and Mickey's blood ran
cold, effectively cooling their desire for her. They
still hesitated, not liking the thought of being forced
to back down, but liking the thought of dying even
less. They were glad that they were a short distance
away from the patio so that no one else noticed the
encounter. It was hard enough on them being
forced to give her up, but if they'd lost face in the
process, it would have been even worse.

"Let her go," Clay ordered in a steely voice, his
gunhand steady. "Then you can take off and go
enjoy yourselves drinking somewhere else. If
not . . ."

Leo and Mickey looked from the gun to the man
holding it and knew he wouldn't hesitate to use it if
it suited his purpose. They were particularly fond of
being among the living, and the thought of facing
this mean-looking hombre down, left their knees
weak and shaking. Intimidating a woman was one
thing, taking on a gunslinger was something else.
They hadn't wanted any bloodshed, just a little fun.
They suddenly felt a driving need for a strong
drink and decided to release Reina and go find one
. . . somewhere else far away from here.

"You can have her," Leo finally spoke up in
disgust.

"Yeah," Mickey groused as he and Leo backed
slowly away, never taking their eyes off his gun, "she
ain't worth gettin' killed over, that's for sure."

"You're probably right, gentlemen," Clay said sarcastically, watching until they had completely disappeared from sight down the street. That threat
dispensed with, he holstered his weapon and turned

his full attention to Reina. His mood was near savage as he stared at her, and glacial was too warm a word for the regard he leveled on her.

Reina was completely unaware of the hostility of his feelings. She only knew that he'd arrived just in the nick of time to save her from what would have been a terrible fate. She was trembling uncontrollably from the terror that had not yet had time to abate.

"Thank God, you came along when you did!" she gushed, ready to launch herself gratefully into his arms.

Clay was not about to have any of it. When she tried to embrace him, he did not return it, but took her by the upper arms and pushed her coldly from him.

"Clay? What is it? What's wrong?" She looked up at him in wide-eyed wonder as he held her away. It was then that she saw his expression.

"Nothing's wrong," he answered curtly.

"Then let's go back inside and—"

"Your friends, there, said you wanted to join the party." He nodded in the direction Leo and Mickey had fled. "A spoiled little lady like you should always get exactly what she wants. She should never be disappointed." His words were biting and taunting.

"No, Clay, really, I . . ." She tried to move away from him, but his hands stopped her, tightening on her arms.

"Smile, Reina. You're going to enjoy yourself tonight," he ground out. "If you wanted to join the festivities so badly that you climbed down off the roof, well, then, I don't think I should be the one to deny you that happiness."

The joy she'd felt upon seeing him was rapidly

fading as she remembered that he was her captor, not her savior. When he took her by the wrist and led her back to the crowded dance area, she had no strength left to deny him.

"We haven't danced in quite a while, have we, Reina?" Clay said softly, dangerously as he pulled her against him. His arms were around her like iron bands, keeping her close, letting her body feel the rhythm of his as they moved to the beat of the music. "Is this what you were so eager to do?"

"No . . . I . . ."

"Do you remember the last time we danced?" he asked huskily, whirling her around.

Reina wondered how she would ever be able to forget that night at the Randolphs'. She had thought Clay was perfect then. She had thought that he cared about her as a woman, and she'd even thought she was falling in love with him.

"I remember," she whispered, lifting her gaze to his.

"So do I," he replied.

She caught a glimpse of some flaring emotion in his eyes before his expression suddenly turned grim and he looked away. The beat of the music was fast and sensual, and Reina instinctively followed Clay's lead as if she'd been made just to be in his arms. The throbbing, heated pace heightened their physical awareness of each other.

Clay knew he should march Reina back upstairs, tie her to the bed and keep watch over her until their boat left port. But for some reason he couldn't fathom, he was driven to do this. He'd almost lost control when he'd seen her dancing with the other men. She'd told them she wanted to enjoy the party. Well, he was going to make sure she did.

When the music ended, Reina was breathless

from the exertion. Clay took her hand and practically dragged her to a table at the edge of the dance area. He signalled for drinks to be brought to them.

"Leave it," he ordered tersely as he paid the man for the bottle of whiskey and two glasses.

The servant scurried away, and Clay splashed liberal amounts of the cheap liquor in the two tumblers, then handed Reina one.

"I really don't want it," she said, not picking up the glass immediately.

"It's what you had with your other companions, isn't it?"

"Yes, but—"

"Then drink it, Reina, or I swear I'll pour it down your lovely throat."

His threat was a cold angry one, and she knew she'd better do as she was told. She took a sip of the terrible whiskey and grimaced.

"Drink it all. Now. You're the one who wanted to join the party. Aren't you enjoying yourself?"

Holding her breath, she downed it, then glared at him furiously. "There! Are you satisfied?"

Sudden icy contempt flashed in his eyes. "Not yet, my dear. How about another one to celebrate your near escape?" He didn't give her time to answer, but poured more in her glass and added some to his own. He drained his without even seeming to notice the potency of what he was drinking. "You don't seem very happy, Reina," he remarked derisively. "Would you like to dance again?"

"I don't want to dance, and I don't want to drink anymore," she said through clenched teeth, wanting only to escape the surrounding revelers.

"I don't care what you want. I insist."

Clay drew her to her feet and led her out onto

the dance floor again just as the music stopped. They had to wait a moment for another tune, and when it began, Reina was dismayed to find it was a slow melody. Obsessed with proving his point, he pulled her tight against him as he began to move.

Reina didn't want to dance with Clay, and most certainly she didn't want to like dancing with Clay. The potent liquor was beginning to affect her, though, and the temptation to relax and enjoy the feel of his warm, strong arm around her and the easy fluid motion of his lead was growing. She struggled against it, determinedly. Yet, even as she fought her conflicting feelings for her captor, she realized that he had saved her from Leo and Mickey. Whether she was willing to admit it or not, she'd needed him. She might have been dead by now if he hadn't stepped in.

The fact that Clay had been so fierce in protecting her to the point of being willing to kill for her sent a shiver through Reina. She wondered if he'd rescued her because of the money or because he cared about her. The thought troubled her. Her heart longed to think that he'd saved her because he felt something for her. But logic pointed out that he was a man for hire, a man with a job to do. Reina wondered why that thought pained her so badly, and she refused to think about it further.

The whiskey's magical potency began to work upon her beleaguered senses then. Her better judgment suddenly seemed to have lost influence with her, and she found herself relaxing and enjoying being with Clay without fighting. The headiness of the slow dance and the sheer pleasure of being held so close against him set her senses reeling. She wanted this. She wanted him. She let her eyes close as she imagined in her alcohol-induced fantasy that they were far away from here and the ugliness of their current situation. It was a pleasant dream, and she clung to it.

Clay sensed the subtle change in Reina as he felt the tension ease from her. He glanced down, wondering at her mood. He expected to see anger and rebellion in her expression. Instead, what he saw reflected on her lovely face shocked him. Her stubborn expression was gone. There was no look of defiance, no look of hatred. She looked positively radiant, and her eyes had drifted shut as if she was truly enjoying the dance. Clay stifled a groan of defeat as his gaze shifted lower to her mouth, for her lips were moist and soft and slightly parted, as if she was breathlessly waiting for his kiss.

A sudden, near violent need to crush her to his chest and kiss her possessed Clay. He didn't understand it. He only knew that he had to have her. Now. Anything that had gone before between them was lost in his obsession to make love to her. He continued to dance with her, but he slowly made his way toward the hotel. Reaching the walk that led inside, he didn't speak, but merely stopped dancing and took her hand in his to lead her off.

Reina's senses were attuned to his. As he drew her with him with a gentle yet firm touch, there was no balking, no fighting. She instinctively knew what he wanted, for she wanted the same thing herself. She wanted to belong to him in every way.

Neither of them spoke as they crossed the lobby and made their way to their rooms. Clay did not even bother with her door, but went straight to his own. Unlocking it, he swept her up into his arms and went inside. He kicked it shut behind him, pausing only long enough to lock it and then give her a lingering kiss.

Reina returned his embrace with a passionate fervor of her own. When he moved to the bed to lay her upon it, she kept her arms around his neck and drew him down with her.

Clay could not stop kissing her or touching her. This thing between them was elemental in its strength. Like the winds of a storm or the crashing waves of the sea, it could not be stopped or controlled. It was love, the most powerful force on earth, and sharing it as they were only increased its potency and its need.

His mouth moved over hers, parting her lips and tasting of the honeyed sweetness there. As his hands sought her breasts, she whimpered softly in excitement. She clutched at his shoulders, her nails digging into his back as he unfastened the buttons of her bodice. Clay parted the material, baring her breasts to his caresses, and she cried out to him in ecstasy as he sought out the sensitive, passion-hardened crests. When his lips followed the path his hands had traced, she arched against him, longing to be closer to him.

Their clothing was a barrier against the intimacy they both craved, and Clay moved slightly away to unbutton his own shirt and strip it off. Reina's eyes were glowing as she stared at the broad expanse of his chest. She sat up slightly, shrugging free of the remnants of her dress so she was bared to the waist and then leaned forward to press kisses to that broad, hard plane of muscles.

Clay groaned aloud at her move, and he tangled his fingers in her hair and pulled her back so he could kiss her. The feel of her velvety breasts against him sent his desire soaring, and he knew he could wait no longer to seek that perfect union with her.

They broke apart and shed the last of their clothing, then came back together in a blaze of passion. He slid over her, seeking her lips as he fit himself to her. It thrilled him when she adjusted for him, and he moved deep within her, filling her with his love. Reina welcomed him eagerly. She held him close, taking all he had to give and returning it full measure.

In exquisite harmony, they began the tempo together. They were on fire with the need for that glorious rapture that came only with fulfillment. The heights of passion beckoned them onward. They ascended, scaling the peak to the crest where enchantment burst upon them in a sparkling rainbow of delight. Enthralled, they cried each other's name, acknowledging in that moment of splendor, the power and depth of their need.

The turbulence of their desire sated, they kissed once more. It was a tantalizing, lingering kiss, a kiss of promise and of the unspoken emotion neither of them would admit. Clay cradled her near, savoring the softness of her against him.

Reality was blurred by the haze of euphoria that surrounded them. Whether liquor-induced or not, neither cared. They lay in each other's arms without speaking. Touching and kissing, cherishing and loving, until at long last a blissful peace enveloped them both, and they slept.

It was the middle of the night when Reina came awake to find herself lying quietly on her side next to Clay, one leg entwined with his, her hand resting over his heart. Thinking of the perfect beauty that had transpired between them, she realized with a deep sadness in her heart that she had fallen in love with him. It was a terrible truth, a miserable truth, but the truth nonetheless.

Reina wasn't sure how it had happened, and she supposed it didn't really matter. All that mattered was that she loved him and that it could never be, for he didn't love her. He had merely taken what she'd offered.

A tear trickled down her cheek, and a great sense of impending doom overwhelmed her as she realized how completely hopeless her situation was now. There would be no more chances to escape. Her best attempts had proven futile. She was condemned to the life her father had chosen for her . . . a life spent married to a man she couldn't stand.

A ragged sigh tore from Reina as she fought to keep from crying harder. She didn't want to awaken Clay. She didn't even want to talk with him again if she could help it, for she feared that she might accidentally give herself away. She didn't want him to know how she felt about him. He worked for her father. He was his ally, not hers. No matter what they had shared physically, he was not her friend.

Withdrawing from all contact with him, she moved as far away from him as she could and then huddled in misery there under the blanket. In just a few short weeks she would be at Rancho Alvarez. It used to be that there was nowhere else she'd rather be than home, but now the prospect filled her with despair. Her future stretched bleakly, endlessly before her, and she wondered how she would ever suffer through it.

Reina lay for what seemed like hours before she finally got back to sleep, but even then, it was a fitful, restless slumber that did nothing to ease the grimness that now possessed her soul.

Clay awoke shortly after daybreak to find Reina sleeping by his side. He marvelled at her loveliness and had to resist the urge to touch her again. He lay back, staring at the ceiling, a forearm resting across his forehead as he went over in his mind all that had happened the night before.

Reina . . . she was so beautiful and so responsive to his lovemaking. Even now, heat filled him as he remembered the ecstasy of being buried deep within her body. It was almost as if they were made for one another, so perfect had their lovemaking been.

Vaguely, Clay wondered how he could allow himself to feel this way about her. She was the object of his search. She was the treasure that had to be returned to its rightful owner. Yet, somehow, somewhere along the way, he'd allowed himself to care about her. Her beauty and intelligence and pure grit impressed him. She was nearly indomitable. He was lucky that he'd been sharp enough to keep up with her. Any ordinary man would have been run ragged.

A small, proud smile curved his mouth as he turned his head to gaze at her again. Asleep, she looked innocent and almost unearthly beautiful, but he knew better. She was filled with more fire than ten other women, and the fire in her had ignited a hot, flaming blaze within him. Something stirred within his heart, too, something he couldn't quite put a name to, but that moved him deeply.

It shocked Clay to discover that he felt this strongly about Reina. He knew it was ridiculous for him to care. He knew without a doubt that she despised him and that she was already pledged to someone else. He'd only be making a fool of himself if he allowed these feelings to come to mean anything to him. There could be no future for them. No matter what he felt for her, there was still Dev to consider.

At the memory of his friend, Clay left the bed and, after pulling on his pants, he went to stand at the window and stare out at the rising sun. Soon they would be back in California. Soon he would give Reina back to her father. Dev would then be freed, and they would be able to get on with their lives.

As he thought about it now, though, Clay was filled with a terrible guilt at the prospect of turning Reina over to him. He glanced back at her where she lay so quietly, so defenselessly, and a great ache expanded within his chest.

Sternly, he denied the emotion that threatened. Only Dev was important. His own feelings meant nothing. Reina didn't need him or want him, and she'd already proven what a survivor she was. No, things would be fine once he delivered her home to her waiting father.

Chapter Thirty-one

The week since he'd married Molly had been the happiest Dev could ever remember. He had moved in with the Magees, and it seemed that almost overnight they had truly become a family in the finest sense of the word. His life, once so unsettled, now took on a firm, secure base. He belonged. He was loved. He'd started his job with the sheriff, and with the regular money coming in now, Molly took great delight in quitting her job. When Dev wasn't working with Macauley, he labored on the property, trying to make the improvements he'd envisioned before.

In spite of all his joy and contentment, though, Dev still felt a nagging concern about Clay. His friend had been gone a long time, and with each passing day his worry grew. Finally, unable to deny his disquiet any longer, he decided to have a talk with Luis Alvarez. He hoped the rancher would know what was happening with his friend.

Dev admired his surroundings as he rode up the drive toward the sprawling, attractive main house. It was easy to see that Rancho Alvarez was a very successful operation. As he reined in and dismounted in front of the Alvarez home, the young boy, Carlos, appeared out of nowhere to take his reins for him. Dev was impressed, and when he was greeted by Consuelo, one of the maids, even before he had time to knock on the door, he was even more so.

"Welcome to Rancho Alvarez, sir. Can I help you with something?" the middle-aged, slightly rotund servant inquired.

"Yes, I'm here to see Luis Alvarez, please. The name's O'Keefe . . . Devlin O'Keefe," he announced.

Seeing the deputy's badge on his shirt, Consuelo didn't hesitate to invite him inside and direct him into the parlor. "Please wait in there and make yourself comfortable. I'll tell Señor that you are here."

"Thanks." Dev took off his hat as he entered the house, and he went on into the room she'd indicated. He did not sit down, however, for the richly decorated room left him feeling decidedly out of place.

The news that O'Keefe had come to see him was no surprise to Luis. He'd been expecting him to show up asking questions about Cordell, ever since he'd heard that he'd been cleared of the murder charges against him and released from jail. He hurried to join him in the study.

"Mr. O'Keefe . . ."

At the sound of Luis's voice behind him, Dev turned to face the old Californio who had just closed the door for privacy and moved easily into the room. He had an aura of command and confidence about him. It was evident that he was a man used to luxury, and he seemed very at home here in the sumptuously appointed sitting room.

"Mr. Alvarez . . ."

"Yes, what can I do for you?" As he studied Dev, he noticed his badge and said with some surprise,

412

"Deputy, now, is it?"

"Yes, I've been hired on by the sheriff."

"Well, congratulations. That's quite a turnabout in your situation, isn't it?"

"Yes, but that's not why I'm here."

"This isn't official business, then?"

"No," he assured him. "I just rode out here to check with you about my partner, Clay Cordell. I know that you hired him to do a job for you, and I was just wondering if you know how soon he'll be back?"

"No, I'm afraid I don't know where your cohort is, Mr. O'Keefe. He left here weeks ago, and I haven't heard from him since."

Dev frowned. He didn't like this, not at all. "Well, do you have any idea where he might have gone?"

"None whatsoever," he replied firmly, not wanting to discuss Reina with this man.

His evasiveness irritated Dev, and his tone hardened. "Look, Mr. Alvarez, Clay is my friend as well as my partner. I'm concerned about him. I want to know where he is."

"As I told you . . ." He didn't get to finish as Dev interrupted.

"I know he's searching for your daughter. Surely, you gave him some suggestions about where she might have gone."

Luis was angered to discover that he knew about the search for Reina. "That is confidential information."

"That's what Clay told me, and I've respected that. But after all this time, I think you should be growing a little concerned, don't you? I mean, he's only tracking down a runaway girl. How difficult could that be? He should have been back with her long before now."

Stiffening at his words, he glared at Dev and then said with imperial disdain and not just a little touch of pride, "You obviously do not know my daughter, Mr. O'Keefe. She is not just 'a runaway.' She is a very beautiful young woman, but she is also resourceful, headstrong, and determined."

"Then shouldn't you be worried? What if there was some kind of trouble? What if something's happened to the both of them? Have you ever given that a thought?" he challenged.

Luis's façade cracked for just a moment under his prodding. "Of course, I've thought about it!" he answered, his tone agonized. "I've thought of nothing else for weeks now!"

"Then tell me where they might be. I can help look for them . . . for her," he offered.

"I'm sure she's left California. Had she been here, your friend would have found her ages ago. The only thing I can believe is that she went to New Orleans. She has friends there, friends who would help her if she was really that serious about staying away."

"New Orleans . . ." Dev was startled. No wonder Clay had been gone so long.

"If Cordell followed her there and managed to catch up with her, they should be returning here at any time now. If not—" He moved away from him and went to stare out the window at the vastness of his rancho. "If not, then I don't know what I am going to do . . ."

The terrible thought that he might lose his beloved home tore at his heart, but that pain was outweighed now by his fear for his daughter's safety. Surely, Reina was all right, but if she was, why hadn't she given up this folly and returned home. Where was she?

"Do you know how he traveled to New Orleans?"

"No."

Dev became frustrated as he realized there was absolutely nothing he could do but sit and wait. "There's no point in my going to Louisiana looking for them. But I want you to let me know the minute you hear anything, all right?"

Luis faced him. "I will, Mr. O'Keefe. If there's any word from Cordell, I'll notify you."

"I'd appreciate it."

The rancher walked him to the door and bid him good-bye. He watched as Dev rode off and then was about to turn around when a cold, savage voice rang out in the empty foyer.

"So, Reina's run away, has she?" Nathan's words were a vicious snarl.

"Nathan . . ." Luis said his name in despair and humiliation as a cold, sickening feeling washed over him and settled in the pit of his stomach. What little serenity he'd had left in his soul was destroyed, and he was left in shock.

"Yes, *Nathan,*" he said harshly.

"How did you get in here?"

"If you must know, your servant was kind enough to let me wait in the study while you spoke with your other guest. But what does that matter, and why change the subject, Alvarez? Let's talk about what's really going on here. Where's Reina? Where's my precious fiancée?" he thundered.

Luis was cornered and unsure of what to do. He didn't know just how much Nathan had heard.

"Don't try to lie your way out of this. I'm sick of your lies. I want to know where she is," he demanded.

"I don't know," the Californio managed.

"What do you mean, you don't know?"

Luis's temper flared at being spoken to in such a way. "If you eavesdropped on my entire conversation, then you know very well just what I mean. She has run off, and I hired Clay Cordell, the bounty hunter, to find her. I haven't heard anything yet."

"How long ago did she leave?"

"Weeks," he admitted.

"Weeks," Nathan repeated angrily. "You mean you've been lying to me this whole time?"

"Now, just relax, Nathan." He tried to calm him. "As I was telling O'Keefe, my daughter is very strong-willed, but she isn't stupid. She'll be back. I assure you the wedding will go on as planned."

"Oh, I'm certain of that, Alvarez," the greedy American told him. Just because the woman was unwilling, didn't mean the marriage wouldn't take place. It didn't matter to him what Reina wanted. It only mattered to him what he wanted, and he wanted Rancho Alvarez.

Luis brightened at this news. "Then you still want to marry Reina?"

"Of course," Nathan answered sharply. "Do you think I can afford for this to become public knowledge after the engagement celebration and wedding announcement we had? No, I will still take your lovely daughter as my bride, Luis. Mark my words."

Luis knew he should have felt relieved that Nathan wanted to go through with the plans that had been made. It meant that the rancho would be safe. But even as he rejoiced inwardly at the good fortune, he couldn't help but feel there was something far more sinister behind his determination.

"I am looking forward to it, just as I've always been," Luis replied, trying to ignore the sense of alarm that was growing within him.

"Good," he said coolly. "You'll keep me informed?"

"Yes."

Nathan started from the house. "I'll be expecting to hear from you soon."

When he had ridden off, Luis remained standing in the foyer, lost deep in thought. He was developing a great dislike for Nathan. There was something about the man . . . something about his arrogance and the way he pushed, that set his nerves on edge. For a moment, he considered that possibly Reina had been right in her judgment of him, but he pushed that troublesome thought away.

Luis knew he should be pleased with the way things turned out. The worst thing he had feared could happen, had happened. Nathan had found out that Reina had fled. Yet, despite the revelation, the repercussions he'd expected from him after learning the news, hadn't occurred. Nathan had been angry, but not enough to call off their arrangement. Luis told himself that things were going to work out fine, yet even as he tried to convince himself, there was an edge of hesitancy to his conviction.

Nathan was filled with rage and a violent ugly hatred for Reina as he rode for Monterey. Had he been able to get his hands on her right then, he might have strangled her. It infuriated him that she would run away like this and risk damaging his reputation. He could hardly wait for her to return so he could show her just how he expressed his displeasure with people who crossed him.

A cruel smile thinned his lips as he imagined the punishment he would mete out on her sweet, young body. He was a master at inflicting pain in ways that never left any marks or scars. He was going to enjoy every minute of her suffering. She deserved that and more, but he had to be careful. Humiliated though he might be by her defection, he still had a larger goal in mind. He wanted Rancho Alvarez, and he intended to have it, even at the cost of being forced to marry the recalcitrant Reina.

At least, Nathan reflected as he reached the outskirts of town, Alvarez had had sense enough to keep quiet about her disappearance. No one else besides the bounty hunters knew that she'd fled, and no one else ever would. He would see to that.

Tense and aggravated, he changed his mind about returning to work and urged his horse in the direction of Lilly's place instead. She somehow always knew just what to say and do to ease his moods. As angry as he was, he knew a relaxing visit with her was just what he needed.

Clay's mood was as dark as his expression as he strode the deck of the ship carrying them north to Monterey. It would only be a matter of days until they made port, and though he should have been thrilled at the prospect of almost being done with Alvarez, he was not. Nothing was right in his life any more.

No matter how hard he'd tried since they'd made love that last night in Panama City, Clay could not deny that he cared about Reina and that he wanted her with a nearly consuming passion. She was a fire in his blood . . . an addiction from which he feared he would never be free. Every time he was close to her, he could barely stop himself from taking her. Somehow, he had managed not to touch her since they'd boarded, but it had taken a major effort of will on his part, especially since they'd been forced by circumstances to share a cabin again.

Clay knew that if he made love to Reina again, he would never be able to let her go, and that was an impossibility. Dev's life hung in the balance. He had to take her back. He had to.

That realization was upsetting enough for him, but the change in Reina, herself, since they'd left Panama, had affected him even more. No longer was she his arch rival, fighting and sparring with him as she constantly matched wits with him and tried to get the upper hand. Now, Reina had finally done what he'd told her to do. She'd accepted the inevitable. She'd realized he'd won, and that it was over. But in accepting the truth of her situation, she'd become withdrawn, defeated. She avoided him as much as possible and talked to him only when necessary.

Clay knew he should be glad, for it took some of the pressure off him, but instead it left him wracked with guilt. Her spirit seemed to have been crushed. She refused to argue with him. She quietly acquiesced to whatever he wanted, and it was driving him crazy. He wanted her to be her usual vibrant self, not this icy, reserved, distant woman, who was eating little and sleeping even less. Several times during the nights since they'd been at sea, he'd awakened to find her out of bed, standing at the cabin's window, staring expressionlessly out at the sea. Her mood disturbed him. He wanted to help, but knew he couldn't. He had a responsibility, a duty. He had to save Dev.

Clay paused at the rail, frustrated and tired. He didn't like situations where he wasn't in complete control. He raked a hand nervously through his hair as he glanced in the direction of the companionway that led to their cabin. He thought about returning there, but immediately dismissed the thought. It was torture chamber enough at night, far better that he spend as much time as possible away from her.

The hours were passing far too slowly for Clay, though. The prospect of a stiff drink and some male conversation to distract him sounded particularly enlightening, so he headed for the men's saloon.

Reina was sitting on the bed brushing out her hair, trying to come to terms with the inevitability of her future. It was the same struggle she'd had within herself night and day since they'd left Panama City, and she knew that no matter how hard she tried, it would never get any easier for her to accept. She was going home. She would be forced to marry Nathan. She would live the rest of her life at Rancho Alvarez with a man she didn't love and couldn't bear to be near.

In her mind, Reina tried to picture herself living a happy contented life with Nathan and making love with him. The thought left her shuddering in revulsion. Now that she'd known true bliss with Clay, how could she ever give herself to another man?

Thoughts of Clay besieged her then. He had made no attempt to touch her since the voyage had begun, and his obvious lack of interest only made her realize all the more how little she really meant to him. He did not care for her, and he never had. Money was the only thing important to him . . . just money.

Her misery complete, Reina set aside her brush and went to the small trunk that held her things. Impatiently, she dug through until she found the one item that Emilie had included that had surprised her when she'd first discovered it . . . the rosary from the nun's habit. She stared down at it, wondering if prayer could really help her now. She

wondered, too, if she should consider a vocation
. . . if a vocation could be a way out. As soon as
she had the thought, she denied it. A religious life
couldn't be used as an escape route. It was something much finer and more dedicated than that, and
she knew she was not cut out for that life. She had
to face reality. She went to her knees and began to
ask, humbly, for guidance, help and the strength
she was going to need to get through the coming
days.

Clay was feeling no pain as he returned to their
stateroom long hours later. He had had more than
his share of the saloon's fine bourbon, and numb as
he was, he hoped that at least tonight he would get
a good night's sleep. He needed one.

Reina heard him fumbling with the lock. Surprised by the trouble he seemed to be having opening it, she glanced up curiously when he finally
came in. Of all the things she'd come to expect out
of Clay, being so drunk he could barely walk wasn't
one of them.

The stubborn lock had agitated Clay. He'd never
had any trouble with it before, and he wondered
why it had refused to budge now. When he finally
entered the cabin, he was still a little annoyed and
shut the door with extra force behind him.

The sight that greeted him as he turned into the
room caused him to pause just inside the door.
Reina was sitting on the bed clad only in her
nightgown, the covers demurely pulled up across
her lap, her dark, lustrous hair tumbling gloriously
down around her shoulders. A shaft of lightning
desire jolted through him as his gaze dropped from
her face to her bosom. The chaste gown she wore
revealed nothing, but he remembered all too well

the luscious curves beneath. Only by sheer grit did he manage to look away from her. He felt suddenly like an animal trapped in a maze, and he wondered dismally why he'd returned to the cabin so soon.

Reina was so startled by the state of his drunkenness, that she spoke almost involuntarily, "You've been drinking."

With pride, he lifted the bottle he'd carried with him, showing her that three quarters of the contents were gone.

"All for a worthy cause, I assure you." His cause being a search for painless, temporary amnesia. He'd been trying to use the liquor to wash away her memory. He didn't want to think about the feel of her silken skin beneath his hands and her writhing body bucking under his. He discovered now, to his dismay, that his attempt had proven futile. The bourbon had only enhanced his recollections. His besotted brain was replaying them for him in a vivid, passionate sequence that pounded relentlessly at his control.

For the first time in days, Reina's temper flared. She believed he was celebrating his triumph over her, and it stung. This victory he was so proud of would be the cause of untold misery for her. "I'm sure you believe your cause is worth celebrating."

As if in salute, he took another drink. "And I'm not done yet."

Needing to distract himself from thoughts of loving her, he pulled a chair over to the foot of the bed and sat down. Leaning back, he braced the chair on two legs and then rested his feet upon the bed, his long legs stretched out comfortably before him. He lifted the bottle to his lips again.

"You're really happy that we're almost back to Monterey, aren't you?" Reina asked.

"You have no idea," Clay answered. "You want a

422

drink?" He held the bottle out to her, but she shook her head in refusal, her expression cold.

"No. I have nothing to celebrate."

"Not many of us do."

"You do. Why, in just a few days, you'll have your big reward for bringing me back. That should make you real happy. After all, money is what you've always loved best."

"Don't judge me by your standards, Reina. I find more value in loyalty and honor. You're the one who loves money."

His accusation hurt, and she was embarrassed by the sudden rush of tears that burned in her eyes. "You're wrong about that, Clay, but then you've been wrong about a lot of things concerning me from the very beginning."

She sounded so utterly sad and vanquished, that suddenly for the first time, Clay found he was questioning himself and his motives. *Had he been wrong about Reina?* He wrestled with the possibility, his heart softening toward her, his guard edging down. In a flash of agonized insight, he realized that what he felt for her had gone far past mere caring. He'd fallen in love with her.

Yet even as he admitted to himself the truth of his feelings, he knew it was hopeless. Dev was depending on him. Downing the last of his bourbon, he righted his chair and stood up. Without a word, he strode from the stateroom, leaving Reina wondering why he'd gone.

Chapter Thirty-two

Though Reina had managed to keep her emotions under tenuous control for most of the trip, the sight of Monterey shattered what little composure she had left. She turned away from the stateroom window, glancing frantically around the jail-like confines of the cabin, her thoughts in chaos.

Within the hour, they would be gone from the boat, and soon, very soon, she would have to face her father . . . and Nathan. She imagined what would happen when they were finally reunited, and she shivered in dread. She clasped her hands nervously together to stop them from shaking. Staring around her in desperation, she knew there was only one last hope left to her . . . Clay. She had to tell him the truth. She had to tell him how she felt about him, even though she knew he probably wouldn't believe her and might even ridicule her and accuse her of trying to manipulate him again.

As Clay strode down the companionway toward the stateroom, it seemed impossible to him that there were only minutes left before they could go ashore. The first week of the trip had been endless for him, but to his dismay, the last few days had flown by. He had wanted more time to think things through. He still had not resolved the conflict between his loyalty to Dev and his love for Reina, and no matter how hard he tried to reconcile the two, he remained torn. Grimly, he realized that there really was no choice open to him. He had to save Dev, his own feelings be damned.

He paused outside the cabin, girding himself for the moment to come. He had to tell her that they had arrived. He had to tell her to pack the last of her things and prepare to go ashore. He would then accompany her out to the ranch where he would turn her over to her father. He grimaced inwardly at the thought of their parting, for he knew it was going to be the most difficult thing he'd ever done in his life. He didn't want to let her go, but there was nothing else he could do.

"Reina, it's almost time for us to leave the boat," he announced as he let himself in.

Reina was standing at the window, her back to him. She'd heard his approach and knew it was now or never. She faced him.

"I know," she answered slowly, drawing a deep, fortifying breath. "Clay . . . there's something I have to say now before we go. It's something I should have told you long ago."

"I think we've said about all there is to say, Reina." Clay didn't want to talk, he just wanted to get this over with as quickly as possible.

"No, we haven't even begun."

She lifted her gaze to his, and the emotion he saw mirrored there surprised him. He frowned, puzzled and confused by the tenderness he'd read in her expression. His deeply ingrained mistrust immediately reared its ugly head, casting doubt on the small flicker of hope he'd felt.

"Clay, I want to tell you the truth now before we

reach Monterey. I want you to know how I feel."

"There's really no need for this."

"Oh, but there is," she said softly, going to him and putting a hand on his arm. "There's every need."

Slowly, she leaned toward him and pressed a gentle kiss on his lips. She drew back, smiling bittersweetly, and moved away.

"Can't you feel it? Don't you know?"

"Know what?" He watched her carefully, not quite sure what was happening. Reina had done nothing but declare how much she'd despised him from the very beginning, and now . . .

"That I love you." There she'd said it. She watched and waited for a reaction from him, but when there was none, her heart sank.

Clay was stunned by her declaration, and he had to force himself to keep his expression from revealing that surprise. He wanted to believe that she loved him. Oh, how he wanted to believe it, but why had she chosen this particular moment to tell him when they'd had weeks together?

She's an actress! a little voice inside of him reminded. *She'll do whatever she has to, to avoid going home!* the voice taunted. Clay wanted to deny the warning, but she'd tried to trick him so many times before that it was difficult for him to be convinced of her sincerity this time.

"Why are you telling me all this now?" He asked a bit angrily, torn up by the fight going on inside him.

Reina went on slowly, "Because I wanted you to know. You see, when I get home, my father is going to force me to marry a man I don't love— Nathan Marlow. The two of them arranged the marriage without even consulting me. When Father finally told me of his plans, I told him that I didn't love Nathan and wouldn't marry him. He refused to listen to me though, and no matter how hard I tried to explain that I wanted a love match like he'd had with my mother, he'd insisted that I go through with the wedding."

The thought of Reina married to someone else stabbed at him.

"That was when I decided to run away. I just couldn't spend the rest of my life married to a man whose very touch makes my skin crawl." Her shoulders slumped in defeat. "I didn't mean for this to happen, but it did. I think I've loved you ever since the day of the stage robbery." Reina was a proud woman, but she put her pride aside as she begged, "Clay, please, if what we've shared has meant anything to you at all, don't take me back to my father."

She sounded so earnest, that he felt himself wavering. He was caught between Dev's very life and his own happiness. "Reina, I can't go back on my word. I have to do this . . . I . . ."

Before he could say any more, a loud knock at the door sounded. It didn't matter to Reina, though, because she'd already heard his answer. He couldn't do it. He wouldn't do it. He didn't love her. He didn't care.

Clay answered the door, expecting it to be someone from the boat. He was shocked when he came face to face with Luis Alvarez flanked by two big, burly ranchhands.

"Alvarez!"

Reina stiffened, her head snapping up as she heard the familiar sound of her father's voice.

"Do you have my daughter, Cordell?" Luis demanded.

"Yes, I've brought her back." He stood aside to let him enter.

427

The old Californio stepped into the stateroom to find Reina standing across the room, regarding him with regal bearing, looking as lovely as ever. He'd been nervously anticipating her return, and he'd set men to watching the stage depots and the waterfront. He couldn't believe his luck that he'd happened to be in town on business today when the ship had arrived. He'd sent a man out to check with the captain to see if anyone by the name of Cordell or Alvarez had been on the passenger list, and he'd been thrilled to find that a Mr. and Mrs. Cordell were registered. He was anxious to make sure she was all right, and it pleased him to find that she seemed fine.

"You're all right?"

"I'm fine." Reina remained unmoving, her head held high as she met her father's gaze. She felt chilled to the very heart, for she knew any hope of happiness she'd ever had would be gone the moment she walked out of this room. A part of her wanted to cry for the loss, but the woman in her refused to show either man any weakness. Gathering the tattered shreds of her pride, she prepared to leave.

"Here's your money, Cordell." Luis pulled a thick envelope from his coat pocket and offered it to him.

Clay suddenly seemed as if he was taking blood money. When he reached for the envelope, he could feel Reina's eyes condemningly upon him. He knew he couldn't let that stop him, though. He had Dev to worry about. "What about O'Keefe?"

"You'll find him right where you left him, quite safe and quite comfortable," he answered easily. "Reina? I think it's time we returned to the rancho, don't you?"

She nodded with all the dignity she could muster, then she strode sedately across the room to stop before Clay. For just an instant all that she was

428

feeling was poignantly revealed in her eyes . . . the hurt . . . the betrayal . . . the love. She leaned toward him to kiss him gently on the cheek.

"Remember me, Clay," she whispered, and then she swept from the room without looking back. She did not allow the tears that blurred her vision to slow her or the twisting, roiling pain in her breast to show in her expression.

Clay watched her go, her father and his men following after her carrying her things. A terrible sense of loss nearly overpowered him when he closed the stateroom door behind them. He stood in the middle of the cabin feeling more alone than he ever had before. He ran a hand over his eyes, struggling to focus on what he had to do next. The worst was over. Now it was time to get on with his life and see to it that Dev got on with his. Gathering his things together, he left the boat.

Dev was tired. It had been a long, dull day, and he was glad it was nearly over. In another hour or so, Macauley would show up to work the night, and then he would head home to a nice hot meal and Molly.

A grin split his face as he thought of his wife. They'd been married for over two weeks now, and as impossible as it seemed, things had only gotten better between them. He was enjoying being around Jimmy so much that he could hardly wait until he and Molly had children of their own. She would make a wonderful mother, and he knew he would love being a father.

At the sound of the office door opening, Dev glanced up, thinking it was the sheriff arriving early.

"You're early . . ." he began, but the sight of his

long-lost friend had him on his feet and racing across the room to greet him. He'd been waiting forever for this moment, and he was thrilled Clay was back.

"Clay! I don't believe it!" He threw his arms around his astonished partner and hugged him tight.

"Dev?" Clay pushed away to take a good look at him. "What the hell are you doing out here? You're supposed to be rotting away behind bars!"

"Well, I was for a while, but now I'm—" he began, but Clay went on.

"A deputy? You're wearing a badge?" he stated in disbelief, looking from the badge up to his face and back again. "What's been going on around here?"

Dev threw his head back and laughed at his shock. "A lot," he assured him, clapping him soundly on the shoulder. "Sit down. I've got a whole helluva lot to tell you. So much, in fact, I don't know where to start."

"Try the beginning," he said drolly as he sat down before the desk and Dev took his own seat again.

"First, you tell me about you. Did you find the Alvarez girl?"

"I just handed her over to her father," he answered stiffly.

"Any trouble?"

"Nothing serious," he dismissed his concern not ready to talk or think about Reina just yet. "Now, tell me, how did you manage to get out of jail and get yourself a job as a deputy? When I left, Macauley seemed dead certain that you were his man. I thought you were on the verge of being hung."

"I was lucky, very lucky," Dev began, and then he went on to explain all that had happened from Denton's escape attempt to the sheriff's arrest of Stevens for the Santana murder.

430

"So he let you out of jail and hired you on to help him?"

"That's about it. There is one other thing that happened, though . . . uh, something else I have to tell you." He hedged, but at Clay's questioning look, he went on, "There's Molly . . ."

"Molly? The girl from the restaurant you saved from Denton?"

"Yes."

"What about her?"

"Well, while you were gone," he hesitated again, then just blurted out the truth of it. "I married her."

"You got married?" Clay was truly surprised by all that had transpired, and he found, a little annoyed. Here, he'd been worried that Dev was in mortal danger, and all along he'd been cleared of the charges for weeks and was now happily married to boot. Relief spread through him as the burden of concern he'd shouldered for so long was lifted from him. He was happy for his friend. He wanted only the best for Dev.

"I know this is all a shock for you," Dev was saying, trying to ease the blow of his defection, "and I'm sorry I had to spring this on you this way. But Molly and I fell in love, and I didn't want to live another minute without her. You haven't been in love yet, but when it happens, you'll know what I'm talking about."

Clay didn't want to tell him that he knew full well exactly what he was talking about. He wondered vaguely that if he'd known Dev was free, would he have kept Reina from her father. He knew it was useless to debate the point, but the thought of her married to another man because of him, left him filled with impotent rage.

"That's why I took this job with the sheriff," Dev explained. "I knew I couldn't have a home and a

431

family and keep working as a bounty hunter. Molly and I hoped you'd understand."

Clay managed a smile. "I understand. I would have done the same thing in your place."

"Thanks, Clay," Dev's words were heartfelt as he clasped his friend's hand. "I want you to come to the house for dinner tonight. I want you to meet everybody. I've already told them all about you. You can even stay with us if you like."

"I'll take you up on the dinner offer, but I've already taken a room at the Perdition."

"Ah, you want to renew old acquaintances?"

"Could be," he answered, but in truth, the last thing he wanted was one of the girls from the saloon. There was only one woman he wanted, and she was now lost to him forever.

Before he'd gone on board the ship to claim Reina, Luis had sent one of his men to hire a carriage for the return trip to the ranch. As he guided Reina to the conveyance and helped her to climb in, he cast her a sidelong glance, trying to judge her mood. She looked perfectly at ease, unruffled by all the upset that had surrounded her disappearance and now, finally, her return.

Luis's emotions were in a state of total havoc as he picked up the reins and urged the horse toward home. He was overjoyed that Reina had been returned safely to him, but he still harbored anger over her disobedience. The conflict between the two was wearing upon him. He'd realized while she was missing just how very dear she was to him, and he wondered, now, if they would ever be close again as long as Nathan was in the picture. He knew they were going to have to talk about everything that had happened when they got back to the rancho, but it was not a confrontation that he was looking forward to. They rode in silence for quite a while, before he finally spoke up, breaking the icy barrier that had existed between them.

"You look well."

"I am."

"I was worried about you," he ventured.

"Really?" Her tone left no doubt in his mind that she didn't believe him.

"Yes, really." His own hot temper flashed. "You are my daughter."

"I thought I was more your chattel, something you could sell or trade as you pleased."

"This marriage could be a good thing, if you gave it half a chance. Nathan is not a bad man. He would treat you well. He's rich. You could have everything you ever wanted."

His words raked over her like sharp claws. Clay had believed the same thing about her. The two men in her life she loved, the two men who meant the most to her, didn't know her at all. They both thought her a mindless fool who loved riches above all else.

"Money has never been important to me, Father. You're the one who loves the power it can give, not me."

"I respect the power it brings," he defended himself.

"Power and money are both the same. Neither are important."

Her attitude angered him further. "You can say that because you've never been poor. You've never done without."

"Maybe not, but I do know that money can't buy happiness or contentment. If you continue in your quest to have me marry Nathan, I will be rich, but I will not be happy. I don't love him, Father, and

433

no matter how hard I try, I will never be able to love him."

"Love! Bah!" he scoffed. "What do you know about love?"

"I know that you loved Mother, and she adored you. I know I want that kind of marriage. I want a man who loves me, not the ranch I bring as a dowry."

"Nathan loves you."

"Nathan loves only Rancho Alvarez. There is no love in that man. He's cold and he's cruel."

"You're wrong about him, Reina," Luis argued, but even as he did, he felt a sting of conscience.

She grew tired of the same old argument for she knew she'd never win. "If you say so, Father. I know there is no point in going over this again. You've won. You've brought me home. I will respect your wishes in all things as I have no other choice."

Luis fell silent. He knew he was forcing her into this, but he could see no other way out of his dire situation. An alliance with Nathan and his wealth would insure the continuity of the ranch. Reina would understand someday, he hoped . . . He also hoped that he never lived to regret his decision to go forth with the marriage plans.

Nathan had had his own men keeping watch for Reina. Word reached him quickly that she had returned and had left for the rancho in the company of her father. The moment he heard the news, he headed out after them. With each passing mile on the way, his mood grew increasingly wicked and savage. She had thought to escape him, but she'd failed. Once they were married, he was going to teach her a thing or two about obedience and

434

respect for one's husband.

Reina and Luis had barely had time to settle in when Nathan arrived at the ranch. Consuelo directed him into the parlor and then went to the study to announce him to Luis and Reina, who had, themselves, only just arrived a short time before.

They were startled by his unexpected appearance. Luis had hoped to have some time alone with Reina before reuniting her with Nathan, but it seemed that things had been taken out of his hands. He did not like the feeling.

Reina shot her father a pleading, almost wild-eyed desperate look as Consuelo announced him.

"Father, please don't do this . . . don't force me to go through with this . . ."

"I'm sorry, Reina, but it's all been arranged. The wedding will go on as scheduled."

"You would really sentence me to a life of misery?"

"Trust me in this, Reina. It won't be as bad as you think. In time, you may even come to love him."

"Why can't you trust me, Father? Why don't you respect my judgment?"

"Show Nathan in, Consuelo," Luis overruled her, rising to greet his honored future son-in-law.

Nathan was aggravated as he entered the study. He did not like being kept waiting, but he took Luis's hand just to keep up images. It would not do to alienate him yet. He swung around to Reina then, his gaze coolly assessing as he regarded her.

"I'm glad to see that you're well."

"Thank you, but you had no reason to be concerned. I was quite safe the whole time." Though she sounded very calm and collected, Reina was really quite frightened. She'd sensed the viciousness in Nathan long ago and didn't trust him one bit. For a moment, she let herself long for Clay, but then almost immediately pushed the thought away. He was gone from her life now. She would have to be brave and handle this all on her own.

"That's a relief to know now, but it didn't help your father or me during all the time you were missing. We were quite worried about you." Her poised, self-confident attitude annoyed him greatly, and he grew determined to bring her to heel, now. She was a little too cocky, a little too self-assured. He wanted to see her groveling before him. He wanted to see her crawl. Women were meant to be submissive, and it was time little Miss Alvarez learned that.

Reina knew she should apologize, but somehow, seeing the coldness in his eyes, she couldn't bring herself to do it.

Nathan was furious by her lack of response, but when he turned to Luis he appeared the perfect gentleman. "Luis, I wonder if my future bride and I might have a few moments of privacy?"

"Of course," Luis agreed, understanding the need for the two to be alone. He quickly left the room. He could feel Reina's desperation but he ignored it. This man would soon be her husband, she needed to learn how to get along with him.

Chapter Thirty-three

When Luis had gone, Nathan turned on her, his eyes burning with the fiery heat of his anger. "Well, my darling fiancée, it would seem that you and I have a lot to talk about."

"I can't imagine what," she replied haughtily, though, in truth, her self-confidence was badly shaken.

Nathan jerked her around toward him, forcing her to look at him. "I'll tell you what, little girl," he snarled. "First, there's our wedding. Then there's our life together."

Reina tried to break free, but he held her easily.

"And we will have a life together, Reina. A long and prosperous one, I should think." His smile was evil, tinged with cruelty.

"I'd rather be dead!" she spat back at him.

"That could be arranged if you continue to defy me," he threatened, tightening his grip to bruising strength. "I like spirit in a woman, but I'm no lovesick swain where you're concerned. You're nothing more than a commodity to me, a means to an end. Remember that." He released her, but the imprint of his fingers would mar her delicate flesh for days to come. "Your father has given you to me, and once we're married, you'll be mine . . . all mine, to do with as I please."

"Why do you want to do this? If you feel nothing for me, why don't you just let me go? Forget this marriage. Tell everyone it was your idea to end the engagement. I would gladly suffer the blow to my reputation than suffer endless years married to you!" Reina knew she had nothing to lose by telling the truth.

Nathan chuckled. "There's more at stake here than just the marriage, my dear. If you think I went into this arrangement because I wanted you, you're sadly mistaken. You're only a bargaining chip to be used and discarded as I see fit."

Reina lifted her chin defiantly. "Then you intend this to be a marriage in name only?"

"I didn't say that. You do hold some physical appeal for me. There is, however, one thing I want to be sure of before our wedding takes place."

"What?" She felt chilled by the look in his eyes as he studied her.

"My sources tell me that you were booked on the ship from Panama in one cabin under the names of Mr. and Mrs. Cordell. I just want to make certain that you're still untouched before I make you my bride."

"You what?" Reina was shocked by the crudity of his revelation.

Nathan could see that he'd shocked her, and he gave a low, ominous laugh. He lifted one hand to caress her cheek. She felt like cold alabaster beneath his touch, and he wondered if there was any heat or excitement in her. He wondered, too, if she would be that cold and unresponsive in bed.

"I want to make sure you're worthy of the honor of being Mrs. Nathan Marlow."

He took her by the arm and pulled her against him. Brazenly, he fondled her breast through her clothing and then let his hand slip lower to the juncture of her thighs. Reina tried to break away, but to no avail.

"Let me go, Nathan!"

"Not until I make sure of your innocence, my dear. Or perhaps you'd like to have me bring in the doctor to check? That certainly could be arranged, although the damage to your reputation might be irreparable should any indiscretions in your past come to light."

Reina saw the very real, intimidating promise in his eyes and knew she couldn't bear to suffer his hands upon her, ever. There was only one thing left for her to do—alienate him in whatever way she could by whatever means possible, even if it meant lying.

"You don't have to examine me," she told him proudly. "I'll tell you exactly what you want to know."

"Oh?"

"I'm no virgin. I gave myself to Clay, and I'm glad I did. We shared the cabin on the trip back as lovers. I love him, and I'm pregnant with his child right now! If my father hadn't forced me to return home, I would never have come back! Never!"

"You're what?" Nathan's wrath was an awesome thing, and he struck out at her, brutally backhanding her.

Reina staggered backward, uttering a small cry of surprise and pain at his ruthlessness. She cradled her cheek and bloodied, swelling lip with one hand as she drew herself up to full height to face him contemptuously.

"I'm going to have another man's baby, and I couldn't be more thrilled. I love him as I could never love you."

"You little slut . . ." He took a menacing step toward her, but she held her ground almost daring him to hit her again. He realized the precariousness of his situation and restrained himself. He told

439

himself the wedding would take place soon, and then he'd make her pay, and pay dearly.

"Now, if you'll excuse me—" Without another word, Reina quit the room with a dignity befitting her name. Once she was out of Nathan's sight, she ran as quickly as she could to her own chambers to seek solace there.

Nathan stood in the center of the study, his temper raging nearly out of control. *So, she was pregnant, was she?* he thought angrily. Well, this changed things considerably. He didn't relish the idea of taking some other man's whore as his wife or some other man's bastard as his own, but for the right price he could be convinced to do anything.

He wondered if Alvarez had any idea of his daughter's whoring ways, and he decided the old man didn't. Smiling to himself, Nathan went to seek him out. It was time he learned of his daughter's debauched behavior, and he knew it would be interesting to see how he responded to the possible thought of her reputation being sullied by spreading rumors around town concerning her indecent state.

"Luis?" Nathan found the older man in the parlor.

Luis was surprised that they had finished talking so soon. "Where's Reina?"

"I believe she's gone to her room."

This sounded bad to Luis, and he wondered what had happened between them. "Did you settle your differences?"

"That's what I need to talk to you about."

"Oh? Is there a problem? Whatever it is, I'm sure we can work it out."

"I'm afraid, Luis, that this is more than just a simple problem to be worked out."

"I don't understand."

"Obviously, your daughter has not told you everything."

"Everything? What are you talking about?"

"I'm talking about the fact that she's pregnant with another man's child." He dropped the news with particular delight, and he enjoyed watching the old man turn a sickly shade of gray.

"Cordell . . ." Luis uttered his name in a hoarse rasp. Guilt riddled him as he realized what he'd done. He was the one who'd thrown her together with that lowlife gunslinger. He was the one responsible for her current state. It was all his fault. It was no wonder that Reina hadn't trusted him enough to tell him the truth about everything. Look what he'd done to her! "I'm going to kill the bastard!" he declared, seething.

"Don't do anything drastic, Luis," Nathan urged calmly. "I have no objection to saving her reputation. I'll go ahead with our plans and make her my wife, but first I'd like a change made in our original agreement."

The old Californio, a man of honor and pride, held himself rigid as he listened to Nathan's proposal. "Such as?"

"Such as, I'll agree to marry Reina and call the child mine, but only if you deed the ranch over to me before the wedding."

"What?" He was astounded by his greed and conniving. If Nathan had been a man of honor, if he had really cared for Reina, he would have made no such demand. The unsettling dislike he'd felt for him before now turned to a full-grown hatred.

"Let's face it. Reina is no virgin. She's whored herself around to God knows how many men, and now she's carrying someone else's bastard . . . a bastard she's going to want to pass off as mine! I think I deserve some extra compensation for this humiliation. If not, the deal's off. Do I make myself clear?"

Luis was livid. In that moment, if he had had a

gun, he would have used it on Nathan. How dare he stand before him in his own home and say such things?

He realized then that, regardless of what Reina had done, she'd been right all along in her opinion of this man. For all his money, important contacts and business dealings, Nathan had no honor. He was filth. He wasn't even good enough to clean out the Alvarez stables, let alone marry his precious daughter.

"You make yourself all too clear, Mr. Marlow," Luis stated firmly, "and as far as I'm concerned any dealings we had are now cancelled. You may consider yourself relieved of your obligation to marry my daughter."

"You're going to let this deal slip away?" Nathan was shocked.

He ignored the younger man's question as he continued, "I will see that the necessary people are informed of the change in wedding plans. You, sir, are no longer welcome in my home or on my land. Do I make *myself* clear?"

"What about your land, Alvarez? Are you prepared to lose it? I thought this rancho meant everything to you?"

"I have just discovered that there are things in life far more important than riches. To my sorrow and shame I almost had to lose them before I realized their true value," he told him, thinking of his daughter and how much he needed her love and respect.

"Right now you may think there are more important things than riches, but I wonder if you'll feel that way once you've lost everything," he taunted.

"The state of my affairs is no longer any of your business. I suggest you take your leave."

"You're going to be sorry, Alvarez."

"I already am, Mr. Marlow. Good-bye."

442

Luis had cut him dead, but still Nathan refused to leave.

"Mr. Marlow," the rancher said with slow precision, "will you leave my home of your own accord or will I be forced to call some of my men to assist you from my rancho?"

Nathan's eyes narrowed dangerously as he regarded the old man. "This ranch will still be mine!"

"Rancho Alvarez is mine and will ultimately belong to Reina. You'll never lay your filthy hands on it! Never! Now get out of my sight before I forget that I'm a gracious host and take great pleasure in seeing your back bloodied before you're thrown bodily from my property!"

Nathan was furious as he strode from the house and mounted his horse. "You haven't seen the last of me, yet!"

Luis, however, ignored his shouted threats. He watched him ride away into the night with great relief. When the rage of the moment had passed, he sighed deeply, then went back inside.

He knew he had to speak to Reina, but he was afraid. He had ignored her pleas for understanding. He had overruled her at every turn. Now, he had to go to her and tell her that she'd been right all along. It was a difficult thing for him to do. He would have to swallow his pride to do it, and his pride was all he had left right now. Knowing he could not put it off, he started down the hall that led to her bedroom.

Reina was sitting at her dressing table with a cold compress pressed to her cheek when she heard the knock at her door. She cringed at the thought of anyone seeing her this way. "Who is it?"

"Reina, it's your father," Luis answered. "May I speak with you?"

"Please, Father, could we talk in the morning? You've won. I'll do whatever you want, but I really

443

need to be alone for a while."

She tried to put him off, but he would have none of it. What he had to say, needed to be said right now.

"Reina, please, child, it's really important. Please open the door."

She'd never heard him sound so humble, and it bothered her. She wondered if he was playing some sort of game with her or if he was really having a change of heart.

"All right," she conceded, laying the compress aside as she went to answer the door.

Luis was completely taken aback by the sight of her injured cheek and lip. "My God!" He was overcome by the thought that she'd been hurt this way, and tears stung his eyes.

"I'm sorry, Father, I didn't want you to see me like this."

"He did this to you?" he asked, his tone hoarse with emotion.

"Yes," she answered softly.

At her response, he felt even more embarrassed by what he'd almost done. He had nearly forced his precious daughter to marry a violent, woman-beating fiend. The man deserved to be horsewhipped.

"Reina, child . . ." his voice was choked as he reached out to her. He was surprised when she allowed him to hold her. It had been so long since they'd shared any affection. "Reina, I'm sorry . . . so sorry. I almost made an unforgivable mistake, but I've taken care of that now. You'll never have to concern yourself with Marlow again."

"Father?" His words surprised her, and she drew back in total confusion to look up at him.

"You were right about Marlow all along. I was just too desperate, too worried about losing the rancho to see the truth. He's an amoral, manipulative bastard, and he's not worthy of you! In fact,

444

I'm not worthy of your love. When I think that I almost sold you to Marlow—"

Tears of relief and joy filled her eyes. She was thrilled with the news. When Luis saw the happiness in her gaze, he was relieved. He held her once more, his throat constricting with the power of his emotions.

"But Father, what are we going to do?" she asked, thinking that they might now lose the rancho.

"It'll be all right," he told her earnestly, thinking about her pregnancy.

"It will?"

"Yes, and I understand."

"You do?"

"Yes, Nathan told me all about it, so you don't have to keep it from me any more."

"Nathan told you?" For a moment she didn't realize what he was talking about, and when it suddenly dawned on her, she turned decidedly pale. Luckily, the way he was holding her with her head against his shoulder, he couldn't see her face.

"Yes, he told me about your delicate condition, but don't worry. I won't fail you this time. I want you to tell me exactly what happened, then I'll decide what I'm going to do. Did Cordell force you or hurt you in any way?" he asked as they moved apart. His dark gaze searched hers for some sign that the bounty hunter had mistreated and taken advantage of her, too, because if he had—

"No . . . no, it wasn't like that at all," she quickly denied, swallowing nervously as she tried to think of a quick way out of this one. She'd lied to Nathan about being pregnant just to get rid of him, and it had worked. She had never dreamed that her father would find out. She'd just thought that the other man would leave in a huff of self-righteous indignation and that would be the end of it. Obviously, she'd been wrong.

445

"Then how was it?"

Reina knew she was cornered. If she told her father the real truth, he would be furious with her. If she let the lie stand, there was no telling what he would do. To save herself, she finally told him what she considered to be a partial truth. "I fell in love with Clay, Father."

"Does he know about the baby?"

"No. I couldn't tell him, not knowing that I had to marry Nathan once we returned."

"Does Cordell love you?"

"No!" Realizing she'd answered too quickly, she toned down her reply, "I mean, I don't know if he does or not."

Luis fell silent for a moment, and Reina's nerves were on edge as she waited to see what he was going to say.

"Do you trust me enough to let me handle this, Reina? Will you give me another chance to prove that I have your best interests at heart?"

She was caught and could see no way out. "Father . . . I don't want Clay to be coerced into anything."

"Don't worry. I'll take care of everything."

"Promise me you won't force him to marry me!"

"I give you my word that I won't force him to do anything he doesn't want to do." He went to her and pressed a tender, fatherly kiss to her forehead. "You rest and take care of your cheek. I'll be back as soon as I can."

Reina was filled with dread as she watched him leave her room. She was trapped in a web of lies of her own creation and things were getting more and more entangled with every passing moment.

She lay down upon the bed, but found rest impossible. Her thoughts were consumed with worry about how Clay was going to react to the news her father would be bringing him. It was all a lie, of course, and she would tell him so just as soon as she saw him.

Reina went rigid as it suddenly occurred to her that it might not be a total falsehood. She had not had her monthly flux since they'd left Panama City. She glanced down at her flat stomach and wondered if Clay's child was growing deep within her. She was surprised that the thought actually made her smile, and she relaxed a little, resting her hand on her stomach.

Luis had put on the good show for Reina, but his mood was far from calm as he strode through the house after leaving her. He had promised he wouldn't force Clay to do anything he didn't want to do, and he would keep his word on that. He just had to make sure that Clay *wanted* to do the right thing.

"Consuelo!" He summoned the maid, and then ordered in a stern voice, "Have my horse saddled and brought around! I'm riding into Monterey."

"Yes, sir!" She rushed to do his bidding.

He went on into his study and stalked straight to the gun cabinet. Taking out his most powerful rifle, he loaded it, his expression grim and determined. A loaded gun could be a very persuasive tool.

"Is there trouble?" Consuelo asked concernedly from the doorway. She'd come looking for him to tell him his mount was ready and waiting outside and had been surprised to find him arming himself.

"Nothing I can't deal with," he answered curtly as he strapped on his gunbelt.

"Do you want some of the men to ride with you?"

"No. This is something I have to do by myself." He did not want anyone else to know of Reina's situation. "Is the damned horse out front?"

"Yes, that's what I came to tell you."

"Fine. See to Reina's comfort while I'm gone. I'll be back."

Luis left her without another word. Mounting up, he rode from the rancho at top speed. He was lost deep in thought as he headed for town. It was late but he didn't care. He had to find Cordell and set things straight.

Chapter Thirty-four

"Your Molly's a lovely young woman, Dev. I know now why you didn't want to wait for me to get married," Clay told his friend with a chuckle as they made their way to the Perdition Saloon much later that night.

The evening he had just passed with Dev's new family had been a pleasant one, and he knew Dev was a very fortunate man. The loving warmth of his new home, however, had left Clay feeling even more alone. He'd been glad when Dev had suggested he accompany him back to the saloon so they could share a few drinks before calling it a night.

"Molly is special. Outside of you, she was the only one who believed in me while I was locked up. I had some damned dark days, and her faith in me meant a lot."

"I can imagine how rough it was for you. I kept thinking about you the whole time I was tracking Reina all the way back to Louisiana."

"You never have said much about your little adventure. How did it go?"

Clay shrugged. "She was very good at disguises . . . quite the actress, really."

"I take it she had you going for a while?"

"She tried, but I finally caught up with her at a party outside New Orleans."

"Did she give you a bad time once you found her?"

"I'd have rather brought back three Ace Dentons and a rattlesnake single-handedly," he admitted with a smile. "She was quick, sharp and gorgeous. It's a lethal combination."

There was something in Clay's tone that caused Dev to glance at him curiously, and, though nothing showed in his expression, it left him wondering if Reina Alvarez might have something to do with his troubled mood. Earlier during dinner, he'd sensed that there was something bothering Clay. He'd decided to join him at the Perdition for a while on the pretense of celebrating his return, in hopes that he would open up and talk about whatever it was.

"You sound like you've come to care about her," Dev said, trying to get his friend talking.

"You're getting to be a romantic now that you're a married man, Dev," he scoffed, trying to distract him from the subject of Reina. "Don't go getting any ideas. I did a job for Luis Alvarez. I found his daughter, and I brought her back, that's all. Reina's a very beautiful woman, but she's not for me."

"Oh, well, what are you planning next?" He let it drop, knowing it was better not to push.

"I'm not sure. Alvarez certainly paid me enough to keep me in style for quite a while. I told my father I'd come back for a visit some time soon. I think maybe this might be the time . . ." Clay said as he led the way into the Perdition.

Nathan was in a vile mood as he stood at the bar in the Perdition drinking straight, double-shots of whiskey. He was not used to having his plans thwarted. A seething hatred for Reina churned within him. She'd been so arrogant . . . so proud of what she'd done — pledging herself in marriage to him and then giving herself to the lowlife bounty hunter her father had sent to find her.

Nathan wanted to beat her within an inch of her life. He wanted to see the fear and terror in her eyes as he punished her for daring to cross him. He wanted to see her suffer. He knew he would never be able to get his hands on her now, but there were better, even more cunning ways to bring about her downfall.

Slamming his glass down on the bar, he waited impatiently for George, the graying, overweight, good-natured bartender, to finish taking the order of the two men who'd just come in. After giving Frenchie and Josie a bottle of bourbon and two glasses to serve the men where they'd settled in at a table, the barkeep quickly hurried down to the end of the bar to refill Nathan's glass. Nathan thanked him with a grunt of acknowledgment and downed the whole thing in one deep drink. The burning liquor felt good as it slid down his throat, fortifying his fury.

"Give me another one," he ordered before George could walk away.

Surprised by his thirst, he asked as he splashed more whiskey into his tumbler, "You celebrating something or just plain thirsty?"

"I'm celebrating," Nathan replied, deliberately speaking in a loud voice so his words would travel and others would hear.

"Oh? Got some good news, did you?"

"Real good," he gloated, ready to reveal Reina's betrayal to all who would listen. He wanted to blacken her reputation so completely that she'd never be able to show her face in town again.

"What good fortune befell you, friend?" George urged him to talk. It had been a long, quiet night, and he needed some good conversation. Nathan was

451

a pretty important man about town, and anything he had to say would probably be real interesting.

Nathan had hoped he would ask. "I just saved myself from a marriage made in hell," he announced.

"I thought you were all set to marry that good-looking Alvarez girl," he remarked, a little astonished. "I know I was envying you and so were half of the men here in town. You were going to have it all . . . a beautiful wife and a fabulous ranch."

"Goes to show how wrong we all can be. A pretty face has long been man's downfall, and I'm no exception," he lied, wanting to make himself sound betrayed. "Those sweet good-looks hid a whoring heart, George. The girl's a slut. I'm just lucky I found out before the wedding."

The barkeep was stunned. "Reina Alvarez!? A slut!" He was so fascinated that he didn't notice the way the tall, dark-haired man at the table with Frenchie and Josie suddenly looked up in their direction at the mention of Reina's name. He was too caught up in wanting to hear the rest of the story.

"That's right. She ran off with one of those bounty hunters who was in town a while back, then has the nerve to come home and want to keep to our wedding plans."

"She did?" George's eyes were wide with avid interest.

"That's right. But you know why she was so hot to go on with this wedding?"

"No, Nathan, why?" he asked, waiting eagerly for his next pronouncement. He was hungry for every terrible detail, for he knew the cancellation of the Alvarez-Marlow marriage would be the talk of the town, and he wanted to get all the facts straight.

* * *

Clay had planned for the evening to be a quiet, relaxed one, sitting and talking with Dev while they enjoyed a few drinks. He'd even been glad to see Frenchie and Josie again, though only on a friendly basis. He felt no passion for either woman now. He'd thought that strange at first, and then realized it was all because of Reina. He loved her. No one else held any appeal for him. There was only Reina in his heart.

They had just started to savor their first bourbon when Clay had heard the man at the bar mention Reina's name. He wasn't sure exactly what the man had said, but he intended to find out. He wanted to know why someone would be bandying Reina's name around in a saloon.

"Frenchie, who's that man at the bar?" Clay asked in a low voice, not wanting to draw any attention to himself.

"The man talking to the bartender?" At his answering nod, she replied, "That's Nathan Marlow."

Clay went cold inside. Nathan Marlow. Reina's fiancé.

"What is it?" Dev wondered at the sudden tension that had gripped him.

"Listen . . ." he said softly, discouraging him from talking, and it was then that Nathan announced Reina's delicate condition.

"Because she's carrying the other man's kid," Nathan confided in a particularly loud voice.

George and Nathan were so caught up in their conversation that they didn't see Clay come abruptly to his feet, his expression suddenly deadly.

"Alvarez's daughter is pregnant?" George said it over again, unable to believe it.

"That's right. I'll be damned if I'll put the Marlow name on somebody else's by-blow! The girl's no-good, and I'm glad I found out ahead of time. I'm well rid of her."

453

The news that Reina was carrying his child filled Clay with joy, but the fact that this bastard was holding her up for public scorn left him furious enough to kill. He was tempted to pull his gun and put an end to Nathan's miserable life right then and there, but he thought better of it. He wanted to beat the man senseless and enjoy every minute of it. He barely had himself under control as he stalked toward the loud-mouthed Marlow.

"I think it's the other way around, Marlow," Clay said coolly, butting in on their conversation. "I think Reina's the one who's well rid of you."

Nathan gave him only a cursory glance. "I don't remember asking your opinion. So why don't you just move on along and mind your own business?" He turned back to George.

"Reina Alvarez is my business," Clay stated with deceptive calm, as he moved within striking distance. At Nathan's surprised look, he added, "You see I'm 'one of those bounty hunters.' The name's Cordell. Clay Cordell."

Nathan had only a fraction of a second to let the truth of his identity sink in before Clay struck. He lunged at him full-force, and they crashed violently to the floor. The other patrons scrambled to get out of their way as tables and chairs were overturned, and glasses of liquor crashed to the floor and shattered. In a savage test of strength, they rolled over and over, each seeking to dominate the other, each seeking to inflict as much pain as possible.

Nathan fought dirty. He threw Clay off and started to go for his gun. Dev had been watching, just in case something like this happened. With the expertise of a gunfighter, he fired once, his carefully placed shot knocking the gun from Nathan's hand. Nathan was stunned, and Clay took advantage of it, tackling him again, pinning him to the ground.

This time, Clay's anger had no bounds for he was

certain that Nathan would have killed him had Dev not intervened. With a ferocity he hadn't known himself capable of, he began to pound him with driving blows. Within minutes, Nathan was pleading for him to stop.

"Stop . . . don't . . . wait . . ." he begged through bloody lips.

Clay heard him distantly through the red haze of his rage, but something primitive in him refused to let him off so easily. He landed several more punishing blows before he felt Dev's hand on his shoulder, urging him without words to quit.

Clay hauled Nathan up off the floor by his shirtfront as he glared at him. "You utter another word about Reina in this town, and you won't walk away from our next fight."

He saw the bloodlust in the bounty hunter's eyes, and he knew he wasn't lying. He hated Reina, but vengeance on her wasn't worth dying over.

"All right, Cordell! I won't," he gasped weakly, every inch of his body suffering from the terrible beating Cordell had just given him.

Clay gave him a rough shake to emphasize his point. "If you ever do . . ."

"No . . . I'll never say anything! I swear! Just lay off . . ."

Clay let go of his shirt then, and Nathan fell heavily back to the floor. Clay got up then and dusted himself off. His knuckles were sore, and he knew he'd be sporting a few bruises in the morning, but he didn't care. If anything, he was amazed that he felt better than he had in a long time. He moved to the bar then, to confront George.

"I don't want to hear that you've been repeating anything he said, either." Clay's icy gaze met his.

"Oh, no, Cordell. I didn't hear anything!" After what he'd just witnessed, George knew without a doubt he would keep quiet about what had happened here tonight. He busied himself with picking up the aftermath.

Frenchie and Josie rushed to Clay to hug him and congratulate him on his victory.

"I'd be dead if it wasn't for Dev. Thanks, partner."

"You're welcome," Dev replied, smiling as he slid his gun back into his holster. "That was a man who was just begging to be taught some manners."

"You're right."

Frenchie and Josie had just thrown their arms around Clay and were trying to kiss him when Luis stepped into the saloon, rifle in hand. He saw Clay first and was thoroughly disgusted by the sight of the two dancehall girls hanging all over him, kissing him. This was the man his daughter loved? From where he stood, he couldn't see Nathan still lying on the floor or the overturned tables in the back.

"I knew I would find you here, Cordell," Luis sneered, dreading the thought of having this degenerate for a son-in-law.

Clay looked up at the sound of his voice. He saw the gun and knew immediately why he'd come.

"There's no need for the gun, Alvarez," Clay assured him. "I was just on my way out to your ranch." Shaking off the girls, he strode straight over to him.

"I'm sure you were," the older man disparaged, glancing back at Frenchie and Josie.

"Take another look, Alvarez." He was in no frame of mind to put up with anything from anybody right now. He'd just found out that the woman he loved was pregnant with his child, and he was worried that she wouldn't have him. She had begged him not to turn her over to her father, and he hadn't listened to her. He hoped she had it in her heart to forgive him, and if she did, he was going to spend the rest of his life making her the happiest woman in California.

There was a loud groan as Nathan hung on the bar and tried to pull himself to his feet. Luis looked in his direction and spotted him for the first time. The sight of Nathan's swelling, bloodied face brought a smile to the old Californio's otherwise stern features. He noticed then the disarray at the back of the saloon.

"So, you and Mr. Marlow have already met and exchanged a few pleasantries?"

"Yes, and it was quite a 'pleasant' exchange, for me," Clay replied.

"I can see that. I would have enjoyed watching, but seeing the outcome is satisfying enough."

Clay wondered at his change of attitude. According to what Reina had told him on the boat, Luis had been quite taken with Marlow.

Nathan saw Luis with Clay and knew it was too late. He'd lost. Pulling himself together as best he could, he left the saloon.

Clay watched Nathan go, feeling quite satisfied that the man would give them no more trouble.

"Are you ready to go to the ranch?"

"Give me a minute, and then I'll be ready to ride with you," Clay answered.

"I'll wait for you outside."

When Luis had gone, Dev spoke up first, grinning as he did so, "I thought there was something on your mind tonight, and now I know what . . . make that who, it was. You gonna tell me all about it?"

"You know too much already," he replied with a matching grin. "I love Reina, and if she'll have me—"

"You don't think she loves you?" he interrupted, surprised. Clay had never had any trouble with the ladies before.

"I'm not sure, but I'm going to find out right now."

"Let me know how it goes."

"I'll see you tomorrow."

Dev clapped him reassuringly on his back as they strode from the saloon. Frenchie and Josie watched them go, their expressions crestfallen.

"I hope their women know how lucky they are," Frenchie sighed.

"They do," Josie replied. "Otherwise those men wouldn't be in such an all fired hurry to get back to them." As they went to help George clean up the mess, they were silently hoping that someday a man like Clay or Dev would fall in love with them.

Clay joined Luis outside, and after retrieving his horse from the stable, they rode for Rancho Alvarez. They had gone some miles before Luis spoke.

"My daughter is a very perceptive young woman," he said obliquely. "She knew Marlow for what he was before I did."

"Which is?"

"A fortune-hunting, amoral bastard," Luis answered succinctly. "She also says now that she's in love with you, but she's not sure how you feel about her."

"I see." Clay was noncommittal.

He was growing agitated by the younger man's evasiveness. "I assume you heard of her, er . . . um . . . current circumstance?"

"Nathan was making a point of letting everyone know," Clay said tersely.

"Oh . . . Well, I promised Reina I wouldn't force you into anything you didn't want to do, but I must assure you that you will either want to marry my daughter or you will not want to marry anyone."

Clay bristled at his blackmail. He didn't need this old man telling him his obligations. He loved Reina. All he had to do was tell her the truth about how he felt and explain to her about Dev's situa tion. Once she understood, everything would work out.

"Look, Alvarez," he snarled as he reined in his horse and faced the old man in the moonlight. I told you when you showed up at the saloon that I was on my way out here, and I was. I love your daughter. I have since the first time I saw her, and I will never stop. I had no idea she was carrying my child, but now that I know, I fully intend to make her my wife. I don't need you to force me to 'want' to do anything. In fact, it makes me mad as hell that you think you'd have to force me to marry her!"

Luis was shocked by this display of honor by Cordell. He would never have expected it of him. Perhaps, he mused, Reina really was a very astute judge of character.

"I apologize if I've offended you."

They glared at each other for a moment, sizing each other up for the first time, not as adversaries, but as potential allies. Where before, Clay had thought of Luis as a hard, arrogant man, he now saw him as a loving, desperate father who wanted only what was best for his daughter. And where Luis had thought Clay nothing more than a fast gun, he now saw him more as a worthy man, capable of caring for Reina and eventually running the Alvarez spread.

Luis realized then, that though his business deal with Nathan was over, if Reina and Clay married, he would still get his American son-in-law and that would insure that the land stayed in the family. He considered that maybe things weren't turning out too badly after all.

Neither man said a word as the edginess went out of them, and they urged their horses onward again through the night, heading for home.

Chapter Thirty-five

The knock at the door roused Reina from her troubled half-sleep. She'd been dreaming strange, tormented dreams of Clay and Leo and Mickey and Nathan, and the interruption left her groggy and a bit disoriented.

"Yes? What is it?" she called out.

"It's Consuelo, Reina. Your father wants to speak with you."

"In the middle of the night?" She wondered what was so urgent that it couldn't wait until morning.

"Yes. He said it was very important that you meet him in the study right away."

Resignedly, she climbed from her bed. "Tell him I'll be there in a few minutes."

"Yes, ma'am."

Pulling on her floor length, gold silk robe, Reina tied the sash belt at her slim waist, then went to her dressing table to brush out her hair. She took care with her appearance, wanting to make sure she looked her best. She knew how proud her father was of her beauty, and now that things were back to normal between them again, she wanted to please him. She tried to disguise her discolored cheek with a dusting of powder, but it did little good. To her annoyance, she realized that this last reminder of Nathan would be with her for a while.

Once she was confident that she looked her best, considering the hour, Reina left her room to meet with her father. She was a little apprehensive as she approached the closed study door. As was her custom, she knocked lightly once, then let herself in.

"Yes, Father? You wanted to see me?" Reina swept into the room, but stopped, one hand still remaining on the doorknob, as she saw Clay standing with her father near his desk. "Clay!" she gasped, her grip tightening on the door so much that her knuckles showed white.

When Clay turned slowly toward her and their gazes met across the room, her heartbeat quickened. He was so magnificently tall and wonderfully handsome that her breath caught in her throat.

For a moment, Reina almost delighted in the fact that he'd come, but then the truth settled over her. A sick, sinking feeling weighed in the pit of her stomach. *Her lie.* He was only here because of her lie.

"Hello, Reina."

His voice went over her like a velvet caress, but she steeled herself against it. She kept her expression closed, her heart wary as she took a step farther into the room.

"Hello, Clay."

"I'm sure you two have things to talk about, so I'll leave you in privacy."

Neither of them said anything as Luis let himself out of the room and closed the door behind him.

Only a single, low-burning lamp illuminated the room, and across the distance in the soft glowing light, Clay could not see her injured cheek. All he could see was Reina clad in golden silk, looking much like a goddess he might have conjured up out of a dream. His gaze took in the cascade of ebony curls that fell around her shoulders, then moved lower to sweep appreciatively over her slender figure. He let his regard linger just for an instant over the still-flat plane of her stomach. The thought of his child nestled there . . . growing within her . . . filled him with a great sense of awe and pride. He wanted this baby, and more than anything else, he wanted Reina.

Reina wasn't sure exactly what Clay had in mind, and she wasn't about to wait around to find out. With a stubborn lift of her chin, she decided to be the aggressor. She would discourage him and get rid of him, just like she had Nathan.

"Why are you here?"

The coldness of her statement startled him. "Because we need to talk. There's a lot that needs to be settled between us before we get married."

"Married? I'm not marrying you, Clay Cordell." It was a definitive statement.

"Reina . . ." he began again. "We have to talk. You have to let me explain."

"There's nothing to explain. I don't want to marry you."

"You're pregnant with my child! It's only fitting that we marry as soon as possible."

His words pierced her heart. It was just as she'd expected. No words of love, no declarations of devotion, just an obligation. It was something he felt he had to do, because of the child.

"That is the worst reason in the world to marry someone."

"I don't think so," he argued. "I intend to be a father to our baby. I want this child. Reina . . ." He lowered his voice to make his point. "You know how determined I can be when I decide to do something."

For one minute, Reina let herself believe what he was saying, but then reality intruded again.

"I said no," she insisted, not giving any ground in their argument. She moved aside, giving him a clear path to the door. "Now, why don't you just leave?"

She made a mistake in shifting positions for in doing so, he caught sight of her damaged cheek.

"Dear God, who hit you? Not your father. . . ?" Clay was outraged as he quickly grabbed her by the upper arms and hauled her to him. She tried to wriggle free of his gentle, yet restraining hold, but he would not let her go. With one hand he tenderly touched the bruised flesh.

"No! My father would never lay a hand on me!" she quickly defended Luis.

"Nathan . . ." he breathed his name in a curse.

"Yes, it was Nathan, but it doesn't matter any more. He's out of my life forever."

"I'm sorry I wasn't here to protect you," Clay said softly.

"I don't need your protection, Clay. I handled Nathan just fine on my own."

"So I see."

"It's not that bad. In fact, it was worth it just to be done with him. I hope I never see him again as long as I live."

"You won't." Clay replied with certainty. Then unable to resist, he cupped her chin and tilted her face up to his. Without saying a word, he bent and kissed her injured cheek. "Once you're my wife, I'll see to it that nothing ever hurts you again."

The touch of his lips on her cheek sent a shiver of delight through her. She struggled to ignore it as she fought to deny any claim he might put on her.

"I am not going to be your wife," she declared, and when she tried to pull away from him again, he let her go.

"Reina, I love you. I want to spend the rest of my life with you."

"Why don't I believe you?" she taunted, her sarcasm hiding the pain in her heart. He'd finally said the words she'd been longing to hear; the only trouble was, it was too late. She was certain he was only saying it as a way to convince her to marry him. If he'd really loved her, he wouldn't have let her go that morning.

"Look, I have no intention of leaving here until you agree to marry me." Clay was growing exasperated. He had never been in love or proposed before. He'd waited until he'd found the one woman he treasured above all others—Reina. He thought she loved him. After all she'd just told him so on the boat that morning. But now here she was, turning him down, refusing his marriage proposal. He was confused, to say the least.

"Then you're going to be here for a long time," she retorted angrily. "Because I have no intention of marrying you or anyone else!"

"You can't mean to raise my child by yourself? Don't you realize what that would do to your reputation, not to mention how the child would suffer?" He was horrified that she could have such a radical idea.

Inwardly, Reina groaned. *Why couldn't this man just leave her alone? How in the world had she gotten herself into this mess?* "It'll have me and my father."

" 'It,' Reina? You're talking about our son or daughter," Clay said persuasively.

Bitterly, Reina realized how deeply she'd dug herself into this hole of lies and that the only way out of it was by telling him the complete truth. "Damnit! Why did you come out here, anyway? I didn't want this to happen!"

"What are you talking about?" Clay feared she was growing despondent over her pregnancy.

"I'm talking about my lies . . . all of them."

"Lies? What lies?"

"You want the truth, Clay? Well, here it is! I'm not pregnant, and I never was. I just made it up to

464

get rid of Nathan, and it worked. The only thing that went wrong was that you got dragged into the middle of it."

"You mean you lied about being pregnant? You're not carrying my child?"

"That's right. So you can just go back to your saloon and celebrate. You don't have to marry anybody." She turned away from him, hoping that he would leave without another word.

"What about this morning on the boat, and what about what your father told me on the ride out here from town? He said that you'd told him you loved me. Were you lying then?" Clay had to know the truth of her feelings. If she loved him, it didn't matter if she was pregnant or not. He loved her, and he wanted to make her his wife.

"What do you think?" she bit out caustically. "As desperate as I was to keep from marrying Nathan, I was ready to try anything. I am my father's daughter, you know." She kept her back to him, so he couldn't see the hurt in her eyes. She wouldn't marry him just because he thought he was obligated to do it.

Reina waited, her heart wishing and praying that he would take her in his arms and declare his love. She wanted him to sweep her off to the altar, telling her that it didn't matter if she was pregnant or not, that he loved her and that nothing else was important. Her mind, however, was telling her to prepare herself, because he was going to walk out and never come back. That he'd only come to her because he'd thought she was in trouble, and now that he knew she wasn't pregnant, he was going to go off on his merry way, without giving her another thought. The minutes ticked by as she waited to see what he would do next.

Clay stared at her, seeing the stiffness and defiance in her stance, and nearly unbearable pain shot through him as he accepted her truth. *She'd been lying. The whole thing had been a lie.* She must have loved having him dancing to her tune this way. He'd made a damned fool out of himself, but he realized miserably that it really didn't matter. Nothing mattered right now. Nothing. He thought of his mother, and the cruelty she'd wreaked in his and his father's lives. It was a galling, agonizing comparison.

"Yes," he finally said slowly, "you most certainly are a lot alike." And as he said it, he wasn't sure if he was comparing her to her father or to his mother. "How will you explain to your father that we're not going to marry?"

"Don't worry about it. My father loves me. Now that he knows what kind of man Nathan really was, he'll understand when I tell him the truth."

"I see," he replied tightly, the ache in his chest expanding to almost excruciating proportions. "Well, I'm glad everything worked out so well for you."

"Yes, it has, and now that you know everything you can go on and go. I'm going to be just fine."

"I'm sure you are, Reina."

She heard him leave the room, and her tears began to flow. As his solitary footsteps echoed down the hall, she whispered, "Good-bye, Clay."

Luis was in his bedchamber when he heard the sound of a rider on the drive. He frowned, wondering who'd left. He'd expected Clay to stay on so they could make the necessary arrangements in the morning. Curious, he left his room to find out what was going on.

The sight of the study door standing ajar caused him to pause. He hurried forward to push it wider and found his beloved Reina, sitting in one of the leather wingchairs, crying brokenheartedly.

"Reina! What's happened? Where's Clay?" he asked as he rushed to kneel before her.

She raised tortured, tear-filled eyes to his. "He's gone."

"Gone?" Luis was totally perplexed. "Where did he go?"

"I sent him away."

"You sent him away? Why?" Luis stared at her in bewilderment. "He did propose to you, didn't he?"

"Yes," she managed in a choked voice, "but I turned him down."

Now he was really baffled. "Why, in God's name did you turn him down? He wanted to marry you. He told me so."

"He only wanted me because he thought I was pregnant, Father, and I didn't want him under those circumstances."

Luis heard something in her words that troubled him. "Because he 'thought you were pregnant'?" he repeated back to her.

"Yes . . ." she confessed sorrowfully. "I'm sorry, I know I shouldn't have lied to you. I should have told you everything."

"What are you talking about?"

"The truth, Father. I'm not pregnant . . . or at least, I don't think I am," she admitted humbly.

"You're not . . ." He digested that bit of surprising news slowly.

"No. You see, I made it up because of Nathan . . . of what he threatened to do to me."

Though he was still a bit angry over her lie, this was the first he'd heard of any threats from Nathan. "Just what did Marlow threaten to do to you?"

Reina quickly went on to tell him of his need to confirm her innocence before their marriage.

"That son-of-a-bitch! It's a damned shame Clay didn't kill him while we were in town."

"What?" she asked amazed.

"Clay didn't tell you that he ran into Nathan at the Perdition Saloon?"

"No."

"It must have been quite a one-sided fight judging from the way Nathan looked when Clay got done with him."

"Clay beat up Nathan?"

"Soundly, and, in defense of your honor, I might add. He loves you very much, Reina."

"No. He doesn't love me," she denied, not believing that it could be true.

"I think you're wrong. He loves you. I'm sure of it."

Her expression turned downcast again. "And I'm just as certain that he doesn't."

"Why? After all he's done to prove to you that he does, why do you refuse to believe it?"

"Because of this morning . . ."

"What happened this morning?" he urged her to tell him what was bothering her.

"It was right before you showed up at the boat to bring me home. I was scared. I didn't want to go to Nathan. I knew I couldn't marry him, feeling as I did about Clay, so I told Clay the truth. I told him that I loved him, and I begged him not to take me back to you, but it didn't matter."

Luis's heart was breaking as he listened to her. Hearing the very real anguish in her voice he stood and drew her up from the chair into his warm, loving embrace. He soothed her, just as he had for all the years of her childhood, holding her close, enfolding her with his fatherly love.

"Didn't he offer to explain?" he finally asked, when she'd calmed.

"Explain? What was there to explain?" she countered heartbrokenly. "If he loved me, he would have done anything for me."

"Sometimes, there are situations in life when

things are not as simple as they appear. Did you give him a chance to tell you about his friend?"

"He said there was a lot he wanted to explain to me, but I told him I didn't want to hear it."

"I think you should hear it now . . . from me." Luis had the good grace to look a bit shame-faced. "I had more than a little to do with what happened this morning. Don't judge Clay too harshly."

"I don't understand."

"You will. You see, I was the reason Clay couldn't just tell you that he loved you and run off with you this morning. I had Clay trapped. He had to turn you over to me. There was nothing else he could do."

At her questioning look, he went on.

"When you first disappeared, I was frantic. At first, I searched everywhere myself, but when I couldn't find you, I became desperate. That was when I attempted to hire Clay to track you down. Initially, though, he refused me. He wanted no part of searching for a runaway girl. Even after I told him that he could name his price, he was adamant."

"So he didn't do it for money?"

"No. Obviously, money isn't very important to the man."

This thrilled Reina, but she still didn't understand what had forced him to take the job. "If it wasn't the pay, then why did he finally agree to do it?"

"He forced me to become more inventive in finding a way to 'encourage' him to take the job."

"What did you do?" She knew her father, and she was horrified as she realized what lengths he'd gone to, to get Clay to bend to his will.

"The details aren't important," Luis glossed over his more dastardly deeds, and Reina knew better than to ask. "The important thing was that his friend, Dev, was in jail. He'd been arrested, accused of Pedro Santana's murder, and he looked to be pretty guilty. I made it my business to personally assure Clay that his friend would be safe in jail, but only if he agreed to locate you and bring you home."

"You blackmailed him!"

"Yes, I did," he told her, not at all proud of his actions now.

Reina was amazed as she began to see Clay's words and actions in a whole new light. He couldn't save her from her father because he was afraid his friend would die. Her heart sang as she realized that he really might love her.

"He told you he loved me?" she asked, needing to hear it confirmed again.

"When I found him at the saloon, shortly after his fight with Nathan, he told me he was just on his way out here to see you. On the ride here, when I tried to persuade him, in a not so subtle fashion, to do the right thing by you, he got very angry. That was when he told me that he didn't need to be coerced into marrying you. That he had loved you from the first time you met."

"Clay really said that?" Her eyes were still brimming with tears, but they were tears of happiness now.

"Yes, he did. He loves you, Reina, and he's a fine man . . . a man of honor."

"I know . . . Oh, yes, I know," she told him, a happy laugh bubbling up inside of her. "Father, I have to go after him! I have to find him quickly and tell him I'm sorry!"

Luis chuckled as she moved out of his embrace. "Get dressed then, while I have the carriage brought around."

"I don't want the carriage! That's too slow! Have them bring my horse. I've got to get to Clay as fast as I can."

"It is the middle of the night, you know."

Reina flashed her father a triumphant smile as she headed for the doorway on her way to her room to get dressed. "Would the lateness of the hour have stopped you from going after Mother, had she left you?"

"No," he answered, remembering how he'd felt about his dear wife.

"Then how can you expect me to sit here and wait for a suitable hour? I am your daughter, you know."

"Yes, Reina, my love, you are my daughter."

With a light-hearted laugh, she raced from the room, leaving her father smiling happily behind her.

Chapter Thirty-six

Clay sat at a table in the nearly deserted Perdition, an open bottle of bourbon and a half-empty glass before him. *Reina had lied. Everything had been a lie* . . . The words kept tumbling through his mind, taunting him, scalding him with the white-hot truth . . . the truth that had been burned into his consciousness by his mother long ago and that he should never have forgotten.

He realized now that he'd been wrong to ever have imagined things could be different. There was only one kind of woman that could be trusted, and that was a woman like Frenchie or Josie. They, at least, were honest and upfront about their motives. You paid ahead of time in cold, hard cash, and you got exactly what you paid for. Involvement with them didn't cost you your very soul as it did with women like his mother or Reina.

Clay felt isolated. It was difficult enough dealing with Reina's deception, but now he didn't even have Dev. He thought of home, of his father. He understood then that they were far more alike than he'd thought. For all his vows that what happened to his father wouldn't happen to him, it had.

The recognition of his weakness was not a soothing one, and he took another stiff drink. As he downed the liquor, he thought it odd that he'd been sitting there, trying to drink himself to forgetfulness for the better part of an hour, and he had yet to feel any effects from his efforts. Reina still dominated his thoughts . . . Reina and his love for her. It irritated him. He poured another glass.

Frenchie had been surprised when Clay had returned to the saloon that same night. She hadn't expected to see him again so soon. She'd figured he'd be on his way to the altar with the rich Alvarez girl by now, and she found herself wondering if something had gone wrong. The temptation to approach him was powerful, but his earlier coolness kept her waiting at the bar.

"What do you think, George?" she asked the bartender quietly. "Think I should go talk to him?"

George turned pale. "I wouldn't mess with that man, if I were you, Frenchie. He's a hard one, and he looks plumb mad to me."

She glanced over at Clay, seeing the hard set of his jaw and the tense line of his body that was not betrayed by the way he was sitting slumped in his chair.

"You always were a coward," she told him with a soft laugh. "I like Clay, and I'm going to find out what's going on." Taking her own drink with her, she moved off across the room to come stand beside Clay. When he didn't look up right away, she slid into the chair opposite him. Her greeting was a sultry, "Hi, Clay."

"Hello, Frenchie," he answered distractedly, his thoughts preoccupied.

"You're looking lonely, sitting here all by yourself. You want some company?"

Clay was of a mind to decline, but then thought better of it. Frenchie was a good-hearted woman. He knew what was on her mind. "Sure, why not?"

She leaned forward, giving him a clear view of her cleavage as she spoke. "Is everything all right with you? The way you rushed out of here before with old man Alvarez, I kinda thought we'd seen the last of you."

Clay forced a smile. "I'm fine. Why?"

"You look a little down, is all, but I'm glad there isn't anything troubling you."

"Not a thing," he lied. "Want a drink?"

"Sure." She held out her glass while he poured her a healthy shot. She took a drink, then gave him a flirtatious smile. "Good stuff, I like your taste in liquor."

"Thanks."

"I like you, too, Clay." Frenchie paused, her eyes meeting his, letting him read there exactly what she was wanting. They had had a good time together all those weeks ago before he'd left town, and she was eager to have him back in her bed again. "You want to bring the bottle and come upstairs with me? We could have some fun . . ."

Clay wanted to go upstairs, but he wanted to go to his own room, alone — just him and his bottle of bourbon. He liked Frenchie, but Reina was the only woman he desired. In spite of everything, he still loved her. There would be no point in trying to erase her memory with another woman. He knew without even trying that it wouldn't work.

"I think I'll go on up, but I'm going alone, Frenchie," he told her affectionately. "You're a gorgeous woman, but tonight I just need to be by myself." He pushed his chair back and stood up.

"You sure?"

"I'm sure." He picked up his bottle and glass and started to leave.

Frenchie wasn't about to let him go that easily. She got up, too, and grabbed his arm when he would have moved off.

"Good night, Clay," she said as she looped her arms around his neck and planted a warm kiss on his lips.

Clay accepted her embrace. He felt no rousing passion, no driving need. When she let him go, he gave her a sweet-sad smile.

"Good night, Frenchie." With that, he headed up the stairs to his rented room.

The saloon girl watched him mount the steps, thinking it might be worth her effort to wait a few minutes and then go knock on his door. Worst that could happen would be that he'd tell her good night again.

Reina rode like the wind through the starlit early morning hours. Her heart was pounding excitedly as she anticipated seeing him again and telling him that she loved him. The miles melted away as she gave her horse full rein. She knew she was driving her mount hard, but she didn't care. Only Clay was important now . . . only Clay.

When the lights of Monterey appeared ahead of her, she was thrilled. Soon, they would be together! Soon, she would tell him the truth and everything would be fine.

Her father had told her that Clay had taken a room at the Perdition Saloon, and so she rode directly there. She knew she was going to have to be brazen to enter the place. Lord knows, ladies of her stature in the community did not frequent these types of establishments, but she knew the prize waiting for her there was worth it.

Reina reined in before the saloon and slipped from the saddle. She was trembling as she hurried toward the entrance. As she neared the swinging doors, she paused, wanting to get a look inside before she went rushing in. As she peeked over the top of one door, she gasped. There in the middle of the room stood Clay, and one of the saloon girls was kissing him!

Anger seared her. But it was not anger with Clay, it was anger with herself. It was all her fault that he was kissing someone else. She'd driven him to it. She'd be damned, though, if she was going to let that other woman have him. Clay was hers!

A hideous prospect penetrated her indignation. She might claim Clay as hers, but what if he didn't want her? She almost wouldn't blame him, after all the trouble she'd caused him, but she intended to make it up to him, just as soon as they talked and straightened everything out.

Reminding herself that Clay had told her he loved her when he'd proposed, bolstered Reina's confidence. She glanced inside again, just in time to see Clay disappear upstairs, alone. The saloon girl was watching him from the foot of the steps.

Reina wasn't sure if his going upstairs ahead of the girl was good or bad. Was he really going to bed for the night or was he expecting her to follow him a little later? She wasn't sure how these things were arranged by men in this type of situation. When she saw the girl start up the steps after him a moment later, she knew she wasn't going to wait around to find out. If Clay wanted a woman, he was going to get one — *Her!* Assuming her proudest, most arrogant manner in the hopes that no one would dare interfere with her, Reina walked right on into the saloon.

"Which room is Mr. Cordell's?" she asked George, regally.

The bartender looked up, shocked, to find the fine Miss Reina Alvarez standing in the middle of his saloon. He had seen her from a distance before, but never up this close, and he decided that she was even better looking than he'd thought. She was wearing a white blouse, leather riding skirt, matching vest and riding boots that hugged her shapely calves. The outfit emphasized her luscious curves, and her hair . . . oh her hair! What a man wouldn't want to do with those silken tresses . . . George gulped twice trying to find his voice to answer her.

"Well?" Reina demanded, wondering at his speechlessness. Her brown eyes were flashing at him now in impatience.

"Twenty," he finally answered.

"Thank you," she said curtly.

A moment before Reina had entered, Frenchie had started up the steps just to see if she couldn't change Clay's mind. Seeing the Alvarez girl now, though, she knew she didn't have a chance. She stopped, hand on the railing, and waited for Reina to pass by.

Reina, her head held high as if daring anyone to stop her, strode purposefully across the room. As she passed the saloon girl on the steps, she'd intended to give her a frosty look, but the other woman's expression was so friendly and so amused, she found she could only smile at her.

"It's on the right, three doors down," Frenchie offered helpfully.

"Thanks," Reina whispered in reply.

"Make him happy . . ."

"I'm going to try," she promised, then hurried the rest of the way up to the top and moved out of view down the hall.

Frenchie returned to the bar and waited patiently while George poured her a drink. "Lucky woman," she sighed.

"Lucky man," the bartender answered.

They both took one last glance up the staircase, then turned their thoughts to other things.

Clay lay on the bed, the lamp turned down low,

his mood even lower. The knock at the door both startled and irritated him. He'd thought he'd made it plain to Frenchie that he wasn't in the mood. He didn't want to be bothered right now. He just wanted to be left alone.

"Yeah?" he called out, not even wanting to get up and answer it.

"It's me, Clay," came the muffled woman's voice in answer. "Open the door."

He expected it to be Frenchie, therefore, he didn't even consider that it could be anyone else. Exasperated by her persistence in the face of his refusal, he got up and went to open the door so he could tell her that it was nothing personal, but that he just wasn't interested tonight.

"Frenchie, I told you downstairs that I needed to be alone tonight. Why—" He stopped in mid-sentence as he swung the door wide and came face to face with Reina. His eyes widened in shock. She was absolutely the last person he'd expected to see, and the one person he'd longed to see. His heart leapt at the sight of her. "Reina?"

Reina's heart nearly burst with joy at his words. He hadn't wanted the other woman! She was thrilled.

"Hello, Clay," she said softly. "May I come in?"

He studied her for a moment, not wanting to question his good fortune, then stepped aside and waved her in. "Why the hell not?"

"Clay . . ." She heard the coldness in his voice and turned to him beseechingly. "Clay . . . I came to tell you that I love you, and I'm sorry."

He looked profoundly stunned by her announcement.

"Look," Reina rushed on. "I know you have absolutely no reason to believe me, but it's true."

"Sure, it is," he drawled derisively, remembering all too vividly the little scene just a few hours before in her father's study.

"It is!" she insisted. "I love you, and if you love me . . . really love me like you said . . . I want to marry you." She paused only long enough to draw a deep breath before rushing on. "I know you don't trust me, but if you'll just listen. I want to explain, now, before this goes any further."

"Go on." Clay was fighting down the urge to take her in his arms and kiss her. It was hard for him to believe that she'd changed so completely, so quickly.

"I honestly didn't know about your friend being in jail. My father just told me about that after you'd left the ranch. See, I didn't think you loved me, because you let my father take me from the boat. I didn't know he was blackmailing you."

"I see."

He still sounded disbelieving to her, so she went on, "I also didn't know how you really felt about me until just a little while ago. I thought you'd only proposed because you thought I was pregnant. I didn't want you that way, Clay," she entreated, boldly going to him and putting a hand on his arm. "I didn't want to think that you'd been forced to marry me. I wanted a lovematch when I married, not an arrangement." She gazed up at him soulfully, seeing a warming in his regard and feeling a first bud of hope. "Clay? Can you ever forgive me for sending you away? Can we start all over again? From the beginning?"

"I don't think the beginning is a good place. I don't think I'd want to be the cause of Sister Mary Regina forsaking her vows."

Reina heard a note of humor in his voice and smiled for the first time since she'd entered his room.

"Maybe we could just start from here . . . from tonight . . . from my love to yours?"

"From my love to yours, Reina. I love you,

darling. I always have and I always will." His words were a groan of deep emotion as he took her in his arms.

Pushing the door shut behind them to ensure their privacy, he bent to her. His lips met hers in a deep, passionate kiss of promise and devotion, of infinite tenderness and love everlasting. It was yesterday and tomorrow. It was the beginning and the end.